# THE THINGS GODS BREAK

## MORE FROM ABIGAIL OWEN

### THE CRUCIBLE
*The Games Gods Play*

### DOMINIONS
*The Liar's Crown*
*The Stolen Throne*
*The Shadows Rule All*

### INFERNO RISING
*The Rogue King*
*The Blood King*
*The Warrior King*
*The Cursed King*

### FIRE'S EDGE
*The Mate*
*The Boss*
*The Rookie*
*The Enforcer*
*The Protector*
*The Traitor*

### BRIMSTONE INC.
*The Demigod Complex*
*Shift Out of Luck*
*A Ghost of a Chance*
*Bait N' Witch*
*Try As I Smite*
*Hit by the Cupid Stick*
*An Accident Waiting to Dragon*

# THE
# THINGS GODS
# BREAK

**#1 NEW YORK TIMES BESTSELLING AUTHOR**

## ABIGAIL OWEN

RED TOWER
BOOKS™

This book is a work of fiction. Names, characters, places, and incidents are the product of the author's imagination or are used fictitiously. Any resemblance to actual events, locales, or persons, living or dead, is coincidental.

Copyright © 2025 by Abigail Owen. All rights reserved, including the right to reproduce, distribute, or transmit in any form or by any means. For information regarding subsidiary rights, please contact the Publisher.

Entangled Publishing believes stories have the power to inspire, connect, and create lasting change. That's why we protect the rights of our authors and the integrity of their work. Copyright exists not to limit creativity, but to make it possible—to ensure writers can keep telling bold, original stories in their own voices. Thank you for choosing a legitimate copy of this book. By not copying, scanning, or distributing it without permission, you help authors continue to write and reach readers. This book may not be used to train artificial intelligence systems, including large language models or other machine learning tools, whether existing or still to come. These stories were written for human connection, not machine consumption.

Entangled Publishing, LLC
644 Shrewsbury Commons Ave., STE 181
Shrewsbury, PA 17361
rights@entangledpublishing.com

Red Tower Books is an imprint of Entangled Publishing, LLC.
Visit our website at www.entangledpublishing.com.

Edited by Liz Pelletier
Cover design by LJ Anderson and Bree Archer
Edge design by Bree Archer
Edge image by duncan1890/Gettyimage
Case design by Elizabeth Turner Stokes
Case images by Anton_Tokarev/Gettyimages, and
Endpaper design by Elizabeth Turner Stokes
Endpaper image by lyubava.21/Shutterstock, and VasyaV/Shuttestock
Endpaper original illustration by Kateryna Vitkovska
Interior map design by Elizabeth Turner Stokes
Interior map images by Nadia Murash/Shutterstock, and ekosuwandono/Shutterstock
Interior design by Britt Marczak

Hardcover ISBN 978-1-64937-853-8
Ebook ISBN 978-1-64937-642-8

Printed in the United States of America
First Edition October 2025

10 9 8 7 6 5 4 3 2 1

RED TOWER
BOOKS™

*To the mean girls in high school who I let convince me to stop writing for years because they told me I was weird for this passion... welcome to Tartarus.*

*To the writers, the readers, the storytellers, the dreamers... never, ever let someone else take away your passion.*

In *The Things Gods Break*, the Greek gods walk among us and the Titans are imprisoned below us—and they are all as unspeakably beautiful as they are deadly. As such, this story features elements that might not be suitable for all readers, including blood, gore, violence (human, god, and monster alike), perilous situations, heights, injury, vomiting, neglect, bullying, isolation, imprisonment, torture, death, grief, use of hallucinogens, graphic language, and sexual activity (including domination and choking). Readers who may be sensitive to these elements, please take note, and prepare to enter Tartarus…

**AUTHOR NOTE:** *A GLOSSARY OF THE GODS AND TITANS AND THE (SOMETIMES TWISTED) ROLES THEY REPRESENT IN THIS SERIES IS AT THE BACK OF THE BOOK.*

# PREVIOUSLY IN THE CRUCIBLE

Who the hells could have guessed that, after competing in a series of twelve potentially deadly (and honestly pretty fucking twisted) Labors, I would *win* the Crucible Games. Me, a lowly office clerk for the Order of Thieves, cursed by Zeus to be unlovable. I won not only the throne of Olympus for Hades, but his heart. And along the way, I was made a goddess myself — Queen of the Underworld. That should have been the happily ever after to our story.

# PART 1

# WELCOME TO TARTARUS

"As far beneath the house of Hades as from earth the sky lies."
~*The Iliad*, Homer

# 1

# WE'RE SO SCREWED

### LYRA

Fuck the universe. I knew it hated me. I just didn't think it would be this *petty*.

Besides, becoming a goddess should've come with perks. Sparkly powers. A throne. Maybe a brief vacation somewhere that didn't drop me onto a stone bridge suspended over nothingness, with a yawning abyss on either side and a door looming in the distance like a punch line I've already heard.

Not that it matters what it looks like. I know where we are.

Tartarus.

Not because I recognize it, but because I was standing on the other side of the double doors of the massive gates to this place when one opened.

Worse? I dragged Boone in with me. One of my few friends—who already died once thanks to me and the Crucible Games. Sure, I won and pulled his soul into godhood, so yay, happy ending. That only lasted a few weeks.

Now he's here. Again. With me. In this hellhole.

I shoot him a quick side-eye, but he doesn't turn. Just grits his teeth and stares forward. Which is code for very worried and pretending not to be.

I take a breath. The air tastes like iron on my tongue. Or maybe that's dread. Because I don't have to ask who yanked us through the gates. I already know that, too.

Cronos.

King of the Titans.

By all accounts, the mold all assholes have been made from ever since. After all, his son Zeus had to get it from somewhere. This guy swallowed all his children the day each was born to subvert a prophecy that he'd be overthrown by them one day. I mean, I've heard of crappy fathers. Mine wasn't exactly a poster boy for Dad of the Year. But Cronos was next level.

Is.

Not was.

Is. He's standing right in front of us. As tall and muscled as the hero of a novel, with hair as black as onyx only touched by silver at the temples, and a thick, dark beard that hides the cut of his jaw.

And gods, he looks like Hades. Not in the way parents sometimes do, but bone-deep, uncanny—like looking at an older, more brutal version. No wonder Hades always carried a shadow he couldn't name. This is where it came from.

But if the gods are beautiful, I'd say Titans are radiant. Like, it's actually hard to look directly at Cronos.

I'm not sure there's a word to describe how remarkably, overwhelmingly, hysterically bad staring at *this* Titan is. My heart is pounding so hard I can hear it in my ears, my rib cage expanding and shrinking visibly with every panting breath.

*Keep calm, Lyra.*

Something hits the gates at my back. "Lyra!" The shout is so faint, I can barely make it out.

I spin around and flatten my hands on the double doors carved in scrollwork that looks like thorny vines. Oh gods.

*Hades.*

My soul reaches for his through the barrier between us, but there's no way through.

No way to him.

*No, no, no.*

I swipe an impatient hand across the tear sliding down my cheek. I can't lose him. I *won't*. Not after we just found each other. I suffered in silence with Zeus' curse that no one would ever love me all my life, and still I survived the damned games the gods make us mortals play in their stead. I *earned* immortality and a life of happiness at Hades' side. He deserves happiness, too.

This can't be happening.

Only I know, down to my marrow, that there's no possible way for even the mighty god of death to fix this. Yet I'm still silently screaming for him to get me out of here.

A sob breaks free as two thoughts strike in rapid succession. First... he'll blame himself for this. It's a truth as inescapable as Tartarus.

And second...I should have paid more attention to Rima's prophecy during the Crucible—a vision of Hades burning down the world. A future I honestly thought we'd stopped from happening. What else did Rima say?

The pounding gets more and more violent, until I feel the shake of it in the narrow bridge of solid rock beneath my feet. I think for a wildly hopeful minute that the gates might give way, and then...the pounding stops.

And so does my heart, leaving me hollow inside.

I try to feel Hades, feel a flash of emotion from him to tell me that he's still there, but the effect of him giving me his blood during the Crucible— allowing me to sense what he's feeling in any given moment, especially the strongest emotions—has already worn off almost completely. Nothing comes to me.

"Lyra!" Hades' voice is even quieter now, muffled, like he's farther away. What are the others with him doing? Dragging him back?

I curl my fingers into the metal door like I can dig myself out or keep him here. "Don't leave."

But only silence answers.

I can no longer hear him. Putting my ear to the door, I close my eyes, listening for the smallest hint that he's still on the other side, that he hasn't left me.

"Hades." His name is a whimper.

"He's still there," Cronos says behind me. Or murmurs really.

Even that quiet, I tense. Hard.

The Titan *sounds* like Hades, like his firstborn son, although the deep tones are rougher, raspier, like he's been breathing in brimstone for too long.

"It's the wards that prevent us from communicating with the outside world," Cronos informs us, still speaking softly. "You won't be able to hear him anymore."

I drag my forearm across my wet face, then turn to face the King of the Titans, meeting Boone's dark gaze on the way. The newly made god of thieves is ready to fight if we have to, jaw rigid, hands in fists at his sides. I give him the tiniest shake of my head. Fighting seems like a guaranteed path to sudden, instant, and even irreversible death. But that leaves one single thought circling my mind.

How do we get out?

The answer is simple. We can't.

This is godsdamned—literally—Tartarus. Maybe if I think it enough times, reality will sink in.

Not even the Titans have managed to get out in millennia, and I have no doubt they've tried. Pandora's Box was a gamble. A last resort. And it was supposed to let out only one person.

Persephone.

Speaking of… Where in the name of Olympus is the goddess of spring? She was supposed to be waiting on this side to escape, but Cronos is the only one with us.

What'd he do? Eat all the others like he did his children?

Cronos smiles at me. Sharks have more inviting smiles. Worse, he reminds me of Hades so much my heart keeps skipping beats, confused about what I should be feeling right now. Not attraction, of course, but certainly some sort of affection. Or maybe I'm slowly and quietly unraveling.

I let a single, sharp laugh escape. "Out of everyone you could've pulled through, you chose the two most useless to you. Nice work."

Or maybe I'm unraveling fast and loud.

Boone tenses ever so slightly. Then gives a short whistle, the kind thieves use to communicate.

A warning.

One I ignore. I learned early on in the Order of Thieves—where Boone and I both grew up—that the way to deal with bullies is never to back down, and, when challenged, double down.

Cronos checks carefully over his shoulder, presumably at the doorway behind him. Checking what, exactly? Is he waiting for backup?

I lean to look around him. There's no one else in here and no place for them to hide. The small doorway at the other end of the bridge leads off into a tunnel, maybe. Hard to tell in the light of the torches that burn in sconces around the room.

"You need to be quiet," Cronos whispers, still turned away. "Or you'll wake them."

Ominous and mysteriously vague. My two favorite things. "Wake who?"

"Shhhh." Cronos goes very still, continuing to look down the tunnel across the way. "They always get worse when you arrive."

What?

I exchange a glance with Boone. The Titan has been locked down here a very, very long time. Clearly, it's had an effect. Something to look forward to if we can't get out.

Cronos jerks around to face me, and I straighten as his eyes twinkle, his lips tilting in a growing grin.

Yeah, that's not creepy as fuck. "What?" This time I ask the question aloud.

"You think you're useless?" Cronos says in a tone like a kindly uncle, but it's still a whisper. "Seems like *you're* the one not thinking clearly."

I glare. "I *think* you're a total, raging—"

Boone shoves his elbow into my side in the universal signal to shut up before the Titan smites you, and I wince.

Cronos moves faster than anything I've ever seen, and that includes the gods and several monsters. In a blur of movement, he doesn't come for me. Instead, he gets Boone by the throat and slams him into the gates. I yelp at the sound of Boone's head striking hard metal.

Cronos drops Boone like a rag doll and not the six-foot-two grown man he is. Then the Titan turns back to me like nothing happened.

Horror building, I stare behind him at Boone's limp body in a heap on the ground. His chest moves up and down. Thank the stars. One arm is bent under him at a bad angle, golden blood, the ichor of the gods we now are, trailing from a cut above his brow. I shudder. He looks so breakable like that, god or not. Like someone who never should've followed me through any door, let alone *this* one.

"Why did you do that?" I ask, fighting the urge to rush to Boone's side. Something tells me I need to keep my eyes on the Titan if I hope to get us both out of here.

Which is when I remember my weapons. I reach up to grab the double axes strapped to my back. Only…they're not there. I grab again, but I didn't miss. They're...gone. The straps still crisscross my chest, but the sheaths are empty.

When he sees what I'm doing, Cronos sighs. "The gates of Tartarus strip all who enter of their weapons, Lyra." He's still speaking barely audibly.

As I lower my hands limply to my sides, the last part of what he just said sinks in. I blink slowly at Cronos, a new band of fear ratcheting down on my lungs. "You know my name?"

He lifts his brows—can brows be disappointed? "Obviously."

Right. "Um...how?" I ask, a tad distracted, and who can blame me.

"We've met."

I rear back before I can bury the reaction.

Met the godfather of world-ending daddy issues? "Nope. Not even a little bit."

I should just stop talking to him altogether. I'm not going to get sensical answers—just cryptic declarations and Titan-size ego.

My mind scrambles for options to get Boone and me out of here. Escape routes. Diversions. Bribes the universe might actually take. I don't even know how we got here entirely. One second, we were standing on the threshold—and the next, we were in the lion's mouth.

How the hells am I supposed to carry Boone out of Tartarus if he doesn't wake up?

My mind finally relays the fact that I might not have my axes but I do have my tattoos. The animals Hades gifted me are buried in the skin of my arm, and surely no one can take those away. I go to wake them up, except Cronos is already there, moving too fast for even my goddess eyes to see. He scoops me up under the armpits, holding me with my feet dangling off the ground, his grip firm enough that I can't reach my arm to touch it and access my animals.

"Your tattoos are gone, too, along with your weapons."

"I don't believe you." I kick out at him, but he doesn't so much as budge at the impact.

"You are always so quick to fight," he murmurs softly. Like he's proud of me.

"You've only known me a few minutes," I say. "How would you know that?"

Maybe I can try to teleport. My skill in that area sucks—Hades has been trying to teach me—but I can't dangle here like a hooked fish, either.

I will Boone to wake up. To move while the Titan's back is turned.

"I know you well, Lyra Keres," Cronos says. Then grows scary serious in a way that makes me still. "You will be our savior."

My mind abandons teleporting. Just drops it.

Adrenaline floods so fast it feels like my skin's turning inside out.

Because I believe him. Gods, I do. He knows me. Really knows me. It's there in his eyes—too certain, too familiar. Like I already belong to some plan he made ages ago and forgot to mention until now.

"You're wrong about being useless," he says, still calm, still quiet. "You are very useful to me. And I will punish anyone who harms the one who will free me."

I shake my head, stomach lurching. He hurt Boone…because he *elbowed me*? Because he thinks I'm going to free a *Titan*? And not just any Titan. The absolute worst one?

A bell chooses that moment to chime. Clear. Cold. Final. Like it's counting down to something I won't survive.

Cronos doesn't let go. Just turns his piercing gaze toward the dark tunnel again.

"What is it?" I whisper.

The bell *keeps* chiming, and it sounds…off. Like it's supposed to be a happy sound, akin to toy shops at the holidays, but instead is in a minor key.

"Son of a bitch." With no warning, Cronos swings me around so abruptly that my feet fly out in an arc only to dangle over sheer nothing.

The abyss that edges both sides of Tartarus' walls—that pit full of monsters—looms below me like the open maw of a kraken.

Fear claws its way up the back of my throat, and I start thrashing for real.

"It might be safer down there anyway," Cronos says. "I hope you do not die this time."

Then he fucking lets go.

# 2

# LIVING ON BORROWED TIME

LYRA

I scream.
Of course I scream.

It rips right out of my throat as I flail, my stomach bolting for the exit while I plummet into the chasm. Above me, I see Cronos leaning out over the edge of the bridge. That damned Titan is watching me drop the same way a cat might watch a bug flounder in a pool.

After another breath, his shrinking face disappears entirely, swallowed by an impenetrable darkness that consumes me. Which is about when I realize that I'm *still* falling and not hitting anything.

It's also when it strikes me that I'm a fucking goddess. Not all that great of one yet. But still…

*Get your shit together, Lyra.*

If Hades were here, he'd be watching with his arms crossed and that impatient look that furrows his brows when I'm not immediately grasping whatever he's trying to teach me. We haven't had long to practice, but I've already seen that look a lot. Goddess lessons have gone about the same way thief lessons used to go.

That all clicks in at the same time, and I cut my screams off sharply, leaving my throat feeling raw and only the sound of air rushing in my ears as I fall…and fall…and fall.

Rabbit-hole style.

Then, out of the oppressive darkness, I see…something.

I squeeze my eyes shut, then open them again, and it's there. Bigger.

Closer. Something moving with me? Or maybe to me?

I have only a second to take in what appears to be a crystalline crack that reminds me of a geode rock, but I'm not falling past it. It's floating *with* me.

"What the hells—"

The thing rushes me. Only instead of making impact or crushing me, it doesn't touch me—it's not solid. And it swallows me whole.

My question gets absorbed by a silence so oppressive, it's like sound no longer exists. Everything is tinted red as movement flashes all around me, like I'm running so fast that the world blurs.

Then the space around me changes abruptly, and rather than falling endlessly through a dark abyss, I'm standing on one of the delicately carved bridges in Hades' water garden in the Underworld. The transition is so jarring my head spins for a second, and I put a hand out on the trunk of a nearby tree until everything stops spinning and the world comes into sharp reality.

Home.

Sound returns in a flash, and I'm surrounded by the soothing gurgle of running water, the fragrant scents of jasmine and honeysuckle, the perfect cool air on my skin. I'm surrounded by the brilliant, glowing colors of Erebos, where Hades' castle-like home stands. It's in a cavern so massive, the ceiling looks like a star-studded night sky.

I'm *home*. My new home in the Underworld.

Or…maybe this is a glamour. What in the fields of Asphodel just happened?

"What in the name of Olympus are you doing down here?" A low, snarling voice sounds from behind me. "This is the worst possible timing."

An achingly, wonderfully familiar voice.

Heart thudding with euphoria, pretty sure I'm glowing, I whirl around.

"Hades," I whisper, then almost sob with the emotions bubbling up.

His entire body goes dead still as he stares at me, taking me in with a single sweep of his gaze. "What happened?"

Everything off about this moment gets buried by the crash of relief that slams through me. I'm across the space between us, my arms around his neck in a heartbeat.

"Thank the gods," I whisper and kiss him.

He jerks against me, going rigid in my arms as he draws his mouth away from mine. Only far enough to search my eyes. Confusion slices through my relief like one of my axes. Holding still as well, I stare back.

What I see in his eyes isn't relief. It's angry bewilderment.

But…as our breaths mingle, his hand draws up the small of my back, pressing me closer, and my confusion turns to a wanting so familiar, I smile.

Hades catches his breath, and then his mouth is on mine. Gods in the heavens, it feels like the first time we kissed. Only…more.

Commanding but still soft. Demanding but questing. Like he's claiming and savoring this as something he's thought about for a long time.

How long was I trapped in Tartarus, anyway?

As for me, I'm so happy that I got out of that pit of vipers and back to him that I'm kissing him like I thought I'd never see him again. Because part of me, a deep-down part I was trying not to listen to, was worrying that he knew. That he knew Tartarus was my fate, maybe even exchanged me for Persephone.

When we slow, we're both breathing hard, and he puts his forehead to mine, eyes closed, hands at my back still holding me pressed up against him.

"You've never kissed me before," he says.

It takes a second for the words to burrow past my bubble of relieved happiness. I've never…what? "What are you talking about?"

As if my question knocks him upside the head, Hades rears back, looking more shaken than my god of death ever allows himself to.

"Your hair is long. You're my future Lyra, aren't you?"

Confusion feels like I'm trying to swim through rapids, getting flipped around in the rush of water. Future? My hair? What is he talking about? I put a hand to my head, and sure enough, it's wound up in a low bun.

I have no idea what is going on or why my hair matters. "Hades?"

His brows draw together in an intimidating scowl. "Damn it, Lyra. You're in the middle of Poseidon's Labor right now. I shouldn't be leaving you to deal with that alone."

"What? I don't understand."

"You told me to—"

Without warning, that blood-colored crystal thing passes over my head in a blur, and after a soundless, red-tinted moment, Hades is gone. I can still feel him against me, the sensation slowly fading, but I can tell the instant it disappears again, because of the darkness and the swish of air as I fall.

Trapped in the darkness of the abyss once more and still plummeting.

I don't know if I should scream or something else. I flail, a sound bubbling out of my throat that I cut off just as abruptly.

Because screaming won't fix shit.

*Think, Lyra. How do you get out of this?*

# 3

# AT LEAST ACT LIKE A GODDESS

LYRA

Wrangling my crashing heart as best I can, I force myself to close my eyes—not that it makes a difference in the dark, but so far, it's the only way I've managed to teleport the few times it's worked.

The memory of Hades' smooth voice rings in my head.

*Focus.*

Harder to do when a large part of me is bracing to splat when I hit bottom.

*Draw on your power until you feel a tingling under your skin, like energy.*

It takes longer this time, fear ripping the sensation away before I can get a good hold of it. My stomach is churning. But eventually, I feel it.

*Then pull it inward until you feel pressure in your chest.*

It never works that way for me.

The tingling gathers at the base of my spine, the same way pleasure does when Hades makes me…

*Picture where you are going.*

The memory of his voice in my head sounds more urgent now.

*Because you're still falling, Lyra. Focus.*

But where do I try to go? If teleporting worked to get out of Tartarus, the Titans wouldn't still be here. Instead, I picture Boone's limp form heaped on the bridge in a tangle of limbs. I'll try to get back to him and then get us both away from Cronos and whatever that bell meant.

*Release the power.*

An act that tends to blip out on me. Like the electricity turns off right when I need it most.

I let the tingling burst through me, trying to hold the image of where Boone is in my head. The wind in my ears stops, and I jerk my eyes open, heart tripping because I think, for a second, that I managed to do it on the first try for once. Without the side effects.

Disappointment might as well be a slap in the face.

No bridge. No Boone. No Cronos.

But I'm also not falling anymore. I'm standing...

Wait. When did I land? How?

Actually, the more important question is, *where* did I land this time? I frown, spinning in a circle to take it in. A cramped room with rock walls that is achingly, horribly familiar.

My room in the Order of Thieves' den in San Francisco.

It looks the same. My cheap metal desk is set up with my computer — only allowed for the clerks. My bed is a neatly made mattress tucked into a rounded recess carved out of the rock of our underground lair. Piles of loot from recent scores that I have to catalog are stacked as orderly as they can be. It even smells the same — cave, rock, and laundry detergent. I have a thing about mold, which can be an issue when living underground near the ocean. Keeping everything frequently washed is how I deal with it.

"What in the name of Tartarus?" I ask aloud, voice hushed. Is this even possible? Did I truly escape Tartarus? I'm still tingling like I haven't teleported yet, though.

I look down and stare at the jeans and my favorite long-sleeve shirt from my days in the den. Nothing special. Just gray, but soft, dry-fit material that was always comfortable. It's consistently cool underground, even in the summer. I wore this often. But I wasn't wearing it when I came into Tartarus.

Did I start over in my life, back at... Well, not the beginning, exactly. But out of that cursed place?

My shoulders slam back. Hades. *Does he know I'm in San Francisco?* I bolt for the door.

"You have entered the Lock of Hestia."

I screech to a stop and whirl into a defensive crouch at the sound of the voice behind me, only to jolt at the sight of a woman dressed in flowing traditional Grecian clothing. A golden laurel is woven into her crimson hair, which falls in waves down to her waist.

It can't be.

I stare at her hard as I come out of my crouch slowly. I've only ever seen carvings and paintings of this goddess, who is said to have died during the Anaxian Wars, when the gods and goddesses of the Greek pantheon knocked Zeus off his throne, then battled each other for the position. Scholars theorize that it was her death, not the destruction of Olympus, that finally ended the war.

"Hestia?" I ask, uncertain.

Goddess of home and hearth. Oldest child of Cronos and Rhea. What is she doing in my room?

Her smile is so full of natural warmth, I actually feel myself relaxing enough to smile back, a second sliver of hope wedging into my panic and fear, even if I'm still as confused as if I waded into the River of Oblivion. It's a good sign she's here, isn't it? It has to mean I made it out of Tartarus somehow. "Can you... Can you help me?"

"I am a reflection of the goddess who created this Lock," Hestia says.

Lock? She said that word already. Hestia's Lock. I frown, glancing around. How is *my* room a lock? "I don't understand."

Hestia flickers, like a signal got interrupted, and yet she still looks so... real. Would she feel solid if I touched her?

I don't try it.

She holds out her hands, indicating the room we're in. "Welcome to the Labyrinth."

# 4
## HESTIA'S LOCK

### LYRA

Shock hits, clean and sudden. I must have misheard the goddess.

"Labyrinth?" I glance around but only see the walls of my familiar bedroom back in San Francisco. "We're still in Tartarus?"

She enunciates each word as though speaking to a child. "The only way out of Tartarus is to open the Lock."

My first illogical thought is, *Thank the gods. There* is *a way out of Tartarus*. Immediately followed by thought number two...

"What do you mean by lock?" That word feels eerily synonymous with *captive*, and my stomach pitches. "What is a lock? How do I open it?" I shoot the questions at her like Artemis' arrows. "Is it part of a maze?" The Labyrinth is a maze, isn't it?

Hestia's ghost, or projection, or whatever she is, flickers again. "The Lock tests your innocence. I wish you luck in this. My Lock will test the power of your deepest unfulfilled desire."

My head is reeling. "What the hells does an unfulfilled desire have to do with innocence?"

The goddess blinks at me, and then the first smile she offered pins to her features again. This time, it's not giving me any warm fuzzies. "You have entered the Lock of Hestia."

I frown. "You already said that."

Another blink. Another flicker.

"Welcome to the La—"

"You said that, too."

Flick. Blink. Flicker.

If I wasn't so damned confused, I'd say it's been a while since anyone talked to Hestia's…recording?

"Welcome to the Labyrinth," she finally starts again.

*"Eirene help me,"* I pray to the goddess of peace, since technically there is no one to pray to for patience.

With a sigh, I cross my arms and wait to see if, without me interrupting her, Hestia might provide more information. Sure enough, after yet another smiling beat, she says, "This Lock can only be opened by one willing to give up what they want most."

*Damn.* This sounds *exactly* like the godsdamned Labors the gods and goddesses created for the Crucible. But this isn't so bad, I try to console myself. One simple test. I made it past *nine* Labors in the Crucible. Surely, I can open one measly lock and meander through a labyrinth.

I nod and open my eyes again, ignoring the racing of my pulse. I offer Hestia my own sinister smile. *Bring it.* "Let's do this."

But she's not done. "In the Lock, you will be tested without your powers."

Fuck *me*. Then the rest of what she said hits me… "No!"

I shoot out a hand like I can stop her. She is *not* taking the powers that Hades *sacrificed* to give me, that saved my life. I have a bad feeling that I'm really going to need them down here.

She snaps her fingers.

The lingering sensation of tingling from my teleporting attempt gets… stronger. And stronger. And stronger. Not pleasure now, but pain. Until it feels as though I've stuck my finger in a light socket.

I fight it. Or I try to. Fist clenched, I hold on to the sensation at the core of me that I think of as a piece of Hades—warmth, light, brightness in the dark—I try to hold on to it with everything I am.

A jolt ricochets through me.

Electric.

Then another, so violent that I pitch forward on a gasp. My grip on my power slips as, with my hands on my knees, my vision closes in on itself, the edges turning black until all I can see is a pinpoint of…light.

I *know* this light.

I am awash in it, everything around me radiant. It is everywhere, within me and without. My power. Hades' power. Only, unlike when Hades made me a goddess, this time it lifts away from me, as if I'm watching a train going farther away down a tunnel. As it gets smaller and smaller, all warmth disappears, leaving me chilled to the bone.

My vision clears and I come back to myself with a blink and a shudder, lungs heaving with effort and sweat trickling down my temples, only to find that I haven't left my room and creepy AI Hestia is still standing there with that inane smile on her face. Wrapping my arms around myself, I try to control my breathing.

I'm already sure of what just happened, but I test it anyway. The only thing I've mastered in the little time I've had to learn is turning lights on and off. I focus on my sad, wonky desk lamp and swish my finger like a wizard's wand.

Nothing. Not a flicker of the lightbulb. Not even a poltergeist.

I'm human. A frail mortal without a weapon. Worse, she stole the only part of Hades I had left with me down here. Son of a bitch.

"Now for your test—"

"Whoa, whoa, whoa." I throw up a hand. "Cronos threw me down a hole, and I ended up here. I do not want to go through any Lock or take a test."

She flickers and blinks, clearly not computing.

Useless.

"Just send me back the way I came," I beg. "I don't want to do this."

Another episode of flickering and blinking, and then she settles again. "The only way out is forward."

Godsdamned gods with their "only way out" and "you have no choice but to compete" bullshit. I *earned* the right to never play a game or be tested again. This can't be happening.

"Your sacrifice is to be granted your deepest unfulfilled desire," Hestia says.

I glance around. Did I hear that right?

"Err... You mean you take it away, right?"

Glitch. Flicker. Blink. Glitch.

I don't know why I keep bothering with questions.

"When you cross the threshold of this room, all that is will no longer be, and everything you want, you will have in its place."

"Uh-huh," I mutter under my breath as I start to search the room for anything I can use to fight my way out. A grappling hook, maybe? Can I climb out of here? "Riddle me something else, Batman."

Like she finally decides to answer one of my questions, she rephrases it. "Everything that currently is will be stripped from your memory, replaced with a new history and what you've always wanted most."

I straighten to stare at her. Anger twists like writhing snakes in my belly at being put in this position again, then goes limp under another onslaught of panic. It keeps coming in horrifying waves. She's going to take away everything. Including…Hades?

*Oh gods.*

*Oh hells.*

*Olympus be damned.*

I scrape my brain for a thousand different answers. A way out of this. A way back up to the bridge. Cronos probably already left, assuming I'm dead.

But I'm also asking myself…

What have I always wanted most? That's easy. My heart is screaming Hades. *Hades* is what I want most—to get back to him and the life we were trying to start together. That has to be it, right? I'd gladly give up being a goddess if it returns me to him.

"You have a choice," Hestia says now.

"Finally." I fling my hands up on a wave of sharp relief.

"You can accept the life you've always dreamed of inside my Lock. Or you can unseal this Lock and return to your real life."

The relief abandons me so fast my shoulders slump. That's not the choice I was hoping for. "How do I open the Lock?"

"You must willingly choose to walk away from the alternate life your hopes and dreams create, even if it breaks your heart and your mind." She shoots me one more fake, glassy-eyed doll's smile. "You may start…now."

Hestia's AI ghost disappears without a sound or trace. I narrow my eyes, frowning as I stare at the lamp on my desk. Why does the light look… fuzzy, hazy? I rub at my eyes, but it doesn't help. The entire room has this romantic softness to it. A knock sounds at my door, unexpected, and I jump.

Then pause.

Do I open it?

"Lyra?" That's Felix.

How does my boss in the Order even know I'm in here? Then my brain kicks in. This is part of the Lock. This is an illusion. The instant that thought occurs, a sharp pain pierces through my head, right behind my eyes. I wince.

Another knock. "Lyra? Good news." I try to focus on the words and how wrong they are. I don't think Felix has ever used that term in his entire life. The basic concept of "good" is lost on that man.

I point at the door, calling out to the invisible goddess. "This simulation got that part wrong."

Another stab of pain is the only answer I get. I understand her reply all the same. Holding on to reality, to the truth…hurts in here.

Another knock.

I still hesitate. Hestia said that one bit about crossing the threshold of this room. So I probably shouldn't do that. Right?

Except the only way forward is through. She said that, too.

A choice that is not really a choice. I have to go through this. The thing is, if Hades is on the other side of that door, even if it's an illusion, what if I can't make myself walk away from him to get back to the dumpster fire that is my reality?

Mental note for when I escape this place—lodge a complaint with the gods about their cruelty and shitty instructions in all things locks, labors, and games.

"Lyra?" another voice calls out.

I gasp so hard I splutter.

Was that…?

I'm only vaguely aware that the pain disappears thanks to a flutter of nerves taking off in my stomach. My feet carry me to the door, and I jerk it open to find Felix standing there with a grin as cutting as the rest of him. Behind him, haloed in pink glowing light that almost makes them appear angelic, are two people I used to dream and pray about every night from the age of three, when they handed me over to the Order of Thieves so I could work off "our" family debt.

But the reality is, thanks to the curse Zeus gave me as a baby—to be unlovable—they were using the debt as an excuse to abandon me. Or so I've always thought.

"Mom?" I croak around a throat that is threatening to clog up with tears. "Dad?"

# 5

# NEVER DREAM

### LYRA

Brad and Jessica Keres. They're here. They came for me finally. Not Hades but my parents.

Another stabbing sensation rips through my head, and my heart might as well tear in two. Until I met Hades, I only ever wanted three things—to lose my curse, my freedom from the Order, and a real family. Is the wish Hestia is granting me the one I've ached for the longest?

"You've grown up so much," Mom whispers.

The haze in this illusion makes it hard to collect details, like walking through a dream, but I still greedily absorb everything I can about both my parents. My mom is petite, her brown hair graying at the roots, but she does have green eyes like mine with gold at the center. My dad is tall with a belly that reminds me of Santa Claus. I get the raven-black shade of my hair from him. Brown eyes, though. I didn't seem to inherit any of his other features.

I used to put myself to sleep imagining this exact moment. When they came back for me.

My father holds a trembling hand out to me. "We've come to take you home, baby."

His eyes brim with hope, but worry lines bracket them, etched deep as if carved there by time. Is this an act? Or did they miss me every single night the way I missed them? Did they wonder what I was doing? Picture me thieving? Pray for my safety?

*It's all a lie*, I try to tell myself, and I flinch with the pain. *Don't believe it.*

But it feels so...much better...to believe this. It doesn't hurt. It feels... warm and more real by the second, and convincing my mind that it's fake is getting harder.

The only way they'd be here in the den is if they came here to pay off our family debts and take me home... Maybe I was wrong. Maybe they do care.

"You're really here?" I ask.

Is that my voice?

I sound...off. Like an automaton reciting scripted lines.

Besides, that's not what I should have asked. I want to ask how in the name of Hades they could have left me here so long. I want to demand why they thought a three-year-old should be paying off debt of any kind. I want to ask why they blamed *me* for Zeus' curse in the first place. My mother is the one whose water broke in his temple, pissing him off. It's her damned fault.

So many other questions.

My mother nods, dropping her hand from her mouth to smile at me through the mist of tears. "Yes, baby," she says. "We're really here."

She steps closer, opening her arms, beckoning me.

Something pinches in my head, like the start of a headache. Pain means something, doesn't it? But the reason why is slippery. Didn't Hestia say something about a threshold? Maybe I'm remembering that wrong.

Swallowing hard, I manage to keep my feet where they are, but I still reach out and grasp her hand. Then close my eyes as even that small touch sends happiness through me on a surge of pure warmth.

All the pieces of my heart that chipped off—year after year, each time they didn't come—rush back in and snap together. Whole again. Like nothing was ever missing.

A tear squeezes out to run down my cheek. Grief doesn't always come from losing someone—it also comes from realizing they were never really yours to begin with.

I was *so* angry with them, but now all I want is for this to be true. I can have both, can't I? Them and Hades? Another pinch of pain—duller, though—and in the back of my head, a small voice, barely audible, whispers that something is wrong. That this isn't right. Isn't real. I have new dreams and a new family.

But it's such a little voice. Distant and far from me and growing softer and hazier by the second.

My mother squeezes my hand. "Let's go home, Lyra."

A small part of me is still fighting this…compulsion…but only a small part, and I step through the doorway and into my parents' arms, and what was left of that little doubting, warning voice flies away.

Everything that's happened recently—the Crucible, Hades, Tartarus— suddenly, it becomes so obvious that all of that was just a dream. A nightmare, most of it. I'm still in the Order, still cursed, still paying off our debt…and yet my parents have come to free me and take me home.

"Come on, sweetheart," my dad says in a voice wobbly with tears. He clears his throat.

Before they can lead me away, Felix gives me a big hug. It's a little uncomfortable, since Felix is not and has never been a hugger. But I find myself hugging him back.

"My little master thief," he says in my ear.

Master thief? I try to pull away, the ache behind my eyes growing again. Because that sounds wrong. I'm not a master thief. I'm a…

His face blurs a little more, turns rosier, and the warmth takes away the headache.

And I suddenly remember things are different. Or…not suddenly. More like the knowledge just…is. I *belonged* here.

Felix looks over my shoulder at my parents. "You should be proud. She's one of our best. Second only to Boone."

I…am?

Pride swells in my chest as memories of my scores flash through my mind. I *am*. I'm one of the best master thieves they've ever seen.

I pull back and grin at Felix. "You only want me to come fix your spreadsheets."

Spreadsheets? I don't do spreadsheets. That's the clerks' job. Why did I say that?

A sharper shot of pain stabs behind my eyes, and for a flash, the space it takes for a hummingbird's wing to flutter once, I think Felix's face morphs into something…not human. Are there…teeth? Did I see jagged teeth?

But even faster, he's back to smiling. No pain, either. Must've been a trick of the pretty lighting.

He shakes his head with a click of his tongue. "You will be a sore loss to the den."

Which makes me tear up. So many years in one place will do that.

As I step away from him, my mother takes my hand and my father wraps an arm around my shoulders. Together, they lead me away down the long natural stone hallway, navigating the various twists and turns of the den secretly buried underneath the city of San Francisco.

We get to the area where the newest pledges are required to stock rubber boots and flashlights for the thieves coming and going from our underground tunnels. I help my parents find pairs that fit them before I grab one of the lights. Which is when the slap of running feet has me glancing back.

Then straightening.

Boone.

"Lyra," he calls.

The second he says my name, the edges of my vision feather and fuzz and another wave of memories comes at me. Boone and I…

We're partners.

Best friends, but more than that, when Boone and I work together, we're unstoppable.

# 6

## MY HEART'S FAR, FAR AWAY

### LYRA

The details about Boone are crisper in the rosy light than everything else. He's dressed in dark jeans and a hoodie, like he's been out casing a score. When he gets to me, Boone glances over my head at my parents, dark-eyed gaze sharp on them. He knows how long I've been waiting.

Boone has never waited for his parents.

The way he talks about them, on the rare occasions he has, I'm pretty sure he thinks of them as evil incarnate. The look on his face tells me he's worried my parents are the same. I hear my father clear his throat, shift on his feet.

My father is not a small man. I seem to remember he was a mechanic, and those years have left him in good shape other than the belly. I don't blame him for being nervous. When he wants to be, Boone is intimidating as hell. His size, the muscles, the recently shaved scruffy beard a shade darker than his brown hair. Add that to his usual get up of biker clothes—leather and jeans—combined with a palpable vibe of fuck around and find out, and most people avoid him on the street.

Which is hilarious, because really, he's a big squish. A squish who can handle himself and is the best master thief the Order has seen in several centuries, but still...

As if dismissing my parents as insignificant, Boone focuses on me. "You were going to leave without saying goodbye, Lyra?" he asks quietly.

With my free hand, I tug on his jacket so he'll lean down.

"I figured you'd come find me," I whisper.

Official partnerships within the Order are strictly forbidden. Dating, too, not that Boone and I have ever entertained that. They don't want their pledges distracted by personal bonds, and they want to use all the combinations of their resources that they can. So Boone and I manipulate things behind the scenes to suit ourselves. The truth is, he's taking a risk, meeting me like this.

Although neither Boone nor I have ever been too worried about breaking rules.

He looks over my head again. "Excuse us for a second."

Boone pulls me away, backtracking to a turn in the corridor. Then he swallows. This close, I see his throat move with it, the details clear. "They came for you?" he asks.

"Just now."

Boone tugs on my long hair, which just for a second makes me frown. Wasn't it just up in a bun? Or...didn't I cut it? It shouldn't be long.

The flash of pain disappears quickly when Boone distracts me. "And me?" he asks.

Which gives me a different pause, my hair forgotten. I study my friend's face. He is *never* vulnerable. Part of that is training as a thief all his life, and part of that is how Boone is. I can see a hint of worry in his eyes all the same. Because he *lets* me see it.

"I couldn't exactly ask Felix where you were." Not without making things harder on Boone, who has to stay here. "I planned to catch you on your way topside to scope your next score tomorrow night. The diamond place, right?"

His broad shoulders ease slightly. "You knew about that?" We don't talk jobs we don't partner on.

"What do you think?" I raise a single eyebrow in challenge.

He offers a narrow-eyed half smile. "But I haven't even reported that one yet."

I shrug. "I'm damn good at what I do."

Boone breaks into a wide grin, eyes gleaming at me over his crooked nose—broken before I met him, when he was still part of the Dallas den. But then he slowly sobers. "So this is goodbye?"

We've never talked about what would happen when one of us left. But he's talked about going legit when he gets out, putting his skills to use and opening a private security business.

"I was thinking…you might need a hand with that new business of yours."

Boone backs up, searching my face like he thinks I'm joking. "Are you being serious?"

Does he hate the idea? I shrug. "I mean, I know a thing or two. And I'm better at office work than you."

*Office work.* The hazy light wavers behind him and around him on another flicker of pain behind my eyes. Why would I know anything about office work? The dens have clerks for that.

But then Boone grins again, and this one doesn't fade away. "I'm in, partner," he says.

I laugh because that's what I said to him the first time he offered to team up on a score.

He's nodding to himself, and I can see he's already plotting out how this will work. "The gods must have plans for us, Lyra."

*Gods…*

*The gods have plans…*

Another flicker in the haze, and a twist of pain hits as those words rattle around in my head. An image of mercurial silver eyes in an unsmiling face flashes through my mind.

*Hades.*

But as quickly as it appears, the image is gone, along with the sharp ache it brought, returning me to that odd, fuzzy feeling. Almost…feverish.

"So…" I rub my hands together.

We're doing this. I have plans for my future. A fear I've been stuffing down deep my entire life—what I would do when I finished with the Order of Thieves—is no longer a fear. "Tomorrow night, after you scope your next job, we can talk. Figure out what I can be doing while we wait for you to pay off your debt."

"You won't have to wait long," Boone says.

His track record as a thief is unrivaled, so I'm not surprised. I let out a silent breath of relief. "When?"

"I'll see you tomorrow."

I rock back on my heels, not sure what he means. "To talk through plans?"

He shakes his head. "I paid my debt off two years ago."

"Two…" Holy shit. How did I not know that? I mean, I should have assumed, given how good he is, but I'm just as good.

"I have a stash saved away where no one knows. Enough for us to get a solid start." His lips tip. "More than a start."

So do I, for that matter. I frown over that. "Why didn't you leave?"

"I didn't have anywhere else to go." He shrugs.

Gods, the things the world does to us sometimes. The Order hasn't been awful, but it hasn't exactly been all candy, Christmas, and pats on the head, either. And he didn't have anywhere else to go.

At least I have my parents.

"I'm sorry," I say softly.

But he shakes his head. "Don't be. Hermes gives his thieves what they need. So I figure he brought us together for this. I couldn't make my business idea work all on my own anyway."

He needed me. That's what he's saying. That I'm needed.

My heart feels like one of those symbols on computers showing the battery level. It was close to full, thanks to my parents, but now I'm practically glowing I'm so charged up.

"So…" My whisper is embarrassingly choked. "Tomorrow?"

He sticks his hand out for a shake. "Tomorrow, partner. I'll come to your parents' home, and we can talk. Figure out how to start a business. Okay?"

A new life…

Family. Freedom. The future.

It's like all the holidays landed on my birthday and I'm getting everything I ever wanted.

The headache that keeps threatening pushes outward with pressure and a new shooting ache.

*Not everything.* A tiny voice tries to wave a red flag. And I shake my head like I'm attempting to rattle something loose that I can't quite remember. There's something else I want more. Isn't there? Something right out of reach in my mind. Something to do with Hades…

But Boone grabs my hand to shake it, and the feeling goes away as I laugh and squeeze back, even while the pain behind my eyes remains. I ignore it.

*No way am I not soaking up every single second of this.*

Maybe I have a migraine coming on? I've never had one, but I hear they can make you light sensitive.

I'm probably only thinking of the god Hades because he's associated with omens of endings. After all, it's hard to believe this won't all be taken away from me. I should be ecstatically happy, so why do I feel like something is off? Maybe everything that's happening is so good, so perfect, that I can't quite believe it. That has to be it. Right?

Boone grins one last time, then gives me a small push toward where my parents are waiting to take me home, probably wondering what happened to us. "I'll see you tomorrow."

As I turn the corner, I see my parents down the hall. They're standing in shadows, the rosy light not quite reaching them, so it has to be my mind playing tricks again.

Because, for a heartbeat, I swear I see a blank space where their eyes should be.

# 7

## HOME'S A LIE

### LYRA

My father steps out of the shadows, nearing one of the sconces that light the halls. Blue flame—a gift from Hermes of undying flames to light all his thieves' homes. It casts more of that pink haze over his features.

I was definitely seeing things, because Dad's eyes aren't blank sockets. They're normal. He's even grinning, making them crinkle at the corners, which makes my own eyes ache.

"You ready to go home?" he asks.

Home.

The *finally* of this moment settles into my heart, into my soul, wrapping around me like the softest, warmest blanket. I take a deep breath. "I am."

I grab one of the flashlights and lead my parents through several more twists and turns in the dark until we get to a solid-looking cement wall.

"Did you ever meet Hermes in person?" my mother asks curiously as we pass through the hidden door into the human tunnels where his image is painted.

"No—"

A sharp sting of pain in my skull comes just before a vague image, one that feels like a memory but couldn't possibly be. Because in it, I'm standing on some kind of platform surrounded by mountains and white temples. Lots of them.

And standing in front of me isn't Hermes but Hades, wearing jeans, a blue button-down shirt rolled up at the sleeves, and work boots.

Hades.

This feels like a memory, but I'm certain I've never met the god.

I close my eyes, applying pressure to my temples as I try to force other images into some kind of order. Try to force them past the growing ache. There's a vague feeling that the place I was standing in was Olympus. Which doesn't make a lick of sense. Humans don't go to Olympus.

The harder I try to remember it, the worse the pain gets, building and building and making my stomach roll, and so do the images until I'm left feeling like I'm drifting in a sea of confusion.

"We've kept your bedroom exactly the way it was when you left us," Dad interrupts my thoughts to tell me.

I drop my hands, letting the images go, and immediately the pain fades. It's probably better that I stop trying to force memories that aren't there. I'm sure it was just a dream anyway.

I swing the flashlight my dad's way.

Only to pause.

Teeth.

I saw jagged, inhuman teeth in the dark a flash before the full beam of light hit his face. What is happening? Trying not to be obvious, I peer closer. But the details of his face stay the same, if slightly fuzzy around the edges in the darkness.

"We hoped you would come home sooner," he continues. "But since we weren't able to get enough money until now, we thought it might be nice if you chose all new things." I blink at the lopsided, slightly sheepish smile he gives me. No jagged teeth.

Terrific. Now I'm seeing things.

It has to be the shock of all this happening so quickly. I'll settle in soon enough. In the meantime, I won't say anything to my parents. They'd only worry.

Dad takes me by the hand and tugs me along. "I'm pretty sure you're not going to fit in the bed we had for you when you were three."

I chuckle. "Probably not."

Then we're standing in a hallway in a home. My previous home. For a disorienting second, if feels as though I closed my eyes and when I opened them, we'd moved, but the longer I think about it, the more I remember walking out of the tunnels, then hailing a cab home, the drive, all of it.

Gods. I guess excitement is making me lose it a bit.

I follow my parents down the length of the narrow space but pause to stare at the pictures on the wall. I don't remember what used to be here, but now there is image after framed image of…me. All from far away, all different ages.

Me growing up.

I reach out to run my finger over the smooth glass, biting down hard on my lip. They've always been watching?

Mom rubs my back, and I have to keep myself from flinching away, not used to touch. "We knew we weren't supposed to, but…"

I swallow hard and nod.

Then I let them lead me to the room at the end of the hall and pause in the doorway.

"There's enough room for a king-size bed in here," Dad says, looking over my shoulder from where he's standing behind me.

Mom slips her hand into mine and gives it a squeeze. "I only caught a glimpse of your room in the…errr…den, but it looked like a smaller bed. Maybe you'd like a little extra space to start with."

With another zap of a headache, a crystal-clear image flashes through my mind. This one of a king-size bed in a masculine room, floor-to-ceiling windows with a view of San Francisco, gray silk sheets. Did I do a job in some rich asshole's penthouse? I don't remember it.

"Lyra?" Mom asks.

Her voice clears away the pain like it never happened, and I shoot her a smile. "A king seems awfully large for one person. Maybe a queen would be better."

Queen.

That word means something else to me, doesn't it? Something new?

As Mom exchanges a glance with Dad, her shoulders drop slightly, like my answer was…a relief.

The size of my bed is a relief?

Maybe they can't afford a king and are just trying to make up for all the years we've lost.

"Now that I think about it, a double would be better," I say. "After so many years in a small bed, I think I'd feel lost in a bigger one."

The lines around her eyes ease. "Anything you want, honey." Mom inhales and lets it go. "Is spaghetti still your favorite?"

Anything that doesn't taste like sawdust is my favorite. The Order is cheap when it comes to feeding their pledges. I don't tell her that. "Absolutely."

Her eyes light up. "I'll go get that started." And she hurries down the hall.

Dad watches her go with a smile tinted with sadness.

"What's my real name?" I ask. The question comes so out of nowhere, even I tense a little.

Dad frowns. "You don't remember?"

I shake my head slowly. "I was too young, and I've been Lyra ever since."

"Right. Of course," he mumbles to himself, casting his gaze around in darting little moves.

Does he not remember? How could that be—

"Alani."

I straighten. "Alani?" I try out the sound of it, strange in my mouth, but sweet, like a song.

He nods, watching me closely. "Your mother's idea."

"I like it."

That earns me a new grin. Did my parents always smile this much?

*They just got you home. Of course they are extra smiley.*

What is wrong with me? I've been in the Order too long, had things like faith and trust trained out of me. That's what it is. I'm the problem here.

"Do you want us to call you that?" The hopeful note in his voice is unmistakable, but…

"I don't think so," I say slowly. "I'm used to Lyra now."

"Of course." He holds his hands up. "Anything you want."

"Brad?" my mom calls from the kitchen.

"Coming," he calls back. Then Dad gives me an awkward little wave and leaves me there.

I turn around and wander my room. They really did leave it the same. The small twin bed that is more toddler size than a full twin. I squat down, picking up a dark-haired doll that I remember. Three-year-old me always thought she was so beautiful, with curling locks and big brown eyes and grown-up clothes. Current me sees the tatters. She was second- or third-hand. I still don't care. She was my favorite.

"Nice to see you again," I whisper, then smooth her hair and set her back down beside her faded plastic house.

Getting up, I turn around in a slow circle, hands on my hips. What changes do I want to make?

Nothing too expensive, but maybe paint the walls a simple white. Blue has always been my favorite color, so a bed with blue sheets and maybe a white or darker blue bedspread would be nice. Or maybe…gray silk.

Another lightning strike of pain zings my brain, and I can picture that bed again, even more clearly now. Visceral details come with the image. The silky feel of them against my skin, the smell of lying in them—fresh linen, chocolate, and…smoke? Like a campfire. Why smoke?

More details come at me fast, so real that I start breathing harder—a strong arm stealing around my middle, pulling me back against a solid chest. The low rumble of a voice in my ear that makes me both shiver and sigh at the same time.

But I can't make out what he says.

Just that I…am happy.

Who? There is no one. I've never had anything like that with anyone. Ever.

I press my palms into my throbbing temples and squeeze my eyes shut.

"You couldn't even wait until morning?" I murmur in the memory and can hear the smile in my own sleepy voice.

Then I roll over and freeze.

# 8

## BEFORE MY TIME

### LYRA

A lock of raven-black hair falls into silvery eyes that stare at me with sleepy adoration.

Hades.

My heart stutters, then jagged pain bursts through my head like fire burning away the underbrush and clearing the haze with the truth as the veil of the illusion rips from my mind.

Hades.

My home is with *Hades*. My life is with the god of death, the King of the Underworld. No...not king anymore.

I am queen.

I spin around my little-girl room and see incandescent shimmers of glamours and enchantments everywhere now. This version of me, of my life... It isn't real. Exactly like she said she would, Hestia made me believe that none of that happened. She showed me a different future. Yes...one where I got everything my younger self dreamed of for so very, very long. One where I could even have been happy.

But it's *not* my future.

Not the one I choose for myself. Not the one I desperately need to get back to on the other side of those damned gates.

Not anymore, and it never will be.

I squeeze my eyes shut, trying to wrestle with the abrupt disillusionment. The ache in my head turns into throbbing, like reality is still battling to keep the false narrative out. Because I did want this once—the love of my parents. The bigger shock, reverberating through me like an earthquake shaking the very foundations of San Francisco, is that what I will regret giving up most is...

"Lyra?" Boone's voice sounds from behind me.

I whirl around to find him in my doorway, my parents' worried faces tucked in behind him on either side.

My hand creeps up to my throat like I'm trying to contain my own sorrow as my throat closes up at the sight of his face.

This alternate life blends with what really happened, and I know, beyond a shadow of a doubt, that Boone is only my friend from my life before—we were never partners, never best friends. Those were things I wanted. Desperately, at the time.

But that's not what I want now. I walked away from those dreams with ease the second I gave my heart to Hades.

*This* Boone must see something of the truth in my face because he reaches out almost reflexively. "We're supposed to start a business together—"

I shake my head. "It's not real. None of it was."

"Please," he chokes out. "You're the only true friend I have. I can't do this alone."

"I'm sorry." I twist my lips around the words and the threatening burn of tears.

I'm sorry because now that I can see the glamour of Hestia's test, I know the future she showed me would never have happened. My parents were *never* coming back for me. Even if I'd paid off the debt, I don't think they would have taken me in. I'm not sure they ever loved me, or missed me, or thought of me once they shucked me off to the Order, able to go on with their lives debt free and no longer burdened with a cursed child.

But Boone...

That future with him *was*...possible. My skills as an office clerk would have made me ideally suited to help him start a business. Was that what he'd wanted? His dream?

He closes his eyes, because he knows I won't change my mind.

I take a step back, lifting my gaze to the ceiling, looking anywhere but at him. "Okay, Hestia!" I call out. "I've made my choice. Let me out."

A hissing sound comes from the direction of the doorway. Behind

Boone, my parents' faces…melt. Like candle wax. The colors of their skin and hair and eyes drip away with it. My throat was already raw and tight with emotion, but now it closes even more with gut-churning horror, making it hard to breathe as I see what lies beneath.

Because my parents aren't an illusion…they are Nightmares.

*Oh. My. Gods.*

I'm not safe in my dreams here. I was being hunted.

I thought the creatures of antiquity were eradicated from the world around the same time the Titans were locked up in Tartarus. I guess they've been stuck down here, too, waiting for more victims.

And Cronos fed me to them like chum in the water.

The illusion melted away, they stand behind Boone in their true form. Sickly pale, grayish-white skin stretches over an anthropoid shape—lanky and long-torsoed with humanish heads, they stand on two overlong legs and with two arms that nearly scrape the ground. That's where the resemblance to humans ends.

Their sinewy chest muscles blend into something that looks like tree roots under their skin, growing around their collarbones and leading up their necks to their faces, which have wrinkles where a nose should be, smooth sockets for eyes, and high foreheads that mold into what looks like a ridge at the back of their heads. Their mouths are human-looking but filled with jagged teeth.

I wasn't seeing things before.

*Trust your damned instincts, Lyra.*

In sync, they both open their mouths wide, and it only gets worse—those jagged teeth protrude on what, to me, looks like a beak. Pink and raw, their beaks are lined with those teeth along the entire length, snapping at me.

On sheer instinct, I reach behind me to grab the axes strapped to my back only to get handfuls of empty air. Which is when I remember that the Gate of Tartarus stripped me of my weapons and Hestia stripped me down to mortality.

*Shit. Shit. Shit.*

Keeping my gaze glued to the snapping creatures, I try to think.

Is there anything in here that can help me?

Unless you count the doll—I mean, those plastic pointed toes could be used to stab—there's nothing I can use to fight the Nightmares. Shit.

Maybe I can run past them if they come in the room. Except Boone is blocking the doorway.

I pull my thinking up sharply.

Boone, who isn't covered in a film of glamour, who has been crystal clear the entire time I've been down here. I squint at him. Why hasn't he melted into a monster yet? Is he an NPC in this illusion? He's holding still with his eyes closed.

One of the Nightmares lifts a long limb, and the hand at the end changes shape into something akin to a sword. Holy hells. The bastards are shape-shifters? It's not entirely about glamouring?

I take up a fighting stance—feet wide, hands up, ready for it to come at me—but the thing that was my mother moments ago steps back and aligns the point of the sword with Boone's spine. Then, even without eyes, I know it looks directly at me.

A threat.

Boone is *real*.

Did Cronos throw him down here with me, too?

What an asshole.

Holding up both hands, I don't move. "Boone," I whisper.

His eyes open slowly, and he stares at me, kind of hazy and confused. Oh my gods. It's *really* him. Boone is here with me. Since when? The entire time?

*Focus on the important stuff.*

I think Boone is still caught in the fantasy, his eyes glassy and unfocused and slightly accusing. I do the only thing I can think of…

I whistle.

It's one of the signals all pledges know—the warning to drop.

At the same time, I whirl and grab the doll, chucking it at the sword-armed Nightmare, but I miss and hit Boone right between the eyes.

Because he didn't fucking drop.

His head snaps back. Before he can straighten, I tackle him, trying to take out his legs so he'll fall forward instead of back. Which works great, except he lands on me with an *oomph*, though I'm not sure if it comes from him or me, because all the wind gets knocked right out of me.

"What the hells, Lyra," he groans. "You don't have to tackle me to—"

A flash of a weird, gray-fleshed sword comes from overhead, and, despite still struggling for air, I manage to roll me and Boone together, slamming my back into the doorjamb, but at least the Nightmare misses us. Its sword arm slams into...

Rock.

Not carpeted flooring.

The glamour of the bedroom and the house and the entire world of San Francisco melts away like an oil painting melting in a fire, and instead we're lying on the ground in a huge space that reminds me of a pie wedge—wide at one end, which boasts a curved wall, and narrowing to a point at the other. There is no ceiling, or maybe I can't see it, since the top is so high up. Smooth stone walls climb into the darkness of the abyss. The space is lit only by a glowing orb that floats in the center close to the ground.

And scattered around the floor are bones. Bleached white like they've been in the sun.

Or picked so clean there's nothing left.

Fuck.

"Move!" Boone, sounding more himself, wraps around me and rolls us both over and over and over as more than one sword arm flashes by, thudding against the ground with sickly noises as they miss each time. Using a flipping technique, Boone has us on our feet, with him bodily between me and the two Nightmares, his arms stuck out to keep me from coming around him.

I lean over, getting a better look at their entire bodies. The rootlike growths around their shoulders and necks also extend down their legs. I shudder. Those things were my parents only a few moments ago.

With an otherworldly screech of sound that reminds me of nails being dragged down giant chalkboards, the two creatures charge. Boone drops a shoulder and barrels into one of them, backing it up even as it pummels at him with its sword arms—but the swords are too long and it's only hitting him with the fleshy part.

And the second Nightmare is coming straight for me.

My early years of training as a thief, including self-defense, kick in hard, and I manage to deflect its stabbing motion, grabbing it by the forearm and turning to bring its elbow down across my shoulder. The arm bends the wrong way with a satisfying crunch, and the Nightmare screams. The sound seems to trigger its friend into a rage.

Across the room, the other Nightmare lifts Boone up, holding him lengthwise overhead like it's lifting a barbell, not letting go no matter how much he thrashes. The thing has to be eight feet tall at least, and its arms are even longer.

Another screech—this one different, almost shocked—sounds from the Nightmare at my side.

At first, I think it's because of me, but then I realize that it's looking behind me with those eyeless sockets. Then it drops to its belly on the ground, trying to scoot away, like it's hiding.

I jerk around to see what it's hiding from. Another one of those red crystal things is coming at me fast. I get a better look at it this time—glittering in a deep red sheen of jagged minerals, like a bloody gash ripping through reality. Bypassing the Nightmare, it swallows me whole.

In the next instant, after a new round of silence and blurring red, I'm standing in Hades' office in our penthouse.

The shock is followed by a rush of relief that is like diving into the bracing cold of the Pacific Ocean. My hands fly up over my mouth as I stare around me at the familiar space.

Wait. Is this real? Or another Nightmare illusion? Is Hestia trying again? She got my deepest desire wrong and is trying to fool me again.

But this isn't hazy like before. No rose-colored sheen to it. No pain in my head when I think of him or anything that was real. Which means *this* is real. I'm actually *here* in the penthouse. Just like I was in the water garden with Hades.

No fucking clue how. Or maybe all of this is a glamour. One giant hallucination.

Only…I can *smell* the bitter chocolate of him. Faint but here. My body lights up at the familiar scent.

This is real.

It feels like yesterday when I woke in his bed, the scent of him all over my body. Or like he'll show up any second, stealing his arms around me from behind, feathering his lips over the curve of my neck. Coaxing. Teasing. Calling me his star. Making me burn.

I run toward the door.

"Hades!" I call out. "Hades—" I stop mid-step and stare at something that is…definitely wrong.

A chill slithers through me, stealing all the warmth of his scent from the room.

I'm facing his trophy wall. That's what I call it. It's a wall of glass shelves, brightly lit to show off the antiquities he's collected through the years. Including…

"That's not possible." The words scratch in my throat.

Because a matched set of weapons is displayed inside—two axes with golden handles, the bottom halves of which are wrapped in turquoise leather. The blades are silver with golden markings. A circle with a symbol of Odin's head divides the larger axe blade from a smaller one on the backside that's shaped more like a tip of a spear. There are other symbols. Norse.

A gift from Odin to Cronos' eldest child.

Our axes. Mine now.

Stripped from me when I entered Tartarus.

My hands start to shake. Did Hades put them here after I disappeared? I haven't been gone *that* long. Have I? He wouldn't give up on me so fast. He couldn't.

Forcing my trembling fingers to work, I open the case but only have time to lift one of the axes before a shimmer of glittering red light catches my eye and the crystalline form passes over me again. After another freaky soundless second, I find myself back in the rock pit with the Nightmares. It's like I didn't leave at all. One is still cowering on the ground, and the other is holding Boone in the air.

The one closest to me springs to its feet and reaches for me.

I don't hesitate, slamming the handle end of the axe into the side of its face. The creature crumples to the ground in a heap of long limbs. Not dead, though. I don't think. They're stuck down here just like me. I won't kill them unless I have no choice.

Across the room, the Nightmare holding Boone aloft screams so horrifically I want to put my hands over my ears, but I can't. It goes to break Boone over its knee, and, in that split second, I hurl my axe at it. I swear I hear the *whomp, whomp, whomp* as it turns end over end in the air before striking the Nightmare in the shoulder, lodging deep with a sickening crunch and suck of bone and blood and flesh that I can hear from across the chamber. Throwing axes is the only thing I got any good at as a thief, so I hit exactly where I aimed. Not a kill shot.

The Nightmare stands there, still holding Boone in the air and staring at me with its creepy-as-sin blanks for eyes for a long second before it collapses.

Boone manages to roll away from the thing, coming to his feet in an enviably slick move, then hops out of the way as fuchsia-colored blood leaks from the wound I made in the Nightmare's shoulder, pooling on the ground. Not dead but wounded enough to stop it.

Boone yanks the axe out and runs to my side, handing over my weapon and taking up a position at my back.

"They can't be the only ones," I say.

Boone doesn't bother to argue. We turn in slow circles, looking up into the darkness, waiting for more of those things to come at us.

But they don't.

Instead, a slow clap has both of us crouching tensely and looking behind us toward the curved back wall of the pie-shaped space. There, where solid rock used to be, an archway intricately carved with all the symbols of Hestia—a heart and fireplace, a chaste tree, and a kettle—parts the wall. And on the other side, in another massive room, stand a number of people lined up in a semicircle. Cronos isn't with them, but I can take a decent guess at who they are.

The Titans of Tartarus.

The rest of them.

# 9

# MISTRESS

### LYRA

A now-familiar chalkboard screech sends fear shooting over my skin, standing every hair up on end like toy soldiers. Then another screech, followed by another, and then more. All coming from high overhead.

We don't even have to debate it. Boone and I take off at a sprint. The screeches turn into a cacophony, drawing closer and closer, along with a low, rhythmic thumping that I realize is the beat of wings. Those fuckers can fly. One swoops down on our left, and Boone throws an elbow without breaking stride. I swing my axe at another and miss. Then together, we hurl ourselves through the doorway to land at the Titans' feet.

"Congratulations." Hestia's voice comes from the doorway behind us. "You have unsealed my Lock."

That's when my power returns.

Before, when I was made into a goddess, I basically died first.

That time, a pinpoint of light in my vision grew larger and larger, followed by heat that spread everywhere, and finally pulses of power, as if a defibrillator was being used on me.

Not this time.

This time it's like being woken from a dead sleep by ice shooting directly into my spine with a long, thick needle. The heat is still there, but the cold sizzles through my veins so fast, I might as well turn frozen solid.

About the time I hear Boone grunt, the sensation disappears, like it never was to begin with.

"That's new," a woman murmurs. Whispers, more like.

A Titaness. Some accounts have only the Titans down here. But history, especially ancient history written by men, often overlooks women. Clearly, they got this part wrong.

"What's new?" I grumble as I gain my feet. "Gaining goddess powers never hurt before?"

"Not that," she says.

I look up at the woman not ten feet from me. She's tall and slender, and the upper part of her chestnut-skinned, hollow-cheeked face is hidden behind a mask shaped like an owl and the same color as her brown hair. I only know of one masked Titan. She's got to be Mnemosyne, mother of the Muses, Titaness of memory and stories.

She points a finger that reminds me of a talon. Not at us. Behind us.

I jerk around, axe raised, ready to take on another Nightmare, only to see the creatures—there must be hundreds of them—at the doorway, standing in rows, glaring at us with their unsettling eyeless heads, mouths open in silent, jagged-toothed shouts. Except they're not coming through. They're just standing there. Motionless.

Behind me, another Titaness whispers, "How does she have a weapon?"

And a different Titan, sounding a little pissy, says something about how "right now the bigger issue is them."

The Nightmares still staring me down? "Yeah," I toss over my shoulder at him. "I'd call them a big godsdamned issue."

"For the love of the cosmos, keep your voice down," one of the others whisper-hisses at me.

Cronos said something like that, too, right before that bell. Loud noises apparently wake something even Titans fear. Awesome. This just keeps getting better and better.

The Nightmare at the front steps forward, and Boone and I both step back.

Only, instead of attacking, one by one, they bow.

To…me. Us?

At least I think they do.

Um…

I look at Boone, who shrugs, then glance around to find the Titans watching all this with stoic faces. Or is that god-level shock?

"Have they ever done that?" The grumpy-sounding Titan speaks again. Quietly. I get the sense that quiet is not his normal mode.

He's wearing white knee-high athletic socks with sandals, shorts, and a bright salmon-colored shirt. Like the worst kind of tourist. Iapetus, I think? One of the four original pillars of the earth who held up the four corners of the skies.

He was the pillar of the west. Iapetus' hair is dark gray shot through with silver, reminding me of storm clouds, striking against deep brown skin. He's the Titan of controlling life and pain and considered to be the father of mortals. I'm not sure if his clothes represent the mortals part or the pain part.

His question was muttered to masked Mnemosyne, who stands closest to him.

She puts a hand to her temple. Do Titans get headaches? "Never," she says. Or…did the owl's mouth move instead of the Titaness's? Either way, I can't tell if she's grim or pleased.

Right now, with my arm starting to shake from holding my axe at the ready, I'm just trying to keep up.

*"You are the only one worthy of us, Lyra Keres,"* a hissing and yet sweet voice says inside my head.

I swing my attention back to the Nightmares, who rise from their bows in an oddly uniform motion.

*"When the time comes, we will follow you, Mistress. You have only to command."*

I don't know what that means. Yet another question mark. Those seem to be piling up around me like sand dunes today.

I'm tempted to command them to get me out of Tartarus. The only thing that stops me is knowing that if they could have escaped before, they would have already.

The one Nightmare in the center of the group nods its head, like a smaller bow. Then, with a swish of air, the archway closes with the Nightmares behind it, leaving us here.

The wall right in front of us, where the arch was, closes, suddenly appearing solid except for Hestia's symbols carved into the center. Before my eyes, a new, glittering golden symbol appears in the stone.

Two flames coming up out of a two-legged table.

The icon for the goddess Hestia.

It glitters at me as if lit with an inner fire.

"Well, at least she was fast this time." I hear a whisper from one of the Titans.

Right. One threat is no longer a threat. We should be facing the one that still is.

# 10
# MEET THE TITANS

### LYRA

In unison, Boone and I slowly turn to find the Titans surrounding us in a semicircle, having apparently crept closer while we were distracted. We're like lobsters in a pot slowly being brought to a boil.

Tension ratcheting through my body, threatening to pull a muscle with each breath I take, I lower my arm slowly, switching my axe to my other hand.

I take a quick look around, trying to get my bearings.

We're in a massive, high-ceilinged cavern running in both directions past where I can see around a bend. Best guess, it circles the cylinder that makes up the abyss—bridge and gates at the top, Lock or Locks at the bottom, and where we stand outside is separate. In here, across the opposite rockface that's more like a craggy mountainside, offshoots of multiple human-size tunnels appear to lead away from here and from the abyss.

Switching my focus to the Titans, I count, then frown and count again. We're missing a few.

Because they are no longer worshipped, likenesses aren't exactly thick on the ground in the Overworld, but their appearances help. Iapetus and Mnemosyne, I think I already got. But the others...

I count. Five Titanesses and four Titans, rather than six of each. I don't see Cronos, and...

"Oceanus isn't here," I whisper to myself.

"Curse that traitor," Mnemosyne snaps, though quietly.

Not too surprising. Oceanus is missing because he was never imprisoned. He's the only Titan who refused to fight in the war against the gods, or, for that matter, against their father, Uranus, and the other Primordials in the war before that one.

"Where is Cronos?" I ask next. It's a bad idea not to be aware of where *all* my enemies are. Especially the most dangerous one. "I have a bone to pick with him."

"He saved you from the Pandemonium." Iapetus' smile sends a slither of dread over my skin.

At a guess, the Pandemonium is the thing that sound wakes up. Doesn't take a genius to figure that out. But Cronos dumped me somewhere worse.

"He almost killed us, dickhead," I snap.

If it's possible, his scowl gets so deep, shadows crease his face, like storm clouds rolling. "Watch it. I'm not a patient Titan, and we can always start over."

"What?"

"Shut up, Iapetus," Mnemosyne says. "She's not ready for that yet."

Is this what Alice felt like when she landed in Wonderland and nothing made sense? I was never a huge fan of that story for that reason. It always made me feel...adrift.

Boone whistles the signal for me to *ease up*, inching so he's standing more between me and them. He does that a lot. We need to have a chat about that later.

Iapetus points an accusing finger at Boone. "*That's* new, too."

"Shut up, Iapetus," more of them snap in unison—it's clearly a catchphrase for the Titans. Only made weirder because of all the whispering.

Beside me, I can hear the way Boone's hands ball into tight fits, knuckles cracking. I don't blame him.

"Indeed, he is new," a different Titaness says.

This one, I know for sure. I'd have guessed based on her eyes alone. The mercurial swirling silver, just like Hades', are a dead giveaway, contrasting with her rosy-cheeked ebony skin. The small diadem nestled in her tight, black curls is another clue, marking her as Rhea. Cronos' queen. Hades' mother.

The same as with Hestia earlier, her smile invites me to relax, to trust.

I straighten my spine, determined not to give in.

"Anything new is bad," Iapetus insists. I have to say, he's even more dour than Ber, Cerberus' grumpy head. I didn't know that was possible.

I'm also kind of proud of myself for keeping all these thoughts inside today.

"No," Rhea says. Her voice is like her smile. Serene. "Anything new is good. Otherwise, we're just spinning our wheels."

How in the name of the Underworld does she know a modern phrase like that after being stuck down here all this time? Same with Iapetus' clothes.

*Focus on the problem, Lyra.*

"Maybe we should throw her in the next Lock now," Iapetus says.

The *next* Lock? As in more than one? Hestia said *this* Lock, implying one. But there's another? Fuck me.

Mnemosyne raises her hands. "Agreed."

In unison, he and the others drop into threatening crouches, like they're preparing to attack. The move is so in sync, they make a collective sound, like soldiers clicking their heels when standing at attention. Power crackles over every single one of them like electricity zigzagging from spark to spark.

Rhea, however, in a blur of speed, suddenly stands before us. *Between* us and them. She doesn't crackle. No power on display.

The Titaness of generations and all things that flow as a woman—blood, birth waters, milk, and time—stands between us. I'm not sure what she can do against all of them, but she doesn't seem remotely worried. She merely raises her hands like that'll be enough to fend them off.

I don't know why she's helping me. I don't care. Right now, survival is top of my priority list, followed by escape. Maybe between the three of us we can—

*Wait. Where's Boone?*

A quick, panicked glance around reveals he isn't here anymore. The Titans don't seem to have noticed, all focused on Rhea and me. My heart is already crashing in my chest, but realizing he's gone puts me into a gear that might cause a stroke. Dots start to dance across my vision.

"Don't make us go through you, Rhea," Iapetus warns in a low snarl.

Damn that Titan and the horse that brought him here.

Any trace of her tranquil smile melts away, leaving Rhea scary-intense, the way Hades can sometimes get. "Throwing her in the second Lock now is too soon," she murmurs calmly. "Listen to her. She's hyperventilating."

No shit. I close my eyes and focus on controlling my breathing. Another Lock. Another Labor. Another catch. Always with death on the line. It's never enough with gods, is it?

And Rhea is just as much a part of the problem, but I'll take any port in a storm, it seems. Leaning around where she stands between us, I open my eyes, point to her, and wheeze, "Voice of reason."

"Shhhh…" they all warn me. More than one glances back toward one particular tunnel. Does the doorway at the top of the bridge Cronos kept looking at lead all the way down here to that entrance?

"That attitude and that mouth are part of the problem." Something ripples across Iapetus' skin, dark but also fiery, reminding me of peeks of lava under a cooled blackened crust. "Getting her to do anything we want is like watching glaciers move."

Dickhead.

"I don't think I'm the one with the attitude problem here," I whisper through clenched teeth, mostly to keep them from chattering. Fear is rising with every extra-rapid pump of my heart, the taste like heavy metal coating my mouth.

*Boone. Where are you?*

The others don't do anything new, but Rhea slowly ushers me behind her. I take a jerking step sideways and raise my axe overhead, gripping it with two hands, ready to hurl it. There's no way I can beat them all, even with her help, but I can take at least one out before they get me.

"Don't react." Boone's low voice is right by my ear, and I jump a little at the sound. "I'm here. I have a plan."

# 11

## AS TIME GOES BY

### LYRA

It takes everything I have not to twitch, let alone to keep from shaking on an inhale of relief.

Thank the fates. Boone's here. I'm not alone.

Although...he's also *not* visible. When did that become a thing?

Collectively, they all take a menacing step toward us, and fear shoots up my spine like Zeus slammed one of his lightning bolts into me. I imagine all the hairs on my body spiking up and out, like a wolf raising its hackles.

When every gaze trained on me shifts behind me, for a second I think Boone must be doing whatever he planned to get us out of here. It takes me too long to identify the fear that crosses the Titans' faces. Because fear makes no sense.

More than one backpedals in the other direction. But not Iapetus.

"Lyra, run," he whisper-yells.

I think Rhea reaches for me, but she misses as I whirl around to see what they're all cringing away from.

I have a split second to realize another one of those red, glittering slashes that look like something ripped through the air with claws, leaving a jagged cut, is coming straight at me. "Not again—"

Another oppressive silence as it swallows me. Almost as quickly, sound returns as whatever the fuck those crystal things are disappears from view in a glittering crimson halo, and I can hear Hades' voice somewhere nearby. It only takes a glance around to figure out *exactly* where and when I am.

Oh gods. I know this.

It's impossible *not* to know.

This was one of the worst moments of my life.

White, fluted Corinthian pillars lead up a pathway to a set of floating stairs. Literally floating, not attached to one another or the ground. I'm standing well up the path to Hera's quartz-adorned observatory, the pink glow from the lanterns inside casting a light over the scene below me. Where I am, half hidden behind one of the columns, no one can see me.

But I can see them...

See *me*.

What's happening inside these crystalline forms narrows down to one of two possibilities.

Either they could be some kind of strange glamour, meant to mess with my head, probably to make me do the Titans' bidding or break me or something.

But what's seeming more likely, especially as I watch *myself* with Hades across the way...

This is time travel.

I'm being taken back in time when I get swallowed up in the crimson light. That's it. It has to be. I am going to the past.

*Fuck me.*

The past version of me standing before Hades is a mess thanks to Athena's horror of a Labor. My shoes are covered in bug guts, both from killing bugs and from running through their remains inside the glass maze she made out of the Roman Colosseum. There are holes in my clothes where the spiders and the bullet ant pierced through. My face is so pale, I could apply for permanent specter status. And there's blood on my shirt. I try not to think about whose blood.

I look like a sweet spring breeze could make me disintegrate as I face down a furious Hades, with Charon and Cerberus looking on like worried mother hens.

Charon, who was against the idea of us using Pandora's Box to get Persephone out. No way did he know what the result would be, but damned if he wasn't right.

Hades takes a step toward that girl from what feels like lifetimes ago. "Lyra—"

"Don't," she says calmly. To the current me, past me sounds like a recorded voice, like a robot, as I slowly move away from him. "You don't want to come anywhere near me right now."

He stops.

Gods, even now, knowing that he was pushing me away for real reasons, he seems so…remote. So cold.

I gave him myself, all of me, and he shut me out the next morning. Yes, I knew there was no future in it when I was still human, but I didn't expect him to make me feel…used. To discard me so carelessly. I don't think I could have done that to him. Made him feel worthless, like nothing, after what we shared.

The biggest fear I've been holding back since I ended up in here with no Persephone in sight rears its ugly head and lashes at my insides like acid rain.

Did Hades know?

"Was that what last night was about?" Past Lyra asks him. "Boosting my confidence or something to try to get me to win? You feel nothing for me. I'm just a tool."

"I—"

"That wasn't a question."

Lyra takes another slow, careful step back, even though he doesn't move. I remember so well just wanting to get away. To not be there. To not hear the truth or see it in his eyes. That he cared nothing for me, but even worse, that he'd made me believe he might just a little bit as some part of a manipulation or bigger plan.

He did that to a girl who'd never felt love.

I look away, not wanting to see this again.

"I thought I could see you," I hear Lyra say. "The real you. But it was all a calculation."

And I can't help but look back. The two solitary figures stare at each other. Even knowing how this ends, even having gotten an explanation from him that he had to break my heart so that my curse would stay intact enough to get through the sirens, resentment flares inside my chest.

Hot. Heavy. Full of the heartache that he put me through.

Made worse now by where I've ended up.

Lyra drops her gaze to a spot at his feet. "You made me burn for you."

And just like it did then, my heart breaks all over again.

Tartarus and time have me questioning if any of it was real. Questioning us. Did I let him off too easily when he explained why he did all those things? Did I believe him too readily? Did he do all that not just so that

I'd win the Crucible, but because winning meant he'd get the box to get Persephone out? Did he know I'd end up stuck in Tartarus? Did he not care as long as it was a chance to save her?

Was I his pawn in more ways than I ever realized?

I don't want to believe it, but seeing the way he was in this moment again... It *hurts*.

"Fuck," Hades mutters. "Lyra, listen to me—"

She shakes her head, and even from here I can see the fear on my own face. The denial. The need to protect my heart from more damage, a heart so desperate for love it's still a terrible ache inside me.

"I don't want to hear what you have to say," Lyra says. "I lost today."

"I know," he says.

"I can't win the Crucible."

Hades doesn't respond.

"I can't make you king, so you don't need me anymore." Past me looks down at her feet.

Hades takes a step closer, eyes turning to molten silver. "The crown isn't out of reach yet."

Lyra blinks, then raises her head to stare at him, and I know what she's thinking. For her to win, her friend and fellow competitor, Diego, would have to die. She searches his face for any hint that what he's saying bothers him at all. "And you think being an asshole is going to make me want to win?"

An emotion flickers over Hades' features, but it's gone too fast to catch, even when I know what I'm looking for. "Make me king, and I'll grant you anything you ask for that is in my power to give."

Anger whips through me for that girl I was. For me *now*.

"Do you want to be back with your parents? Done." He snaps his fingers. Does he know my parents never loved me? What he'd be sending me back to? "Do you want to be rich? Done." Another snap. "Rule a country? It's yours."

I forgot he'd offered those things. Afterward. Forgot that he'd shown how clearly he didn't know me.

A heaviness sets up camp in my chest.

"I don't want anything," Lyra tells him.

She's begging him not to keep going. With her eyes. The way she leans away. She should throw a rock at his stupid head.

Hades prowls closer. "Everyone wants something."

She backs up. "Not from you."

There's only the slightest pause in his steps, and then he keeps coming. "That's pride speaking, Lyra. Get over it and take something for yourself."

Lyra slips two fingers in the small, zippered pocket where I kept the pearls he gave me. "Come closer, and I'm gone."

He jerks up hard at that, fury and a sort of shocked denial whipping across those beautiful features.

And betrayal.

I want to shout at him. Even now. Even as that heaviness in my chest worsens.

A shadow streaks by overhead, and Hades' gaze shoots past her.

Past me from that awful day gasps.

I remember why. Because I felt Hades' fear in that moment.

*For* me.

It pulls me up sharply now. Fear doesn't make sense, but I think having felt that from him is why I blocked out a lot of other things about this moment. About how he'd been. To me, later, after I won, after all the explanations, his fear in this moment was proof that he loved me despite all the terrible things he said.

But now…doubts are winding around me like a snake, smothering me.

"No!" Hades shouts as the winged Daemones land, two on either side of past Lyra, and take her by the arms. I remember this, too. How they took me away and locked me up, and how my heart was too broken to even care.

I watch this living rerun of the worst episode of my life, wishing I could turn it off. But I can't, so I grit my teeth as the Daemones take off into the sky, dragging Lyra away from the mountain. And Hades shouts a string of profanities into the skies after me, his voice filled with rage and doom and death.

But when past Lyra is out of sight, Hades goes quiet…and very, very immobile. Painfully slowly, his head drops forward until his chin is on his chest. The stillness that descends is like the hush at a funeral. He stares at the ground, then waves one hand at Charon and Cerberus, who haven't moved. "Leave me."

Though they are both visibly reluctant, they do. They walk back toward the narrow stairs that wind down from Hera's observatory, leading away from where I still hide among the pillars on the pathway above them.

There's a red crystal shimmer of light coming from just above the mountaintop. Coming for me. I don't have long, and maybe the push of time running out is why I'm down the stairs in a rush.

"Why did you do that?" I have to know.

Hades goes even more still, if that's possible. Michelangelo couldn't have carved anything more perfect out of marble if he'd had a hundred years to try.

The god of death and King of the Underworld doesn't turn before he speaks. "Lyra."

The sound of my name is low…and off. Too low for me to tell if he's angry or shocked or something else.

I stop just behind him, far enough away that I don't do something foolish like reach for him, heart twisting. "Why did you do that?" I demand again.

"Are you kidding me with this?"

What the hells is he talking about? "I gave myself to you, and you ripped it all away. I know it's to keep my curse intact for the sirens, but you were cruel. *Unnecessarily* cruel—" I choke on the last word.

And Hades says nothing. Does nothing.

*"Why?"* I demand again.

"Because, Lyra…" His head comes up, and he faces me, jaw tilted at an arrogant angle and eyes nearly black. "Because *you* told me to."

I only get through half a shake of my head before I freeze. "No."

"You *did*. It happened the same way it always happens with you." Now I can identify the emotion in his voice. Resentment.

He stalks toward me, hurling accusations. "You show up out of the blue after ages, tell me things that are impossible…"

I back up as he keeps coming.

"…You mumble unintelligible things about glamouring. Tell me to do things I don't want to do, and—"

My back hits the rock of the mountain, and he cages me in, hands on either side of me, eyes flashing like steel honed to destructive sharpness.

Only his gaze drops to my mouth, his next words deadly soft. "…And like a *fool*, I listen."

Having him so close when I'm still so mad, and he's so mad, and the words he's throwing at me make no sense—it's making my head spin.

I told him to?

*No.* The denial rips through me so hard my chest aches. None of this makes sense. None. Even if this is time travel and I've visited him before, why would I ever do that to myself? To him?

I'm shaking my head over and over. No. This has to be a glamour. The Titans or Tartarus—someone is fucking with my head.

And maybe Hades sees my panic, or maybe his own anger drives him, but he mutters, "Gods damn it."

Then his mouth is on mine.

Heaven. And hell.

A sob rips from my throat as I melt into his touch. With a groan, Hades buries his hands in my hair, knocking the length of it loose. With another groan, he wraps his fist in it, his other hand at my neck, not squeezing but cupping my chin, controlling me as he consumes me.

The only thing controlled about him.

Everything else is like he's been…unleashed. A tiger who has lived its entire life in a cage, to then finally have its keeper accidentally leave the door open with an innocent lamb waiting on the other side.

But this lamb is happy to be devoured by this particular tiger.

I return every ravenous kiss with my own, taking his heat and giving it back to him stoked higher, tangling my tongue with his, moaning into his mouth. I want to wrap him around me, crawl inside his arms, hold on to him so tight Tartarus can't take me away again.

But his desperation, while it echoes mine, is different. Harsher.

The hand at my chin drops, tracing my curves on the way down, teasing and merciless. He stops at my hip, where his fingers dig into the flesh, pulling me flusher against him so I can feel exactly how hard he is.

The whimper that escapes me makes him growl with an answering possessive satisfaction.

All my doubts melt away under the heat of this onslaught.

He couldn't touch me this way if he didn't mean it. Hades doesn't do anything he doesn't mean.

And, gods above and below, the things my King of the Underworld can do with his mouth alone. I know all the wicked, wonderful, wild things he can make my body feel. How he can make pleasure sing through my veins, explode in my depths. How he holds me afterward, gentle, whispering the sweetest words that make my heart more his with every passing moment.

I still don't understand…anything…really. But here in his arms, where I'm supposed to be, I don't care.

Hades nips at my lower lip, running his tongue along the small sting in a way that makes me suck in a breath, and I feel him smile against my mouth.

But when I smile back, he goes suddenly still.

His lips are a hairsbreadth away and still too far from me, but neither of us move. We're both breathing hard.

*Don't stop*, my heart is begging him. *Don't let me go.*

"Hades?" I whisper.

"I can't fucking do this." His words are a low, tortured groan.

My heart drops, my fingers compulsively digging into him as he goes to draw away. As he pulls his hand from my hair, his thumb brushes over my cheek, and he stills again. Just for a second.

A different kind of stillness.

"Shit," he says. "Don't cry, my star." He's kissing me again. My lips, but also the tracks of my tears. Like he's trying to erase my pain and fear. He whispers, "Don't cry," with each sweet touch.

I open my eyes to beg him—to keep kissing me or to help me, I'm not sure which. Only those damned red glitters of light catch in the corner of my vision. I have seconds at most.

*No. Not yet.* Not ever, but not yet.

I snake my arms around Hades' neck, burying my face in his chest and holding on as tight as I can. So tight.

"Fuck," he says in my ear, his arms coming around me. "You're shaking."

"I don't want to go," I whisper.

He tenses against me. "Already?" he demands in a rough voice. "Are you fucking kidding me?"

Time consumes me before I can reply or even breathe.

He's gone.

Or, more accurately, I am taken away.

When I regain my senses—with my arms curved up in the air like I'm still wrapped around Hades, but now holding nothing—I'm exactly where I started. I'm back in Tartarus with the Titans.

# PART 2

# MONSTERS

Seriously. What the fuck is happening?

# 12

# A FATE WORSE THAN DEATH

### HADES

I pound on the fucking indestructible gates of Tartarus. The ones I helped create to hold back the Titans for eternity. With the wards, I know Lyra can't hear me on the other side, but I scream her name anyway.

She's trapped with the Titans. They'll destroy her. First, they'll play with her, like a killer whale plays with its food, and then they'll eat her alive. Just like my father did with me.

"Hades?" Charon puts a hand to my shoulder, and a tsunami of shock barrels into me, obliterating any control I have left. I lash out, throwing him away from me.

"Lyra!" I pound the door.

Then I pound harder and harder, the violence of my fear shaking not only the Gates but everything around them, like the earth shifting its plates. Fuck the consequences of releasing those bloodthirsty, conscienceless bastards on the world and having to face fighting them again.

I have to get her out.

I have to.

I'll obliterate everything and everyone who gets in my way, dismantle the world a stone at a time if I have to. End it all. Take it back down to nothing.

To chaos.

Sucking in hard breaths, I close my eyes, pressing my palms and forehead against the gate. This is the prophecy come true.

Lyra was wrong.

I don't have enough control to keep my promise. I ball my hands into fists against the cold, hard steel and pound again. And again. And again.

Something slams into me from the side, and I'm thrown onto my back. All three of Cerberus' heads get in my face as the massive hellhound pins me to the ground with his weight. Before I can toss him off like the traitorous rag doll I'm about to make him into, rock and earth cover me. Demeter. She was with us for Persephone. She doesn't just control the plants of harvest. She controls the soil, too, and she's burying me alive.

I shake my head, only partially covered, and spit out some dirt. I didn't know my little sister was this strong.

Then Charon is leaning over me. "You've got to stop."

"Let me up!" I put all the command of the King of the Underworld in my voice. As chthonic beings, both Cronos and Cerberus are unable to deny me.

Except they do nothing.

Because I'm not their ruler anymore. Lyra is. I gave her my throne to save her. And even though I replaced Zeus as King of the Gods, I can't order them. They obey only one ruler.

The wrath inside me has nowhere to go, and I shout one long, thunderous, "Fuuuuuuuuuuuck!"

Then I go deadly quiet. Only the sounds of my ragged breaths fill the cavern as I try to figure out how to get them out of my damn way.

"Got it all out of your system now?" Charon chides.

"I could kill you where you stand." I damn well mean it.

He gives me a hard stare. "Look up."

What?

He points. "Look the fuck up, Phi."

When I do, it's to see that the entire roof of the chamber surrounding Tartarus has collapsed and fallen in one piece, looming practically on top of us.

A swift glance shows Demeter standing nearby, one hand raised to the roof, holding it off us, the other pointed toward me, holding me down. She's shaking so hard, I can hear her teeth chattering.

"I can't fix it until I can let you go," she says, voice strained.

"You're going to bury Lyra down there if you keep this up," Charon says baldly. And I flinch, the rocks on top of me digging into my flesh.

*"She wouldn't want this."* Cerberus' most serious head, Cer, nudges at me. *"You know she wouldn't."*

Which is when I remember…

A day a long time ago, when she told me I could choose not to fulfill my grandfather's prophecy. She was so sure that fate lines can be broken. She also once said that she was strong enough to get her own ass out of trouble if it ever came looking for her.

Did she know? Did she know then what was going to happen to her?

If she did, then why in the cursed name of all the Titans did she come with me down here? She could have broken that fate herself.

I want to rail at the world. Fight my friends, even kill them if I have to, to get her out. But Cer is right. She wouldn't want that.

I close my eyes, seeking any kind of peace I can. But it's so hard to find under the fury and terror. And then I picture her green-and-gold eyes and how she feels in my arms. Her kindness. Her intelligence. The way she says everything that pops into her head. *Her.*

And it's over.

No burning down the world, but that doesn't mean giving up. She'd want me to find another way. So that's what I'm going to fucking do.

"Let me up."

# 13

# BOTH OPTIONS SUCK

### LYRA

I heave forward, hands on my knees.

The wild swing from Olympus in Hades' arms to being trapped in Tartarus again is like running full tilt into a wall of cement. It steals any remaining air from my lungs.

Yet I still manage to mouth his name.

The bitter chocolate scent of him is abandoning me, even in this place, and I want to trap even that much of him down here with me.

Just a piece to hold on to while I try to get back to him.

Rhea is in my face, forcing me upright with a firm grip on my shoulders. "Hades? What did you tell him?"

I blink at the Queen of the Titans, who, up until a few seconds ago, seemed to be my ally. Now her face looks like she's ready to kill me with the rest of them.

With a scowl, I try to shrug off her hold, but she doesn't budge.

"What the hell was that?" I demand. Bravado is all I have left.

Where is Boone? A quick glance tells me he's still invisible… I don't think he would have abandoned me. Or did he get sucked into the past, too?

I look at Rhea. "What did that crystal-looking thing do to me?"

Just like her oldest son, Rhea's silvery eyes turn dagger sharp, and I want to cry at the similarity. I was *with* him. A heartbeat ago. Yelling at him. Blaming him. Kissing him.

I still want to kiss him. And yeah, yell at him some more.

Instead, I'm here. *Back* here. Trapped. Probably about to die. Or lose myself in this place where reality has clearly unraveled.

Maybe the only answer is to let Hades unleash on this world that can be so cruel. But I can't make myself wish that on him, even as that stolen moment is feeling more and more like a dream.

I'm staring my nightmare in the eyes.

"Answer me," Rhea urges.

"It's okay," Mnemosyne says from behind Rhea. "We're still here. Nothing changed, thank the cosmos."

I'm *not* thanking the cosmos that I'm still here. "Someone explain what the hells is going on." I need a real answer. "Did I just time travel?"

Rhea passes a hand over her eyes, then glances back at the others.

"She's not ready for more," Mnemosyne says with a pinched face—or the lower half under her mask is pinched, anyway. "Look at her. She's close to snapping."

*Oh my gods.* I force myself to straighten. "That's it. I *did*. I fucking time traveled."

I'm not sure if that's better or worse than being glamoured. Both still make sense. They could be lying to me now, but all those moments in the three times I've been taken away so far are adding up.

"Shit," Iapetus mutters.

Rhea reaches for me, but I jerk away, so she brings her hands up. "Easy."

"Screw easy. Start talking."

"See," Iapetus says. "I told you she could handle it."

"Shut up, Iapetus," all of them hiss.

All except Rhea, who is studying me, brows puckered and what looks like motherly concern in her eyes. "Those cracks are broken time. Cronos broke it long ago trying to get us out of here. They take you to the past."

To the past. To right after Athena's Labor. Right after I survived Poseidon's Labor, too.

I think I'm going to be sick.

*That's* where Hades went?

After the Labor was over, he said he had something to take care of. I'd just been devastated by Isabel's death, the first champion we lost, and he left me to go talk to future me.

Iapetus, oblivious to the thoughts trying to suck me into a whirlpool and drown me, gives me a sarcastic bow. "You, Lyra Keres…are prophesied to be our savior someday." Then that asshole grins. "Personally, I'd like for that to be sooner rather than later. Which means you go in the next Lock. Now."

I don't have time for a "what the fuck?" before the Titan rushes me, and the only thing that stops him is Rhea. One second, he's a blur of speed. The next, he's flying across the room to slam into the door of Hestia's Lock, then dropping to the ground with a dull, thudding bounce.

The others take that as a signal to come at me, too, blurring in a blink.

Which is when I feel a hand on my shoulder gripping tight, and my vision goes wonky, like everything is in black and white.

Everything except me...and Boone.

A gasp spills from my lips, but before I can ask questions, he slams a hand over my mouth, muffling the sound.

Iapetus pulls up sharply from a second charge but still bounds past Rhea to wave his hand through where we were standing. Where we are *still* standing. But his arm passes right through us. "I'll be damned!"

He sounds as clear as a bell, despite how I'm currently feeling like I'm watching an old black-and-white TV show. Then the Titan they used to call the Piercer, thanks to his legendary, deadly spear, stares directly into my eyes but doesn't seem to see me. "Wait. Where's the other one?"

I don't move to check, but I'm pretty sure Boone has a grin on his face.

Iapetus straightens abruptly with a scowl so deep it's gouging lines around his mouth. "There're only so many places they could go in this amount of time."

"Split up," Rhea says, still so utterly calm it's unnerving. "Find them."

"Kill the man if you have to," Iapetus tacks on.

Rhea shoots him a cold look. "That is—"

The chime of a bell—the same one from earlier—cuts her off.

And every single Titan I can see goes as pale as if death sucked them dry.

"Run," Rhea orders them.

A Titaness—the one holding on to one of her sisters all this time—becomes water so fast, she splashes as she hits the floor, becoming a puddle.

In a dizzying swirl of speed, they scatter, taking different tunnels. Any except the one they kept checking. Only Rhea remains. "If you're still here, Lyra, follow me."

Boone doesn't so much as twitch, and I know he's thinking the same thing I am. Like hells we will.

She glances around as if hoping we'll reveal ourselves.

"Otherwise, I hope whatever you did to hide is enough to protect you from the Pandemonium. You won't be able to see them, but whatever you do, don't let them touch you."

Then she blurs away in an instant bolt of speed.

# 14

## PILLARS OF THE COSMOS

### LYRA

"Don't move," Boone whispers.

All ten Titans and Titanesses are gone, and the Pandemonium—whatever they are—are coming. Something even Titans fear.

"I want to make sure they're gone before we move," Boone says. "Okay?"

I nod. "Aren't you worried about whatever they are afraid of?"

"If they can't see us or feel us, whatever it is can't, either." He sounds so confident that I roll my eyes. "Trust me."

I don't hesitate. I've always trusted him. "With my life."

But...nothing comes.

Boone doesn't move. Doesn't speak.

I can sense him turning his head slowly, scanning for a threat. I glance from one side to the other, also searching. It's been a minute or two, and still nothing comes, and I start to lower my guard. The longer we stand like this, the stranger it feels to be in a world painted all shades of gray. It's disorienting.

"We can't stay here forever," I point out. "Can you teleport?"

"I've tried. I don't think this place allows it."

"Oh." Makes sense. It's a prison.

"So we'll have to pick a tunnel and walk out." His grip on me tightens. "Ready?"

Not really. We start walking, and I find myself cringing at the tiny sounds our feet make with each step. But nothing comes at us, so we keep going.

"How are you already so good at this?"

"Haven't you learned yet?" That cocksure grin is rife in his voice. "I'm good at everything."

Good grief.

A scream pierces the air, and Boone's grip on me tightens. The sound shoots down one of the tunnels to the left of where we stand—one of the Titanesses, by the timbre. She sounds as if she's being ripped to shreds. Then the pitch abruptly changes, and instead of screams, animalistic snarls roll toward us.

But the growling isn't stopping, and it's getting louder. "It's coming our way."

"I know."

It's coming faster than we're moving, and he speeds us up. He'd better be right that nothing can see us, but now the hushed sound of our steps is more obvious.

We're not quite to the tunnel we're aiming at when someone… some*thing*…shoots into the chamber from a different tunnel.

Boone stops us, keeping us preternaturally still. This time I do hold my breath as I stare at something that was a Titaness only minutes ago. Theia, I think, Titaness of insight and healing, mother of the original gods and goddesses of the moon, sun, and dawn. She's supposed to glow.

She almost doesn't look real now.

With light hair and flowy robes along the ancient lines, she's hunched over, her curls wild around her face. Fangs flash bright and deadly in her open, panting mouth, and her hands are dagger-sharp claws.

What did Tartarus do to her? Or is this the result of the Pandemonium that we still haven't seen a trace of?

Boone has us take a single, careful step closer to our escape.

She doesn't seem to notice as she grunts and snarls and paws the ground while she searches the room, like a rabid wolf hunting prey.

Yet another step.

I can see light slipping out between her claws, coming from her palms.

Another step.

We're so close.

Two more, and she disappears from view, blocked by the wall of the tunnel we're in now. But we still move slowly and carefully down the arched passageway carved into the natural rock leading us well away from the chamber. Once we turn a bend, it's so dark that Boone has to feel along the wall as he tugs me after him. I pull my axe in closer. A clank of metal on rock will definitely have whatever the Pandemonium is coming for us. Theia, too, for that matter, or whatever monster she turned into.

Light forms a small arch ahead. One that grows larger as we near it until we come out of the tunnel into…

*Wow.*

Maybe I whisper that aloud, because Boone nods along as we both crane our necks to look up, and up, and up, forgetting for a second the danger at our backs.

We're standing in a semicircle of mountainside that opens up into what looks like a nightmarish land of burning. This is the image so many mortals think of when they picture various hells. Dark rocks, the hazy undulations of lava and fire, everything jagged and blasted with heat. The lands stretch long beyond the horizon as far as I can tell.

But that's not what we're looking at.

Rising between the tunnel-riddled, underground mountain we came out of and the burning lands in the distance are four massive, free-standing pillars that shoot upward so high, I can't see the tops. Only they aren't pillars, really. They're more like wildly different-looking tree trunks or… roots.

*Oh my gods.*

I once heard a quote from an ancient text describing Tartarus as a void beneath the foundations of everything where the earth, sea, sky, and fire have their roots.

It's *true*.

Boone lets go of me. Instantly, like an old-fashioned movie being remastered in Technicolor, the world is painted in bright hues again, and I gasp at the violent beauty of the pillars.

The earthen pillar closest to where we stand, though still a good distance away, looks exactly like tree roots wrapped in vines of greenery and flowers every color imaginable all the way up. The sweet scent in the air is so heavy it's cloying.

The sky's pillar, to the right and even farther away, doesn't look like roots but like a swirl of color. The swirl reminds me of soft-serve ice cream, but the colors are brilliant. At first glance, there are bands of pristine blue, then white, then various shades of gray from light to dark, followed by large bands of black that seem to glitter, and then narrower bands in yellows, peaches, purples. All the phases of the skies? Day and night. Sunset and sunrise. Glittering stars, but also fluffy white clouds and roiling storms. And those swirling bands are moving up the sky pillar, like they are feeding into the world.

The ocean pillar to the left, even with the sky, is comprised of waves. They defy gravity, climbing sideways up the column, spraying mist down to where we stand. The colors of the oceans don't move in bands like the skies but instead have…lanes, I guess I'd call them. Some are a fathomless deep blue, some crystal-clear turquoise, some a muddier brownish blue, some black. All with cresting white as the waves climb and climb.

And finally, farthest from us and smaller in the distance, is the pillar of fire. It looks like a tornado, but in a perfect cylinder that doesn't move and doesn't produce any smoke. And the heat has turned the flames more blueish purple than red and gold.

Another scream sets off, this time from overhead, and Boone and I both crane our necks to realize that the way we got here isn't the only way. Tunnels pockmark the sheer face of the mountain at our backs.

"Hide quickly," a soft, familiar female voice says.

Boone snatches my hand, and color disappears again just as Rhea peeks out from a tunnel off to our right. I know she can't see us, but that doesn't seem to bother her.

"I thought Theia might have driven you this way," she whispers.

So that *was* Theia. That feral thing in the chamber near Hestia's Lock.

Rhea steps fully out of the tunnel, then waves a hand, and color slams back into the world. With a mere thought, she stopped Boone's power to make us invisible.

"I have a place I can hide you that the others won't find quickly," Rhea whispers before we can run or fight. "But we need to hurry." She beckons us to follow.

I glance at Boone, questioning, and he shrugs. But we don't speak. Do we have a choice? This place is too foreign and too filled with dangers we don't know yet. It's worth at least a look. Boone gives a tiny whistle, and I nod.

When Rhea runs…this time, we run, too.

## 15

## SAFETY IS RELATIVE

### LYRA

I'm basically expecting Rhea to take us down more tunnels to some kind of dungeon-style room with torture equipment, or at least chains on the wall that magically keep a god and goddess from running.

But Rhea doesn't bolt down a tunnel. She runs for the pillars.

Gods, she's fast. So fast that even at my own goddess speed I can hardly keep up, the world blurring by in flashes of color then black and white as Boone continues trying to keep us hidden.

She circles to the back of the massive pillar of earth and stops there. Not breathing even a little bit hard, she presses her hands to the root, and like a baby bird opening its beak for its mother, the treelike roots split themselves apart. Vines and flowers crawl out of the way, the wood itself untwisting and separating. The sound it makes is a creaking and brushing. Soft. Almost impossible to hear above the roar of ocean waves and blaze of fire from the other pillars. They may be a mile apart, but they're so big, that doesn't matter.

The splitting and moving stops, and she ushers us into a chamber inside the earthen column that looks like the hollowed-out center of a tree. Not by any means the size of the full root. More like the wood drew back to form a tiny, wonky-shaped chamber just for Boone and me, big enough for us to stand up or lie down in.

The creaking starts again as Rhea closes the three of us inside.

Immediately, a tiny blue flame appears in Boone's palm, lighting the dark space. Hermes' never-ending fire that doesn't burn what it touches—a gift to thieves. But now Boone is the god of thieves, so I guess it's his fire to control. At least we'll have light in here.

In the next instant, he whirls on Rhea, hand to her throat. "No more cryptic shit. Explain."

Rhea's lips flatten a bit, and she doesn't answer, instead giving his hand a pointed look.

From the tension that ripples across his shoulders, Boone is debating what to do. His eyes narrow. "We can't escape you," he admits slowly. "And I doubt we can kill you."

"It is a conundrum," the Titaness murmurs, like he isn't still gripping her by the neck.

He grunts, an angry growl of a sound. But he also drops his hand.

As if none of that happened, Rhea adjusts her pale-pink dress, brushing off an invisible piece of dirt. "You will be safe here for now."

"Safe?" I laugh at that. The sound pops from me like I fired a gun. "From what? *You?*"

We're only *safe* with her because she's allowing it.

"From the others," she says.

"That's not threatening as fuck," I mutter as I glance toward the place we entered, now a wall of tree roots, almost expecting to hear pounding as they try to get in.

"And," she continues, "from the Pandemonium."

"Okay, what is that?" Boone asks before I can.

He's loud enough that the Titaness flinches. Not from fear of us. Her swift glance at the closed "door" to this hidden place tells me it's fear of whatever is out there.

Rhea studies my face, and I frown at her, which is when she finally answers. "When you hear that bell, the Pandemonium are unleashed throughout Tartarus. They are one of the many measures to keep us down here—we think to keep us in our cells."

We glance at her. Other than rabid Theia, we didn't hear or see anything. "Do you mean the Titans go…wild?" Boone asks.

She shakes her head. "There is an onyx obelisk in the tunnel that leads to the bridge over the abyss where you entered Tartarus at the gates," she says. "All we know is that when the bell goes off, the sound comes from inside that structure, and the onyx…vibrates. Nothing seems to emerge, but when they touch us, like they did Theia…" Rhea shudders. "The Pandemonium can't pass through doors or walls. So whenever you hear that bell, hide somewhere you can shut yourself in for a few hours. The closer you are to that obelisk, the faster you need to run."

"I don't believe you," Boone says, hard-voiced. "Shouldn't the Pandemonium have come right by us? We saw nothing. Heard nothing."

"That's what makes them so dangerous. They are invisible, soundless, no smell, no warning. Just one touch and…" Another shudder racks her.

What she's saying should terrify me, probably, but I think I'm starting to go numb from everything being thrown at me—the Pandemonium, that I'm the Titans' savior somehow, Hestia's Lock, what I saw inside those red cracks—I don't know what to believe.

Boone's shaking his head, though, still doubtful. "You said it takes hours for the Pandemonium to clear. But we were only in Hestia's Lock for thirty minutes at most."

"You were in there for a full day," Rhea corrects.

He rears back like she hit him, but I…I feel nothing. Numb is kind of nice, now that I think about it.

"I shouldn't stay with you," Rhea says. "I'll return when it's safer for you out there."

Boone crosses his arms, eyeing her like he doesn't believe a word coming out of her mouth. "You just told us to hide from things that induce violence. You'd risk going out there so soon?"

Rhea's calm cracks the tiniest bit, cut through with irritation. "I can see you are going to be an interesting addition. Perhaps I should separate you two—"

"No!" I grab Boone's wrist just as he takes a menacing step forward.

"If you think you're splitting us up," he snarls, "you'll have a fight on your hands."

She glances at me, then at the way I'm holding on to him, and a frown of what looks like motherly concern mars her brow.

I don't let go of him. His is the only face down here I trust.

And I sink further into numbness.

Rhea sighs, eyeing him like he's a recalcitrant child. "Fine. I won't separate you. But I do need to be with at least one of the other Titans or they'll know that I've hidden you away and have a better idea of where to come looking."

"No." He slashes a hand through the air. "You stay with us, or we find our own way—"

He stops talking when I tug on his wrist. "Where's Cronos?"

"When the bell went off before, he got you two safely into the Lock. But he wasn't able to get himself out. The only way off that bridge is to jump in the Locks or go down the tunnel past the obelisk the Pandemonium come from. We were able to subdue him. He's locked in one of the cells."

"Cells?" I ask.

She nods. "The tunnels are the prison part of Tartarus."

Oh.

"Wait." Boone holds up a hand. "The effect wears off?"

"After a day or so," she says. "Sometimes longer. We're...dangerous... like that. Even to one another. It's better—"

"Both Cronos and Iapetus said I was your savior." I cut her off in a voice that doesn't sound like my own. Like I'm far away and watching from outside myself. "What did they mean?"

I catch the way Rhea winces, and she takes a very long time to answer, clearly thinking through her words. "You're our only way out of Tartarus. Phoebe has seen it."

The quiet words, even gently delivered, are like a thunderclap.

*Phoebe* saw it.

The Titaness of *prophecy*.

Merciful gods in all the heavens. Iapetus said something about a prophecy. Am I prophesied to release the Titans from Tartarus? Unleash them on the world?

Me?

How? Why? Although the answer to why I'd release them is already obvious—accidentally, while trying to escape myself. Is releasing the Titans my only way out?

"Lyra's path will always lead her here," Rhea finally says. Quietly. There's even a hint of apology in her voice.

Always.

I *always* end up down here.

"Lies," Boone snarls.

I jerk my gaze to him. He's looming over Rhea now, fists clenched. Utterly sure. He's right. He has to be right. We can't believe anything they say.

Rhea's watching me closely, and something like grief passes over her features—or fear, maybe—before she turns her attention to Boone. "I can't tell you more now. She's too close to breaking. It happens when she learns too much too fast."

She steps toward the part of the wall we came through before and places her hand to it, and with the same creaking and brushing sounds, louder in here than it was from the outside, the roots start to part.

"Fucking Titans," Boone mutters. "You're going to drop a bomb on her like that and just leave?"

She doesn't stop what she's doing. "If I say more, it ends badly."

I feel Boone staring at me, but I don't look away from Rhea. I already know what he's thinking. Are we really going to let her close us in here with no way out?

Honestly…better in here alone than out there with them.

She steps outside and closes the gap until there's only a sliver of her face showing. "Oh, and stay away from the cracks of broken time," she warns. "If you do or say the wrong thing to someone from the past, you'll reset time for everyone."

Then the roots close us in.

# 16
# LOSING MY SHIT

### LYRA

"Resetting time," Boone mutters. "More bullshit." He prowls the tiny space, running his hands over the walls, the floors, every inch. "Are we even going to be able to breathe in here?" he asks me over his shoulder.

I'm only vaguely aware of his question. My mind is spinning. Broken time. Resetting time. Starting over…

Wait.

Why not reset things? Then we won't end up down here.

The bubble of elation that rises pops just as quickly. Rhea said that I always end up in Tartarus.

I *always* end up here.

"The gates enter into a foyer of sorts," Boone mumbles nearby, and I watch as he lowers to one knee in front of me to draw a circle with the bridge over it. "The drop leads down to the Locks."

Somewhere in the back of my mind, I know what he's doing. The first thing thieves do when scoping out a potential score is to understand the layout of the location. Every nuance. Every blind spot. Places we can get trapped or hide. Exits and entrances, even the ones normal people don't think about.

But I can't…focus.

Cracks of time. I look at the axe still in my hands and remember a conversation with Hades. *About ten mortal years ago, I thought I lost one*, he said. The next time he saw it was in my hands during the Crucible…

because years before that, it had appeared in my bedroom in the den and wouldn't let me get rid of it.

*Oh. My. Gods.*

Meanwhile, Boone is nodding to himself. "Definitely more than one Lock, but we don't know how many."

Then he traces a line around the circle, creating the cavern that sits outside the bottom of the Locks, where we just came from. "I assume this goes all the way around."

He glances at me but doesn't seem to notice when I don't respond.

I look at my axe again.

If I was able to take his axe…did Hades *remember* me showing up in the water garden? Remember kissing me? Have I gone to other earlier times in his life that I don't know about yet? The night I thought we first met, when he stopped me from chucking a rock at Zeus' temple—that night he demanded, a few times, if I knew who he was.

I thought he was being an arrogant ass, making sure I knew the powerful being I was dealing with. Was he asking if I actually remembered him? From before?

But why didn't he say something?

The implications hit me in a thousand different ways, like being tossed around in a storm-ridden ocean. Hades never said a single word about any of it.

He didn't tell me.

My damned god and his damned secrets. If I get out of here, he and I are going to have a reckoning.

I lower my axe, staring at the dirt floor.

Boone is still mapping out what he knows of Tartarus. "Tunnels that hold the prison cells run throughout the surrounding underground mountain. We'll have to figure out if that also goes all the way around the abyss and Locks." He frowns, then mutters, "We know this part is different." He erases the mountain face to make another semicircle shape, then draws in the pillars where we are now and the lava fields beyond.

He leans back, looking at his map. "We'll need to explore the tunnels first. Good for hiding. Seems like the best place to start. What do you think, Keres?"

He looks up at me and goes quiet, finally realizing that I haven't said a damn word.

I swallow, trying to hold on to the way I could hear Hades bellowing for me, the slamming of the gates of Tartarus as he tried to break them down to get to me. The same way I want to get back to him. No. I *need* to get back to him. And I will.

"Lyra?" Boone's tone is soft. Tentative, even. Not very Boone-like.

I suck in a sharp breath. "I can't be here," I whisper harshly. To myself as much as to him. "I can't do this. I can't be here."

I *won't*, damn it.

There's got to be another way out.

"Lyra?" he checks again.

"I don't want to talk about it," I say in a whisper. Any of it.

Immediately, he comes back with, "We'll figure it out." His voice doesn't even wobble. He sounds so sure of himself. Of that truth.

It helps.

Not that he should be that confident. Neither of us points out the obvious—that if there was any other way out of here, the Titans have had enough time, power, and intelligence to solve it long before we got involved.

*No matter what, I end up down here.*

"I can make it brighter in here if you're still afraid of the dark."

"I was never afraid of the dark," I whisper.

He nods. And then I stare at the floor, not moving. I'm not sure how long I stand here just…not processing…before my skin starts to crawl. Like spiders and bugs are all over me, even up in my hair, making my scalp tingle.

Pivoting hard on my heel, I make Boone hop out of my way as I start to pace the tiny hollowed-out space. My thoughts are going to drive me off a cliff if I don't give them some physical release. Back and forth I go, and all the while, I can feel him watching me.

Because I'm acting like this.

I kick the root, which shivers, making a hissing-type noise. Which only pisses me off, so I kick it again. When I go to do it a third time, Boone is suddenly there, putting himself between me and the roots.

"We don't have to talk about any of it yet," he says. "But I need to know that I'm not alone, Lyra."

My frown is slow. "I'm right here." The words come out kind of grumpy because it seems pretty obvious to me.

He shakes his head. "Your body is here," he says. "But the way you're shutting down... I can't get us out of this place on my own. Not without help. If you need to freak out, then take a moment and freak the fuck out. But you only get a moment." He gives me a long, hard look. "I need you, Lyra. Do you understand?"

He needs me.

Not in the way Hestia's illusion tried to play off my childhood dreams of being needed. This is about survival and escape.

Boone doesn't push. He doesn't ask. He doesn't lecture. He just waits. Steady.

And I guess being needed is something that past me must've really craved. This isn't just about me. I need to help get Boone out of this, too.

The bands of numbness that were wrapping tighter and tighter around my chest like steel belts ease, and the small voice in my head that I don't think I'd even realized I was listening to—telling me that we're fucked and should just give up, telling me that I can't do this—goes quiet.

Or quieter.

Boone dips his chin, his gaze going hard and serious in the way I've seen him do when he's ready to really dig in and start planning a score. When he gets like that, all the joking, all the teasing disappears, and you'd better be ready to keep up because he's going to get shit done. With or without you.

Something about the familiarity of that look and what it means settles in my chest. Staying stuck down here for eons is *not* an option.

*Get your shit together, Lyra, and start working the problem.*

I take two long breaths, letting them out slowly. "I'm here," I say.

A sudden rumble sounds, and the floor beneath me...vibrates. It doesn't shake. Not like an earthquake. Having grown up in San Francisco, I know what those feel like. This is different.

"The noise is coming from all over," I say.

Boone hitches his chin toward the wall. "It's shivering."

I turn my head and see it shaking just slightly. "Are the Titans trying to get in here?"

We both stiffen at that idea and jerk our gazes to the spot where Rhea made her doorway. But then the rumbling stops.

I'm already shaking my head. "There was something off about that."

"Yeah."

"It's not good, whatever it is." I leave him there to go run my hands over the wall where Rhea's door opened.

Seven swears on the Styx. "What we need is a plan," I say mostly to myself. Something we can do while we wait.

"What we need," Boone says from behind me, "is to get away from here."

"How exactly do you think we're going to do that?"

"Like this…"

"Like what—"

A slight red glow sends glitters of light across the room. With a frown, I half turn.

Boone grabs my hand and yanks me through the broken crystal shard of time I didn't see coming at us. Apparently, unlike the Pandemonium, those things do move through walls.

That oppressive silence presses in as colors flash all around me.

## 17

# FAMILY TIME

### LYRA

When the sensation of being pulled through time dissipates, I am standing between the side of a building and thick woods that abut it. No Boone to be seen.

I whip around, searching for him, but don't call out. I have no idea who else might hear. "What in the name of Zeus' folly did you do, Boone?" I mutter to myself.

The Titans are afraid of the broken time for a reason. Rhea said I *always* end up in Tartarus. What if I cause world-ending paradoxes or something?

But I can already hear Boone's arguments in my head. We don't know who or what to believe in Tartarus. What if they're trying to keep us from learning that we can get out this way? On the flip side, they could also be the ones controlling where time takes us, trying to manipulate us.

So the question is…what do I want to do now? Hide and wait for time to swing back by, like catching a trolley? Or try to find out more?

I take stock of where I am.

The building is huge and far from modern. It's several stories tall, and I think I see a hint of smooth columns on the side farthest from where I stand. It doesn't look like the pristine white Greek-inspired temples of my current day. Instead, it's painted all sorts of colors—maroons, yellows, blues, blacks.

Beyond that, I catch the glint of sparkling sunlight off dark-turquoise-colored waters. Waters reflecting the blue of a perfect, cloudless sky.

The Mediterranean, maybe. Definitely the past. Will Hades show up in this past, too? A sharp burn of anger stirs in my chest all over again. I still can't believe he never said anything about meeting me before. *I kissed a version of you with long hair in the water garden, Lyra* seems like a conversation we should have had by now.

A shout of laughter comes from the opposite corner of the building from where I am now. More toward the water. Curiosity—possibly my worst flaw, now that I'm lovable—tugs, and my feet follow the sound.

Just a little peek. I have thief training. I can get in and out without being seen, right? Besides which, time will take me back eventually. What's the worst that—

Oh, hells. Was I seriously going to think *what's the worst that could happen*? Maybe Hades is right and my sense of self-preservation is broken.

Moving carefully, I focus on not making a sound as I creep all the way around the building and into the stubby trees that are thick on the ground here, moving outward and then back in toward the sounds of people.

A childish giggle reaches my ears, and I stop where I'm partially cloaked in the shade of a particularly dense set of bushes with shiny dark leaves. I have to go up on tiptoe to see over the shrubbery. The sight that greets my eyes requires me to slap my free hand over my mouth to swallow back my gasp, and then I wince and wait for discovery.

It doesn't come. Letting out a slow, silent breath of relief, I rise back up and look.

Cronos, Rhea, and their children are enjoying a day together as a family. Honestly, when I first looked, I thought it was Hades tossing an angelic-looking baby boy high into the air, garnering adorable, high-pitched squeals and giggles. But it's not. It's Cronos.

Younger than the one in Tartarus, without the silver. Without the lines around his eyes and mouth, either. The baby he's tossing has a shock of white-blond hair. No need to guess—Zeus.

As I watch, Cronos gives the baby an extra boost into the air, and when Zeus reaches the pinnacle, lightning surges from his body with an immediate clap of thunder. Cronos has to jump to the side to avoid being struck directly but also manages to catch his son on the way down. He gives a great, chortling laugh, throwing his head back in obvious delight.

"You threw him too high again," a familiar, patient voice chides gently from somewhere off to my right. "You scared him."

Rhea.

Cronos cuddles baby Zeus, tickling him under the chin. His pale-blue eyes, like his son's, are twinkling. "He's not scared. He's showing off."

"Uh-huh," Rhea murmurs from somewhere I still can't see.

"You aren't afraid of anything. Are you?" Cronos coos at the baby. Even from here I can see the delighted grin Zeus beams back at his father as he babbles with baby talk that the King of the Titans seems to understand, nodding along.

"Well, you're scaring *me*, my love." The gentleness has left Rhea's voice, replaced by affectionate exasperation.

"Fine. Fine. Not so high," Cronos grumbles. Then to Zeus in a low voice, "Your mother is too easily scared."

"I heard that," Rhea calls.

"Mama!" a small voice cries out from the sea beyond. There's a spit of beach leading from the water to a half-moon white-rocked cliff, and atop that cliff, the family of immortals sits in a field.

Squinting, I spot Poseidon's long, blue hair first. He's maybe twelve years old. With a wave of his hands, two dolphins flip out of the water, their chirping noises audible from here.

There's a sound of clapping off to my right followed by, "Wonderful!" from Rhea, and even from a distance it's easy to see the way Poseidon puffs up with boyish pride.

I lean to my left, pulse hammering in my ears as I search for Hades, but I don't see him.

Instead, I spot a younger Rhea sitting on a rough brown cloth spread out over the ground. The Queen of the Titans is clad in a tunic-style dress similar to the pink one she was wearing in Tartarus, but in black this time with a simple geometric design embroidered around the edges. Beside her, Hestia, maybe in her mid-twenties, is helping unload a basket of food. In Rhea's lap, she cuddles a small girl of three or so who is already going to be an obvious striking beauty. Hera.

Everyone knows newborn gods stop physically aging in their twenties, so they really are these ages. Although the Titans have aged slightly in Tartarus, so maybe it's not a full freeze. Not that it matters. The bigger question is…

*When* is this?

When does Cronos swallow his children? I would rack my brain for the historical dates taught to us in school, but I'm too distracted, still looking for Hades.

"Come eat!" Rhea calls to her family.

"Yay, bread!" A small girl with copper-colored ringlets is closer to where I hide, already golden in the way she shines. She bounces and claps her hands. Demeter.

But where is…

"Hades?" Rhea calls.

I lean farther, searching for even a glimpse.

"Do not move," a low, shiver-inducing voice growls from…all around me.

Heart pounding, I freeze, not even breathing and honestly not sure I could if I tried.

Then my god of death—a younger Hades, probably in his late teens, maybe even twenty—appears in front of me in a swirl of black smoke that evaporates from him in wisps, as if he brought a piece of the Underworld with him when he teleported.

He grabs me by the wrist. "Who are you—" His silvery eyes flare with what almost appears to be recognition, but that's not possible, not when he was this young. Except his next harsh whisper proves me wrong.

"…*You.*"

# 18

# TIME IN A BOTTLE

### HADES

The intruder, the *threat* to my family, might as well have taken the axe strapped to her back and chopped me down with it.

Green-and-gold eyes.

I *know* these eyes. I've dreamed of her eyes all my life.

She frowns, her confusion impossible to mistake. "Me?" she asks. "Do you know me?"

Doesn't she recognize me from that day? True, I was a small child at the time and don't remember it myself, beyond a memory of her eyes. That was years ago, so I look much different now, but how could she forget saving me when my grandfather tried to kill me? He tried to drown me on the beach we can see from here.

I hate coming to this home in the mortal world. It never feels quite… safe…to me.

The woman drops her gaze to where I've wound a rope of smoke around her wrist, holding her captive, and her eyes widen. Then she smirks and cocks an eyebrow at me, like she doesn't fear me. Is she trying to die?

"I see Hades, Mama!" I hear Demeter's high, excited voice. "Over there."

Then my mother's voice follows, sharper. "Demeter. Come back here—" She can't hide the fear in it. Hasn't been able to for a long time.

*Damn.*

I give my captive a hard look. "If you value your life, do not move or speak while I deal with this."

Giving her no chance to respond, I turn and step partially out of the bushes, drawing the woman behind me so that she's still hidden by the dense leaves. She tugs once against my rope just as Demeter runs up with a childishly eager face. I tighten the smoke binding around the woman in warning and feel her go still.

Still...but I don't think afraid.

What is wrong with her, to have that kind of reaction to being captured by the god of death? My very touch can send even gods permanently to the Underworld.

"Mama bids you come eat." Demeter holds out a hand to me while she waves toward the happy family gathering around the basket of food.

I can't touch my sister. Not without risking my power escaping my control. I could kill her in an instant—the worst possible result and not worth testing. Her sweet little smiles will fade away when she finally learns to fear me like Hera and Poseidon already have. A day I should help come sooner, for Demeter's protection.

But I can't make myself hurt her like that. She'll learn. In the meantime, I'm careful.

I drop to one knee so I'm on Demeter's level. I'm still tied to my intruder, who doesn't move or speak, but I *feel* her watching.

"Remember we can't touch," I remind my little sister gently.

My little sister looks at her outstretched hand, then at me, and lowers it with a frown.

"I am not very hungry," I say.

Demeter bounces on her toes. "But there's fresh bread."

Her favorite treat. Already her powers as goddess of the harvest have manifested. Young to get them, like me. But hers don't kill.

Or make her family look at her like she's a monster.

"Tell Mama I'm going for a walk."

Demeter is my kind of stubborn, which has always given me a bit of a soft spot for her. "But Mama said—"

I turn one hand up, still holding on to my rope and captive with the other. In my free palm, I do one of the few things I *can* control. Smoke and blue fire manifest, then swirl together, re-forming and molding into a tiny sheaf of wheat that is charred on the outside but glitters with inner light.

I place the gift—a bribe, really—on the ground between Demeter and me, and she claps with delight.

"That's enough of that, now, Hades," my father calls out as he walks Poseidon, who's come up from the beach, and Zeus toward where the others are.

His voice is even sharper than Mother's was. But he also sees more of the things I've killed without meaning to than she does. Or used to. I stopped going to him with my failures four years ago, when I was fifteen. He can't help, and it only adds to the lines of worry around his eyes.

I give him a stare that says I was being careful, and he glances away. I think I'm the only creature alive that can make the King of the Titans look away like that.

Heart as heavy as the center of the Earth, I nod at Demeter to go. She scoops up my little gift and runs off with a laugh.

I take my captive and disappear.

At a whisper of my will, we reappear not far away, just at the other end of our home, on the back side. I face her now, my rope of smoke binding us together and a column of smoke swirling around us, creating the strangest sensation of being entirely alone in the world…just her and me. Together.

I shake off the sensation. The rightness of it.

Connection is not something I allow myself to have with anyone. Even powerful Anubis fears me sometimes when he comes to help me work on my control.

But *she* didn't try to run. To escape. To put distance between us. She's also *not* mortal. I can see the glimmering of the power marking her as a goddess all around her, like sunlight glinting off ripples in the sea.

I know *all* the goddesses of the world, and she's not one I'm familiar with. "What are you?" I demand. "A witch? A fate?"

I *will* her to obey, to answer.

But she doesn't. Instead, her lips twitch. I narrow my gaze on that small tell. "Answer me."

She crosses her arms, seeming uncaring of the rope wrapped around her wrist, dangling between us. "You're being rude."

I suck in sharply. Her voice is honey sweet but with a slight rasp to it. The kind of voice that makes people want to listen. But more than that, it's a familiar sound. Like I've heard it before. Did she speak that day on the beach all those years ago? I don't remember.

"I'm rude? You're the one hiding in the woods, watching my family," I point out, voice tight with irritation. Gods and Titans alike cower in my presence and obey my every word without argument. Mostly because they are too terrified of setting me off. But not this woman.

She lifts her hand, tugging at the bond of smoke. "You can lose this. I won't run."

She ruins the effect by glancing beyond me, in the direction of where my family is enjoying time together without me. Does she think she's safer with them? She'd be correct. Then she glances off to her right, shifting nervously on her feet.

Lies. Her words are lies. She's definitely going to run. Everyone runs from me eventually.

I ball my hands into fists at my sides, gripping the rope tighter. "I thought you were a guardian angel."

Damn her. I did not mean to say that. Not out loud.

"I'm...not," she says slowly, like she's testing each word.

"It was you that day on the beach when I was a child, wasn't it?"

Her brow furrows in confusion. "I...don't know."

Well, that makes no fucking sense. Nothing about her does. "Are you here to harm me?" Others have tried. Assassins. The prophecy is known. My grandfather's death and the following war between Primordials and Titans made sure of that. No one wants me alive except my parents, and I've been aware for years now that even they are second-guessing that choice.

Her frown is all angles. "Of course not."

The way she says it feels like I'm the odd one for suggesting such a thing. I am *not* the odd one here. "Did you come to harm my family?"

"I don't want to harm anyone."

"Then why are you here?"

"I can't tell you."

I slash a hand through the air. "Not good enough."

"For you and me both," she snaps. Then she glances away, muttering something under her breath about, "Not like I have a choice."

She uses such strange words. Gods can understand all creatures and languages, but her phrasing is unusual. Plus all the things she says make no sense. "No choice? Did your feet walk you here without asking the rest of you?"

Amusement sparkles in her smile, and my heart, which I've tried so hard to turn into an unfeeling lump inside my chest, pumps. Once. Hard.

I don't like it. "You need to start explaining—"

"Why don't they want Demeter coming near you?" she asks out of nowhere.

She might as well have asked why I always dream about her eyes. I stare into them now, so serious and full of concern and *real*. All this time, I'd thought the woman from the beach when I was a child was a conjuring of my imagination. But she's not. She's here, and she needs to be warned to be wary of me. "I can't control my power and have killed…things…that have touched me. They just want to keep Demeter safe."

Her brows draw together, green eyes darkening. "And they think you'd kill her?"

"Not on purpose—"

"I saw you with her." She points off toward where I found her. "You were so careful."

She noticed?

My heart pumps again. Even harder this time. It…aches. I need to put an end to this. Now. Hand her over to my father and be done.

"Is it always like this?" she demands. "You all alone, and them watching closely?"

Yes. "No."

Her eyes narrow. "So it *is*. That's not right."

It sinks in that she's angry. Not with me but with them.

"I don't need your pity," I say, yanking the rope. A warning.

She doesn't take it, chin jutting out. "It's not pity—"

"Or your advice. My relationship with my family is mine to deal with." I tug her closer.

I should stop when she's still a safe distance away, but I'm too fascinated, caught by the fluttering of her pulse in her neck, the slight widening of her eyes, so I reel her in, drawing her nearer. Gloriously green eyes. I've dreamed of an angel with those eyes watching over me, but I'm having anything but an angelic response to her now. This stirring in my veins is scorching…and treacherous.

Is this the way spiders feel as their prey tiptoes across the trap of their web?

I want to dig into her soul, discover her secrets, hear her confessions, and be the one to dole out her punishments…and rewards.

What kind of feeling is this?

Insidious. Wrong. I'm always wrong—

There's a pop of sound, and I wince a heartbeat before my three-headed hellhound puppy tackles me to the ground. He hasn't learned to teleport silently yet.

"Cerberus, down," I command.

The serious head, who is most often in charge, gets right in my face. *"Your heart is beating hard. We must relax you."*

The hellhound the size of a small wolf hasn't figured out that pinning me to the ground is not relaxing. But, already made of death, he's also the only creature alive immune to my killing power.

"Cerberus?" I hear the woman ask, and the dog and I both jerk our gazes to her.

"How do you know his name?" I demand.

At the same time, she steps closer. "What are you—"

She cuts off when two of the three heads growl at her in unison. Even with his tongue lolling out of his mouth, the goofier head is dead serious.

Honestly, I expect her to shriek or faint or try to run—the natural response to meeting my pet. Instead, her eyes go all sweet and glassy. "You're just a puppy!"

What in all my hells?

Is she making a jest? The way a grin lights up her face, I know she's not. She doesn't even blink when the grumpier of the heads snaps in her direction. A clear warning. All she does is hold up her hands. "Hey, little fella."

*"Little?"* The goofy head huffs.

Fates, grant me patience. "Get off me," I snarl at the dog.

The serious head is still focused on me, nosing at my chest. *"Your heart—"*

"Is fine."

He growls. *"Is not. You could do bad things."*

No way am I admitting that my heart rate is entirely due to a certain green-eyed witch of a woman who seems to have a death wish, the way she runs headlong at the most dangerous things.

She called Cerberus "puppy" like he's soft and cuddly, which he's not. She's a menace.

The dog is also not going to let this go.

With a sigh, I close my eyes and focus on controlling the beats, erratic at first, then steadier and steadier, until Cerberus finally grunts and steps off me. *"Cerberus stay?"* he asks. *"Maim goddess?"*

He's still young and learning language.

"No. Home," I command.

With an obedient woof, annoyingly happy that he's done his job well—something I can't be angry at him for—Cerberus disappears with a pop as quickly as he arrived.

"What was that about?" my guardian angel asks as I pick myself up off the ground.

I sigh as I dust off my purple cloak. "A gift from my father, trained to detect my heart rate and help me calm down before I kill something." I eye her narrowly. "You, in this case. You're lucky he didn't attack you."

She snorts a laugh, waving that comment away like an amusing fly. "The service animal trained to keep you from killing things is going to kill me? I don't think so."

"He also protects me from those who want to see me dead."

"I'm no threat." She tilts her head and studies me, no fear in her gaze. "Besides, you would have kept him from hurting me."

So sure of herself—like she knows me better than I do. The thing is... she's right.

But she shouldn't fucking believe that. She has no reason under any of the heavens or the hells to trust me. "Did you not understand earlier?" I demand. "Even gods can't touch me without risking death. My family secretly thinks I'm a monster—"

She suddenly closes the gap between us and sets a hand on my arm.

I yank away so violently that she gasps. But she doesn't...die.

My power stayed inside me.

Shock holds me as still as the dead under my care, and I stare at the place she touched. Skin to skin. The feel of the softness of her fades slowly away.

I want...*more*.

But wanting more only ever leads to disappointment. A flash fire of anger sweeps through me—anger at myself for wanting touch, for wanting her, and anger at her for putting herself in that kind of danger. The emotion ignites in a physical burst of flames over my body, blue tipped, hot enough that I sense more than see her stumble back.

"You're not a monster, Hades," she tells me quietly, but also in a rush, like she's running out of time.

I hear her voice despite the inferno around me. If recognizing her when she first arrived felt like an axe to the chest, her words now are like one of Zeus' thunderclaps, leaving my head ringing. My flames are doused as quickly as they came, which never happens. And I'm not sure which shocks me more.

"What?" The word rips from my throat.

"*Hades?*" Cerberus is here again, staying well back. I once accidentally singed the fur off his tail in my anger. He's still got a bald patch.

I hold up a hand toward the dog but keep my gaze trained on her. "I am fine."

She stares right back at me, the moment drawing out between us, full of heartbeats.

"You're unharmed."

She frowns slowly. "Of course I am."

She glances past my head, her eyes widening slightly in what looks like surprise or even fear. The first flash of fear I've seen from her.

I look, but there's nothing. "What—"

The feel of her hand against mine has me tensing so hard I flinch. But this time I don't pull away…because the fire doesn't come.

My power doesn't even twitch. And I can *feel* that it's not her doing. It's mine. I don't want my power anywhere near her, so I stopped it.

*I* stopped it.

I face her, meeting eyes that are so soft, I want to dive into them. Then I slowly lower my gaze to where she's still touching me. Such a small touch, just her fingertips against the back of my hand.

"That was dangerous," I say, my voice hardly above a harsh whisper. "You risk too much."

"I needed to show you."

She slides her fingertips slowly around, then across my palm to lace our fingers together, and I'm breathing hard, feeling that innocent touch in every part of me.

And it feels so…good. Such a simple touch.

My fingers tighten around hers compulsively. I don't want to let her go, even if I should.

"Hades."

I shiver at my name on her lips and reluctantly drag my gaze from our entwined hands to her eyes.

"You're not fine." Her words are as gentle as her touch. "You're far from fine right now, but you *will* be. You're not a monster, Hades."

Even the second time around, those words rock through me.

Then she offers me a smile, the kind only my mother tries to give me every so often. But Mother's are always filled with guilt or pity or worry. *This* smile is filled with…certainty and trust. No fear or pity to be seen. "One day, you'll do the hard things no one else can. But that is only possible when you master your powers. Which you *will*. You just need to have faith in your own heart."

That very heart squeezes tight before beating like a trapped animal inside the cage of my chest.

*"Hades,"* Cerberus warns.

I ignore him, focused entirely and utterly on her. On green eyes that seem to hold nothing but kindness and something warmer…and yet a distance, too, like she's holding herself back.

*This* is her holding herself back?

No one has ever said words like that to me. *Never*. Let alone dared to touch me after my powers manifested completely and raged out of control.

What if she's the only one I can touch like this?

"I don't believe you."

She winces, gaze flicking over my shoulder again. This time, her eyes flare and she takes a step back like she's going to try to run. I pull the rope taut between us.

She sees the gesture, and what flashes through her eyes is indecipherable—a thousand emotions I couldn't begin to untwist. Like she wants to tell me things…but she's stopping herself. Why?

"I wish I had more time to convince you," she says.

"So stay." The words drop between us. I shouldn't ask her to stay. No one should be near me, but…

"You are *not* dangerous." The words rush out of her now as she backs up another step. I tighten my grip, stepping with her.

She gives me a pained look. "Stop fearing yourself, Hades. Fear will always make everything worse."

She goes slightly hazy around the edges in the strangest way, and I shake my head, trying to make her come into focus.

"I'm sorry," she says, her voice sounding like it's coming from far away. "I have to go. I…wish I could stay."

She fades even more, and I tighten my grip on her and the rope, but it's like holding on to water as she turns more hazy. She's leaving, and I can't stop her.

"What's your name?" Desperation jerks the demand from my lips.

I *have* to know.

Her smile falters as she hesitates several more poundings of my heart.

"Lyra Keres."

And then she's gone.

As if she never existed. All that's left of her is the sound of her name floating on the wind and the feel of her touch fading from my skin.

# 19

# SOMETHING WAS TRUE

### LYRA

One second, I was with Hades, longing to tell him everything, to pour it all out, and struggling so hard not to, even while I tried to help him. He seemed so…lost.

In the next instant, I was standing in the hole inside the pillar of the earth.

"Shit, Lyra," was the first thing a shaken-looking Boone said as he ran a hand over his face. "You told him your name?"

But nothing reset. So…no harm, no foul? And Boone, apparently, wasn't picked up by broken time, left behind to wait for me. Figures.

Regardless, we've been stuck in here ever since.

The ground shakes beneath us, and I barely crack an eye to see if the tree roots of the earth pillar are shivering with the quake. "There's another one," I mumble sleepily.

Boone doesn't even shift positions, lying with his back to me. "Yeah."

The quakes have been happening every so often in the days we've been stuck in this painfully boring space. At least we think it's been days, but really, we have no clue how much time has passed with no light outside the small flame Boone keeps stoked at all times. It's not like phones work down here, and neither of us is wearing a watch.

Or the earthquakes could be lies like all the rest.

A thought train on loop in my head for days now. What if this is real? What if it's a lie? What if it's something else, like a glamour, to entice me to let them out? They use truth to tell lies down here. A thief's trick.

We have yet to see the Titans, though. So that's something.

The shaking stops, but that's when a new sound—a strange sound, not hissing, but raspy and soft—makes me go still as I strain to hear it better. Then I bat at Boone's back. "Hey…"

He sits up. "Was that outside?"

I don't have a chance to answer because the noise gets louder, now reminding me of how nylon ropes sound when doing a rapid free rappel. We're both on our feet in an instant, facing the place Rhea made a door before. I think. It's a round-ish room formed by roots, so who can tell.

"It's not coming from inside," he says.

We slowly move to the center of the space, standing back to back, listening and watching for…anything.

"Boone," I whisper, pointing.

A tiny crack has appeared in the wood of the wall I'm facing, and something is trying to wriggle through. Something…green.

The color registers as the break in the wall grows and vines burst their way inside. They keep pressing outward, making the hole bigger and bigger, but no one comes in. Boone and I look at each other, then he leads, and I follow him outside. It takes a second of blinking in the brighter light of the lava and fire from the wastelands beyond for my eyes to focus after days in the dim.

No one is out here, either.

However, the vines and flowers covering the outside of the pillar are still moving. Almost like the flow of a lazy river, but they're going up rather than down, in an undulating swirl of lush greens with pops of color.

Boone puts a hand on my wrist when I go to move closer. He whistles the signal to *keep a lookout* just before he scoots back and to the right, carefully leaning over, only to jerk away abruptly, his back going ramrod straight. He stands there, blinking at whatever he saw around the bend of the pillar, as the still-moving vines continue rasping and shooshing quietly.

"What?" I ask.

"There's someone up there," he says.

I frown, glancing between him and the pillar. "A Titan?"

He shakes his head.

Frowning at his back, I scoot around him and carefully lean over like he did…just as a petite woman with big doe eyes comes into view.

She stops as soon as she sees me, hovering in the air, suspended by the vines. Her wide-eyed gaze takes me in, then slides over my shoulder to Boone.

Then, with zero warning, she smiles.

And she might as well have floated in on a cloud of magic wearing a sparkling pink ball gown, like Glinda the Good Witch of the North. Because the effect is the same. Utter captivation.

She's pretty in an ethereal way down to the last detail, with deep-brown skin and endearing freckles. Her hair is midnight black at the roots but turns a rich burgundy rose that fades to pale pink at the tips, which hang in curls down her back to her waist.

Flowers are woven into a crown around the top of her head, and her sundress is white with embroidered flowers. She's barefoot, her delicate toes painted a glittering rose pink that matches the tips of her hair. And eyes that are more lavender than blue remind me of a baby doll, wide with thick, curling lashes. The scents of honeysuckle and jasmine float on the still air between us.

She needs no introduction. I know *exactly* who this is.

The woman Hades is supposed to have been love-obsessed with and grief-stricken over but who in reality is more a beloved niece. The goddess who made him put flowers in the Underworld and decided how Elysium should be run. The partner he made Queen of the Underworld by pact rather than marriage. Before he met me. The same goddess we were trying to rescue when we got sucked in here.

*Persephone.*

"I managed to get out of the room they put me in the first day," she says in a voice that sounds as delicate as flower petals. "What's wrong with you?"

# 20

## THE FAIREST OF THEM ALL

LYRA

Behind me, Boone mutters, and I don't entirely catch it. But the gist seems to be along the lines of *they're really fucking with our heads*.

His mumble draws Persephone's glance, and for half a beat, I swear shock ripples across her expression the same way the earthquakes make the ground shake. But I second-guess that when she beams at him.

"So you really are stuck in Tartarus." It's the first thing that comes out of my mouth. I've been wondering for the days we've been stuck in here if Persephone was a lie perpetrated by the Titans to get Hades to do what they wanted. To get me in here.

"I really am," she says, pulling her gaze back to me.

"How?" I ask next.

She shrugs. "Your guess is as good as anyone's."

Too flippant. I have to unclench my jaw to answer. "Not good enough."

Her smile might as well have sunbeams and butterflies attached—it's that perfect. "You don't like me now," she says. "But trust me, you and I are going to be great friends."

I give her a flat look. "You got the first part right."

My rude comment doesn't even faze Persephone. Instead, she just aims the beam of her smile over my shoulder. "You're new," she says in a voice laced with cheerful interest, cocking her head to eye Boone. "They told me Lyra brought a friend this time."

"This time—" I snap. And I almost go into grilling her about what *resetting* and *this time* really mean around here. But I won't trust her answers. Not yet. So I change it to, "Where were *you* this time? You were supposed to be waiting at the gates of Tartarus."

Persephone cringes, and even that's adorable. She's not drop-dead gorgeous like Aphrodite, who, like the Titans, has the kind of beauty you can hardly stand to look at. It's more like she's…attainable. The kind of pretty that makes you feel warm and cozy just to be near her but not like you're imposing on her perfect world.

Which only makes me resent her more.

If she's Glinda, then—with my green eyes and long black hair twisted haphazardly on my head, thanks to no mirrors—I am clearly the Wicked Witch of the two of us.

Awesome.

Love that for me.

"I am sorry about that," she says slowly, as if she's carefully choosing her words. "If you knew what I know, you'd understand—"

Boone glowers at her. "You set a trap for Lyra."

Persephone blinks, like she's not used to anyone confronting her. "I wouldn't call it a trap exactly."

Boone's grunt is disbelieving. "Did you somehow send a communication to Hades that you would be waiting at the Gates when he used Pandora's Box to open the one-time-only back door out for you?"

"Well…" Her gaze skitters between us. "Sort of—"

"And instead, you sent fucking Cronos." Now his voice has gone deadly quiet. It's rare to see Boone pissed, but that's what he is right now. Or "pissed" isn't quite right. There's an odd edge to the blame he's throwing her way.

Persephone attempts a conciliatory smile. "That's not—"

"Yes or no," he demands. Even quieter.

For the first time since she appeared, her smile dims slightly before she glances away. "That's how it ended up. Yes."

"Then fuck you."

Even I throw him a startled look. Boone doesn't swear at women or children.

Persephone's lavender eyes widen, then darken with a lost-little-girl kind of hurt that makes even me want to hug her. And, since he's close, I can tell that Boone stiffens, too. But he doesn't take it back.

Not that he needs to. In the next instant, Persephone's hurt disappears like mist clearing in sunshine, and her smile brightens several watts. "When I tell you why, *then* you'll forgive me." She nods like this makes everything better.

Boone scoffs. "I doubt that."

So do I.

"Why, then?" he demands next.

She purses her lips. Seriously. She's like an anime character, she's so damned cute. "I can't tell you yet."

"Uh-huh."

He and I plant our hands on our hips at the same time, and Persephone stares between us again, amusement drawing up one corner of the cupid's bow of her lips. And all I can think is, *Of course the person Hades is supposed to be in love with is this flawless.*

In fact, come to think of it, maybe Zeus didn't curse me to be unlovable after all. Maybe he actually cursed me to be unlucky, and I've had it wrong all this time.

"Rhea warned you that if Lyra learns too much too fast, she can reset time."

We both lean back. "She didn't say it quite that way," I mutter.

Damned Titans.

Persephone shrugs. "We have to be careful not to trigger you too much." Another sunny smile. "Generally, it's much better when you figure things out on your own."

More fun and games for me. This place blows.

"I have to show you something important," she says.

Suddenly, vines whip out, and before I can blink, I'm wrapped in greenery and being lifted up the side of the pillar alongside Persephone.

"Hey!" Boone snarls in a tone that says what she just did lands somewhere between obliviously naive and dangerously foolhardy.

I glance down in time to see him grab a handful of vines, craning his neck to look up at us.

Persephone doesn't stop, tossing words over her shoulder at him. "I thought a god of thieves would have faster reflexes than that. Try to keep up."

"Will these vines let me?"

She brushes a fingertip over a broad, shiny leaf that seems to nuzzle into her touch as she passes by. "Because I tell them to, they will."

"Then do it," he snaps.

A half second later, Boone is lifted upward to follow us. "I don't like this." He's still snarling.

Persephone shrugs. "You need to see something."

She's looking up. I don't like not being able to see her face. It feels like she's hiding things. She's like an evil little pixie trying to convince us she's made of light.

We all fall silent as the vines quietly rasp all around us. Tendrils wind and unwind from around my legs, my feet, my waist as the greenery passes me from one level to the next, but so gently I can't decide if I'm in danger or not. Anything strong enough to carry all of us up so high is also strong enough to kill.

My axe is in my hand, though, and Boone is with me. Those are the only reasons I'm not asking more questions.

As we continue to rise, I can see more and more entrances to tunnels that end at the sheer face of the mountain, but there doesn't appear to be rhyme or reason to their layout. No levels, no patterns. Where could so many possibly lead?

I really, really want to ask about that. Rhea's use of "cells" implies individual prisons, but so far, we've only seen ten Titans down here, plus Persephone. That's a lot of tunnels for only fourteen cells. Persephone doesn't even give the tunnel holes a glance, and it's not important enough yet to take that side quest.

She keeps going, us trailing behind, and several times I look down to find Boone staring with stony determination, arms crossed, and not moving as the vines raise him higher. Which is when I finally remember…he's afraid of heights. I've never been sure because I think he hides it, but now it tracks. That makes his fall off Hephaestus' tower in the Crucible even worse. The third time I glance down, he gives me a tiny whistle telling me to *stop*. So I face upward and quit checking.

We're lifted up until we get to the top, where the rock that forms the underground mountain merges into the ceiling. The pillar seems to keep going into the rock, punching through. These truly are the pillars that formed and feed the cosmos. There's a flat, narrow balcony without a railing that circles the pillar just below the ceiling, so we can walk around up here.

But I'm not looking at where the root punches into the rock and, I assume, keeps going. I'm looking at—

"What happened here?" Boone demands, and I turn to find him coming up over the ridge, gaze glued to what I was just staring at.

Persephone follows his look to the marks—scorch marks, blast marks, claw marks—all along the stone where the roots penetrate.

Permanent scars of violence.

"Oh." She waves an uncaring hand at them. "The Titans have tried everything to get out of here."

## 21

## CRACKING UP

### LYRA

"Boone," I whisper.

"I know," he whispers back.

Because Persephone basically just pointed out the visible proof that the Titans couldn't get out in thousands and thousands of years. And she did it so casually, like this doesn't confirm that there's no fucking way we're making it out ourselves.

"Come on," Persephone calls from across the way. "We don't want to stay here too long. Using Pandora's Box, or possibly your arrival here, always seems to make the Pandemonium set off more often."

And I guess they can get up here. She doesn't say it, but we both understand just the same.

With one last glance at the damage, we both trail over to where she's standing. She scoots around the thick back side of the pillar, then points up, which is when I see the crack. It's not like the other damage wrought by the Titans. Theirs looked very different. This is a golden, glittering seam, like a vein of ore in a mine, part of the very rock.

"It's beautiful," I say slowly. "What is it?"

Persephone lowers her hand to her side. "It's a break."

Boone's gaze traces the fracture, eyes sharp. "What do you mean a break?"

"It appeared a long time ago…" She trails off, making a face and visibly thinking about how to word it. "Something happened that shook Tartarus—"

"What?" I immediately ask.

She makes the same face, nose wrinkling deeper. "I can't—"

"What's the point of showing us this if you can't give us any information about it?" Boone asks.

Another wince, and then she considers me closely. But I'm not shaking yet. I don't think.

"It appeared the first time Lyra ended up down here," she finally says. "And it's getting bigger. Time resets put everything back as it was, but not this."

Dread drops into my stomach like small stones into a still lake, creating larger and larger ripples. A crack in the very heart of the world isn't enough? Now it's getting worse?

Persephone takes a deep breath. "If we don't get out of here soon…" Another breath. I don't think she's faking the fear that blanches her skin. "Come see." Now she takes us to where we can see the pillars of sky and ocean and points to more cracks along those. "I think Tartarus itself is breaking."

A larger rock of dread drops into my stomach. "Are you saying the world is teetering on the edge of collapse?"

Heavens save us.

Are we about to be buried alive down here? Is that what she's saying? And we're immortal. Would we live through that only to be pinned down for eternity?

That's…

I don't even want to think of what that would be like. Hades' punishments for the wicked would look like vacations in comparison.

"I'm saying we don't know." She says this quietly. But the fear is still here, bracketing her mouth in lines now. "But do you really want to wait around to find out?"

Fuck.

Lots of fucks. Because sometimes one just isn't enough.

How is it that I manage to find myself at the heart of a story about the end of the world? Seriously. I have to be the unluckiest girl alive. Definitely the wrong curse.

"Is this what's causing the rumbling we've heard?"

Another doubt-filled look. "We don't know that, either. It's always been a little rumbly down here, but there's been more of it lately."

Great. Just great.

"How did *you* get down here?" Boone demands. "A straight answer this time."

Persephone blinks at him. "I...don't know that, either, and neither do the Titans."

"That's damn convenient," Boone says.

He really does not like her.

Apparently oblivious to that, Persephone reaches out and pats his hand, making him jerk away from her like a startled animal.

"I wouldn't call it convenient at all," she says, lowering her hand to her side slowly.

Boone sets his feet with a glare. "What would you call it, then?"

"Frustrating."

"That doesn't make it any less convenient."

She tips her head, considering him more closely. "Stubborn is kind of adorable on you."

His face goes blank beneath the days-old scruff. Then he opens his mouth.

I rush to cut him off. "Why weren't you there to greet us with the Titans when we came out of Hestia's Lock?"

She doesn't take her gaze from his face, but she also doesn't answer.

Boone huffs an unamused laugh. "Can't tell us?"

"Introducing me to Lyra too early, when she has so much to learn about down here, never goes very well."

"Bullshit."

I agree with him. We still don't know what to believe. For all I know, Persephone is on the Titans' side and always has been.

"What better way to gain access to Tartarus than to befriend the King of the Underworld?" Boone asks, his thoughts clearly in lockstep with mine.

Persephone tips her head again, studying him like he's a particularly difficult flower to grow. "I like you despite yourself, Boone Runar."

Hades is right about her, and so is Charon. The young goddess is essentially sunshine in a bottle. The question is, is it genuine? Or a front? A way to gain trust when what we should be doing is running the other way?

Wait... How does she know his name?

I glance at Boone, surprised he isn't asking the same question, but he's too busy glowering at her.

Persephone reaches out a fingertip and touches it to the scar of gold. Vines burst out of the rock and proceed to wind up the break, pushing in and out of granite so hard it should be impossible for the plants to find a way. But they do. They crisscross the scar back and forth, all the way up, like stitches, and then the vines grow and grow and grow until they cover the entire crack. Even then they don't stop, not until flowers bloom with petals of vibrant gold, as if they drew their color from the ore of the scar.

She holds out a hand to a flower, which leans in and nuzzles her fingers like a beloved pet might, and her soft smile is once again tinged with that strange sadness.

"We're all trying to hold this place together somehow," she says. "Until we can be freed."

Then she looks at me, and for the first time since meeting her, she lets me see not the bright, glowing woman, but the goddess she truly is underneath—one who is powerful and determined. "You have to save us, Lyra."

We. Us. She's definitely with the Titans now.

Will that happen to me, too?

Oh gods. "How?"

They haven't really told me yet. Not really. Just tried to chuck me into the pit. Best guess is I have to open a bunch more Locks. But how many, and why me? Or is there something else they need me for?

"First, you need to trust us."

"Well, that's not going to happen," Boone grumbles. "What else you got?"

"Just…this." That's when she glances behind me. So quickly, I almost don't catch it. Not before she shoves me hard.

She sends me tripping backward, my arms windmilling…

Right into Iapetus.

I didn't even know he was here. But as he knocks my axe from my hand and scoops me up under the knees, I catch the look of horror on Boone's face. He doesn't even get a chance to form the word "no" with his mouth before Iapetus wraps me up in a bruising grip and tumbles both of us off the edge.

He doesn't need vines, taking the landing at the bottom like he just jumped out of bed. The second his feet hit the ground, he's running. My struggles don't even make a dent as we blur through the pillars into the mountain, down tunnels all the way to the chamber where the door to Hestia's Lock still glitters with her symbol. But we blow past that and into another tunnel.

The one they all kept looking at with fear any time I spoke too loudly.

We slow suddenly, and he clamps a hand over my mouth as we pass an onyx obelisk. The source of the Pandemonium, according to Rhea. And I don't know if it's the way the Titan is holding me so hard or the vibe that thing gives off, but I don't try to escape while we go by.

As soon as we are well past it, Iapetus is running again, and the world is blurring. And all I know is the tunnel seems to be circling its way up inside the mountain.

When we come to a stop, the pissy Titan and I are back where Boone and I originally started with Cronos—on the bridge by the massive double gates, with the drop into the abyss at my back. My heart, already tripping, sprints away like a racer off the starting blocks. Self-preservation kicks in, and I jerk against his grip. When that doesn't budge anything, I jam my knee up into his groin.

Nothing.

And now my knee is throbbing like I rammed it into solid stone. What happened to my immortal strength?

Iapetus doesn't bother with the threats or talking it out. He just takes me by one wrist and dangles me over the abyss.

I'm flailing like a snared rabbit. I have no other weapon at my disposal except words. I fling them at him. "Maybe Oceanus isn't down here because you killed him the same way you're trying to kill me."

The world has always wondered. Because the Titan who legend claims wasn't imprisoned has never been seen since. But that's not why I say it. I'm trying to make him stop, rethink, and I saw the way all the Titans tensed at the mention of Oceanus' name before.

"Curse that traitor." Iapetus repeats Mnemosyne word for word.

He draws me in closer, and for a second, I have hope that my gambit worked. Because, for the strangest moment, I think I see regret cross his features.

But I know I was wrong when he gives me a grim smile. "If you survive, you'll thank me when you come out."

Then, just like Cronos, he lets go.

## 22

# THE SECOND LOCK

### LYRA

When Iapetus drops me into the abyss, I try to teleport out. Even with my undeveloped skills, I should at least be able to stop the downward trajectory, so I try again. But it's like gravity has a fist around me and is yanking down hard.

I don't give up, though. At least this time I'm not screaming and bracing for death.

I have a feeling that will come later.

Suddenly, with no transition whatsoever, I'm not falling anymore. Instead, I'm standing on what feels like soft dirt that's been tilled until it's fluffy, and I sink deep, it's so thick. My eyes go wide as I take in my surroundings. If my heart wasn't already pounding from the fall, it would start now.

Is that...sky I see?

I appear to be inside a long hallway that has a series of arches leading outside. Maybe twelve of them, with a larger one in the center. Each arch is closed by a wooden gate that comes up about four or five feet, leaving the top of the arch open to the outside.

Outside. Like I'm in the Overworld.

There is a cloudless, perfect blue sky. I'm so taken with that, a few seconds pass before I register the rest. The stalls, or gates, or whatever they are, seem to lead into the center of a structure that reminds me a lot of the Roman Colosseum where we played Athena's game in the Crucible. But...this isn't quite the same.

Instead of circular, from what I can see from here, the structure is oblong and bigger. It has stands with stadium seating built all around it, only they aren't ruins, like the Colosseum. They are in pristine condition… and as empty as a wise man's tomb. I'd guess it's at least fifteen hundred feet from where I stand to the other end and maybe two hundred feet across at its widest point. There's a large walled platform in the middle decorated with towering statues and maybe even more seating. It effectively creates a center divider like a spine.

A track? Is it a racetrack?

Boone appears so suddenly beside me that I yelp, hopping back.

When I realize who it is, I peer at him more closely, reaching out to poke a finger in his arm. "Are you real? Or are you part of some new illusion?"

He doesn't even look at me, let alone notice the poke, scanning the area like I just did. "Real," he says grimly. "It wasn't exactly hard to guess where Iapetus was going to take you."

"He's an unoriginal bastard. That's for sure."

I swallow hard as I realize Boone intentionally jumped off the bridge to follow me.

I take in his new clothing, then glance down to find I'm similarly attired. "What are we wearing?"

Leggings, a tunic over them, both in a rough-hewn material. His is black, mine close to white. Leather strapping binds around our chests and stomachs and thighs, and we're wearing leather gauntlets around our wrists and close-toed shoes that are a cross between half-boots and flip-flops, with the woven leather strapping covering most of our feet, but with patches and holes in between. My axe is gone, but there's a curved knife in a sheath strapped to my leg. Boone has one, too.

"Looks ancient in style, but…" Boone sniffs at his gauntlet. "This leather is brand new."

"Something a soldier might wear in ancient Greece, maybe?"

Now we're both looking around. Hestia showed up pretty much immediately when I arrived in her Lock. Are we going to get a different god or goddess this time?

"What is this place?" I ask.

Boone shakes his head. "It reminds me of the Circus Maximus in the movie *Ben Hur*, when they race—"

Hades appears before us not ten feet away. I suck sharply and take a step toward him, a move that feels as natural as breathing, only to get pulled up when Boone grabs my wrist.

"Don't," he says in a low voice.

What my heart wants to do is tug against him and argue that it's Hades. That he's here. But I already know that's not true.

Not real.

Because the Hades standing before me is *not* my Hades. Like Hestia, he is a copy, a recording, or whatever they are down here.

He looks only slightly older than he did when I saw him with his family—twenty-three, maybe. Not much younger than he looks in present day. But I can see the differences even so. And his clothes are not modern but like ours—a tunic and leggings with leather strapped shoes, I think. It's hard to tell because he's wearing a dark-brown hooded cloak that covers most of what he wears. It's giving Obi-Wan vibes.

"Going to try again, are we?" Hades is at his most arrogant and taunting.

Wait...he doesn't sound pre-recorded like Hestia did.

"Try again?" The words just sort of pop out. "I haven't been down here before."

I wait for him to glitch. To start over. But he doesn't. Instead, he tilts his head, lips tipped slightly up. "You always say that, little goddess, but I assure you that you have attempted to unseal my Lock many times."

"The fuck you say." Boone growls those four words.

Hades' silver eyes flash to him and narrow. "You, however... This is your first time."

How is it possible for a recording to know that? Hestia flickered and blinked her way through the same generic message and couldn't stray from it. At least that's the impression left on my very befuddled mind from that encounter.

But Hades...

He feels so *real*. I know I should be terrified, particularly of whatever comes next. After all, the Titans implied that there are multiple Locks. This is the second one. Another test. More deadly shit.

I know the Hades before me is *not* real.

But he sounds like him. And he looks like him. Even the sharp narrowing of his eyes is him. And an ache is setting up in the middle of my chest that makes me want to rub at the spot.

*Because* it's not him.

"I know you are not really Hades," I say, jaw tight, frustrated by all the unknowns. "But you should know that he fell in love with me and made me Queen of the Underworld. He wouldn't want you to put me through whatever this is. He wouldn't do that to me."

Hades' gaze returns to me, and for maybe a second, I think it softens. I *know* it softens, the silver turning from a knife's edge to silk. Only to sharpen again as his face hardens into a stubborn cast. "Sometimes you say that, too," he murmurs, almost too soft for me to catch. "But no matter."

No matter?

He's not going to unseal this Lock and let us out without testing us. I wouldn't even have to know him that well to see that much is true.

And to him, it's no matter. *I'm* no matter.

I close my eyes, because I need to *not* see him when I say this next part. I need to not believe that it's my Hades putting me through yet another potentially deadly trial.

"Then get it over with."

## 23

## RUN, LITTLE GIRL. BANG.

### LYRA

There's a distinct snap of fingers.

This time, I know to brace for the electric jolt that reverberates through me, strips me bare, and steals the strength from my limbs, the sight from my eyes, and the air in my lungs.

"Gods damn." I hear Boone's groan of pain off to my right. A sound that cuts off abruptly.

And I force my eyes open to find him doubled over, but the next jolt brings that light, obscuring my vision. My powers are getting sucked out of me, stolen away so that I can only face what happens next as a mortal.

By the time my vision clears once more, I'm on my knees and trying not to heave as a wave of freezing cold chills me to the marrow of my bones.

A team of four horses now stands before us, rearing in their traces.

Horses made of…smoke.

Jet-black and billowing, their manes and tails flow up and around them, streaming away and dissipating in the air. Intricately etched black metal armor is layered into their smoky flesh like bony growths. And through those plates, at their very centers, I can see through the smoke of their bodies to their hearts beating inside their chests. Hearts that look like coal burning bright blue, pulsing in time to the glowing blue blood visible in their veins.

"You've got to be shitting me!" I jump back just as Boone grabs me and swings me around fast, putting his back to the team, his body between me and harm.

But nothing happens to either of us, and we both straighten to face them. The horses remain where they are, stomping and snorting, eyes of fire trained on us.

Hades' lips draw up into a smile that is pure challenge. "My test is to survive the poison of evil that can affect all mortals."

"Sounds ominous," I mutter.

He lifts a single eyebrow. "All you have to do is beat my hell horses in a race. Seven laps."

Gods, he's so damned frustrating. Even down here. And what does a chariot race have to do with evil poison? "It can't be that easy," I say. "Unless you're making me try to win the race on foot."

*Shut up, Lyra. Don't give the recording ideas.*

"You will drive a chariot. You may pick any of the teams that draw from any god's or goddess's powers that you can think of. All you have to do is call out their name and power, and horses will appear, drawing a chariot."

Despite the fact that I've never driven a team of horses in my life, it's still too easy.

I roll my eyes. "What's the catch?"

Hades smiles. No dimples, though. "These creatures are what they are made of. For example, Hephaestus' lava horses are all things passion, all things destruction, and they will decide who to bless and who to kill indiscriminately."

Always a godsdamned catch. Never trust the gods. Even if I'm one of them now. "Do I have to use the same horses for the entire race?"

He tilts his head. "I swear, little previous mortal, you ask the right questions faster each time I see you. Perhaps you truly can remember those other visits and just don't know it."

"Answer her question." Boone is back to growling.

The animated copy of my god of death gives a nonchalant shrug like none of this matters anyway. "You can change teams as many times as you wish."

"And me?" Boone asks. "Do we both have to cross the finish line ahead of your team of horses or just one of us?"

Again Hades' gaze slides to Boone, turning sharper like my friend is the whetstone to a dagger. "My team only has to lose," Hades says. "It doesn't matter to whom. Seven laps. The first horses to cross that finish line, no matter who is driving them, determines the winner. Lyra wins, she opens the Lock. You win, you open the Lock. I win, you—"

I wave him off with an angry flap of a hand. "We die. We know."

Another curious tilt of his head, slower this time, reminding me of a snake coiling to strike. "It is not wise to be rude to a god."

I scoff. "I'm not being rude to a god. I'm being rude to the King of the Gods, who also happens to be my lover."

"King?" Hades gives an annoyingly dark chuckle that snags at my already tattered nerves. "Your stories get more creative every time I see you. I look forward to our next encounter, Lyra Keres."

And then he's gone.

The smoky horses remain, stomping their hooves and neighing with impatience.

"What's our plan?" Boone asks without even a beat of time to react to any of this. Straight into get-shit-done mode.

It helps settle me in an odd way. "Let's each start with our own horses. We'll figure it out from there."

"Double the chance to win." He gives a sharp nod. "Smart."

I grab his wrist. "Just nothing that could kill a mortal. No lightning. No fire."

He grins back at me, challenge sparking in his eyes. "Damn. I was planning on picking a tornado and just laying waste to the entire place."

"You have ten seconds to choose your horses." Hades' disembodied voice rings through the stadium. "Ten. Nine. Eight—"

"Shit," Boone mutters. "Go!"

We take off toward the arched gates to the right of Hades' horses, and my mind is tumbling through gods and goddesses and powers and elements. Sun, lightning, tempest—all are too dangerous as a mortal. And what good are wine, harvest, childbirth, or even Persephone's vines in a race against smoke-and-fire hell horses?

Boone beats me to the lineup as Hades counts down. "Five. Four."

A whip of smoke lashes out from the demon horses to grab Boone around the waist and hurl him through the arched gateways. Because of the wooden gates blocking my view, I don't see how he lands.

I'm also not going to make it to my gate in time. Desperation is a terrible place to start from. "I need horses made of Nike's power of victory," I yell as I run.

"Two."

A team of four gold, winged horses appears instantly, already standing proudly in their traces. Not just golden haired. I mean solid gold, as if a master craftsman molded them from the metal and shined them to gleaming.

No idea what I expected when I picked that power, but it wasn't this.

"One," Hades says.

Then a series of pullies yanks the gates up, and Hades' driverless horses spring forward on a sound that could be either a scream or a growl.

I leap into my golden chariot, grabbing the reins, not that I know how to use them. "Go!" I cry out.

Thank the ever-living daylight out of the gods, because the magical horses listen.

They bolt so hard and fast, I have to drop the reins to keep from being flung backward and out of the open back end of the cart. I'm still trying to just stay in the carriage as we fly past Boone, who is lying on the ground, unmoving.

I whip around to check that Boone's okay. His prone form gets smaller and smaller as we race down the long length of the course.

"Get up. Get up. Get up," I whisper, willing him to move.

My cart lists wildly to the right, and I am forced to face the front, throwing my weight to the left as I realize we've already reached the sharp hundred-and-eighty-degree turn around the center divider. We straighten out just as abruptly, hauling ass down the other side after Hades' horses.

"Oh, gods. Oh, fuck." If Boone doesn't move out of the way, they're going to trample him.

The smoke rising off those damned hell horses is filling the air and obscuring my sight. The jet-black team moves in close to the center divider and whips around the bottom turn, where the carved feet of a towering statue of some hooded figure draped in wicked-looking chains jut out into the track. Their chariot goes up on one precarious wheel behind them. As soon as they are out of sight, I can see that Boone isn't in view.

"Please don't have been dragged under their wheels," I mutter to myself even as I grit my teeth and lean again while we also round the aggressive turn.

I don't see him anywhere.

"Where is he—"

There's an odd trill of sound, high-pitched and so loud that for a second, I take my hands off the bar in front of me to clap them over my ears, only to unbalance and have to grab for it again.

As I do, I see one of seven carved onyx owl statues perched on a metal bar in the center divider drop forward.

Some small corner of my brain catalogs the fact that the sound they made is one screech owls use. Hades' sacred animal.

Those owl statues must be counting off laps each time the team in the lead passes the dead center of this side of the track. One lap down. Six to go.

Across the track from the owls, situated in the main stands, there's a covered hall decorated by fluted columns. I narrow my eyes, searching inside the covered pavilion as we whip by. I think maybe Hades' copy sits upon a dark throne inside. Watching. Is he using that sound—a trill used by mating pairs of screech owls—to taunt me with what I said about me being his queen?

Damn, he can be so cruel.

I love him, but damn.

My hands curl around the bar I'm holding on to as realization sinks in deep, even in the middle of all this chaos. I can't die in here. If the real Hades ever found out, he'd blame himself.

As if survival wasn't enough—mine *and* Boone's—or, for that matter, the possibility of getting out of Tartarus—which has been implied, but I still don't understand how—a new purpose strums through my blood in licks of fire. The sun glints off the pure gold of my horses, which are already running so hard for victory. We have to win.

I *have* to win.

To try to escape.

To keep us from dying.

And to save Hades from guilt and heartbreak.

## 24

# FLESH, BONE, & CIRCUITS

### LYRA

One hand at a time, I take the reins, moving with the rhythm of the horses I'm driving. I've only ever seen clips of movies that tell me anything about how to do this. Jaw clenched against the wrenching violence of the motion, I snap the reins. "Go!"

As if they were only waiting for the signal that I was ready, my team of horses finds a new gear, gaining on Hades' team just as they round the turn.

When I fly around the same turn, not only are Hades' horses ahead of us, but I catch sight of another team. Glowing neon green.

That's all I see before Boone's around the far turn so fast that I wonder if I saw what I saw.

When we round the end this time, we're close enough to Hades' team that the smoke around us thickens and my lungs are burning as I cough and my eyes water. But I squint against the sting. The hell horses pull to the inside of the track. The shorter path.

Screw them. I go wide. We veer wildly for a second. That's when I see Boone's horses behind me.

"Holy shit!" The words burst from me.

Because they are…digital.

Neon green on a darker green or maybe black, their bodies are made of squares, like pixels. Electricity seems to travel the outlines of those pixels like it's zapping across electric wires, sparking and glowing.

"Hermes!" I realize.

Boone picked the power of the messenger god known for speed. Boone may have taken Hermes' status as the god of thieves, but Hermes kept all his other abilities, and now Boone is using one. Not just physical speed but, in this day and age, also the speed of digital communication.

Fucking brilliant.

And they are fast! Boone's already closing the distance between him and us.

Grinning like a demon, I urge my horses faster and faster until we draw even with Hades' team just as the second owl drops with another tremulous trill that fills the stadium.

As if that sound was a signal, the instant it stops, something shoots up out of the ground directly in front of me. I swear it's a hand, but we flash by it before I can tell. Then another. And another. I jerk us to the left to avoid yet another.

One of the hands, or whatever those things are, rises up with a spear the size a giant would wield and stabs it through all four of my golden horses in one fell swoop. On a heart-wrenching scream of pain, my team disappears in a blink. Gone as fast as they came.

I'm flung into the air, arms and legs wheeling as I come down. Thank Olympus for the soft, thick dirt. I manage to curve like a banana when I strike, rolling and flipping before I land with a thump.

*Get up, Lyra. Get new horses.*

But before I can move, another hand bursts from the ground and clamps down over my neck, cutting off my air. Definitely a hand. I claw at it, kicking and grunting, and finally wrest it away from my neck with a sickening sound of a crack followed by sucking.

I throw it off me, jumping to my feet, which is when I see it fully.

Flesh turned a sickly green, rotting, and hanging off the bone I just snapped. I literally pulled an arm off a body that I assume is still buried.

Gross.

The hand jumps up, using its fingers like legs. Because Addams Family style totally makes sense in this moment. It skitters across the ground toward me, and I let out a squeal that a five-year-old would be proud of as I run away.

Yes. Like a coward.

I yell, "I need horses made of Nike's power of victory."

"They're gone." Hades' voice booms out. "Pick another."

"Gone? As in dead?" I ask, spinning around to face the columned structure where I think he sits. Because of me?

Another hand bursts from the ground, grabbing me by the ankle. With a yelp, I jump back. Just as the full body comes up out of the ground.

And a knife of fear slices through my veins.

Zombie. Definitely a zombie. Hades is the god of death, after all. It's made of disgusting rotting skin all over, eyes gone milky white with death. The scent of rotting meat rises up around me.

Nightmare material. That's what this is.

With a series of telltale thumps of rotting flesh bursting through the soft earth, more and more zombies rise.

I freeze for a moment, unable to decide if I should call for horses or run. The meat sack who just put his arm back on makes my mind up for me. His jaw hinging open on a terrible, gurgling scream, he comes at me.

Not slow. He sprints.

I take off running, dodging more who are still rising up out of the ground.

I'm just reaching for the curved knife strapped to my leg when a piercing whistle sounds from behind me—a signal I haven't had directed at me in ages, and yet my body automatically does what I've been trained to do.

I flip around to see Boone's horses bearing down on me, plowing through the zombies. Which, even in the milliseconds I have, I register as disgusting. Parts flying and ripping apart, then skittering. Boone is leaning over the right side of the basket of his chariot, hand extended. I'm pretty sure he's slowed down for me, but damn those digital horses move fast. It doesn't even occur to me not to trust that he'll catch me at this speed.

So I run at him, reaching for him.

The second we grasp each other by the forearms, I'm yanked off my feet and swung violently around. But he doesn't drop me, and I somehow end up in the chariot beside him.

"Gotcha," he says and shoots me a cocky grin.

Hanging on to Boone's waist by the leather straps, I look over my shoulder to yell at Hades. "You didn't say anything about zombies, asshole!"

A dark chuckle rattles around the empty arena, louder than the terrible sounds of the flesh-eating monsters coming after us or the thunder of the horses' hooves.

"Hold on," Boone shouts.

I grip him tight and lean with him as his team takes us around the turn fast and hard. The second we straighten, I can see that there are no zombies on this side. Yet.

Boone whistles, and apparently these digital horses are AI, because they understand thieves' signals. They kick their speed up to an impossible level. The obelisk and statues down the center divider blur as we whip past.

We're just coming to the turn when the third screech owl sounds.

Three laps down. And we're behind.

I'm racking my brain for any possible combination of power and horses that could be faster than the ones Boone has come up with. But I've got nothing.

"Lyra!" Boone nods down.

Trying not to get in his way, I lean over the edge of the basket to look down. Sure enough, half a zombie body is climbing up the side, trying to get at us. I grab at my knife.

"Hold on!" Boone yells as we whip around the turn.

As soon as we stabilize, I hack at the zombie. The crunch and suck of my blade in its flesh is a sound that might haunt me for the rest of my life.

But the thing drops off the chariot.

I check for more as much as I can from this angle and with smoke blowing into my face from the horses ahead of us. Then I straighten as we hit the turn. We skid wide but manage not to tip over, and then we're neck and neck. The rapid thudding of hooves and the rhythmic snorting of the horses as they breathe with the effort is quickly drowned out under the sickening crack, splatter, and screams of the zombies. Only our team is plowing through zombies again, while the things are leaping out of the way of Hades' horses.

He's such a cheater.

The fourth owl's trill rings, and I assume the little statue drops forward, counting down. I'm too busy slashing at several more gruesome things trying to come at us from below.

A whip of smoke lashes across our team, striking our horses. But their pixels just shimmer and shift to fill in the wound.

"Remind me to kiss Hermes when we get out of Tartarus!" I yell.

"Ew," Boone yells back.

Another whip of smoke catches him across the face. The strike is hard enough that he has to drop the reins to keep from being thrown. Which is when I realize that he's tied to the reins that are wrapped around his body.

But I don't have time to worry about that danger.

Another lash of the whip comes for us. This time, I manage to sever it with a slice of my knife. But they keep coming.

"Okay, new plan," I yell, and Boone doesn't stop me when I duck under his arm.

"I need horses of Poseidon," I call out. "Made of ocean waves."

## 25

# HARDER, FASTER, BETTER, STRONGER

### LYRA

Boone has to swerve wide to give space to the team and chariot that immediately appear. They're gorgeous creatures of bright turquoise waters that swell, crest, and crash within and without themselves—their manes and tails, but also as part of their feet, as if they are running through those ocean waves. Salty mist sprays up and over us.

Without taking a breath, I start to climb the chariot's side, only to have Boone grab me. "What are you doing?" he asks.

"Making sure you win."

"Fuck." Boone snarls the word, but then he drops the reins, letting his horses drive where they will, and I find his hands at my waist, helping me up, keeping me steady.

The horses must not like the zombies any more than we do, because we swerve away from the water horses only to swerve back in. This happens two more times while I'm balanced precariously on the edge before Boone swears again, grabs the left rein, and gives it a yank, forcing his horses to trample another few zombies rather than avoid them, bringing us closer.

"Now!" he shouts.

I jump, and he heaves, and somehow, I manage to land in the ocean chariot I'm aiming for. Of course I come down skewed and with one leg straddled over the side bar. Pain explodes through me, probably worse than it seems in the moment, thanks to adrenaline.

"That's going to leave a mark," I groan as I force the now throbbing leg up and over, into the basket with the rest of me.

"I hope to Had—" Nope, can't hope to him right now. Whatever. This better damned well work. "Splash Hades' horses," I command my team.

Immediately, water rises out of them. Not in a whip like the smoke horses, but larger waves that rise and crash toward the charging animals. Those poor fiery horses sizzle at the contact and scream in pain. I grimace at the sight and sound but harden my heart when tendrils of smoke whip out at us. Over and over, the two teams duel as we race around the track.

We scream past the owls that let out their trill of sound, one more falling over. Five laps down, two to go.

And I'm starting to smile as Boone pulls farther and farther away, moving in front of us when he gets enough distance and beating us to the turn by a healthy margin. Of course, that's the instant that two zombies burst from the ground on either side of him, pitching themselves into the spokes of his wheels.

Body parts are thrown everywhere, but it's enough to wrench both his wheels off. The bottom of his cart hits the ground hard and shatters around him. When the parts clear away, I can see that Boone is being dragged through the dirt by the reins he had looped around his waist.

I think I scream Boone's name as I helplessly watch his body skid and bounce along the ground behind his team. But as his horses start to slow and we get closer, I can see him thrashing, struggling to free himself. Can he not reach his knife? I pull mine out again, hoping I'm not going to regret this. It's not the same as throwing axes. As I pass him, I chuck the weapon. It flies end over end, striking true and severing the reins.

Boone's body tumbles to a stop, but his horses disappear entirely.

Holding on with a death grip, I am facing backward in the cart as I watch Boone's prone form on the ground. Just as I hit the far turn, he pushes to his feet.

Relief surges through me. "Thank the gods."

I lose sight of him and twist around in the cart, needing to focus. My own horses are locked in a nasty battle, exchanging vicious blows with Hades' team. The noises all around me—the horses' hooves and screams, the groans and yells of the zombies—almost cover the sound of the owl as we pass the center, where Hades still sits shrouded in darkness.

Last lap. Winning is up to me now.

My horses are holding their own, but is that enough? As I duck to avoid taking a smoke-whip to the head and then hold on as we hit yet another zombie, tossing me around in the cart, I am scouring my memory. What other god's or goddess's power can win this for me now?

Which is when the strangest sound comes from behind me. Not that of an animal. More…elemental.

"What now?" I snap as I look over my shoulder. My jaw drops at the sight of Boone coming at me fast.

Just Boone.

No horses. No chariot.

He's standing upright, a foot or two over the track, and is just floating along at incredible speed, his thick hair whipping around his head. Realization strikes. One of the winds. He harnessed the power of the Anemoi, the four winds who are also called the unseen ones.

That's got to be it.

His horses are invisible. Like wind.

Which means he could win. I just need to slow down Hades' horses more than I already am.

That gods-awful howling noise Boone's wind horses are making grows louder and louder as he closes in on us. All while I'm mentally discarding power after power. I need something guaranteed to stop Hades' team of stallions dead in their tracks.

Wait.

Stallions… They are made of smoke and don't seem to be able to die. Water is only slowing them slightly. But they have beating hearts and can be made to feel pain. What if they could feel…other things?

Animal instinct?

The first clue that I'm in danger is the feel of hands wrapping around my legs. That's all the warning I get before I'm flung from the cart.

I land flat on my back in the soft dirt hard enough to knock the wind from me for a second. But I'm on the side of the track with the most zombies. Even as I'm gasping, I scramble to my feet just as Boone manages to avoid trampling me, blasting past.

"Go!" I yell after him. Because I know him. He'll stop. "I'll slow Hades' horses down for you."

Staying aware of my surroundings, I spin on my heel and run in the opposite direction. If I'm going to slow down those damned horses, it's got to be before the finish line, and I've only got so much time before they round that last turn.

It only takes me about five steps before I really start regretting throwing away my knife. We have mauled and mowed over many of the zombies. A grotesque array of body parts litters the track like gory confetti. But some of those things are still up and moving.

So I run.

Fast.

Or as fast as I can through the thick dirt. And dodge a lot, dealing with an obstacle course of flesh-eating corpses. I'm almost distracted by the sight of the replica Hades—he's out in the opening, leaning forward to grip a rail as he watches.

Breathing hard, coated in blood and brains, and honestly secretly terrified I'm not going to make it, I don't get nearly as much distance between me and the finish line as I would like before the two teams round the turn.

"Damn it," I mutter as I dodge another zombie.

I have one shot at what I'm thinking...

"This better work," I say under my breath. I check around me to be sure that no zombies are too close, then raise my voice. "I need horses made of Aphrodite's lust. Mares who are in heat."

Immediately, I'm standing in the chariot behind a team of cotton candy–pink horses. The mares knicker, cantering forward with a sashay to their steps and their darker pink tails swishing. I swear they give those smoky stallions come-hither looks, batting ridiculously long eyelashes.

Hades' steeds immediately slam on the brakes, skidding to a halt, dirt and smoke flying up around them. Their attention is entirely focused on the creatures of lust I've presented in their path. And it only just occurs to me that I could also be slowing Boone's horses down in the same way. Hopefully having a driver in the chariot makes the difference.

Boone blows past them, and Hades' horses jerk and jolt in their traces, clearly torn between two strong desires—win for Hades or take the mares.

When they start running again, I snap the reins, urging my team to trot straight at the coal-black stallions, adjusting course to stay directly in their path. All four rear up, and I can see their nostrils flaring as they catch the scent of the mares. They go wild, but not to run and win.

Boone blasts past me on a gust of wind so hard it lifts my chariot off the ground—and me with it.

I come down with a jolting thud just as all the horses disappear entirely, which means I end up in a heap in the dirt. The tremulous trill of a screech owl sounds, and the seventh onyx owl statue turns down.

"Ha!" The laugh bursts from me as I scramble to my feet.

All the zombies are gone, too. Thank the gods. Unfortunately, it looks like Boone's momentum pitched him through the air. But it only takes him a few seconds to get to his feet and start walking in my direction, a grin slowly spreading from ear to ear.

"We won!" I shout.

## 26

# & THE TRUTH SHALL FUCK YOU UP

### LYRA

A short distance from me, Boone breaks into a jog, still grinning. And he doesn't stop until he scoops me up into a bear hug, swinging me around.

"Brilliant," he crows, squeezing me tight. "What were those? Aphrodite's horses?"

He sets me back on my feet, and we grin at each other in triumph. "Lust," I say. "And in heat."

Boone tips back his head to laugh at that. "Yup. Fucking brilliant."

Then he sobers abruptly, scanning me from head to foot. "Are you hurt? The zombies…"

"I'm fine." Although I'm guessing a massive bruise is forming where I did the splits on the water horses' chariot side bar. Now I know why charioteers wore leather around their thighs. I wave him off, only to check him over in return. At first, he appears okay, but it's not until I see the streak of dirt covering an entire side of him that I think to lift his tunic. A hiss escapes me. "Oh gods. Boone."

"Bad?" he asks with mild curiosity, like the road rash that basically sheared the first few layers of skin off his torso, leaving long, bleeding abrasions covered in dirt, is no big deal.

"It's not great." It comes out like an accusation.

"It'll heal the second my power is returned."

I carefully lower his shirt, trying not to let guilt churn my stomach. "I guess so."

"Hey." He gives me a pointed look. "I'll be fine."

I frown at him fiercely. "*None* of this is fine, Boone."

"You realize you can leave now?" Hades is standing where I glimpsed him only a minute ago. He's still leaning on a thick rail with both his hands, and he couldn't be more bored.

Then he waves off to his left.

Where the starting gate stalls stand, the taller archway in the center is now intricately carved with symbols of Hades—a bident and scepter, a screech owl, a key, and, of course, Cerberus. And through the now-open archway, standing in the mountain hallway that circles the outside of the abyss's cylinder, the Titans wait like before, watching us.

"Congratulations," Hades says. "You have passed the test of not succumbing to worldly experience and becoming a zombie yourself."

We unsealed the second Lock.

The relief finally hits, and I draw in a long breath.

Beside me, Boone gives a jaunty, slightly taunting two-fingered salute to Hades' double still watching us. "Fuck you very much."

Then, together, we tromp our way through the once-again-pristine dirt toward the exit. And it takes everything in me not to look back.

*He's not real*, I tell myself. *He's not my Hades.*

Looking will only make this worse.

I'm right behind Boone as he exits through the arched doorway, but before I can set even a toe through after him, a hand grasps me around the wrist and gently tugs me to a stop. And I freeze, because I know this touch. I *crave* this touch.

A tremble starts deep inside me.

I thought he was a recording, a copy—more like Hestia—not something that feels like flesh and blood.

"Look at me, little goddess." He says the words softly. Temptingly, even. "Come on."

I don't know what part of me obeys. Maybe the part that needs answers. Or the part that just needs to see his face and hear his voice, even when it's false. Or the part that worries a tiny bit that everything I have with the real him is built on lies. Or the part that just wants to prove myself to him...and to me.

I damned well won this round.

When I meet his eyes, Hades' mouth tilts in a barely-there smile. Then he looks down at my wrist that he's still holding and makes a noise in his throat kind of like a hum. It sounds like satisfaction, maybe. Seeming to be engrossed, he traces a fingertip softly over the two stars of my Orion tattoo that are on my left arm, and then the single one on my other wrist.

"My star," he whispers to himself more than me, and his nickname for me makes my heart squeeze. "Do you know why you're here?" he asks, finally drawing his gaze up to mine, though he continues to hold my hand.

I try not to melt and deliberately narrow my eyes. "If I've been here so often, I have a feeling you know better than I do."

His lips quirk. "I can see why I like you in my future." Why does that wording sound off, like he's more than just a copy?

He sobers, eyes flashing dangerously silver. "You are here for the seven Locks."

Seven. That rings a bell in my memory.

Before Zeus' Labor in the Crucible, I told Aphrodite that Persephone wasn't dead but trapped down here, that we were trying to get her out. And she said...

*Gods.* What were her exact words?

*The only way to open Tartarus requires all seven of the gods and goddesses who trapped the Titans in there.*

And later, Zeus said something about Pandora's Box going *around the seven wards.*

Are the wards these Locks? Do I have to do this seven fucking times? I throw my head back and groan.

"This is the second Lock." Hades slides a hard look over my shoulder at the Titans. "And *they* can't open them."

The Titans can't? I try to control my breathing, to keep my head. "Let's say I believe you..."

I get an immediate, arrogant smirk, and I hold up a hand. "Slow your roll. I'm not saying I do, but for the sake of expediency, if I did... If Titans can't figure out these Locks, then how can I?"

Hades lazily swipes his thumb over the inside of my wrist, and now I'm controlling my breathing for a different reason entirely. "When my brothers, sisters, and I imprisoned the Titans, all seven of us—Hestia, me, Demeter, Poseidon, Hera, and Zeus, as well as Aphrodite—each made a Lock. The Labyrinth down here isn't a maze, as humans seem to believe. It's a series of locks. Safeguards against our parents getting out. Each is a test that must be passed in a certain order. The only way to open Tartarus, to escape, is for someone who is not a Titan to unseal *all* seven."

I suck in a harsh breath as what Hades' copy is saying finally penetrates my poor mind. He's telling me there is definitely a way out. *This* is the way out. A way to get home. Get back to my Hades, the real Hades. We just have to go through five more Locks and not only survive but defeat each test.

*Fuck me.*

"And that's what I did just now?" I ask him. "I unsealed your Lock?"

"You did." Another lazy swipe of his thumb. "Aphrodite's lust was a nice touch."

I swallow down a riot of emotions, so tangled I can't seem to get a hold on what I'm feeling. "I've unsealed two already," I say slowly. "The Titans have had ages down here. Why haven't they escaped? They should easily have—"

He cuts me off. "Because you were once human."

I frown. Why would that matter? Before I can voice that question, another realization hits me harder than the first, and I don't think I move or make a sound, but Hades leans closer, gaze more intense. "What?"

Resets. Time resets. Right? But we know the Titans fear the cracks of broken time.

"You said I've done this before?" I ask through lips that don't want to move.

His grip tightens, then slowly eases before he nods.

"Cronos broke time," I say now. Not a question. It's the only possible answer. "Did he make multiple timelines?"

Hades shakes his head.

Oh. No multiverse. Okay. "Then…"

"I'm not entirely sure, stuck in here and only getting my information from your visits. But time keeps starting over from a certain point."

So it's true. Time can reset. I've been down here before, and Hades… "Does my Hades know? Does he remember all the different times?"

His recording stares at me like he's trying to decide if the answer may break me. "I don't know."

My breath leaves me in a whoosh at that nonanswer.

"The Titans remember, though," he says. "I think they are the ones resetting it to make sure you end up down here, because they believe you're going to free them."

Because of Phoebe's prophecy. Okay. Forget controlling my breathing, which has abandoned me anyway. This deserves a meltdown, starting with a panic attack.

"Lyra." Hades' voice comes from far away, like down a tunnel. "Lyra." He gives me a little shake, and that yanks me out of my head.

"Have I ever unsealed all seven?" I demand.

Another pause, longer this time as he seems to check my expression. Then, "No."

No. Never. Not once.

My heart, which for a smidgeon of a second when he confirmed there was a way out had floated up on a cloud of hope, reverses course and plummets to the bottom of my stomach to churn in the sour bile. "Never." My voice cracks around the word.

"That doesn't mean it's not possible."

*Now* Hades' copy decides to be sympathetic? A slightly hysterical laugh bursts from me. "Yeah. Okay. Sure."

I think maybe he sighs. "You say that we're in love, you and the god I come from, and that he made you his queen."

"What?" I stare at him, my face scrunching up.

"Is that the truth?"

Why is he asking this now? With a frown, I nod slowly.

Through the continued screaming in my head at the situation I'm in, I vaguely watch the way his expression shuts down. "If that were true, then I would have marked you as mine."

He traces a line across my wrist, connecting my stars, and all the way around like a cuff, then up the back of my hand to my ring finger, where he traces around the base like a ring. "Here," he says. "Like this, but a trail of stars."

My already bleeding heart shrivels where it's still lying in the pit of my stomach. Is he trying to kick me while I'm down? Because what he's saying plays into the fears and doubts I've already been trying to hold at bay since ending up down here. "But he *has* marked me as his," I say in a voice gone husky...and shaky. I brush the tip of the forefinger of my free hand across my lips. "Here."

Hades' eyes flash to my lips, then flare wide, darkening to a stormy gray.

Wait. Is it still there? I didn't think until just this moment that maybe Tartarus stole it away, like my axes and my tattoos.

But the way Hades reacts tells me he sees it.

"Satisfaction," I whisper. I remember. "Possessiveness. My Hades would have looked at me in the same way." I tilt my head, studying him. "But does he actually love me?"

The recording of Hades jerks his gaze up to meet mine, and I see the smallest hesitation there. And maybe I expected it, because instead of taking it as a blow, I just sort of nod to myself. If this recorded version of him doubts his future feelings for me, then I am probably right to do the same.

Hades takes a small step back, away from me. "And what about him?" He looks over my head again, but this time I know he's looking at Boone and not the Titans.

"*He* is my only friend down here," I say.

Hades' jaw hardens just a fraction, and I only see it because I'm looking up from below. Then he steps closer again and gently takes my chin between his thumb and forefinger, tipping my face up to meet his gaze, which runs over my features as if he's memorizing them. "I think Hades has more competition than he realizes."

Then, without warning, he lowers his head and kisses me.

And I lean into the touch.

I *want* this touch.

And I try to feel. Feel him. Feel us.

But I don't.

This kiss isn't like our first kiss, when Hades offered me the gift of protection in the Underworld—soft and even tentative before turning to heat. And it isn't like our last kiss before I ended up down here, when he claimed every inch of my body—on fire for each other, unable to stop, an elemental force we both gave in to.

This kiss is…faded. Like this rendition of him.

And my heart, which craved his touch so much, already shriveled from shock and truth, turns to dust. Turns to ash.

This copy of Hades must sense that I'm not with him—body, mind, and spirit all far from his reach—because he stops. When he raises his head, he doesn't move away, only enough to be able to look me in the eyes. Does he see my heavy disappointment? Does he *feel* it?

"What was that for?" I ask.

The smile he offers this time is a shark's smile. Predatory. "I don't like competition."

He means Boone.

I back away from Hades slowly. And his gaze drops to me, a small pucker forming between his brows. "You look…disappointed."

"Not exactly."

"Then what?"

I take another step. "It's just become so clear to me that you aren't him. You're like a carbon copy from the nineteen hundreds—smudged and blurred at the lines."

For the briefest second, I think I hurt his feelings, the way he stiffens. But then he cants his head in the direction of the waiting group outside the Lock. "You'd better go."

"Yeah." I do an about-face a general would have found up to snuff but only make it one step before Hades calls my name.

I pause and glance back, meeting his silver gaze.

"Whatever you do, don't let the Titans out."

# PART 3

# TRUTH, LIES, DAMN LIES, AND DARES

It's all fun and games until someone loses a Titan.

# 27

## THE ART OF NEGOTIATION

### LYRA

As I join the others, I glance back at the replica of the god of death, who is standing at the entrance to his Lock, not twenty feet away, watching us with narrowed eyes.

There's a now-familiar swish of air, and the archway connecting this room to Hades' Lock turns back into a solid rock wall. It stands a full pie piece over and slightly around the bend from Hestia's arch. A glittering symbol, this time in blue, etches into the center of the stone arch.

Hades' bident.

Which is when our powers return.

The sensation is still a thousand kinds of unpleasant, like ice shooting directly into my spine and then outward, turning every nerve to a screaming point of pain. I hear Boone breathe beside me when the ache leaves as fast as it came.

I let out a long breath. "That really sucks."

"Yeah."

"I'm so sorry." Persephone comes from nowhere to wrap her arms around my shoulders. "I'm so glad you made it out okay."

She doesn't seem to notice how stiff I've gone or the fact that I'm not hugging her back.

I pull away from her. "If you think a hug is going to fix what you just did, think again. Luring me out so that Iapetus could fling me into the abyss was a dick move."

Instead of stiffness or guilt, Persephone sighs. "It's so hard to be patient sometimes," she says softly, more to herself than me. "You'll want to negotiate now, I expect."

As she steps away, I frown, because she's right. Boone and I talked out all the possibilities we could think of while we were in the earthen pillar, and we came up with several plans.

"We would, but not with Iapetus." I seek out the Titan's face to find him regarding me with something close to pride.

"You always come out with more of an understanding of what's happening." He indicates Hades' Lock with a nod. "He always tells you, and it never resets anything."

"Yeah. Well, fuck you."

Iapetus rocks back on his heels, and Cronos apparently can't decide what to do with his face. Is he grinning? Is he scowling? Who can really say. The Titan is back among them now, though his skin has a gray tinge to it, like he's been sick.

I turn away from both of them, taking in the others, trying to identify them. Their unusual coloring and markings help. If Iapetus was once the pillar of the western sky, the other three Titans must be the other three corners. One has an aura around him like northern lights. One's skin reminds me of a sunrise, or maybe that's just the glow coming off him. And one is as colorless as moonlight, except his black, black eyes, which are filled with pinpricks of light that might be stars.

Koios. Hyperion. And Crius.

I try to remember more of what I know about them, but my head is starting to hurt. I turn my attention to the three Titanesses in the room and draw a blank.

Never mind. Screw identifying them. I'm tired.

"So, what is it that you want?" Mnemosyne asks, her owl mask opening and closing its beak in time to her words. I still can't tell who's speaking.

She sounds... They all sound...not bored, exactly, but like this is a tedious exercise. I cast my gaze over the gathered Titans. How many times? How many times have they had this discussion with me?

I exchange a glance with Boone. He shrugs. We made several contingency plans.

What I'm about to do is one of them. "I will try to open the rest of the Locks. But I have—"

"Conditions," the sunrise-glowing Titan supplies. "Go ahead. Name your terms."

On the lean side with golden hair, a thick beard, and, of course, the sunrise skin, it clicks finally that if this is Hyperion, he is the Titan of order, light, and the heavens.

"Not here," one of the Titanesses says.

Among the painful beauty of the others, I'd almost say she is plain and pale, with small features that seem to pinch together. Still more beautiful than most mortals. And I love the moving tattoos of the oceans on one arm, the giveaway that her powers are over the seas, winds, and weather—Eurybia, probably.

"I'm not going anywhere until you all agree," I say.

She blinks but doesn't argue, sort of shrinking in on herself. Do they not listen to her often?

"Tell us what you want," Cronos says.

This is going to be interesting. "I want you to prepare me for the Locks. No more tossing me in and hoping I survive."

I glance around. No arguments, no surprise. They already knew that one. "Second, you will all swear an unbreakable oath—"

"You mean to not harm the gods or humans or anyone, really, when we're released?" Crius is holding Eurybia's hand, his voice as cold and crisp as the rest of him. I remember now—the father of the constellations, so…the starlight eyes make sense.

"Crius," Eurybia murmurs, confirming my guess with her gentle warning.

"What?" he says. "She always asks for that."

I blow out a frustrated breath.

He's right—I have zero intention of letting the Titans out, and it wouldn't hurt to have a backup plan in case I fail at that—but I don't love this feeling of them knowing everything and just waiting for me to get through it. It's…creepy.

Cronos waves a hand at the Titans. "We need to be able to defend ourselves if the gods attack us."

"Our children tend to act first and think second," a Titaness says.

Phoebe. Midnight-black hair hangs straight and sleek past bony, honey-colored shoulders to her waist. The black is interrupted by a patch of silver hair that forms what looks like a crescent moon shape around the crown of her head.

That's…sad. "We'll build a clause into the oath for that possibility," I offer.

"In that case, agreed," Cronos says.

I glance around. The thing is…no one argues or protests. I don't trust it. I don't trust any of them. They must be playing along for the moment to get what they want from me.

"And we want better living quarters," Boone adds.

I choke down a laugh. He must also be frustrated by this odd feeling they know everything we're going to say, so he's messing with them, testing their patience, seeing how far they can be pushed, how much they need me.

"Don't we all." Mnemosyne rolls her eyes.

"Done," Cronos says again at the same time.

More than one of the Titans tosses him a frown. Iapetus, of course, is the one to open his mouth. "But—"

"We can glamour them," Cronos says over his shoulder.

Iapetus' jaw works. "I don't think that's a good idea, brother—"

"I'll do it," Cronos says.

"But we need to conserve your strength—"

Cronos slashes a hand through the air, and even Iapetus closes his mouth. Damn. I had no idea a request like that would set them off.

"No glamours," I say. I'm already questioning reality too much. "We'll deal with the living arrangements you have."

They all go quiet.

"So…you're agreed?" Cronos asks.

What? Do I usually ask for more things? He's got me second-guessing myself. Another glance at Boone, who gives a brief nod.

"Agreed," I say.

It's as if the entire group takes a collective breath, all their shoulders dropping from around their ears. Do I not always end up cooperating or something?

They all gaze at one another until Mnemosyne holds out a hand, indicating a tunnel we haven't been down yet. Not surprising. We haven't been down most of them. "This way."

"Where's Rhea?" I ask. Did they think I missed how she wasn't here? "Did the Pandemonium get her?"

Every Titan looks toward Cronos, who stares back with growing discomfort.

"Cosmos grant us peace," Iapetus mutters. "Go get Rhea, Cronos."

Go get her? Did they lock her up somewhere because she helped me? Hells no.

"We can wait," I say sweetly. Then cross my arms. I figure I have a fifty-fifty shot of them tossing me down another Lock just to show who's in control, but I'm banking on them wanting my cooperation. "Although between the Pandemonium, the earthquakes, and the cracks in the rocks, maybe not."

Fear.

It's rare for gods to show it, I've learned. I suspect it's even more rare for Titans, but the emotion seizes every face in front of me. A slow tension starts at the base of my spine and creeps upward like a thief stealing any bit of warmth inside me.

Boone gives a low whistle, the signal for *danger*, and I meet his eyes briefly to acknowledge.

Just beyond him, I see the way Persephone's eyes widen. Did she understand? Thieves' whistles are complex—like Mandarin or Vietnamese, they aren't just about the pattern or cadence but about the tone. Only thieves should know it.

"I'll go get her," Cronos says, distracting me. "Meet us in the map room."

Then he runs off in a blur, and we follow Mnemosyne, the others trailing behind.

Please let this not be leading to disaster.

# 28

# TUNNELS, DOORS, & PUNISHMENT

### LYRA

The darkness in the tunnels is lit by sconces, although several of the Titans glow. The floor here is tilted at an incline, and the tunnel itself feels as though it curves, winding its way up through the rock of the mountain that surrounds the pillars.

We're at least a quarter mile from the Locks before I hear the first sound. It floats down the passageway ahead of me. The distinctive bray of a donkey.

I frown, glancing at Mnemosyne.

She says nothing.

But when we come round a slightly more exaggerated bend, I hear it again. Louder. Coming from a…

"Is that a door?" I ask.

"To a prison cell, yes."

"What's that noise?"

"Ocnus."

I can't help my double take. "What? He's…down here?"

I thought Ocnus was tucked in some dark corner of the Underworld that I haven't been shown yet. The man is condemned to weave a rope out of straw that a donkey eats as fast as he makes it, but there is no record of what he did to deserve such a punishment. Hades will know… Not that I can exactly ask him.

I flip my hand over, tracing the stars on my wrist. Forget wasting time asking him useless questions. I just want to hear him call me his star one more time.

Iapetus shoves his face between us. "Don't go in doors that are marked with an X."

I glance at the door as we pass it. "I don't see an X."

"Oh, Ocnus is…" Mnemosyne purses her lips. "Harmless. He doesn't have an X."

Right. "And the ones that are marked?"

Mnemosyne slides me an annoyed glance. "If you go in, you may not come out alive."

"Resetting *would* be terribly inconvenient," I murmur.

Mnemosyne doesn't just slide me a look this time. Now those green eyes, shadowed by her mask, are uncomfortably direct. "You have no idea."

The heaviness in her voice, in her shoulders, is far from flippant. She really seems…tired. Not physically—more like exhausted in spirit.

Suddenly, I don't want to know that it's real. Because then I have to contemplate how many times I might have ended up in Tartarus already. Or gone through the Crucible, for that matter. Watched Boone die, had my parents give me to the thieves, dealt with Zeus' curse…

*Stop it, Lyra.*

I only see one more X on one of the many doors as we continue, and sounds don't come out of all of them. But the ones that do… Quiet whimpers, labored breathing, and even a quavering, "Who is out there?" reach my ears.

All ignored by the Titans, who hardly seem to notice.

Mnemosyne stops before a door. As she reaches for the handle, one of the other Titanesses calls, "Watch out."

In another blur of speed, Cronos runs by, only to stop abruptly past where Mnemosyne and I stand, whirling to face the tunnel he just ran down, peering beyond us.

I peer with him.

"I'm already here, my love." A quiet voice sounds from the darkness behind him.

Cronos whirls, only to be blasted back down the tunnel by an invisible force coming from the hands of his wife.

"Bastard." Rhea's hair lifts up as though electrified or like she's in a wind tunnel.

She's not being quiet now. None of them are. I guess we're far enough away from the obelisk of the Pandemonium.

"Easy, Rhea." Cronos coughs as he gets slowly to his feet. "It was the only—"

She cuts a hand through the air. "Silence."

His mouth is still moving, but no sound emerges, and I laugh, even though I shouldn't be laughing. This is a serious moment.

But it's like she hit a mute button on Cronos, and damn, that shit is funny.

"At least you're not married to Oceanus," Mnemosyne offers.

Rhea whips her head to stare at her sister. "Curse that traitor," they both say together.

I glance back toward Theia, who seems sickly, the same as Cronos, and is moving with a slight limp. But I'm looking at the Titaness holding her hand like a child.

Tethys, Theia's twin, though apparently not identical. She reminds me of a cold, glassy lake frozen over. Not in looks—red-gold hair and turquoise eyes should be fiery, especially against amber skin, but instead are dulled. The frozen effect is more in her demeanor—unreactive, unresponsive.

The Titaness of nursing and the font of fresh water doesn't appear to react at all to the curses being heaped on her husband's name. Is she broken-hearted? Or just broken?

Beside me, Rhea takes a visible, calming breath, and her hair settles around her face before turning to me with a hostess-style smile pasted to her features. "I am happy to see you survived." She points at the door I'm standing in front of. "This is where we're going."

"Not yet," I say as she reaches for the knob.

"What now?" Iapetus mumbles.

Rhea merely pauses, eyebrows lifting in question.

"Only Rhea, Phoebe, and Mnemosyne can join us," I say.

I see the way Phoebe blinks. She regards me with mysteriously deep brown eyes now shaded with confusion. "Me?"

Iapetus scowls at the same time. "You've got to be—"

I cut him off. "Especially not Cronos or Iapetus. Otherwise, we're happy to rot down here with the rest of you." And I'll visit Hades' past for the rest of my future.

"What did *I* do?" Cronos has the gall to look a little hurt.

"You threw me into two Locks—"

"One." He waves behind me. "Iapetus threw you in the second one."

The beachwear-tourist, age-gap-romance Ken doll scowls. "Because you told me to."

Cronos glares.

Is he for real right now? "Why would I trust someone who decapitated and castrated his own father?"

"For a good reason," he says, his voice a rolling grumble.

"Name it."

He just shakes his head. Stubborn old ass.

Rhea sighs. "If he tells you, time will reset. If you find out on your own, it won't. That one happens every time we've tried." She snaps her fingers. "We start all over again a hundred and fifty years ago."

"When I arrived here," Persephone tacks on.

I don't even glance her way, staying focused on Rhea, who shrugs.

This again.

"Out of curiosity, why does telling me things also cause a reset?"

Rhea shrugs. "Technically, you are part of the outside world, so it has the same effect with you." Another shrug. "We think that's why."

"The outside world." I think that through. "They don't remember?"

Clearly, they don't, or I would know about this already. I would remember doing this before.

Unless it's all lies.

"Only those officially imprisoned in Tartarus seem to remember all the other times," Cronos says, inching closer to his wife. She bats away his hand when he reaches for hers.

*And I always end up here.*

Oh my gods, I'm starting to listen like this is true. I give my head a shake. "Fine. Time does all that, and I'm part of escaping, which is why you pulled me into it. But that doesn't mean I should trust you or like you…" I give Cronos a hard look. "You *ate* your children to keep them from overthrowing you next—"

He straightens abruptly, growing larger and somehow darker as he does. "I. Did. *Not*," he thunders.

I cringe back just a little, surprised lightning doesn't flash around him.

Despite her own ire with him, Rhea runs a hand down his arm, murmuring words softly enough that I can't catch them, and Cronos visibly calms, shrinking again, his shoulders rounding, suddenly seeming…aged. He doesn't look at me.

Then he turns and stalks away down the carved-out tunnel and disappears into the darkness.

In the silence that descends like a wet blanket smothering smoke, Boone points at Koios. "He can come, too."

If a Titan could pull off a hot-nerd vibe, Koios does. Like Iapetus, his clothes are modern, like a gamer in loose shorts and a graphic Metallica T-shirt. The Titan of intelligence and curiosity has a birthmark of stars that trail across his forehead. And then there's that distracting aura of northern lights.

Iapetus frowns. "Why him?"

"Because he's smart enough to just listen quietly," Boone says.

"Come on," Theia encourages her scowling brother as she draws a still-hazy-looking, still-silent Tethys away down the tunnel.

"Just bloody great," Iapetus mutters. But he follows the others, and their glow moves down the hallway with them.

Rhea opens the door, waving me ahead of her.

And I walk straight into a shard of broken time.

"Lyra!" Mnemosyne's voice is still ringing in my ears even through the silence of time travel.

# 29

## ...BABY, ONE MORE TIME

### HADES

I feel her before I see her.

When I'm in the Underworld, I feel *every* soul in my domain. But what makes this one unusual is that she's not dead.

She must be teleporting, because my sense of her is tenuous at best. And she's moving fast, but not in a way that makes any godsdamned sense.

I shove to my feet, and Charon, my ferryman for the dead, here for our daily meeting, raises his eyebrows.

He doesn't show any alarm, but it takes a lot to alarm him. He's not a skeleton or a demon with fire in his eyes, like the mortals portray him — he's very normal-looking. Despite being born at the beginning of time, he looks to be only slightly older than me, still in his twenties. And between his tousled sandy-brown hair and laughing green-blue eyes, many might mistake him for someone who's never serious. I don't make that mistake, even while he lounges in his chair.

"What?" he asks.

"Someone is here."

He taps a finger on the table. "I don't know if anyone's told you this, Phi, but there are a lot of someones here—"

"Living," I snap. "And uninvited."

That shuts him up.

I cock my head, trying to get a solid grasp on her. Where in my hells is she—

Then I feel her again. Closer. "You've got to be fucking joking."

With a mere thought, I teleport away without bothering to tell Charon where I'm going. I don't need his help for one foolish soul. But someone is teleporting right outside *my* home. Whoever she is, she may as well have just declared war on the Underworld. No one living comes here without my explicit permission. Not even my siblings, despite their powers.

How in the name of Tartarus did she get down here in the first place?

Not that it matters. This goddess—because only the gods can teleport—is not going to live much longer.

I blink back into existence in a rocky mountain field right at the base of my castle in Erebos, the Land of Shadows, and summon my bident to my hand with a thought. I raise it, ready to skewer her, just in time for her to appear.

But the way she fades into existence is...off.

I frown, staying her immediate death.

That wasn't teleporting, I don't think. No damned idea what it was. Particularly because of the way she stumbles like she tripped over the void before she landed, which doesn't happen.

"Not again," she says.

That doesn't sound like someone here to kill me.

I flip my bident, standing it upright at my side as she looks around, her back still to me, and take a moment to study her. She's middling height and slender, with raven-black hair, but in the dimmer light of evening, I can't tell if it's short or pinned up.

She's also dressed like she's going to war.

Leggings with a tunic over them. Leather strapping around her chest, stomach, and thighs. Leather gauntlets around her wrists and close-toed boots with woven leather strapping covering most of her feet.

"Damn it all to Hades," she mutters under her breath. "No water garden. This must be a while ago."

*The fuck?*

With no warning, she spins away fast like she's going to run. But she spins right into me. With a flick of my hand, I send my bident back to the in-between where I keep it for easy access. I catch her by the shoulders, now confident in my ability to control my powers when making contact. I steady her, then step back to see her better.

Her head comes up sharply.

And everything inside me goes still.

I *know* this face.

"*Lyra,*" I whisper. The only thing I know about her is her name. Lyra Keres.

All I can do is…stare.

For years, I've dreamed of this face based on the memories of the two times I've seen her before this. Dreamed night after night of the first living being I was able to touch without my power going wild and possibly killing them. How soft her skin was. How her hand felt in mine. A teenage obsession that followed me into adulthood. Although now I look a little older than her. I'm twenty-four, and my aging will essentially stop soon.

Equal footing. Not like last time.

Apparently, my memory wasn't nearly detailed enough.

She has delicate features, with a slightly pointed, stubborn-as-hells chin and hollowed-out cheeks like she never had quite enough to eat. I'd forgotten that part. Her green eyes went wide when I grabbed her, but I'm more distracted by the gold rimming the iris I'm close enough to see now, like the precious metal is running through her and peeking out.

She told me I wouldn't be dangerous.

She told me I would master my powers, to stop fearing myself.

When she showed up near my family home in the Overworld, in the too-short time we had together before she was gone, she told me things no one had ever told me. She touched me like I wasn't unworthy or unsafe.

And now she's *here*, staring right back at me, her pupils slowly dilating. Like she's reacting to me as much as I am to her.

I tighten my grip so she doesn't disappear on me like she did last time.

Or maybe because I have no trouble reading the thoughts flitting across her face. She's trying to decide what to do. I can see the moment she lands on running.

"Not this time."

She blinks. "What?"

Her confusion is so transparent, I have to believe it's real. Doesn't she remember any of it?

I'm not exactly forgettable. The thought makes me sound like I'm a narcissistic asshole, giving a shot of irritation to the fascination overtaking me. Does she flit into unsuspecting people's lives, dropping bombs of wisdom and acceptance on them before flitting away again, so often that she doesn't remember any of them? Some kind of sadistic fairy.

"You came to me on a beach when I was a child," I say, my frustration making my voice quieter. "Then you showed up again years later, in a clearing near my parents' mortal home in the Overworld when I was nineteen, looking just as you had—the same as you do *now*, though with different clothes." I frown. "Now you appear here. In *my home* in the Underworld. A place people only come to by invitation or death."

She swallows.

I'm not sure what reaction I was looking for, but that wasn't it. I don't want her fear.

Everyone else's, sure.

But not hers.

I shake my head slowly. "I won't let you simply disappear again. Not without answers."

The way she drops her gaze, I think she's too afraid to speak, but then I realize that she's gathering herself, like she's putting on armor. Then she cocks a hip and throws me a smirk. "Who says you get to have answers?"

Is she trying to piss me off? I take it back. Lyra might benefit from a healthy dose of fear.

She was the same way before. Irreverent. I'm the god of death and King of the Underworld. Doesn't she know better?

Fuck me, and now I'm stating my credentials in my head. Maybe I *am* that asshole.

I can feel the slow scowl descend over my features.

Shock skitters through me when she reaches out and traces a finger over the ridges between my eyebrows, and my hands on her shoulders tighten convulsively, making her wince.

"You're going to leave a mark," she says softly and nods at where I'm touching her.

Shit. I force my fingers to loosen, stop digging into her flesh through her rough-hewn tunic, but damned if I'm going to let go. "You dare to touch a god in such a familiar way?"

Only Charon comes anywhere near me without flinching, and even he doesn't touch.

She offers me a small, simple smile. "Sorry. I'm a toucher."

No. She's not any more than I am. I have no idea how I know that, but the truth is there in her eyes. "Don't lie to me," I snap.

I hate lies.

"You're right." She gives in fast with a soft sigh. "I'm not a toucher."

Cosmos, I can't get a hold on who this woman is.

She glances past my shoulder like she's making sure no one is coming. She was like that last time, too. Nervously looking in a specific direction.

"Issue?" I ask.

She sighs again. "I'll make you a deal. I can't answer…most…of your questions, but I'll tell you what I can if you help me go unseen by anyone else here."

Unseen. Other than not being allowed down here in the first damn place, why does she care?

I give her another quick frown. "I've seen you disappear at will."

I angle my head, studying her face, thinking through the way she arrived this time—teleporting in theory, but not—and the way she left last time—like she faded away. But if she's nervous of being seen, that means…

"So, you're not doing this by choice," I muse out loud. Not a question. A verbal trap—one she falls into with the slightest widening of her eyes. I'm right, even if she doesn't say so.

"Is someone else sending you to me?" I ask next.

"No." She draws out the word like she's not quite sure.

I nod. Once. "But you are a goddess."

"Yes."

That was unequivocal, at least. But brief. Getting answers out of Lyra is like pulling gold out of Midas' own hand. I hold on to my patience. "Of what?"

She sighs. "Listen, can we play this game of twenty questions somewhere more private—"

"I'm not playing a game with you, Lyra." The words are a growl, low in my throat. And who exactly does she think is going to happen across us here? It's private enough.

"Me neither," she says, giving me a mutinous look that gets right under my skin. "But I'm not answering any more until you hide me."

Another growl rises in my throat. "Watch it," I warn. "I could rend your soul from your corpse and cast it down into the Underworld with merely a thought."

Or kiss her until she turns hazy and warm in my arms. Both have their appeal.

She snorts. "No, you can't."

I rear back slightly. "Now you're challenging me?"

To which she rolls her fucking eyes. "You sound so much like your father, it's not even funny."

At least there's a flash of panic after she says it, though I'm not sure why. Amusement threads through the itch of frustration. "Thank you for that, at least."

I swear her reaction to my response is...relief. Why?

She must catch my closer look, because she tries a wheedling smile. "I react much better to coaxing than orders."

And just like that, I'm back to frustrated. "I don't coax."

"Just a tip."

Is she laughing at me? "Gods, you're impossible."

She can't hold back a grin. The kind that invites me to share in her teasing. "You secretly love that about me."

My heart gives a single painful thump that I immediately resent. All that time thinking about her, and she doesn't even remember me. "Do I?"

She's toying with me. She's never going to give me answers. Not without more incentive. Time to stop playing nice.

Still holding her shoulders, I teleport us both, drawing her closer through the void. I won't risk losing her. Not before I have answers.

When we arrive at our destination, I'm still reluctant to release her as I watch her sweep her gaze over the place, waiting for the dread to flash in her eyes. It should. I've taken her somewhere to put the fear of the god of death in her.

We're standing on a narrow stone bridge, one without walls, that spans a river of fire. Not full-on lava, though. While it's warm, it's not uncomfortable here like it is close to the wastelands in Tartarus. The river of fire feeds into that pit.

The cavern here is carved out of stone, but everything else is built with layers upon layers of the skulls of the damned. They form the walls, the bridge, the arched doorways into the cells. And they are welded together by death, decay, and evil—the truly vilest souls. The souls that I choose to punish with eternal burning damnation are sent to this part of the Underworld.

"Phlegethon? Really?" She sounds unimpressed. "If you're trying to scare me, it won't work."

I smile to myself. "I guess I'll have to try harder."

Taking her by the arm, I drag her across the bridge to a series of dungeon cells, shove her inside one, and shut the door, which automatically locks with a satisfying clink.

Then I walk away.

"Hey!" She runs to the door, grasping the bars to press her face to them. "Don't be an asshole."

No fucking way am I saying for a third time that she just dared something no one else does, swearing at me like that. I don't turn around. "I'm not the one keeping secrets. Let's see how long solitude in this place takes to loosen your tongue."

Then I teleport away, taking her gasp of outrage with me. Music to my fucking ears.

## 30

# TIME IS ON MY SIDE

### HADES

Twenty-three hours. Almost a day. Feels like an eternity.

I thought she'd break in minutes, an hour at most. I can hear and see everything she's doing down there if I close my eyes. Most souls don't last but a few seconds in those cells without confessing everything to me. I'm damn tempted to use my powers to force a confession from her. I can do that. It's how I judge the dead as they arrive. But it doesn't seem right.

Which makes me a softhearted fool.

Although providing her with a pillow and food already proved I am that. At least I held out on visiting her myself—not an easy feat, considering that every fucking minute, going down there to be near her was all I could think about.

Charon, who is seated at my breakfast table, sighs loudly. "Can you stop pacing? You are making me dizzy."

I still and scowl at my feet because I hadn't realized I was doing that.

"She's not going to break." I can hear the resignation in my own voice.

"No," he agrees. Almost cheerfully.

I side-eye him. "You find this amusing?"

He doesn't even try to hide his grin. "I find it fascinating, Phi."

His name for me. A shortened version of Thantophile, which he uses to mean brother of death.

"You won't even tell me who she is?"

It's not the first time he's asked.

I narrow my eyes. "You have never feared me enough, I think."

Other than Lyra, Charon is the only being who has no fear of me, although unlike her, he believes the prophecy. The first time we met, when I was still very young, I asked why he wasn't afraid. He took one look at me and said, "Don't worry about me, Thantophile. If you burn down the world, we'll take care of them down here. All souls come to us eventually anyway."

With an irritated grunt, I snatch the pomegranate right out of his hand, along with the knife he was reaching for. Then I teleport down to Phlegethon and to the woman who is slowly twisting and tying my insides into knots, even while she's sleeping in her cell.

"Here." I shove the fruit and knife through the bars.

She's lying with her back to me. After a second, she turns her head only slightly to glance at me, and then a laugh erupts from her in a short, sharp sound.

"What?" I frown. "You don't like this fruit?"

Her chuckle is dry as she pushes to her feet and crosses the small space to pluck it from my outstretched hand. "Oh, I like pomegranates just fine."

Then, ignoring me, she drops to sit on the floor cross-legged, using the stone surface as a cutting board. She doesn't even look at me as she cuts the top of the fruit off. Then, following the natural lines of the sections, she scores the outside of the skin, which allows her to pull it apart like orange slices. She takes a bite and smiles, humming with pleasure.

Tension curls in my gut at the sound.

"Never seen someone eat one that way," I mutter.

"TikTok," she says. "I was today years old when I saw the life hack of how to eat one of these mess-free."

Maybe I left her down here too long. Now she's speaking nonsense. "What's a tick tock?"

She pauses with a piece of the fruit halfway to her lips, then grimaces. "Never mind."

"I don't stop minding just because you say so," I point out in a dry voice.

"It's been a full day, you know."

I track the change of subject but decide to allow it. "I know. And yet you haven't called out for help, demanded release, or tried to make a deal. Not once." I can't help the confusion leaking into my voice.

"You could have at least given me a book to read or something."

"A book? Is that like a tick tock?"

Another pause. "Never mi—"

"Please stop saying that." This conversation is already a thousand leagues from where I need it to be.

"Yeah, well…" She glances up at me. "It would be nice if you'd stop towering over me." She pats the floor.

Is she serious?

I must make a face, because she laughs.

"You want me to sit on the ground to speak with you?" I ask.

"Why not?"

"Because—"

I stop when she tilts her head, clearly ready for me to remind her of who I am and how afraid of me she should be. Damn, the woman never reacts normally.

I let out a beleaguered breath. "Why not, indeed?"

I sit down outside her jail cell, leaning against the skulls that make up the wall. I stretch my legs out in front of me and cross them at the ankles, likely getting bone dust all over my wool cloak.

"See?" she teases. "Much better."

She's teasing me? There's another sharp twist to my gut, and yet I find myself unable to hold back a low chuckle. Underworld take me. "You are not what I expected, Lyra."

"You remember," she whispers.

I still both at the words and at the way fear widens her eyes the second she says them. But not fear of me, I don't think. Because she glances around as if she's waiting for the ceiling to collapse on us.

While she's distracted, I take the opportunity to study her more closely. She's beautiful. Not perfect, though. That's unusual for gods. But to me, the small imperfections make her more…

Fuck. I almost thought the word "adorable." What is wrong with me?

And yet I can't stop staring.

There's a crease in her cheek from when she was lying down, and her upper lip is a little fuller than her lower lip. There's the tiniest bump in her nose, too. And I was right about that stubborn chin. I could do without the stubborn part. But it's the sliver of a half-moon scar at the outside corner of her right eye that draws my attention most. Gods don't scar unless it's so traumatic our healing can't keep up. What happened to her?

Her swinging gaze suddenly settles on me, and she goes still, staring right back. There is something in her eyes that answers the fascination within mine, turns it to heat.

I've got to get a handle on this—on her and especially on my reaction to her. All I should be caring about is who she is and why she came.

"This is the third time you've appeared somewhere you shouldn't be around me," I finally say slowly, still trying to shake off the strange effect of her. "Of course I would remember that."

She blinks. "You worry I'm a threat?"

"You haven't aged a day and clearly possess powers. Yet you are not a known goddess. Not even from the other pantheons across the world."

Her lips part slightly. "You tried to find me?"

*Tried* to find her? I've scoured the records for her, looked for her at every gathering of the gods, asked a few inconspicuous questions. "Tried" is a weak term. I grimace, more self-deprecating than I should probably show her. "Therefore…" I don't answer her question, continuing with mine. "I have yet to decide what I think of you."

"Fair enough."

"You also speak with an odd turn of phrase."

She laughs. She laughs like her prison bars aren't between us. "Yeah. Sorry about that." Then she reaches through those very same bars to offer me a section of pomegranate and the tattoos on her wrist catch my eye. As I take the fruit with one hand, with my other, I grasp her wrist. Gently but firmly enough that she can't tug away.

"What is this for?" I brush my thumb over the fine black ink of the markings. The two stars on that wrist seem to wink at me in response, and through that small point of contact, I feel her shiver.

The urge to pull her through the damn bars and onto my lap so I can make her shiver more for me rises up like a feral animal, sinking its teeth into me hard.

She distracts me by sticking her other hand through the bars and lining the stars on both wrists up. "They form Orion's Belt. I used to be able to see them from the window in my childhood bedroom."

I stare at the familiar formation—three stars in a row—and this time, instead of my gut twisting, my heart does. I also tracked those stars from my mortal bedroom as a child.

"I wasted a lot of wishes on those stars," she mutters.

Me too.

I swipe my thumb over her tattoo once more, hoping to capture another shiver. When she flutters under my touch…pleased is an understatement. I want…*more*. I always want more when it comes to her.

She tugs, but again I don't release her.

"Let go."

"Not yet."

She tugs harder. "Why not?"

"Because I need you flustered." To get answers, I tell myself. But it's a bald lie. I *like* making her shiver. More than I should.

She glares and tugs again. "You can be such an asshat."

*Asshat.* The words she uses. But she's softened now. Relaxed. Exactly like I wanted her to be when I came down here. For answers.

"You will answer my questions, Lyra." This time, I put the command of the god of death into the words.

The flare of her eyes is followed by another flutter, not just a shiver but a jump in her pulse against the pad of my thumb that captures my entire focus.

Does she *like* being commanded by me?

What started as a simple teenage fascination with an unattainable woman who disappeared flips on its head and roars into a very adult, very dangerous flare of need. One that makes no godsdamned sense. Not when, outside of these cells, she could leave me at a whim. Not with who I am and what I will do one day.

Despite those and a thousand other reasons, I go still, all my senses narrowing in and focusing on her and her alone.

She stares back, holding my gaze for a brave moment, before she drops hers. Not from fear but to hide her response. I see it anyway, and savage satisfaction rips through my chest.

I'm not the only one fighting this thing between us that is so palpable I'm surprised I don't see a visible aura.

She swallows, the delicate column of her throat working, and then more words come tumbling out. "Your home would be so much nicer with water gardens outside the walls."

My eyes narrow sharply. A water garden? I think of where she landed, the flatness of the mountain in that spot, and picture water and flowers and bridges…and Lyra in it. Is that just a fanciful idea…or has she been to my home at some point in the future when there was a water garden?

"Lyra…are you a goddess who wields time?"

## 31

# A QUESTION OF TIME

### LYRA

Shit. Oh shit. I said *would be*, didn't I? I didn't say it was or it had been or will be. How in the name of…well, Hades…did he make that logical leap? He's always been too smart for my own good.

"No." I say it quietly and take a breath. "Only your father possesses that ability."

"And you know my father." Not a question.

Also no hatred. I don't think he's imprisoned his father yet. Which means…if this is truly the past…that whatever makes him and the others do that hasn't happened yet, either.

There is also a layer of satisfaction in his voice that I don't trust.

"Lyra," he prompts.

He wants a confirmation.

"Is *he* sending you to me?" he asks when I don't answer.

Not exactly. Cronos broke time. That's all. "No."

"But you *are* from a time yet to come?"

Gods, this is so hard. I *want* to tell him. I want to curl up in his lap and confess everything and let those broad shoulders handle the weight with me. Let that sharp mind help me find a way through this.

But I can't.

I can't risk it. Not yet.

I swallow. Hard. "All I can tell you is that I would never hurt you. You or anyone you love. That's going to have to be enough. It's too risky to say more."

I *know* Hades. I know it won't be enough for him.

I wait for him to go cold. To release his hold on me and walk away. To leave me here to reconsider what I have to say.

Instead, there is a soft clank of sound—the lock on my cage giving way.

My gaze flashes to his, a thousand questions passing between us.

"Very well." He lets go of me so that we can both get to our feet before he swings the cell door open and beckons me out.

He doesn't back away when I step into the cavern, though, and the warmth of his body seeps into mine as we stand so close, felt deeply despite the fire flowing by. His fingers come under my chin, gently tilting my head up so I can meet his gaze. He leans slowly, inexorably closer, and I hold my breath.

Is he going to kiss me?

Gods, I want him to. I've missed his touch, the taste of his lips, so badly that I ache with the need of it. I quiver.

But he stops just shy of touching. "Break my trust, even once, and I'll throw you down here and forget where I put the key or that you even exist."

What would he do if I tipped forward just the tiniest bit? "Just so long as you realize that there are things I can't tell you and questions I can't answer, and it's not because I'm breaking trust."

His gray eyes glint like molten silver, and he runs the pad of his thumb over my lower lip. The softest brush that makes my breath hitch audibly.

His shoulders rise and fall on a silent breath. "I have the strangest sense, my star, that you are going to be trouble."

When I smile, it presses my lips more firmly against his thumb, and I imagine the way his eyes would flare if I sucked his finger into my mouth. But I don't. Somehow, I wrangle a smidgeon of self-control and don't. Instead, I lean away. "I promise I'm more trouble than even you imagine."

He huffs a short, soft laugh, then abruptly steps away, his shoulders drawing back, spine straight as a lance. "Come."

A hand goes to my elbow, and we blink out, then blink back into an ornate hallway inside a building—all brilliantly painted marble and golden adornments. We're back in Olympus, I guess.

"I can't be seen here." I glance around.

He lets go of my elbow and starts walking. "You won't be."

I follow him through a set of double doors directly in front of us. It's not until I'm fully inside what is clearly an opulent suite of rooms that the few personal touches sink in. I stop dead on the intricate mosaic-tiled floor. "These are your rooms."

"Yes."

"Is that a good idea?" My heart is screaming *yes it is*, but that's not fair to him. To either of us, really.

He stops and gives me a look. "Afraid you won't be able to resist me?"

"Yes."

From the way his shoulders stiffen slightly, I know he wasn't expecting that bald truth. But he doesn't say anything or acknowledge my admission in any other way. Instead, he turns through a doorway that leads to a lush bedroom, fully appointed with, of all things, a sunken tub—or maybe it's a small swimming pool—in the center of the room, already filled with steaming, oil-scented water. "You may bathe here."

Heaven. "Thank you."

He goes to leave but pauses at the door to pin me with another look, this one devoid of any emotion. A look I know is deliberate and probably hiding a whole host of emotions. "I'm not going to fuck you, Lyra."

My throat goes desert dry in an instant, and I give a little cough.

"I won't kiss you. Or touch you in any way that is intimate."

I manage to clear my throat. "That is…" Disappointing? Maddening? Makes me want to channel Aphrodite and see if I can tempt him past his conviction? "Probably for the best."

There's an ever-so-slight crack in his emotionless wall. Did he not like that answer? "As long as we understand each other," he finally says. Then he leaves me alone in this beautiful room.

All I want to do is run after him and break that damned rule he just threw down. But the timeline is clear.

I close my eyes tight and breathe through the urge. Breathe through the realization that this moment is happening ages before he met me that night at Zeus' temple. Before he kissed me to give me safe access to the Underworld and mark me as his.

That first day of the Crucible, he pulled back from that kiss that should have been brief and chaste but turned to flame and desire in an instant, and he murmured, "I wondered."

Was that truly our first kiss? Did he wonder about kissing me before that moment? Did he wonder *today*? What it would feel like? What I would taste like? The sounds I would make for him?

All this time, did he wonder?

The way he was looking at me...

Another deep breath, and I force my eyes open. Just in time for a shimmering, crystalline, bloodred crack of time to swallow me whole, taking me away from Hades and depositing me back in Tartarus.

Only instead of a day having passed, I end up where I left, in the tunnel with the Titans. As far as I can tell, to them, it's been only minutes.

"Fuck," I think I hear Koios say. "Already?"

I'm still trying to process everything. All these stolen moments with Hades, and also that interaction with his replica down here, are mashing up in my head, and feelings are flying around inside me like bullets, leaving me riddled with holes no one can see.

Mnemosyne takes one look at my face, and all she does is put her hand on my shoulder. I'm swimming through my head. She looks at Rhea.

"We can wait to tell you more," Rhea says.

"It's okay," I finally manage. "I'd rather...keep going."

## 32

# SEVEN LOCKS & ONE SAVIOR

### LYRA

As we file into the room, there's a thump, and I look back to find Boone blocking Persephone from entering.

"You go with them," he says, nodding in the direction the others went.

For the first time, a shadow of hurt clouds the goddess of spring's features. "But—"

"Nonnegotiable," he insists. Then steps inside and closes the door in her face.

Turning my focus from him, I take in the room. It has a massive oblong table with no chairs, more a raised slab of rock that appears to be carved from the mountain. At first, I swear there's a faint red glow coming from it, but when I blink, the glow is gone.

Rhea waves a hand over the table, and it changes form, or I guess just reshapes the top to render a 3D structure.

A map.

I glance at the Titaness. "It's a glamour," she says.

They can glamour at that level? Conjure real things and not just visions or ideas?

Boone steps closer, studying the layout. While it doesn't match the map he drew in the dirt when we were hiding inside the pillar, he got pretty close.

"We are here." Rhea waves her hand, and the 3D model moves, starting at the Locks and then cutting through the path we took to this room. Zoomed in, I can make out specific offshoots of tunnels, the way they curve and snake. Some bend back to meet others, and some are dead ends. They go up hundreds, maybe even thousands of feet. Some are deep. And not all of them have cells.

Were the Titans trying to dig out? Clearly, it didn't work.

She waves, and the table flattens and then re-forms, recreating the bridge over the abyss that they keep throwing me into. The perfect circle shows the gates at the top, as well as the bridge across to the tunnel that winds down the outside of the abyss to the cavern at the bottom. Then, at the bottom of the abyss, it shows that the circle is cut into seven larger pie-shaped slices.

Koios points. "Those are the two Locks you opened."

Two of the seven slices bear the glittering marks of Hestia and Hades. I lean over the table, taking in the details. Carved into the 3D relief, a Nightmare stands within Hestia's pie piece, and a team of horses within Hades'.

"Why don't you unseal them yourselves?" Boone asks.

Hades said something about me being mortal to start, and now I'm pretty sure I know why.

"Because they can't."

Boone's head angles my way, gaze confused. "What?"

"They die when they go in one." I look at Rhea. "Right?"

The Titans with us turn as solemn as pallbearers at a funeral, the heaviness filling the room, and I know I'm right. The Locks strip supernatural powers before we are tested. It's happened twice now. Boone and I were born mortal with no powers, so we must've returned to that state. But the Titans are different.

That has to be it.

Savior.

I'm their savior.

I'm their only way out.

Then Rhea takes a breath. "We lost Themis before we realized that."

*That's who else is missing.*

Themis. The Titaness of justice and mother of the Horae and the three Fates. They lost her?

"She thought she could manage Hestia's because they were close," Phoebe says. "But strip us of our power, and we cease to exist."

To kill a Titan, all you have to do is strip them of their power? Is that true of gods as well—the ones not born mortal first, like Boone and me?

No one gave me the fine print to read before I signed up for this goddess job. That's for damn sure. Not that I signed up, exactly.

*They learned the hard way.*

I'm not sure how to address that, or if they'd even want me to, so I move on. "I have more questions about the time travel situation," I say, then give them Boone's theory. "If it takes us to the past, why do we come back? Couldn't we just run away and stay there? Isn't that a way out?"

Rhea crosses her arms. Even that move is elegant.

"Damn," Mnemosyne says dryly. "Why didn't we think of that?"

I shoot her an impatient look.

"We've tried," Rhea says in an overly calm voice.

Of course they have.

"No matter where you go, that crack will find you and bring you back here. Iapetus once made it two years before it found him." Rhea says this almost like she thinks that's impressive. But he was brought back to Tartarus.

Years. I was just gone for a full day, but that time down here seems to have basically been lost.

Can years just be erased?

"So is that why Koios and Iapetus are dressed in modern clothes and you all know modern language?" I ask. "Because you visited modern times through the breaks?"

They all nod.

"But you're afraid of the cracks now?"

Another glance at Rhea. "We have to be careful," she says slowly.

Which is when I realize that when they watched me get taken—twice, now—they weren't afraid for themselves…they were afraid for me. Why? "Does time stop coming for you and start coming for me instead?"

Judging by the way Koios' eyebrows rise slowly, I think that I might have impressed him with that leap in logic.

"We don't know for sure," is all he says, though. "Better to focus on the Locks."

After a shared glance with Boone, we lean over the table, studying it with a thief's sharp eyes.

"Fire for Aphrodite," Boone murmurs, pointing at the icon.

"I'm more worried about this." I wave at Hera's Lock, in which a small child appears to be crying into its mother's lap. There's something…

sinister...about the positioning.

"Yeah." His eyes narrow in a manner I'm more than familiar with. He's planning. Then he looks up at Rhea. "You've taken her through this before. Right? Is it better to focus on one at a time, or are there any we need to start preparing for now?"

For the first time since we landed down here, I think the Queen of the Titans looks at Boone with something akin to respect.

"Like other information, it helps if we don't overwhelm her with what she'll face in all the Locks at once. Poseidon's is worth preparing for more. Otherwise, taking them one at a time is fine. The problem is Aphrodite's." She points.

"Told you," Boone mutters at me.

"Lyra has never come out of it. Obviously, or we'd be free by now."

Boone sobers so fast he might be carved from granite. "What does that mean...never come out of it?"

Rhea's features soften the tiniest bit, like she's trying to figure out how to make this less bad. "She dies in there," she says gently. "And other than a wall of fire, we've never been able to see what she faces."

For a second, I'm pretty sure Boone is about to forbid me from doing that one. But, after shaking his head twice at whatever thoughts are running through it, he says nothing. I relax just the slightest bit. Because I can't fight them and unseal the Locks *and* argue with him, too. I just can't.

"You can't use your strength or speed as a goddess inside the Locks, either," Phoebe reminds us.

Learned that the hard way. Twice.

"And her human muscles are still pathetic, so that's going to be a problem again," a voice says from the doorway.

It's like the Titan couldn't help himself.

I sigh, because there's no point excluding him now. "Any other wisdom to impart?"

Cronos cuts his gaze to Phoebe. "What about him?"

Him who?

She shakes her head. "The thief is nowhere in my visions yet."

Oh, Boone.

"You can still use me," Boone says. "I go in first. If I die, then you still have Lyra to send in after me."

"And if you think that's how that's going to go down, you're as delusional as him." I wave a hand at Cronos.

"We train you both and decide later," Cronos says.

A situation I don't think any of us are happy about, but nobody argues. Boone and me included.

I sigh. "Sounds like a plan."

"Excellent," Cronos says, then claps his hands, rubbing them together. "Time to set up the obstacle course again." He eyes me. "How are you with a sickle these days?"

## 33

# BE CAREFUL WHAT YOU ASK FOR, BECAUSE THIS SUCKS

### LYRA

I still can't believe the Titans can glamour something like this.
A full training course. It's out in the open beyond the pillars and the burning lands, and that makes it hot. It took all of them to create it together and looked pretty impressive when they did. We've been warned of where to try to go if the bell goes off and the Pandemonium come. Like they care. Or maybe the Pandemonium aren't even a thing. Just another control mechanism, like the bogeyman or the thing under the bed. A ghost story.

Not that any of that matters as still, glassy water rushes up at me. Or, more accurately, I fall at it. Fast. And brace, because I already know this is going to hurt.

I don't even manage to flip in the air to hit feetfirst like I was told to do, slamming into the water laid out in a full belly flop after a hell of a drop. The angle I hit at snaps my head back, but it's the immediate shock of electricity that zaps through my body, making every muscle seize, that is the worst. For a horrifying few seconds, I can't move as I float helplessly deeper under water, like a leaf drifting to the bottom of a lake.

It's just long enough for my mind to start panicking about the lack of oxygen before the shock releases its hold on my body, and I come up spluttering and coughing. I learned after the first time to keep my hair pulled back and braided because its wet curtain nearly suffocated me. But at least the electricity stops.

Why did I ever ask the Titans to train me for the damned Locks?

"That was terrible!" Cronos yells down at me from where he stands at the start of the obstacle course while I make my way to the edge of the pool. "Are you even trying?"

I cling to the wall and glare up at him. "I guess I just love getting shocked and drowned over and over," I yell back. "Who knew I had that kink?"

A low chuckle sounds from behind me, and I look back to find Boone leaning a casual shoulder on the post at the end of the obstacle course we're learning to run. Already done. Without a scratch. Dry as a bone. Again. Of course, because years of training and thieving have made him very good at this.

I, on the other hand, haven't made it through once.

I glare at him. "You realize that I would've been eaten by giant electric eels by now if this was really Poseidon's Lock."

That sobers him up, but I swear his lips are still twitching when he holds up both hands.

The god of oceans and waters seems to be a one-trick pony when it comes to his preferred trials. Water and monsters and trying to stay away from both. We don't have to worry about the monsters unless we fall, but then we're dead anyway.

So…you know…the usual brand of divine shenanigans. Oh, those zany gods.

Rhea and Tethys are preparing us for Demeter's, which we'll face before Poseidon's, but they insist they can't tell us much without resetting time *again*, so all I can figure is that it has to do with harvesting something.

"Let's go again." Cronos, who must've run closer, shoves a hand in front of my face and, after I take it, drags me easily out, water cascading off me. "You've managed this before," he says as he walks me over to the starting line of the course. The disappointment rife in his voice raises my hackles like a dog. "What's the problem?"

I answer through clenched teeth. "I'm too short. I can't hold enough tension between the walls."

"Short." He examines me more closely. "That hasn't been a problem before—"

"I swear if you say that one more time, I'm going to gut you." Not really, though. Not yet. The thing is, he *has* been helpful, in his odd way.

The bloodthirsty bastard chuckles but then grabs me by the arm, dragging me over to stand chest to chest with him.

"Whoa—" I hear Boone's hurried steps.

But Cronos simply puts one hand flat on top of my head and brings it to his chest. Even at five foot six inches, I hit him mid-sternum. "You shrank."

Shrank? Really? I take a step back. "Are you saying I've been taller before?"

"By a bit." He frowns. "How is that even possible?"

"You would know better than me."

He nods. "Must've been your upbringing." He raises his eyebrows in question.

I shrug. "My mentor and boss in the Order of Thieves, Felix, used to take delight in telling me how malnourished I was when my parents dropped me off with him."

Cronos searches my expression like he's trying to decide if I'm messing with him or not. "Is that true?" Before I can answer, he casts an assessing gaze over the rest of me. "And you're thinner. What in the name of Tartarus happened to make them starve you, Alani?"

"Are you *blaming* me right now?" I poke him in the chest with a finger. "Talk to your damned son."

He looks at where I poked him almost like he can't quite comprehend that I did. It's hard to tell because his head is bent and the scruff of his beard hides his mouth, but for a tiny second, I think he smiles. That's before he lifts his gaze with another frown. "What did Hades do?"

"Not Hades. *Zeus*."

"Zeus?" He blinks at me.

I tilt my head, giving him a pointed look. "Now that I've met the tree that particular apple fell from, I can't say I am all that surprised."

But Cronos doesn't respond. He's looking at me, but I don't think he's seeing me. There's an emotion working behind his eyes that could be anger but could also be worry. I'm not sure either of those make sense. "What did Zeus do?"

"Your youngest is a dick and cursed me to be unlovable."

Cronos straightens abruptly, his voice raining down on me like thunder. "He did *what*?"

"Rulers of the cosmos." Persephone's words cut through us as she hurries past the nearest pillar. "Be quieter."

"The Pandemonium can't hear us out here," he growls at her, not looking away from me.

I don't look away from him, either, my mind working a thousand thoughts. "Is that new?" I ask slowly. "Is my curse new?"

"Yes." It's possible he tried to gentle that answer.

I'm too distracted to care. Why would my curse make any difference? "What else is new? The Crucible Games? Do I always play for Hades?"

His face takes on a stubborn cast so like his oldest son's that my heart trips. "You can't tell me?" I ask.

"No."

"But I always end up down here. How?"

"We go through one of the broken time pieces and reset it all ourselves if you don't."

"You—" His words might as well have rung a Pandemonium bell inside my head. Heat flares from my gut and into my chest, crawling higher. Flames up the sides of my face. "You—"

"You're our only hope, Lyra." He says it softly, and for the first time this odd, arrogant, maybe-baby-eating jerk of a Titan looks…lost.

"Do you even know what you've put me through? My parents abandoned me when I was three years old because they couldn't love me—"

"They always abandon you."

I whip away, breathing in and out and trying not to let the stinging in my eyes turn into real tears. I promised myself a long time ago I wouldn't cry over my parents. Apparently, that was a good decision.

"I'm sorry. Lyra—"

"Just…" I swallow. "Let's not talk about this anymore." I search for Boone and find him and Persephone standing halfway into one of the tunnel entrances near the ocean pillar. I can't see their faces, and they aren't doing anything unusual. She's talking. He doesn't seem to be saying anything.

But then he walks away from her, and now I can see them both—see him stoically detached as she watches him with an emotion I can't pin down.

"What was that?" I ask when he nears us.

"What was what?"

When I give him a look, Boone glances over his shoulder to where Persephone has now left. "Nothing. I don't trust her."

That didn't look like nothing. But it didn't exactly look like something, either.

Then Boone frowns, his feet slowing as he studies my face for a long beat before his gaze snaps to Cronos. "What did you say to her?"

I really don't want to talk about it. I'll tell Boone later. Not the part about my parents, but the part about the Titans doing much of the resetting on purpose.

I walk away, headed toward the start of the course. "Let's just get me through this stupid thing."

Boone catches up, studying the obstacle course as we near it—particularly the glass cage. "There's got to be a way to get you up that."

I let out a silent breath of relief. Discussing feelings really is not my happy place.

With a glance back at Cronos, who is watching for me the way a tiger waits for a mouse to run out of its hole, I push the anger, confusion, sadness, and all the other things down into my gut. I also study the square contraption made of glass that I have to shimmy my way from the bottom to the top of while it widens as I go. Located in the middle of the course, it's the one spot I can't get past. This last attempt, I tried switching to lengthwise, with my hands on one wall and my feet on the opposite, rather than like a spider, but it still got too wide to reach, and I slipped.

"Maybe if we give me shoes with thicker soles?" I muse to myself. Not so thick that they make the rest of the course difficult, though. Would just another inch make enough of a difference? I look down at my feet, still in the leather-strapped shoes from Hades' Lock, and study the soles. If the Titans can glamour this pool, they can glamour me better shoes. "What do you think?"

"I think that won't work inside the Lock." Boone manifests his blue flame in his palm, then snuffs it out. "We won't have our powers to glamour different shoes."

Cronos, who followed us, touches a finger to my elbow. Oddly gentle for him, so I raise my brows in question when I look back around.

"Parents should love their children," he says slowly. "I shouldn't have..." He trails off like he's not entirely sure what to say.

And, for a second, it's tempting to soften, to appreciate the sympathy he's offering.

Except he tossed me into Hestia's Lock without a shred of regret. So I pull my elbow away from his touch. "You say that, but you swallowed your own children so that they wouldn't steal your power."

Except...I saw them together, none swallowed. Hades and Hestia grown.

"Lyra," Boone hisses.

Because we're playing nice with the Titans right now. Not antagonizing. We agreed that we need them to get through the Locks.

Cronos doesn't blow up at me like he did last time. If anything, he flinches like a puppy I just kicked. "I told you, that's not—" Cronos cuts himself off and shakes his head.

"Still can't tell me?" I mutter.

But I can't get the scene of such a happy family Cronus and Rhea made with their children out of my head. Glamours? Lies? Or was that real?

What is Cronos not saying?

"Try this." He sounds resigned as he waves his hand over my shoes, thickening the soles and drying me off. Then he points at the course. "Poseidon's Lock doesn't always change your clothes, so if we send you in with them, it might work."

I don't make it past the second obstacle, let alone to the glassed-in spider wall, before I hit the water again. The thicker shoes made me lose my footing.

The first thing I think when I break through the surface, spluttering yet again and my body twitching from the shocks, is...*I need Hades.*

# 34

# THE MEANING OF A NAME

### LYRA

"I think it's time for a break," Boone says. And my head goes straight to a single idea that grows larger and larger by the second.

"She's got to get this," Cronos argues while I'm swimming over to the edge.

Boone sets his feet. "I'm not asking."

Cronos' lip curls. "Alani is the key to our escape. *You* are not."

Alani. He called me that earlier. I was focused on other words coming out of his mouth, but it finally hits me…that's the name my Nightmare father called me in Hestia's Lock.

Then there's a softly murmured conversation between the two that I can't make out. A hand appears before me as I get to the side. Not Cronos this time. Boone hauls me out, sopping wet.

Cronos huffs. "She doesn't need anybody's help. Not yours. Not my son's. Not even mine. Something she'll learn soon enough."

"What does that even mean?" I ask, still wondering if I can do this without Hades.

Boone leans in to murmur, "Now that we're gods, let's not do any of this cryptic shit. Let's be clear. Yeah?"

"I was just thinking that."

"Watch it, boy." Cronos is snarling now. "You're only alive because Alani seems to like you."

Boone smirks. One of his hallmark, guaranteed-to-irritate-an-enemy moves. "Her name is Lyra."

Cronos points at me. "Her birth name is Alani. The name her parents gave her, not your Order of Thieves."

I lean back. "That was real?"

His hard gaze falls from Boone to me and softens slightly. "It was real."

"Oh." The word escapes me in a whisper.

So my parents really *did* name me that? How did the Nightmare know? I was born millennia after those things must've been trapped down here with the Titans.

No wonder I fell for Hestia's Lock so hard at first. Thieves are taught that when you lie, you should use as much truth as possible. It makes it feel more real, harder to separate out the fiction, in addition to being easier to remember and less likely for you to mess up.

"Your name means *death bringer*," Cronos tells me. "As Hades' queen, it is your appropriate and true name."

"Death bringer," Boone mutters at me. "Of course that would be what your name means."

I wrinkle my nose at him. "I think it's kind of badass."

And Cronos smiles. Not a smirk. Not in triumph. A real smile. One that reaches his blue, blue eyes and crinkles the skin around them and tries to sneak inside me and make me feel something—kindness, warmth, connection—in return.

Worse, he suddenly looks so much like Hades, he might as well have slapped me.

I shut it all down. Hard.

The last thing I should forget is that the gods locked these monsters down here for a reason.

But the damage is done.

Boone heads toward the tunnel Persephone left down. "Come on. You need to rest."

But I don't follow. I need a break, but not the kind he's talking about.

The thing is…I'm glad I'm not alone down here. It's the most selfish I could be, and if I could make it so he never got trapped in here with me, I would. I'd never wish this on him, but…I don't think I could do this alone, either.

But I need to be alone for a bit. Even in a den full of thieves, I was alone a lot, thanks to my curse. Down here, the Titans do everything in packs, and I think I've reached my limit of peopling. So I lie. "I'm going to keep trying."

I shift my weight, and my shoes squelch. Not Boone's, though. He never once landed in that damned water.

Boone makes a face from where he stopped to wait. "I think you need a break."

"I'm fine."

He snorts. "I'm surprised you're not sparking by now, as many times as you've gotten shocked."

"Oh. Haha. You're hilarious." I know he's just trying to cajole me to rest, but I have something else in mind.

Boone sobers, considering me closely, then sighs. "I'll stay, too."

I shake my head. "I think the audience is part of the problem. Give me a bit to try it all on my own. Send Persephone back down if you're worried."

It's a mean trick, but it works.

His expression goes flat at the mention of her name, so I know he likes that idea even less. "I'll give you thirty minutes," he says. "Then you stop."

"Thanks."

Boone shoots Cronos a look. "Come on, Pops. Your savior needs alone time."

The Titan protests all the way past the pillars and into the tunnels. And then, finally, I'm by myself. The breath that leaks from me is pure relief.

I wait a little longer to make sure they don't return.

I think maybe being around Cronos so much, with all the ways he reminds me of Hades, is starting to get to me. As if every similar glance, every tone of his voice, every move chips away at another piece of my heart, and I just need...

I won't let myself say Hades.

Space. I need space.

Now that I have it, though, the loneliness builds instead of eases. And it's that loneliness that walks my feet to where I left my axe on the floor at the starting line—practicing the obstacle course without it screams of folly, but I won't have it inside the Lock anyway—then out of the area we're in and down the tunnels.

Straight to Hades' Lock.

## 35

## REALITY BITES

### LYRA

Without being stopped or bumping into anyone else, I make it to the chamber that circles the Locks, but I don't place my palm on the etching of his bident. I'll just stand here struggling with the need to see his face, to touch him, even if it's just to hold his replica's hand. I'm even tempted to track down a broken piece of time and jump in it to find the real thing.

But I won't. It's not going to help. Deep down, I know that.

I'm not sure how long I've been standing here when the Lock unexpectedly changes. The etching in the hard rock sparks to life with glittering blue light. Like he knows I'm out here and is inviting me in.

My heart twists around itself, aching behind my ribs.

A sensation I push down deep, where it can be smothered. But I also don't leave, standing with my arms wrapped around me, staring at that symbol, lost in the swirl of my own thoughts and trying not to feel.

"I didn't think you were going to practice more." Boone says the words quietly, and I jump a little.

But I don't turn.

"He's not there, you know," Boone says next.

"I know."

I feel more than see him move to stand beside me, looking up at the symbol that flares briefly, almost like a warning. Message clear: Boone is not welcome in the Lock.

He leans closer, voice low. "I think we need to be careful down here."

"Duh."

"No." He shakes his head. "This place is a mind fuck, and that might be the most dangerous part of it."

I frown at him, because he's not being general right now. "What do you mean?"

He makes a face, like he doesn't love telling me this. "I've seen Persephone before."

That gets me to turn away from Hades' Lock. "What?"

He reaches up a hand, I assume to rub at his beard, because he stops when he encounters smooth skin and drops it again. It's surprised me a few times since Hestia's Lock, when it changed. He's worn the scruffy beard for a few years now.

"She's foiled a few scores for me."

I practically stumble back at that. "What the hells, Boone? That's important information. You should have told me—"

"I wanted to make sure it was...real first. But..." He glances behind us toward the tunnels. "I don't know how to do that. Not down here."

I think through that, and he's not wrong. We don't know what to believe or trust. "Foiled your scores how?"

"I thought she was another thief, maybe from another den who'd earned her way out of debt and went solo. She would show up out of nowhere and do something that would cause enough problems that I'd have to cancel the score, and then she'd disappear like a ghost."

Or like a time-traveling goddess trapped in Tartarus. "That must mean she's gone through the broken time like us, and it took her to you."

Several times, it sounds like. Is this how Hades felt about my random visits? Did he resent me? Not trust me? Hate me, even?

My stomach turns.

"That's what they *want* us to think it means." Boone still doesn't trust anything about those cracks.

"What does Persephone say?"

He scowls. "I'm not talking to her about it."

"Why? Ask her for details and see if her story lines up with yours—"

"Hestia's Lock revealed things I wanted most." He cuts me off. "Things no one else could know. A partner for my business. I never told anyone about that. Not a damn soul. If they know things like that already..."

Persephone could already know about those moments, or they planted those memories in his head to get him to trust her down here.

I see where he's going with it.

I frown. "If you don't believe it's real, then why tell me now?"

He hitches his chin at the Lock. "Because you're here." Then Boone gives me a look that's part pity, part hard truth. "Why are you down here, Lyra?"

Heaviness tries to drag my heart down. "I wanted to talk to someone."

To Hades.

Boone nods. "Then talk to me."

I press my lips together, holding back the words. He's already dealing with enough of my shit.

"I mean it," Boone says.

"Perhaps she doesn't wish to talk to you."

I spin around on a gasp to find that the arched door to Hades' Lock has opened and the replica of my god of death is standing right at the edge. Lounging indolently, more like, leaning one shoulder against the thick stone opening.

"We didn't open the door," Boone says.

Hades picks at a piece of nonexistent lint on his brown cloak. "You were both making such a racket, I couldn't sleep."

I can't help my amusement, because that is just such a Hades answer. He's messing with Boone for the hells of it.

The way Hades' eyes flick to my mouth and the corners of his own draw up just the barest little bit is also him. But now that ache is back.

Because it's not him. Not really.

I expect Boone to snarl back something about apparitions not needing sleep—not that gods truly do, either, and we sleep anyway, or more like rest our minds. Instead, he slips an arm casually around my waist, allowing his hand to drift dangerously close to my ass.

I go stiff because we don't touch like this. It's not our dynamic.

Hades also goes still. The warning kind of still when he's debating how best to strike.

Boone studies him right back with cocky arrogance in a smirk that, as the lengthening seconds pass, grows to a taunting grin.

Then he turns that grin on me. "I don't think he likes me touching you."

I give him a flat look. "Don't use me to poke at a god's facsimile."

A flash of emotion crosses his features, tightening them, and I think it might be hurt. "That's not what I'm doing, Lyra."

"What are you doing, then?"

Boone doesn't remove his arm, but he turns as serious as a reaper. "Proving a point. That *this* Hades isn't real." He points. "He's bound to that Lock. He isn't *him*."

I glance between my friend and a version of Hades that feels so real it hurts.

"Don't trust anything or anyone down here," Boone says.

My heart cracks right down the center. Because Boone is right.

The real Hades wouldn't just stand there silently watching this exchange. He'd put an end to it.

I turn away from this pale imitation, even while everything inside me screams at me to stay. "Let's go."

## 36

# TIME & TIME AGAIN

### LYRA

I lie on the stone floor under a glamoured blanket, my head on a glamoured pillow, staring at the rock ceiling overhead. When I asked about glamoured beds, the Titans only said that they try to save their powers. I didn't know we could run out. But when I asked about it, they hedged. More secrets they can't share, apparently.

Squeezing my eyes shut, I pull my pillow over my head and try to force away the spinning, yapping thoughts.

Not that it helps.

In my sightless and muffled state, I don't know what alerts me that something is off. The silence changes. Turns oppressive.

Slowly, I lift the pillow just in time to see the crack of broken time disappear, leaving me in a small, open field in a forest. Those shards are coming for me. It really feels like it, like they have an agenda of some sort.

Who in the name of the gods is controlling them, though, if not Cronos?

I scramble to my feet.

Or try to.

The concussion of an explosion blows me back off them before I'm even upright. It takes a second of crawling around, coughing in the dust and debris that blew up around me. But I eventually manage to gain my feet again and get out of the clouded air.

And the first thing I see when I do is a perfect sunset sky, all pinks and oranges and purples, and one of the hecatoncheires—the hundred-handed ones—as she hurls bodies into that beautiful sky.

And by bodies...I mean it in the truest sense of the word.

Another boom blasts somewhere nearby, and I duck even as I watch whoever she hurled shoot like rockets toward the ground, then wince when, obscured by trees and hills beyond, the earth spits more dirt and rocks straight up in the air with those pour souls' impact.

"Ouch," I mutter. "I hope to Hades those were not mortals."

Or they'll be seeing him soon.

The only warning I get before lightning cuts across the field is the strangest sensation, more familiar after today's training—an electric ripple over my skin.

"Drop!" someone yells. A familiar voice.

I don't look, hitting the deck flat on my stomach, and I reach for my axe as fire blasts overhead from the mouth of a chimera at Zeus' side. I've strapped it to the leg sheath that held the curved knife during Hades' Lock.

The flames stop midair directly overhead, like the blaze hit an invisible wall. Almost as if something is sucking it out of the chimera, hovering in the air overhead and pulling it into themselves. The fire is extinguished a little at a time. When the intense heat lets up, I look straight up into the pristine blue eyes of a man standing so close I could grab his foot.

"Cronos," I whisper.

A younger Cronos, though not as young as when I saw him with his family, I think. He's started to grow the beard, but there's no silver in his hair yet.

The Titan's eyes widen when he sees me. *"You."* The single word comes out almost as an accusation.

Me?

Given his state of dress—quite ancient in design, as far as I can tell—I'm pretty sure we've never met at this point in his life. Whenever this is. Some point between that family scene and when he was thrown into Tartarus, I assume. Unless he saw me when I witnessed him with his family during that visit to the past. But I don't think he did.

Did Hades tell his father?

Cronos sounds so much like Hades did that day, hard and suspicious, that I feel a tremulous smile try to take hold. It disappears when he says, "You saved my son."

What in the name of all things Olympus and the Underworld is he talking about?

Saved his son? Which one? When? Oh my gods. Is that why Hades thought I was a guardian angel? That's what he said, when I met the teenage him.

*Don't tell them anything.*

"Whoever you are, you may have to save *me* this day," Cronos says. "From—"

Lightning slams into the Titan's chest, catapulting him high into the air and miles away, his shout lost in the wind and distance.

# 37

# KILLING TIME

## LYRA

I'm on my feet in a defensive crouch, axe in my hand in an instant, and thankful that I'm still in the protective leather getup from Hades' Lock.

Zeus has his hands up, but he's not aiming them at me now, and his chimera is also paying me no attention.

"Okay."

Covered in even more ornate armor than he wore the first day of the Crucible—head topped with a spiky, bejeweled crown that would do a witch king proud—Zeus hovers in the air as if the raw energy of his power is making him levitate. His entire body is electrified, and currents of energy spark around him and through him, his white-blond hair nearly glowing.

"Why did you do that?" My voice comes out as bewildered as I feel. "That was unprovoked. He didn't—"

"If you know what's good for you, you'll clear these fields. Save yourself," Zeus snarls.

A warning. He is giving me a warning. Zeus, head asshole of all assholes, is trying to…help me?

Confusion is like a buzzing of bees in my head. Maybe I landed in the middle of a fight, and I didn't see what past-life Cronos did to deserve it, but as far as I can tell, Zeus attacked his father with no warning. And now he's trying to help insignificant, unknown me?

That's not like him at all.

Zeus throws out his hands, and lightning blasts from them with a boom that concusses my ears to ringing before stuffing them with cotton wool. But the electricity doesn't come at me. It shears past me…behind me. I whirl to find Iapetus still on his feet, having managed to avoid the strike.

He's not wearing armor or his loud print shirt—he's dressed like Cronos in ancient robes now. Neither Titan is wearing armor. Unlike Zeus.

"Get the hells out of here." Iapetus, also a younger-looking version of himself, waves wildly at me before dodging another strike.

Now *he* is trying to help me? What upside-down rabbit hole did I just fall through?

Iapetus' focus zeroes in on the god in the sky. "Don't do this, nephew!"

I stumble back. Not just at his words but at the *way* he said them.

There's a desperation in his voice I didn't think I would ever hear from the grumpy Titan who never stops grumbling…who threw me into Hades' Lock without a blink. "We are not your enemies," he calls.

"Lies!" Zeus thunders. "My father swallowed every child he sired except for me, and only because my mother hid me. And you *defend* him."

"Zeus—"

I definitely stumble back this time and nearly off my feet, trying to get out from between the two. Just in time. Zeus flies at Iapetus, tackling him through the air, and even as they blast out of sight, I can see that the Titan isn't fighting beyond defending himself from the deadliest of the strikes that Zeus tries to deliver.

Iapetus does not hit back. He does not use his power.

Zeus was right. I should not be here. Knowing that Iapetus makes it out of this alive—because I know future him in Tartarus—I leave him there and take off through the woods, not sure where I'm going. I'm not even sure if I should do anything beyond hide.

It's obvious now *when* this is. The start, or maybe the end, of the ten-year war between Titans and gods before the gods locked their parents up in Tartarus.

"Hestia, watch out!"

A blur moving too fast to catch details shoots through the woods to my right, zipping around the trees only to come to a jarring halt when Aphrodite slams into Hades' older sister, knocking them both off their feet. I hear the crack as Hestia's head hits a rock so hard the boulder splits into two moon-shaped halves that fall to either side of the goddesses.

The strangest gurgle of pain rips from Hestia's lips.

"Did I hurt you?" Aphrodite sounds frantic as she's on her knees and checking over Hestia.

I can't see Addie's face with her back to me. But Hestia, I do get a glimpse of as she sits up, looking dazed as she shakes her head. There is a shimmer over her face. Like glitter or the way soap is iridescent in sunlight.

Staying where I am, hidden in the trees, I squint, trying to get a closer look.

With a gasp, Hestia raises a shaking finger to point at...me.

I hold very still even as adrenaline and fear pump into my veins with every surge of my heart. Until I realize...

No.

She's *not* pointing at me.

There is a rustle, and Phoebe steps out of the woods to my left. The silvery, moon-shaped patch in her hair is hidden, as the black tresses are gathered into a ponytail. Her expression is a horrified mix of shock and confusion as she stares at the two goddesses. "I would not have hurt her," she says in her musical voice, brown eyes wide. "Not for the world. Not for all the powers of the Primordials."

"She wouldn't, Aphrodite," Hestia murmurs in a bleary-sounding voice. She must've hit her head so hard.

"Your love for her blinds you," Aphrodite hisses, moving into a crouch over Hestia like a mama rattlesnake curling around her unhatched and vulnerable eggs.

Phoebe takes a shaky step farther away from where I hide, circling them.

"You've seen the truth." Aphrodite is talking to Hestia. I still can't see her face. "You've seen what they want to do to us. They will end us if we don't stop them. End the mortals, too."

The odd, shimmery lighting on Hestia's face glints, turning brighter, more obvious. More...familiar.

It reminds me of the odd veil I saw over Zeus' face once, thanks to Eos' tears.

Hestia must listen to Aphrodite. "You are right. You are right, and I just don't want to see it."

Phoebe, now farther from their sides and facing me, raises both her hands—not defensively, definitely not to attack. More a placating gesture. "Don't do this—"

The words cut off in her throat as her entire body goes rigid, head thrown back, and her face spasms into a frozen mask that looks a lot like pain to me. Her body lifts off the ground until only the tips of her sandaled toes touch.

"She's having a vision," Hestia says. "She hasn't had one in ages."

"Attack her now," Aphrodite snaps. "While she's vulnerable."

In unison, like two predators attuned to each other and hunting together, the goddesses stalk toward the Titaness. Death—the intent of it, the violence of it—is evident in every leashed line of their taut bodies.

But before either can lunge for her, Phoebe comes out of her vision, her feet touching back down to the earth.

Her eyes widen at the sight of the two goddesses closing in on her, and the Titaness's chin wobbles. "Who did this to you?" she all but whispers.

Then, carefully, she sets her feet in a fighting stance. When she brings up her hands again, this time it is definitely defensive. "I will not harm you unless you force me."

Then, with visible deliberation, her gaze shifts beyond them to land on me, where I still watch from among the trees. "Your time hasn't arrived yet. But you are coming into your first power. Can you see?"

Aphrodite's back is to me, her focus trained on Phoebe as Hestia jerks around to see who Phoebe is talking to. Her gaze narrows on my face.

"Can you see?" Phoebe makes a gesture, passing her palm over her face like a...

"Veil," I whisper. And stare harder at Hestia.

The shimmering over her features becomes glaringly obvious. Every detail of it. A mesh veil identical to the one I saw covering Zeus' face at the end of his Labor in the Crucible, when he tried to kill me. Eos' tears allowed me to see it before. Or so I thought. But they have long since worn off.

Like before, the one over Hestia's face is all sorts of colors, like looking through a prism, and fitted to her features as if it's been painted on.

Coming into my first power, Phoebe said. I guess time doesn't matter as far as how and when a power presents itself. I know I'm not getting it from this moment or from this place. That the gift was already deep inside me, planted the moment Hades made me into a goddess. He said sometimes powers take years, even ages, to set in and reveal themselves. Maybe it's more that my body and mind are finally ready to handle this one now.

But what power do I have? What am I seeing?

"Alani," Phoebe calls softly. "Hide."

That last word reaches me a heartbeat before Aphrodite attacks and Hestia whirls away from me to join her. Phoebe absorbs the hit, and the three disappear out of sight before I can so much as shuffle my feet to get to her, to help her.

I put my hands to my head like I could physically take away the fog of confusion filling all the gaps and clouding my thoughts.

Do I hide? Do I help?

Given how adamant the Titans have been about trying not to interact with wherever broken time takes me, to avoid resetting things, hiding seems like the better choice.

Besides, if I helped, who would I help? The gods? Or the Titans?

## 38

# TIME WARP

### LYRA

"Screw this," I mutter. "What I need is a higher vantage point." To see everything that's going on.

I turn in a circle, scanning above the tops of the trees until I catch sight of a bluff, treeless and green, overlooking where I stand. "There."

It's too far to run, even at my faster goddess speed, which means trying to teleport. I'm not in Tartarus here. I should be able to. Focusing my gaze and all my will upon that spot, I accept the tingling that gathers at the base of my spine. Unlike in the abyss, when I tried both times, I easily feel myself blink out of existence and then back in again. Pleasure rips through my body and draws a lengthy moan from me. It takes a second to let go of that before I can look around, panting.

I'm not quite at the top. Close enough that I can scramble up the rocks, though.

"At least you got here, Lyra," I mumble under my breath. "Not bad."

When I reach the peak, I can't help the way my hands slide up to cover my mouth, holding in the bile that wants to bubble out of me at the sight that greets my eyes.

The ocean behind me is on fire, waves and monsters crashing into each other with roars of fury and pain. But it's the land all around me— decimated to black beyond a few small green patches like where I arrived and where I stand now—that brings bile to my lips. Large gashes are ripped into the earth as though monsters exploded out or something huge gouged into it. I can see the figure of a man lying very still not too far away, at the bottom of my bluff. Alive, I think. He has to be, because I know him later in his life—Koios. The aura of northern lights that emanates from him is fainter in the daylight but still visible against the black smoke rising around him.

He's missing an entire leg.

Is the Koios I know missing a leg? He wears shorts that I don't think revealed a scar and doesn't walk with any kind of detectable limp or hitch in his stride, and I wonder if Titans can regrow limbs.

Another body hurtles past me, spraying dirt and rocks when it hits, and I duck and swing around to see the wildly waving arms of a hecatoncheir who is out in the fiery sea.

Bile rises so fast I cough on it.

Because the hundred-handed creature's face is covered in the same veil I saw over Hestia's. Impossible to miss at that size, even far away.

Another boom, and I whirl again in time to see Demeter tie up Tethys with vines, just like her daughter, controlling the plants to contain the Titaness. A Demeter whose face is also covered in a veil.

"Oh gods," I whisper as realization starts out as a spark of doubt but quickly catches fire like the seas. And then those words seem to stick on repeat. "Oh gods. Oh gods. Oh gods."

Please don't let this be what I think it might be.

I need to see Zeus.

His face when I saw him before wasn't veiled. But what about now?

"You should not be here."

I jerk my gaze up to find Rhea standing before me. She is covered in blood. Hers or someone else's, I can't tell which, because the figure-hugging draped dress she wears is gold, and so is ichor—the gods' and immortals' blood.

Her eyes widen slightly, then narrow as she takes a closer look at me, her gaze moving from my eyes to my wrists. "Orion," she murmurs. Then her gaze sharpens. "Are you...Lyra?"

What in the name of the cosmos? "You know me?"

"My son told me of you. He told me to lock you in Phlegethon if I ever saw you." Her lips form a barely-there smile. "I must say, he described you exactly. You really do have the most extraordinary green eyes. But the stars on your wrist are what give you away."

Hades spoke to his mother about me? This must be happening after the last time I saw him in Erebos, when he *did* lock me up down there.

Not that this matters right now. "None of you are fighting back?"

The Titaness's shoulders fall. "No. We would never hurt our children."

Shit. I was really hoping for a different answer. One that explained things way better than the off-the-wall explanation my brain is starting to come up with.

"Why are they attacking you?" I ask as I slip my axe back into the sheath on my leg.

She shakes her head. "We don't know. Someone has convinced them that we are monsters."

Monsters. Someone convinced them...

A headache stabs through my skull, and I drop my chin to my chest. Because off-the-wall is starting to ring like the truth, and I can't wrap my head around it. I don't want to hear it.

"I saw a veil," I tell her. "Over Hestia's face. Demeter's, too. Not of cloth but of light."

"Mother Gaia."

I hear her broken whisper and lift my head. She looks like she might be sick. An answering nauseous roll inside my stomach tells me that my wild idea is right. "Have you seen veils?"

"No." She scans the carnage laid out before us in a terrible tapestry, the violence of battle booming across the skies and rending the earth. "Have you seen others veiled before this?"

I hesitate, only because of the timing, during the Crucible. "On Zeus' face. Once before. But Phoebe was here just now when I saw Hestia's. She went oddly rigid and then told me I was coming into my first power."

I'm not sure what response I expected to that, but it wasn't for Rhea to start shaking so violently her dress rustles against the ground. "She told you that?" The words come out of her stiff lips in a harsh whisper.

I nod.

"And then what?"

"Then I could suddenly see the veil over Hestia's face in more detail."

"We need more proof," she says under her breath, then lifts her arm like a perch, and a distinctive cry pierces the skies from above. A few seconds later, a hawk swoops in low to land on the leather gauntlet covering Rhea's outstretched arm, settling to perch there.

Rhea points at a pebble. "That is a mouse. Eat it."

The hawk looks from her to the rock and then ruffles its feathers, seemingly unimpressed.

Then Rhea waves a hand over its face.

"Holy shit." The words are out of me before I can stop them, because now the hawk's eyes are covered in…not a veil, but similar-looking, just over its eyes. Iridescent light.

She points again. "Eat the mouse."

Without pause, the hawk flies to the ground and gobbles down the rock.

Then she leans over, and it's almost like she's peeling the glamour off its eyes—like removing contacts. The hawk coughs up the rock.

After one glance at my face, she doesn't even ask me what I saw. In hers, I see a thousand shades of despair. "Only the god who places it can see the veil, Lyra… I believe you are now the goddess of glamours, with the ability to see them, no matter the source. Probably to manipulate them at some point."

The goddess of glamours?

Of *course* the middle of the battle between Titans and gods is when I would manifest my unique power.

And what a ridiculous fucking power.

Glamours. That makes me the goddess of what? Lies? Fake shit? Mental and emotional manipulation?

I want a different power. This one sucks.

It's also exactly the wild idea I was starting to have on my own.

"Fates be damned," I mutter.

Rhea lets out a short, sharp breath. "My thoughts precisely. What you're seeing—the veils over their faces—means someone very powerful must have glamoured our children."

Hearing it confirmed out loud sends my heart plummeting through the soles of my feet and into the very Underworld itself, where it shrivels in the cold and dark of the in-between spaces.

Because I know what happens next.

What happens to her. To all the Titans.

And if we're right, if the gods are glamoured, then that happy Titan family moment I saw before—that was *real*. The lie is everything the gods believed. Everything the world believed. Still believes thousands of years later.

That the Titans are evil incarnate.

That's the lie.

Oh gods. "Rhea…they don't know what they're doing. You can't stop it—"

Black smoke rises out of the ground, manifesting from nothing, and I know who is coming next.

More smoke swirls around the Queen of the Titans, like two cobras dancing back and forth, winding into each other to form a latticed cage around her.

"Run," I urge Rhea. "Try to run. Hide. Don't let them find you."

Instead of answering, Rhea does something with her hand, waves it, and a tingling rush flows up and over and through me. And I don't have time to figure out what she just did.

Because he's here.

While the cage around her remains, the rest of the smoke dissipates, and standing before her is…

Hades.

## 39

## DEVIL OF A TIME

### LYRA

I stand slightly to Hades' side, and I can see the shimmer now. The veil over his face. Hades is glamoured, too.

"Mother."

Even I flinch. So much hatred. So much rage. He doesn't even acknowledge my presence, as though I'm insignificant, but he has to be aware that I'm here. Right? Does he not recognize me? Has the glamour made him forget me?

"Hades," Rhea implores him. "You are bewitched. You've been lied to."

His shoulders stiffen, but he does not react beyond that, still facing down Rhea. "Don't fight me. Don't make me harm you, Mother. Just come quietly."

The look she gives her son is one filled with a myriad of emotions—quiet desperation, forgiveness before he's even laid a finger on her, fear. A deep-seated fear. That rips at me the hardest. That she would fear her own son that way.

But there is also love.

I can see it in the way she raises her hand to reach out to him only to lower it again when he growls at her. "You let him *eat* me," he snarls, reminding me of a wounded animal in the woods. His body is barely leashed, vibrating with his fury. "I was a baby, and you let Father eat me. Eat all of us."

Hades grows quieter with every word. More venomous. More deadly.

Rhea shakes her head. "I didn't. Cronos didn't—"

He cuts off Rhea's denial with a sharp slash of his hand. "Enough, Mother. It's over."

His voice cracks on the word, and Rhea closes her eyes. "I will go with you," she says. "Because the last thing a mother would ever want is for her child to regret what they did in a moment of brokenness."

"I'm not the one who is *broken*." The smoke cage lifts Rhea off the ground, drawing her closer until he can grasp her by the arm. "Where I'm taking you, you can no longer hurt your children again. *Any* of us."

"No!" I cry out. Without a clue of what I'm doing, I rush forward to wrap my arms around his neck, pressing my palm to his cheek. "Don't do this. Don't do this."

He'll hate himself when he learns the truth. He'll blame himself.

For the tiniest fraction of a second, his eyes clear and the veil that covers his face wavers.

"Lyra?" he asks, staring hard like he can't quite see me. The veil wavers more, like fog blown by wind, and his gaze focuses on me narrowly. "What are you doing here?"

Rhea reaches out and taps her middle finger gently to the center of Hades' forehead. "Sleep."

Her son collapses to the ground, sliding right out of my grasp. All the smoke around her dissipates into a fine mist as he lies there, his chest moving with deep breaths.

Rhea kneels over him and brushes the white curl off his forehead with gentle fingers as tears silently slip down her cheeks. "He used to have nightmares as a child," she says to me quietly, never taking her gaze from his face. "Always about the things he would have to do and be for humanity. Fears that his power would escape him and cause harm and devastation. I got very good at helping him sleep."

She closes her eyes tightly. "Those nightmares stopped after he met you the second time."

I have no idea which time would be the second time for him, but it doesn't matter. I have to swallow down the sadness that tries to choke me—for her, for him. She sighs, then grasps him by the wrist. I don't see what she's doing at first, but then there's…movement.

Movement on her skin. And I gasp when I see what.

My tattoos. Or not mine…but Hades'. The ones he gave me as a gift during the Crucible, to help protect me. I lost them when I entered Tartarus. His mother gave them to him, he once said.

*This* is when she did that? Right before he sent her to the lowest depths of the Underworld.

"They won't live beyond the gates of what our children have built," Rhea explains, giving a sad smile as the spider, butterfly, owl, fox, and panther obediently crawl from her skin to his. The owl waits until last, flapping at her mistress, but Rhea just tips her chin at it, and the owl flies to her son, settling into his flesh before they all fade from view. Then, with a sigh, the Titaness gets to her feet.

"He couldn't see me," I say. "Why?"

"I made sure he couldn't. It would have broken his trust in you. My Hades has never trusted easily, and doubting you, I suspect, would be the end of something important."

My heart beats against the cage of my ribs like a trapped thing. "Thank you," I whisper.

The look she gives me is all things sadness and resignation. "You need to hide. This won't last much longer. We're losing, and we won't fight if it means harming them."

I know she's right. But leaving them here to be unjustly imprisoned feels all kinds of wrong. I swallow. Hard. "Listen to me…"

How in the name of Olympus do I word this without revealing too much, without resetting time?

"If you…lose this war. If you end up somewhere you can't get out of… I'll come for you." No. That's not true. They had to drag me down there. "I'll help you. You'll have to convince me at first, but I'll help you fix this. Phoebe will see."

She's been staring at me like I'm losing my shit, but at those words, the look in Rhea's eyes hardens, turns into a command. "Keep your promise to me, Lyra. Help us."

"I…will. I swear on the River Styx."

Rhea's eyes widen slightly.

Did I really just make an unbreakable oath to the Titans to help them? The world has turned upside down.

Again.

It keeps doing that on me.

"Now hide," she says. "Far from here."

I close my eyes and think of the only place I can go right now. Hopefully everyone is busy with this war and it's empty at the moment.

Also…hopefully I can get that far on my own.

This time, teleportation comes easily and without the tingling surge, as if finally manifesting my power over glamours means I have more control overall. I picture where I want to go, and almost instantly, the cacophony of battle goes dead silent and a perfect breeze drifts across my skin. I open my eyes to find myself in the Underworld, staring at Hades' castle-like home in the subterranean mountains. It is smaller than the version I know in the future. Different. Fewer wings and turrets, more ancient in style.

"Water gardens," I whisper.

Not quite the size and extent of what I know so many centuries from now. But he's started creating the water gardens.

I sit down on the ground under a weeping willow, wrapping my arms around my knees as I wait for broken time to return me to Tartarus.

Return me to the Titans, who have been wrongly imprisoned there for eons in a way I don't even want to contemplate.

Even as I try to squeeze them back in, I can't stop the tears from falling.

# PART 4

# PANDEMONIUM

Make it make sense.

# 40

## TO CHEAT DEATH

### HADES

"What do you think you are doing, Hades?"

I straighten on my uncomfortable throne.

"Fuck," Charon mutters beside me. Because he recognizes that voice, too.

Sure enough, out of the shadows of the pillars, a figure emerges. The god of death who once so patiently shared his teachings with me when I was younger and out of control.

Anubis.

The Egyptian god walks toward me, dressed in a simple linen, kilt-like schenti, his onyx-skinned human chest, ridged with muscles, bare. His head is that of a jackal with inky black fur, his long, pointed ears twitching, and his brown-and-gold eyes are narrowed on me.

One of my siblings must have summoned him.

At least he isn't holding his crook, the infamous staff with its curved end. I take it as a sign that he's here to negotiate, not go to war with the King of the Greek Gods.

"This isn't your fight, old friend," I tell him.

His jackal lips pull back, only slightly showing his teeth. A warning. "It is my fight if you unleash what's down there."

Fuck.

I can't fight my siblings, any other gods their deaths will bring down on me, and Anubis, too.

My skin prickles a heartbeat before another figure emerges from the shadows.

Hecate.

"Not you, too," I whisper. She is both goddess and chthonic being, part of the balance of the Underworld. And she's supposed to be standing in for Charon while he's here with me.

She flinches, but she stands her ground. "I can't let you let them out."

Anubis moves forward, pulling my attention. "If you don't let this idea go, then you leave us no choice. We will have to destroy Tartarus and all the souls within it."

No. Fuck no. He can't do that. "You don't have that power."

"Not alone, I don't," he agrees softly.

Then another figure arrives, and another, and another. They show up in numbers. All the gods who touch or wield death throughout the world position themselves around my throne in a semicircle meant to trap me.

What the fuck do I do now?

My gaze narrows on Zeus, who can't hold back a hint of a smile. He did this. Somehow, while standing before me, he called them here.

"If it's a fight you want, brother," I say, "then you've got it."

# 41

# BUT I'M NOT THE ONLY ONE

### LYRA

When time takes me back to Tartarus, I find myself sitting, arms still wrapped around my knees, in between the pillars of the cosmos. The ground between them is decorated in black-and-white tile depicting the history of the Primordials and Titans in a winding spiral of squares.

I rub at my damp cheeks with my shoulders, although they're already drying from the heat off the lava flows. The stark rock-and-obsidian ceiling overhanging the wastelands is beautiful somehow. Terrifying. But beautiful. Not nearly as beautiful as the sparkly blue constellations on the ceiling of the Underworld that I've been staring at for hours. Or Olympus. Or, for that matter, the Overworld.

Skies the Titans haven't seen in ages.

The question is…was that real?

Did what I saw and felt and heard and witnessed really happen? I had enough time sitting and waiting in the Underworld to start asking myself that.

It felt damned real.

Part of me wants to run to Rhea and Cronos and hug them, to check that Koios has his leg, to make sure Phoebe wasn't harmed by Hestia and Aphrodite. But I gut check that urge in favor of a logical approach.

A crimson form catches the corner of my eye, and I jerk my head around to stare at the broken shard of time floating through the air.

"Not again—" The words stutter to a stop on the tip of my tongue.

Because a figure appears on the floor—and the man is sizzling.

I mean literally. Including a hissing sound coming off him.

"Boone! Holy shit!"

I crawl over to where he's lying on his back, knees bent. His dark hair is standing on end, and some of the strands look melted at the tips. His shirt is torn and charred at the edges, which are singed, and smoke rises off his body. But his eyes are open.

Not in death, thank the gods.

He's glaring at the ceiling thousands of feet above our heads. "What a dick," he mutters.

"Who?" I ask as I check a nasty burn that streaks down his arm in the strangest pattern. What on earth did he encounter?

It's healing quickly, at least. I peer closer and wrinkle my nose. Maybe too quickly.

Boone winces as I gingerly peel up a scrap of shirt that's partially knitted into his regenerating skin. "Sorry," I whisper.

With a groan, he lets me guide him up, and he pulls off his shirt. Two more spots stick in the skin.

I sit back on my heels. "Who's a dick?"

He scowls. "Zeus. Motherfucker threw a lightning bolt at me."

My eyes go wide, and I take in the angry-looking burns with more interest. "I'd say he hit you."

"Glanced off me," Boone insists.

"Yeah. Okay." Male pride is such a sad thing to behold sometimes. "Do you know when you were?"

Blowing out a sharp breath, Boone drapes his hands over his knees, gaze going unfocused as he thinks about it. "Shortly after the gods claimed Olympus, if I had to guess—the clothes, the way Olympus was laid out…"

"You were in Olympus?"

He nods. "At the main temple… You know the one high up, above the waterfalls? Only it looked…different. That god is power hungry. I'll tell you that much."

I believe it. Zeus still is. "What did he do?"

Boone's lips tighten. "I was spotted by Poseidon and Hera as soon as I showed up where their individual fancy houses currently stand in our present day, but instead there was one long, giant structure there. Looked much older. Byzantine, maybe." Like any good thief, he knows his antiquities.

"They *saw* you? Why didn't they recognize you during the Crucible?" Or Hera, at least. Poseidon wasn't much of a joiner after the first Labor, when his champion, Isabel, was killed.

"Who knows." He shrugs, then winces as the action pulls at his wound. "They took me straight to Zeus, almost as if they were afraid to deal with me on their own..." He pauses. Thinking. "No. Not deal with me. If I had to guess, they were afraid of him and what he'd do to them if he found out they'd seen me and hadn't brought me to him."

"That's even worse than he is these days."

"I know. So they took me to the temple, where there's a statue of Zeus out front so large it's almost as big as the mountain the temple is on. And inside, that god is sitting on...get this...a throne. Not just any throne, either. Solid gold. Ornate. I've never seen anything more ostentatious. And lightning everywhere." Boone frowns, thinking. "But the weird part is that it looked like he'd been there a while."

Seriously? "How could you tell?"

"There were plates and bowls everywhere. Goblets. All within reach of him. Half-eaten food. Like they'd been feeding him there. And he was not his usual preening self. His blond hair was longer, hanging in his face and matted. His clothes rumpled."

Zeus is nothing if not a diva. That sounds wrong. All wrong.

"He never once got off that seat, either."

I adjust to sit beside him on the floor. "By any chance, was there a mesh veil made of iridescent light over his face?"

"What? No." He squints at me. "Why would you ask that?"

Which is when I lay it all out for him. When I'm done, we're both still sitting on the ground and he is stone-still and silent. And thinking.

He shakes his head once. A single, jerking rejection of a move.

Then again.

Then sighs. "My initial thought is you're the one being glamoured..."

He says this slowly, brows drawing together, and just as slowly, I feel my stomach sink. I'm not sure why I want to believe all the things I've seen. But...I do.

"I mean..." Boone rubs a hand around the back of his neck. "It would be much easier to glamour one brand-new goddess still waiting for her powers than it would be to glamour a bunch of gods."

"I know." I thought of that, too.

"There's the amount of power that would take." He shakes his head. "I don't think even Titans could manage it. They seem…limited down here… but still."

I nod. "I figured they had to have help, maybe. Or multiple people working together?"

"Maybe. But gods don't like to share power or secrets. If someone did do this, they've sat on the truth for a long-ass time without a single leak? How?"

Also something I thought of. "What if the person responsible glamoured other gods to help them and then forget they helped?"

I wince. Because when I say it out loud, I can tell that's reaching.

Boone's already shaking his head. "Think about it, Lyra. It's not just the Greek pantheon that person or persons would have had to glamour. The gods of the other pantheons—Norse, Egyptian, Sumerian, Celtic, Mayan, you name it—they interact. I don't think Odin would have let the Greek pantheon lock up their parents if he knew the Titans were being wrongly imprisoned."

"*That*, I hadn't thought of yet," I mutter, glaring at a pink flower waving lazily in the breeze at the base of the earth pillar.

Pink doesn't feel like the right color for my mood, which was dark enough when I got here.

"What about Zeus?" I ask. So far, it's the only explanation my brain has accepted.

The way Boone squints, I can tell he's thinking through it but not buying it. I start ticking off my points on my hand. "He became King of the Gods, and that comes with extra power. What if it came with all of Cronos' Titan-level power? I mean, Hades got Pandora's Box because he became king. He couldn't have done that without the crown. So clearly that position gets…extra."

"Okay," Boone agrees.

"And what you just saw…clearly he went a little power wild."

He huffs an unamused laugh. "That's putting it mildly." Then he shakes his head. "What about the other pantheons?"

"As king, Zeus would have more interaction with and access to them?"

"Afterward," he points out heavily.

"Yeah." I drop my head into my hands. "I don't know what to think."

Gods, that headache that started during the battle is only getting worse. Maybe it's a side effect of getting my goddess power?

I pause.

"What?" Boone asks from above me, voice slightly muffled by the way I have my hands over my ears.

I lift my head. "Have you figured out how to glamour yet? Even small ones?"

"No. Why—" Realization snaps in his eyes. "You want to test out your power."

"Exactly. Let's start there."

## 42

## PERSEPHONE'S STORY

### LYRA

We start toward the rooms where we'd been sleeping. Or trying to.

"Who are you thinking?" Boone asks.

"Persephone."

He straightens so hard I'm surprised his spine doesn't snap. "No—"

"She's the only non-Titan down here to ask for help."

"And clearly on the Titans' side." He's shaking his head.

"Do you have any better ideas? We won't tell her why we want to learn this. Just say it's for our own protection."

Boone's jaw tenses. He does not like this idea at all. "Fine," he mutters.

At least now I know why he doesn't trust her. Although, having been stuck in the past with Hades and unable to tell him much, maybe he should give Persephone some slack.

When we get to the rooms, I stand in the doorway to the shared space where all the Titans gather—just a safe place to wait or sometimes to sleep, which is what they are doing now. Boone tiptoes across the Titans littered across the floor—Iapetus snoring loud enough to wake the dead—to shake Persephone's shoulder. I can't see his face, but I do see hers, especially the bleary-eyed fog clearing in a burst of a smile when she realizes it's him. Boone leans away from her, like he's trying to avoid the beam of it touching him.

Dimmed a bit, she quietly gets to her feet and follows him out into the hall where I wait, and even after sleep, her dark-to-pink ombre curls still manage to lay perfectly over one shoulder as she rubs at her big lavender-blue eyes. The woman doesn't have so much as a pillow crease marring her perfection.

When she wasn't in Tartarus, she probably slept with clouds for pillows.

"I need you to glamour something of your choosing," I say once we get down the hallway. "It can be small. You can't ask why."

Persephone blinks. Blinks again. Then smiles, not nearly as bright as a second ago, but still, the hallway might as well fill with rays of sunlight and butterflies. "You want my help?"

Boone makes a choking sound at my back, and I'm tempted to throw an elbow.

"Happy to," she says, then steps away. Her gaze slides from me to Boone, and then she lifts her hand in a flowing motion, like a ballerina.

Boone jerks back, one hand coming up between them. "Not me. No way."

Persephone pouts, even as her eyes twinkle. "You're no fun."

Boone's response is a basic grunt, but he lowers his hand. Not that he relaxes.

With a teasing smile, Persephone waves her fingers, and from behind the flowy skirts of her dress, a tiny little bunny with gray fur and ears so long it almost trips itself tentatively hops out and right into her palm. She lifts it to her face to give it a nuzzle before setting the sweet little thing back on the floor.

I know the bunny itself is a glamour, so I glance at Boone's face. No veil. "Do you see that?"

"Of course he sees it, silly." Persephone laughs, but not meanly.

He still nods.

"Right," I mutter.

"Let's try this." Again, with the ballerina-perfect hand move, she waves her fingers over the bunny. "Today, you are a frog."

Just like Rhea with the hawk, the bunny immediately changes its seated position so that it's upright, front legs straight and back legs on either side.

Then the thing…ribbits.

Or tries to. The sound is like a squeaky version of a ribbit. It tries again, then hops. Not bunny hops…frog hops…across the stone floor.

Boone leans forward, fascinated. "I'll be damned."

"Yes, you will," I say quietly, not nearly the same amount of amused.

He jerks his gaze to me. "You can see it?"

After a breath, I give a jerking nod. Also like the hawk, the covering of light appear over the bunny's eyes as soon as she waved her hand. "But this is a glamour on a glamour, right?"

"Essentially," she says slowly. "But the bunny is more a manifestation. It's real enough, like the training course."

That doesn't help us much if fake can be real and real can be lies. "You can stop it now." I nod at the bunny that thinks it's a frog.

She calls the bunny to her, and—just like Rhea with her hawk—gently peels the glamour from its eyes. That small veil of light disappears as soon as it's removed, and the bunny immediately adjusts how it's standing, no longer frog-like, and it looks visibly confused. She waves her hand again, and the bunny disappears.

A twinge of sadness for the little thing that was "real enough" tweaks in the center of my chest.

"See what, exactly?" Persephone glances between us.

I'm not ready to share that with her yet. "How *did* you get down here?"

Persephone leans back like she wants to get away from that question. "I already told you we don't know, but..."

I'm expecting her to say something about breaking time if she tells us, but she doesn't.

Instead, she drops her gaze to her fingers, which are twisted in front of her. She holds herself very still. "The first time you and Hades came for me with Pandora's Box, trying to get me out that way, I snuck up to the gates of Tartarus alone, as agreed."

Boone and I exchange a look. That's not what I asked about. But I don't say so, waiting for her to keep going.

She peeks out from under the curtain of her hair as if she's checking that we're listening. I've seen false smiles before a thousand times—ones hiding judgment, ones hiding lies or hiding the truth, ones patiently waiting for you to mess up. I don't think I've ever seen anything like hers now. Sadness and a hopeless sort of resignation.

"You have to understand," she says. "Before you finally arrived in Tartarus, Lyra, we already knew you were coming, thanks to Phoebe's prophecy. And Rhea. She always said you'd come."

My heart flip-flips like a fish out of water. I promised Rhea. That was today for me but thousands of years ago for her. Is that something I always end up doing? Do I always go to that moment and promise her? Or did I make that same promise in other situations? What about in the time resets that happened before I ever arrived in Tartarus?

Boone's reaction—since I told him about what I saw and did in my most recent visit to the past—covers my own. Suspicion lends an edge to his voice. "This is the first we're hearing about it."

"You know why." Persephone just shrugs. "We have to be careful not to overwhelm either of you. There's a lot you haven't heard about yet."

She's right about that.

"Anyway, the Titans had time to prepare, to go through hundreds or even thousands of different scenarios. Apparently, I was a bit of a surprise when I showed up down here almost a hundred and fifty years ago." She makes a face. "I wasn't any happier about it than you. But I've learned patience after waiting for Lyra to be born and then grow up enough for Hades to find you and choose you for the Crucible. Only…the first time around, he didn't."

"Didn't what?" I ask.

"Choose you. He didn't play in the Crucible Games at all, like usual. So you didn't meet, you didn't win, you didn't end up here. We had to reset time and try again."

Because of Phoebe's prophecy?

I could really use a seat for this.

"That's—" Boone starts, then waves like he's erasing the question. "Never mind."

Persephone scrunches up her nose. "We've had to reset time a lot, actually. We've been patient. We've prepared, thinking and even going through all the possible futures you might face. Whittling down the perfect combination of events and exact steps to get you here and then get us out."

"Gods above," Boone mumbles.

"I'm not sure those are the gods we should be praying to," I mumble back. We might have a better shot with the gods of death. Anubis, maybe?

Persephone doesn't seem to notice, almost like she's lost in the memories of all the pasts they've experienced. "At this point the Titans have been down here so long that they've learned there are infinite possibilities. They've also learned when to start avoiding those broken bits of time so that they don't accidentally reset things when they don't want to, in order to hurry the future to them faster."

Which lines up with what Koios told us. Persephone wasn't in the room when we talked about how the broken time works.

She gives a small sigh. "I haven't been back to visit the past in a while."

Boone leans forward, suddenly harshly focused. "You're admitting you've also traveled back in time?"

The way he says it, it's like he's accusing her of murder. But I know why.

She opens her mouth, only for him to wave his hand and mutter, "Never mind," again.

The disappointment that crosses her features makes me want to hug her. I am having way too many urges to hug people down here. Dangerous urges. We still don't know who to trust.

"It's better if we don't risk changing things anyway." There is *real* fear in her voice, in her eyes, which shift like she's checking the corners of the room for broken time.

A series of emotions cycles through Boone's eyes—confusion, concern, and then a gradual, hardening anger... I'm guessing because of the concern and that he felt concern at all.

"It's also better if you share anything you know with us," she urges.

"I'm not telling you shit," he says. "I don't trust anyone down here with anything about my past," he adds in a voice I've never heard him use on anyone except maybe Chance, the biggest bully in our den.

Not even the time Boone got into a bar fight with a motorcycle gang—him against them—was he like this. I wasn't even there, but I saw the video because I had to wipe it. He made five rough dudes think a second before coming at him, just with that tone.

The fact that all Persephone does is look down at her hands says a lot about her. When she looks up again, a smile is pinned back in place, though not quite as glowy. "I wouldn't trust us, either," she says, "if I were you."

"And I *don't* need your approval," he shoots back.

With a sigh, she trains her gaze on me. "Like I said, the first time you finally won the Crucible and Hades got his hands on Pandora's Box, we tried to get me out the way we had planned. Instead of sucking me through a keyhole, the door cracked, but it shut before I could go through. The Titans had me try two more times—"

"Wait...they *knew* you were trying to escape without them?" I ask before Boone can.

"Yes. Because I am never part of Phoebe's prophecy. If they could get me out sooner…" She shrugs. "But then they figured out that Pandora's Box was how to get *you* in with us."

Boone's hands clench. "That makes no godsdamned sense. The gods made it to work a specific way."

Her smile wavers, turning serious even as she keeps her gaze on me. "At first they thought, when I showed up, that they'd get you in the same way I got in."

"Which was?" I ask.

"That was the problem. I don't know. Neither do they."

She's said that before. No change in the story.

Boone makes a scoffing sound in the back of his throat. "Seriously—" He cuts off when I kick his foot.

Persephone is frowning. "I remember I had just gone up to Olympus after a several-months-long visit in the Underworld. I can picture laughing with my mother. Hades was there." Her brows furrow even more as her gaze turns inward. "There was something funny about his face."

His face.

A shiver snakes around me. Over my skin, setting my teeth on edge.

She shakes her head. "I went to sleep in my room in Mother's house, and then I have a vague memory of someone else in the dark with me." She screws up her face as if she's trying to force the memories to clear. "Then I woke up in Tartarus."

"Bullshit—"

"Stop," I interrupt, and he just looks at me.

"I believe you," I tell Persephone.

She straightens, smile brightening. "You do?"

"The fuck you do," Boone snaps.

I swallow. "I believe you because of what I can see right now."

Boone flops back in his chair. "Since when?"

"Not before tonight. But as soon as she woke up." I shrug. I've been trying not to stare this entire conversation.

"See what?" Persephone demands.

I hope she doesn't freak out. "You've been glamoured."

## 43

# THEY'RE COMING FOR US

### LYRA

Boone and I balance side by side on a ledge barely wide enough to stand on tiptoe, pinned on the framework of the practice course for Poseidon's Lock between the stabbing swords behind us and the Thor-like hammers ahead, which are flying around like helicopter blades as they swing off a thick center pole above us.

"You can do it, Lyra," Persephone calls from the sidelines.

Like we're friends. I'm still not entirely sure about her. I might be able to see the glamour covering her eyes, but I can't tell what it makes her believe or do. A glamour, by the way, that I attempted to remove. After all, as the goddess of glamours, shouldn't I be able to affect them?

It didn't budge. It's still there every time I look at her beautiful face now. She could be a ticking time bomb. Boone seems determined to not trust her, mostly pretending she doesn't exist.

I needed to physically work off some of the pent-up, confusion-driven energy, so we came down here to practice the course.

Even able to see glamours, I *still* don't know what to believe.

The goddess of irony and I really need to have a chat someday. I don't know why she keeps targeting me, but it feels personal.

So many other questions are a giant knot in my head, like colored threads of yarn that a demon kitten has batted around and snarled into a mess.

*Stop thinking about it*, I tell myself for the hundredth time.

Hyperfixating means losing focus on what's right in front of me. Which is how I've already managed to get a decent slice across my cheek from one of the swords. It was deep enough that, even with accelerated healing, it still stings. The bruise on my forehead is from a hammer and is new, but now at least it doesn't feel like a goose laid an egg under my skin when I touch it.

Goddess healing is pretty awesome.

"Okay," Boone says as we both stare at the swinging hammers. "Last time you paid attention to too many of the hammers."

He's been sounding more and more like some kind of Zen obstacle guru as we practice.

"I should pay attention to *fewer* hammers?" I try really hard not to sound sarcastic. I don't manage it very well.

He gives me a pointed look, to which I shrug.

"Yes, Lyra," he says in a deliberately slow and overly patient voice. "The only hammers you care about are the two or three that are in danger of hitting you. The others are just a distraction. If you get confused, pick the hammer going slowest that's closest to you and step on it so you can ride it. Doing that allows you time to observe."

I snort a laugh. "You seem to think I'm a coordinated person who kept training on the obstacle courses in our den."

"Lyra…you got through Artemis' Labor, including outrunning a dragon. Not to mention Athena's glass labyrinth."

It takes a lot to hide the shudder that hits me hard at the mention of Athena's, the most brutal of the Crucible Games for me. The heads on spikes. The way Dex and Meike died. Not the best memories to hold on to.

"I had help." My tattoos, Zai, Meike, Trinica, Amir, even the other champions from time to time. I miss them all. But nothing like I miss Hades.

The rock inside my chest from his absence never lets up. Even right now, when I'm focusing on not being knocked into electrified water, it's there. Like he's here with me.

What if I keep dying in here because I can't do this without him?

Boone looks from me to the hammers and back. "Okay, new plan," he says. "We're going to do this together. Every time I say *step*, take one step in the direction I tell you. Don't move unless I tell you to, even if I move. Got it?"

Now we're playing a game of Simon Says? This is so not going to work. Another dousing and shock are definitely in my near future, but that's true if I do it on my own, anyway. So we might as well give this a try. "Got it."

"Here we go."

It works for a hot second. The next few moves we take, I focus on the hammers closest to us and move when and where Boone tells me to, and I think I'm starting to see what he means about figuring out which ones to focus on. But it's too fast. My brain wants to take longer to process the trajectory and proximity and where I need to be going to get out of the path. Probably why I catch sight of a hammer coming at me from out of the corner of my eye and flinch, instinct making me take the smallest move away.

"Nope." Boone is somehow right there, shifting me to a safer spot.

"Like a dance," I mutter.

He gives a single nod. "Backward."

And we step.

A hammer whips by with a *whomp, whomp, whomp*.

"Exactly like a dance." He grins. "Lateral left."

We move.

"What do they think they're doing?" Cronos' voice reaches us over the sounds of the obstacle course and the blaze of fire and lava beyond in the wastelands.

Maybe I turn toward him. I've been expecting him to show up, but the timing still surprises me. All I know is I hear Boone say, "Shit," and then I'm being lifted completely off my feet. There's a confusing swirl of motion as I'm swung around. It takes a second for me to realize that he's stepped both of us up onto a hammer that's turning in circles.

"Don't distract her!" he yells at Cronos, somehow managing to keep his gaze on the Titan while we spin.

How is he doing that? I'm getting dizzy and nauseous.

"She wasn't ready for that part!" Cronos yells back.

"She was," Boone insists. "You were holding her back."

In a passing whirl, I catch the Titan's frustrated scowl. "This isn't how she—"

"Let them get through the obstacle first, my love." Rhea doesn't speak loudly. I don't know that she ever does.

She's here? The tiniest gasp escapes my lips as I look around and find her standing beside Cronos. The last time I saw the Titaness's face, it was streaked in silent tears, drawn into despair by a soul-deep sadness and the knowledge that her children had been forced to attack her. To believe she was terrible. To believe even worse things about their father.

I told her I'd come help her.

I *promised*.

She didn't know in that moment how long she would have to wait. How long they all would have to wait. For me it's been instant, but for them it's been thousands and thousands of years.

Every question, every worry, every confused backtrack of the thought process trying to figure this out abandons me at the sight of her face now.

And I realize that, whatever else happens, I'm going to try to keep that promise.

Other than that one small gasp at the sight of her, I don't say anything or do anything else. I don't make another sound.

But Rhea's gaze on me changes. Not sharpens, exactly, but settles.

She knows that I know now.

"Ready?" Boone asks.

I force myself to suck in another sharp breath and mentally shake myself back into focusing on getting through the rest of the obstacle when what I want to do is go to Rhea. Even if she can't give me any more answers than I already have.

I'm almost tempted to jump into the stupid water, but that electric shock is no joke.

So I nod, and we move.

Which is when the damned bell decides to go off. Even out here, near the lava flows and burning lands, with all the noise it makes, it's like it's ringing right beside my ear.

"Shit," Boone mutters and gets us up on another hammer so we can look toward the others on the ground.

"Stay there!" Cronos yells. "The Pandemonium shouldn't be able to get to you there."

Then all three of them run as if their lives depend on it.

Leaving us dangling on the swinging hammer like sacks of food hung in a tree so a bear can't get to them.

"We can't stay here for hours," Boone says. "Let's try to get back to the platform between obstacles."

Which means backing up without getting knocked off. "Is taking that risk really any safer?"

He looks down at me, then over the obstacle course, only to go horribly still.

"What?" I track the direction of his gaze. "Can you see the Pandemonium?"

Nothing is coming from the tunnels, the sight of which is blocked by the pillars between us and the mountainside, so I only get glimpses with each swing. It's probably the blur of motion that hides the initial sparkle of red. But it takes Boone swearing again for me to realize that broken time is coming directly at us.

"Shit," Boone repeats. "Back one."

But I hesitate.

I've learned things in the past that are important—things that the Titans can't tell me in this timeline because I have to learn them for myself. So far, other than Hades' replica in his Lock, everything I've learned has been by witnessing it myself…in the past. As long as I can avoid resetting anything, wouldn't it be better if I went into the breach?

At the same time, we still need to sit down and talk with the Titans. Right this second is so inconvenient to be time traveling.

"Lyra." Boone grabs my arm and yanks me back.

What comes next happens fast. Because we can both tell that the crack in time is moving toward us faster than we're moving away.

Boone reacts, completely in charge. Moving me this way and that, spinning me around, setting me on a hammer so that I swing away from him, only to grab me as I come back by. And all of this is moving us backward through the hammers as fast as he can—away from time.

But it's almost as if that sparkling shard is chasing us. I know Boone sees it, too.

"Hopefully the Pandemonium don't like electrified water," I hear him say as he swings by.

"What?"

In response, he whistles—the signal for *get ready*.

I'm on a hammer by myself. When he whirls by on a different hammer, he suddenly grabs me by the hand. Our combined momentum swings my

legs out wildly. I'm not even a little bit surprised when he yells, "Brace!"
Then lets go.

I'm catapulted away from the obstacle course and out over the pool, dropping fast. But not fast enough.

In the next instant, a now-familiar shimmering light closes over my head—I never even saw the second break in time below me. Neither did Boone, apparently, because I see the shock on his face right before he spins away and the first shard of time swallows him up.

Then everything around me goes silent.

## 44

## A TICKING TIME BOMB

LYRA

Time drops me off right at Hades' feet this time, but I go tumbling to land on my ass on the docks of the River Styx.

"Damn, that's jarring." I rub at my backside where I landed a little too hard.

Hades grabs me by the arm to haul me to my feet and off the dock to stand at the side of the rocks.

There are way too many people jerking me around today.

"Hey—"

"You need to get out of here, Lyra. Now."

His grim urgency cuts through my irritation. "What—"

My surroundings finally sink in fully. Not the river with the swirling, glowing blue currents. Not the stars in the mountain cavern high overhead. Not Charon's pirate ship.

It's the *ships*. As in multiple. There are *dozens* lined up down the river, waiting their turn. And thousands, maybe even tens of thousands, of souls mill about on the shores, already landed.

"What happened?"

Hades doesn't answer for a long moment, too busy peering into the eyes of one after another soul. For most of them, he simply waves a hand, and they disappear. Sent to one part of the Underworld or another. But he pauses at one. "Confess," he demands.

Only because of what I am now—Queen of the Underworld—do I hear the soul speak, see his ghostly features move as though opening and closing his jaw and forming words with lips that no longer exist. And what he says is too horrible, too ugly.

When he's done confessing, Hades leans forward and whispers his judgment in the dead man's ear. The soul's mouth opens on a scream I don't hear because he disappears as well. To the bowels of the hells.

To Tartarus?

Is that asshole down there with me now? Locked in one of what I've estimated to be thousands of rooms off the tunnels, being given a punishment commensurate with his crimes. He'll suffer for eternity no matter where he ends up.

I know Hades will have given him a fair punishment.

Hades continues sending souls away, and I have a chance to study him. His clothes are more ancient-style robes with a hooded cloak thrown back over his shoulders. So, not current day. But when? Why the fuck is he doing this *outside* of the gates to the Underworld?

"You need to get out of here, Lyra," he snaps over his shoulder.

"Why? What happened?" I ask again, quieter.

He doesn't even look toward me. "It's been a long time. Things have happened here that you may not know of yet."

I scan his features and see…he's afraid for me.

I can't explain why he doesn't need to be. "You and your siblings trapped your parents in Tartarus and now rule Olympus. Is that what happened?"

It's rare to see Hades surprised, but from the way he freezes slightly before continuing with the souls, I know he is. "So you do know things."

I glance away. "I know more than I would like and sometimes less than I need."

"Cryptic," he mutters. Another soul disappears at a wave.

My huff of a laugh is entirely sarcasm. "As a god with many secrets, welcome to how it feels on the other side."

There's a sudden dull boom, and the ground under our feet shakes slightly, sending fine dust raining down from the rock ceiling high above. It makes a soft hissing sound as it hits us and the ground.

"What was that?" I ask.

Erebos has never done that when I've been there. It is a haven of beauty and peacefulness. No booming. No rocking.

"Get out of here," Hades snarls.

"Tell me why first."

"I can't do this and protect you, too. We're overrun."

My frown deepens. "Why are so many souls coming to you?"

He can't answer, too busy dealing with those souls.

The boat that Hades has been filtering through moves away from the dock, and another comes in. On its decks, I recognize a figure.

A true pirate.

Charon.

I tuck myself behind Hades, not wanting the ferryman of the dead to see me. In my future life, he never once indicated that he recognized me, and Charon, unlike Hades, has a tendency to offer me the truth. Sometimes more than I need. He would have said something if he'd met me before. I'm mostly sure of that.

"Hades?" I prompt. "Why so many souls?"

The kind of frustration that only Hades can show with a mere twitch of his mouth flits across his features. "My brothers and sisters have decided to fight over the Olympic throne."

My eyes flare wide. The Anaxian Wars. *That's* what I'm in the middle of? I don't say the words, but I do mouth them.

Hades finally looks at me more closely, just for a second, his sharp gaze taking in every nuance before he continues dealing with souls. "What do you know of it?"

I bite my lip. I shouldn't tell him anything. But…he also once said I told him to stop the wars, or deal with them, or something like that. The way he worded it wasn't entirely clear.

"The devastation my siblings are causing is wreaking havoc down here," he says. "Mortals are dying in droves. If there's something I can do, tell me now."

I can't. I can't do it.

Partly because the ending of the Anaxian Wars was the start of the Crucible Games. Trading one terrible thing for another doesn't seem like a solution.

Another boom ricochets through the massive chamber, so violent that a wave rushes through the waters, tossing all the lined-up boats around like they're toys, then coming straight for us.

Hades jerks me into his arms, curling around me protectively, and I'm sure he's going to stop the water. Except, the way I'm angled, I can see

Charon. On the deck of the ship, the ferryman drops to one knee, both hands coming up, and the waters calm.

"Wow." I breathe the word. I didn't know he controlled the Styx as well.

I don't move out of Hades' arms and behind him fast enough. Charon meets my gaze.

And I tense. Hard.

Charon knows all souls, as the first person to usher every single one to the Underworld, and the god never forgets. Mine included.

He knows me. When he meets future me, he knows, and he never said…

Another boom. Charon's hands are still up, so the river doesn't move at all. But an ominous series of rumbles groans overhead.

I drop my head back, searching the cavern high above, just as one last ear-splitting fracture cracks, and then it feels as though the entire ceiling caves in on us.

Hades covers me, so I can't see what he does, but I can hear it. The grinding of rock on rock growls like thunder. Dust rains down on us in a fine layer, but nothing hits. Hades is breathing hard when he grabs me by the shoulders. "I told you to get out of here!" he yells. I swear he wants to shake me, but he doesn't.

I look up to find the ceiling back in place.

"Damn it, Lyra. I can't do this—"

"I can help," I tell him. I can send the easier souls to their destinations, at least.

"No! I'll be too distracted if you stay. I'll worry—" He cuts himself off.

I know he means that. That he'd worry about me, despite the fact that at this point he's only met me a few brief times. Logic is finally overriding the sense of panic the milling souls and constant booms and danger here are generating. I can't show him my power as Queen of the Underworld. He won't understand why I can also do what he does.

"Where?" I ask. Where is safe?

"My room in Erebos." He glances at my lips, and I almost raise a hand to touch them. He knows. He can see that he, or someone, has given me a kiss that protects me down here. It remains on my lips to this day even though I don't need it anymore. He knows I can safely pass through all the nooks and crannies of the Underworld.

"I'll go—"

A howl sounds from just inside the gate.

No. Not a single howl. A *trio* of howls.

"They're overrunning the gate!" Charon shouts from the deck, pointing. "This isn't working. You have to end this."

Hades goes so still and pale. If he weren't immortal, I would worry death had claimed him. He closes his eyes, taking a deep breath. "Fuck," he mutters.

Then he's gone.

I stare at the space where he was—the empty space that the souls rush to fill, trying to push and shove their way to their afterlives.

"Go!" Charon yells from above me.

I meet his eyes again. Eyes with a thousand questions he doesn't have time to ask. Why didn't he ask them when he met me again ages from now? He gave me information Hades would have probably preferred he'd not given me then, but not a single hint that we'd met before.

I give him a single nod, then teleport to Hades' bedroom in Erebos. Our bedroom in the castle he's built in the Land of Shadows. The deathly quiet of the souls drops away for a different silence. It should be comforting, peaceful here.

Instead, it's just empty.

I wrap my arms around my waist, closing my eyes. Because I know what the King of the Underworld just chose to do.

"Hades," I whisper. "I'll wait for you this time."

If I can.

I have a feeling he's going to need me.

Almost immediately, there's an urgent knock at the door.

I rush over and swing it open to find Charon standing there.

He is a little different from the god I know in my current day, mostly because of his clothes—a dark tunic covered with leather across his chest and around his wrists and shins. He's definitely not the gruesome bag of bones most myths depict him as, but in this moment, the approachable guy with laughing eyes is nowhere to be seen.

He also has no problem reading the panic on my face. "Hades isn't dead," he rushes to say. "I'd feel it."

"But you don't know what he's doing?"

He pauses, looking at me closer, then shakes his head. "I wanted to make sure you made it here, so I got Hecate to spell me for a bit. I can't stay."

"Why?"

"I had a feeling he'd want you to be safe."

I snort a laugh. "Liar."

His scowl is so swift and harsh, and so not like the Charon I know, that it reminds me he doesn't know me in return.

Holding back a sigh, I give him a contrite smile. "I'm sure he would, but I'm guessing you're here to make sure that I came directly where Hades said to be and nowhere else."

The scowl lets up slowly. "Maybe," he finally admits.

He checks over his shoulder like he's being called back. There are purple shadows under his blue-green eyes. It takes a lot to make a god look haggard, and he's there. Tension rolls off him in waves.

I swallow. "Can you send Cerberus to him?"

Charon's frown is sharp. "There's no way for me to handle the souls on my own."

"Right." I glance away. So fucking tempting to offer my services. He's seen my face now, but when he meets past me in his future, knowing what she can do later—despite being human then—is going to be a big problem for him.

So I don't offer.

"Do *you* know what Hades is doing?" he asks, voice turning as sharp as his earlier frown.

I have a guess. "Not entirely."

"Why don't I believe you?"

What am I supposed to say to that? Nothing. *Nothing* is all I can do. I'm really not a fan of nothing.

"So you're the one." Charon says the words so softly, I almost miss them.

"What?"

His gaze on me is strangely assessing, curious. "He waits for you. In the water gardens."

The words reverberate through me, not only with shock but as if warmth consumes me in a rush. "He *told* you that?"

"No—" Charon suddenly straightens, cocking his head like he's listening to something far-off, and his shoulders adjust like he just took on a heavier load. "Hells. I have to go."

He disappears so fast, he leaves the door hanging open and the hall empty.

Abandoning me to a thousand new worries and waiting for Hades to return to me.

# 45

# PASS THE TEST OF TIME

### HADES

**N**umb.
The sensation has taken me over—my mind, my limbs, even my skin. The horror of what I just had to do... The only way to stop them was to shut down entirely and let rage consume me.

I haven't felt that in ages.

Not since I mastered my powers.

It felt...*right*. It felt—

I stop dead at the sight of someone in my bed, and it comes back to me finally that Lyra's here. She's been waiting for me, but I never thought it would be in my bed. If someone had asked me any time before this night how I'd feel about that...

But right now, after what I've done...

Fuck.

She should leave. Immediately.

Lyra should get as far from me as possible, to the farthest point in time from me that she can find. Hells, everyone should. She once told me I would be good. I would do the things that no one could but that needed to be done, using power that even I feared at the time. But I bet she didn't think that I'd do something like I did tonight.

But...I can't make her go. I don't want to.

Selfish as always.

So instead, I snap my fingers, instantly clean of the blood *I* spilled, wearing only a tunic to sleep in. Then I slide into the bed on the opposite side.

I don't touch her. Hells, this bed is big enough for Cerberus to sleep in between us comfortably.

"Do you want to talk about it?" Her soft, husky voice breaks the silence.

I tense, tight as a drawn bowstring, but stay facing away. "I don't need one more person calling me a monster today, Lyra."

"Why would I?"

"I leveled Olympus." I hear myself say it like I'm outside myself, my voice dead.

Like I feel inside.

My mother is buried alive in Tartarus with our father. After helping us all to escape his bowels, she still chose him. Olympus was the last remaining thing I had of her. That and… I glance down at my arm where my sleeping tattoos lie.

"Is that the worst consequence you can come up with? Being called a monster?" Lyra asks the question almost idly.

Is she fucking bored? I just did the worst thing I could, and she thinks I'm weak to hate it?

"Not now, Lyra."

I hear a rustle of the wool blanket, the material tugging a bit as she moves around. "I mean…were any mortals harmed?"

I'm not talking about this.

"What about immortals? Did you kill any?" Then she's musing aloud to herself. "I can think of a few I wouldn't mind seeing less of."

Which makes me twitch under the covers.

"Any world-ending, apocalyptic consequences?"

Fuck me. She's not going to shut up about this, is she? "No," I snarl, turning over to glare at her. "And I'm tired of this game."

She purses her lips, nodding like she's some kind of sage, wizened witch. "What I'm hearing is that whatever you did was the only way. If there was any other way to stop your siblings from sending more mortals to you before their time, you would have."

"Would I?" How would she know?

She looks back at me with eyes clear and trusting.

*You shouldn't trust me!* I want to yell it at her. Pound it into her until she believes me. Until she runs and never comes back.

"None of the truly worst consequences happened today," she points out. "So I don't know what you're whining about."

Fuck this.

I move with a violent kind of speed that makes her gasp, but only after I've already pinned her under me on the bed, gripping her hands back on either side of her face. "I told you. Enough."

She bucks against me with a glare. "What did you do? What makes you a monster?"

"Stop."

"What can be that bad?" She hurls the words at me.

"Stop it, Lyra." I give her a shake, my grip around her wrists tightening.

"Confess!" Her voice when she utters the word is not a roar to match her fierce expression, but like a song. Not one voice but legions. A choir raised in angelic music of such beauty even my eyes sting with tears.

It's the same as the voice I use when, as King of the Underworld, I demand the truth of a soul's actions in life so that they might be judged.

And I want to fight it, fight the influence of it.

But I can't.

I feel my face slacken, and my eyes go unseeing. I'm no longer in my room in Erebos but in some place inside my own mind that both exists and doesn't. A place where only the truth can be told. Must be told. I hear myself speak. "The Anaxian Wars are ended. I have wiped the last traces of my mother from the world. Olympus has fallen, and all that remains of Rhea is her rotting carcass in Tartarus."

Then Lyra is here in this foggy place in my mind with me, and I focus on her face as she listens. "What is your judgment, my queen?"

Through the fog, she slips her hands out of my grip to frame my face. Am I… Am I shaking? Fuck, I am. My whole body is as I wait for her words. Her punishment.

But when they come, they are as sweet as honey. "My judgment is that you were the *only* god protecting humanity when the rest of your siblings would have trampled over humans like giants clomping through anthills."

Words that absolve me. Words that forgive me. Words that understand me, even when I'm a monster. I still can't move, still float in this haze, but I feel the cool wetness as a tear slips down my cheek.

Lyra wipes it away with the pad of her thumb. "Your penance is to let go of your guilt, knowing that if there had been any other way, you would have found it."

It's like she punched straight through my ribs to my heart, but instead of ripping it out, she's pumping it for me, keeping me alive while she makes me face myself and what I've done. A guttural yell explodes up and out of me, and I struggle to choke it back down, to hold in my pain. But the haze lifts from my eyes, and she's here.

Lyra's still here with me.

Even knowing what I've done. What I'm capable of.

I collapse around her, pulling to one side so I don't crush her as I gather her up in my arms and bury my face in her hair…and heave with my cries.

Lyra runs her palm up and down my back in soothing circles and lets me work through my penance. She waits.

She waits for me.

And when I draw in a long, uneven breath and finally relax against her, going quiet, she whispers in my ear. "I could never think of you as a monster."

The last of my tension drains out of me in a huff. "Why? You don't even know me." Not really.

"I see you all the same, Hades."

What does she think she sees? "I've just told you that I destroyed Olympus. None could stop me. Do you think they didn't try?"

"I know they would have."

I pull back to glare down into her face. "That alone should have you running from this bed screaming. *Everyone* fears me. Can barely bring themselves to be in the same room. Even my parents feared me, or my father would not have swallowed me and my mother would not have let him."

She shakes her head. "Others fear what would happen if you were to lose control of your power or, perhaps worse, consciously decided to use it to the full extent that you can against them or the world."

"But you don't fear that?"

"No. And tonight is proof."

"Proof?" The word comes out on a scoff.

She gives me that stubborn, determined look of hers. "Yes, proof. You didn't lose control of your power."

"But I did. I let the rage take me."

She shakes her head. "Exactly. You *let* it. The rage didn't control you. There's a difference."

"You didn't *see*, Lyra."

"I didn't have to."

I want to walk away. Leave her in this bed and not come back until she disappears again. But I can't. Because my heart is screaming at me to keep her. To never let her go. Because—and maybe this scares me the most—she's right about the rage, but only partially. My control over it, limiting what I destroyed to Olympus alone—it came from picturing her face. From holding her image in my mind. Not wanting her to look at me with disgust.

And that scares the ever-loving shit out of me.

How, in the course of only a few short encounters across the span of my long life, has she become this…important…to me?

"You're a fool." I don't know if I'm saying that to her…or myself.

"Maybe I am," she murmurs.

I need to make her go. Make her leave me. Never come back. This is getting out of hand…dangerous.

"There are visions of me," I tell her. "A prophecy from long ago. I do *terrible* things. You should have seen their faces today…" My throat tightens so much around those words that I trail off, unable to utter more.

She looks me in the eyes. "Have you done those things yet?"

Confusion sneaks through my self-directed anger. "No, but—"

"Then stop serving penance. Stop feeling guilty for things you have never done."

I grunt as those words hit hard, and yet… No. My grandfather believed this prophecy enough to try to kill me. I am doomed. I should not doom her with me. "What if I do—"

"The Hades I know doesn't sit back and wait. He plans. He schemes. He prepares. Can you do that?"

Just like that, the heaviness that has threatened to drag me to the depths of my own hells, to bury me alive there with my evil parents, lifts. Like sunlight peeking over mountains to chase away the darkness. I stare at her, at her beautiful, stubborn face. "Do you believe I can do that? With my own fate?"

Her smile is so assured it hurts and yet lessens the ache inside me. "Yes."

That simple.

She believes this much that I can master my own fate. The same way she told me that I'd master my powers.

And I did.

I did that.

Heavens, this woman… My torment, my hells, and my salvation are all wrapped up in one person who abandons me over and over and yet lifts me up every time she sees me.

With a shaking hand, I trace the lines and curves of her face, her skin buttery soft under my touch. "You're the only person who has dared to get this close to me. I knew you'd wait for me, if you could, but expected you to be curled up on the floor in the corner with a blanket, as far from me as you could get, and instead you're in my bed…and now in my arms. Yet you don't tremble with fear. Even after I tell you what I did. How can that be?"

Her smile is soft. "I'm here to *sleep*," she points out. "But I think that fear has never been in me when it comes to you."

I want to keep her. I want her to be…

Mine.

The word flares to life inside me, but I douse it just as quickly. Because she can't stay. Because even if she could, I shouldn't let her.

"Have you ever met someone and felt as if you've known them your entire life?" I ask her. "Even though it had only been minutes or hours or days?"

The question surprises her. I can see it in the flare of her eyes. Me too, if I'm honest.

"Once," she says slowly.

"It is a strange, uncomfortable sensation," I say, staring right at the source of that discomfort. "I don't know that I care for it."

"Would it help if I told you that one day you and I will be…friends?"

"Friends?" I taste that word. "I don't have friends."

"You have Charon and Cerberus."

I hum a doubtful sound as I trail my gaze over her face while I consider her as a friend. A mere friend. No. My soul rejects that. It's not enough. "Now, if you told me that we were going to be lovers, *that* is something I would have an easier time believing."

I swear she softens underneath me, so damn trusting in my arms that it hurts…and fascinates.

I trace my fingers from her temple to her jaw. "I wonder… What would it be like to taste you?"

Just a kiss.

A simple kiss.

Only one, and then I'll send her out of this bed and far away from me forever.

I brush my thumb over her lower lip, watching her reaction. As natural as breathing, she lifts one hand and presses it against my chest, then gives a little whimper in the back of her throat. Can she feel how fast my heart is beating?

"Are you a siren?" I whisper. "To bewitch me so easily?"

An emotion passes over her features, too fleeting for me to catch it. Sadness, maybe, or a terrible knowledge. What does she know that I don't?

Can I draw it out of her lips with a touch?

"Lyra." Her name is like a prayer.

Like a confession—

I stiffen, seeing not her features but the memory of a single word uttered by lips I was just about to kiss. My whole body goes cold, and I narrow my eyes as her face comes back into focus. "Confess." I whisper that word.

Unmistakable fear flares across her features. "What?"

"You used my power over a soul's truth." I tighten the grip I still have on one of her wrists. "My. Fucking. Power. You made me confess." I clench my jaw so hard, trying to hold on to the fury burning through me like a flash fire, that a muscle jumps at the hinge of it. "How is that possible?"

She stares back at me like an injured fawn facing a ravenous lion, the pulse in her wrist hammering against her skin. "I can't tell you that."

"Did you *take* the power from me?" I demand, though quietly, in the way those who know me well know to fear. "Is that what you do? Take powers that aren't yours? I thought you had power over time, but to have both that and a power over souls…" I shake my head. "Impossible."

She swallows hard, the sound audible in the dead-quiet room. "I can't tell you anything, except that I don't take it from you. I would never do that."

"So I *give* it to you?" I scoff.

"I can't tell you—"

I'm off the bed, prowling back and forth at the foot, because I have to bleed off the rage somehow. I have to know. If I don't and she leaves, I'll drive myself wild trying to figure it out and not having answers. I want to trust her. I need to. But there's only one way.

I go still. Utterly still. "Forgive me, my star, but needs must..."

Then I whisper a single word, this time imbuing it with power. A word that sounds like choir song. A command her soul cannot ignore. "Confess."

Immediately, her face slackens, and her eyes turn cloudy as she's pulled into the haze of her own mind, to the fog where only the truth is clear.

But she fights me.

I can sense it through the control I have over her. Fuck, she fights me so hard. I've never felt anything like it.

But I'm so much stronger. I will her to accept the command. Accept it and tell me the truth—

"I love you," she says in a soft, sweet voice that is almost dreamy.

The truth.

I stumble back like she hit me.

"No matter when, no matter how, I love you. I love everything about you—the way you care, the way you fight, the way you make me laugh with a dark sense of humor that matches my own, your strength, the way you kiss and do a whole lot of other things, even the way you keep secrets for my own good. But especially the way you love."

The terror that consumes me with every word she utters is like nothing I've ever experienced, even as part of me roars with triumph at the same time. But my fear sweeps away the happiness like a lava flow, not just burying it but obliterating it. It's too much. Her love. She's too precious.

She deserves better than me.

I can't love her back. I won't.

"I will always love you, Hades," she says. Each word is an arrow to my heart. "Forever, no matter what you—"

That's when she disappears, cutting off the sounds of the confession still tumbling out of her mouth.

# 46

# A TIME TO KILL

## LYRA

I cut off my confession to Hades on a yelp as the horribly familiar glassy water rushes up at me. Again.

Because broken time deposits me right where it picked me up before. Over the fucking electrified water.

I have just enough time to yelp and flail before something—or someone—tackles me from the air.

We hit the hard ground and roll. After a stunned second, we both get to our feet to stand beside the pool of the training course. Me…and Cronos.

I thought he ran from the Pandemonium with Rhea and Persephone? Did he come back? We stare at each other with wide eyes, and I'm breathing hard from the scare of being dropped over that damned water out of nowhere.

"We need to get out of—" His gaze jerks up over my head.

I don't even have to look. "You've got to be kidding me—"

The sound of my own words gets cut off in the silence of another broken shard of time. Am I some kind of time magnet? What the hells is happening?

At least I'm not falling when it drops me off in a rocky area surrounded by big boulders. Me only. Not Cronos.

These cracks of time really do seem to be selecting the who, what, when, and where.

"That would've hurt to fall on," I mutter to myself as I look around, trying to get my bearings.

As I round one of the boulders, I pull up short, then tuck myself back behind the rock, where I can see but hopefully not be seen.

Not too far away is a small boy with hair so black it gleams in the sunlight sitting on a rocky beach. He's holding a little creature that wriggles in his hands, and he can't be more than three years old, based on the size of him.

Hades.

Seriously, it's almost like the broken fissures of time have an agenda. At this rate, I'm surprised he wasn't in the room when I took his axe.

I don't move closer. Being seen again is a particularly bad idea, although he mentioned seeing me on a beach. I glance up the hillside to the structure at the top—the same building where I saw the whole family together.

Is this that moment? That beach?

A childish giggle floats across the sea air, brought to me by the gentle breeze, and I smile because even as a child Hades' giggles are reserved. It's also clear that whatever he's holding is delighting him.

The beaches are empty, other than him and me, so I sit down on a flat rock, mostly hidden by the larger boulder, and draw my knees to my chest while I just watch and wait. I used to do this in San Francisco. Go to a spot along the Pacific coast that was lonely for lack of human company, sit, and stare out at the ocean. One of the few places where I felt safe or peaceful. At home, though, the breeze was chilly, coming off the colder water. Here, it's near perfect. I tip my face up to the sunlight, soaking in its warmth.

"No!"

The shout has me snapping my eyes open to find little Hades on his feet. He's turned slightly sideways now, and I get a better view of whatever is in his hand. An octopus, I think, based on the tentacles that drape out of his fingers. The creature turns black, even as I watch, and Hades is crying something in a language I don't know, but just like every time I've visited his past, I understand him anyway. Some power of the gods, I guess.

I know what he's saying. "It's dead. It's dead. I killed it. I'm a monster."

Small shoulders are racked with sobs that I can feel from here, each an arrow to the heart. Then, beyond where he is, the sea suddenly and violently rises and reaches for him like a giant, translucent fist.

Self-preservation abandons me, and there's only one thought in my head—*get to Hades*. I run so fast that the world blurs around me, and then

I'm scooping him up. If I had both my axes, I'd use them now, crossing them at the hilts to create the force that blasts things away from me. But I only have one, so I do the only thing I can think of and jerk around, placing my back to the water and bracing for the crash of the giant wave to slam into us.

Only it doesn't come.

After a second, I jerk around to find a man I'm not familiar with standing between us and the angry ocean, his arms raised high, bare back rippling with muscles. "I will not let you harm him, Father."

The water, as tall as a three-story building at this point, falls straight down with an enormous splash, and the Titan between us and the sea holds it at bay again as it rushes around us, touching us only with a fine, salty mist. When the water recedes, a man with white hair and a time-aged face stands on a rock outcropping exposed by the receding surf.

"Open your mind, Oceanus," he calls. Not a boom, not a yell, but a plea. "Let me show you."

Oceanus? I jerk my gaze to the Titan, studying him. *This* is the traitor who abandoned Tethys in Tartarus, who refused to fight as the gods imprisoned his own family?

The two stare at each other, the water turning more and more calm between them. And then the older man—he must be Uranus, the Primordial father of creation and the Titans—sags, his shoulders dropping, although I can't tell if it's in relief or sadness. "Don't you see," he calls to his son. "We have no choice."

For his part, Oceanus turns slowly to look not at me but at Hades. The sadness written across his features is like a story I can read without words. Whatever his father showed him, he believes it. "Whoever you are, you have no part in this," he says to me. "Set the child on the ground and leave now."

Cheeks wet with tears and ocean spray, little Hades buries his face into my neck on a whimper, and I tighten my grip around him. "I will never let you harm him."

Neither Primordial nor Titan hesitates, both raising their hands. "You made your choice, woman," Uranus says. He even sounds sad about it.

As I back up slowly, struggling not to trip on the rocks, the only thing I can think to do is try to run, but these are a Primordial and a Titan. Even at goddess speed, I doubt I'll be faster.

The water, when it comes at me, rushes so wild and hard I don't even have time to take more than a few steps. For the second time, I turn my back to take the brunt of the impact and pray I can hang on to Hades in the violent torrent.

Also for the second time, nothing happens.

Instead of the roar of ocean spray, the silence is almost obliterating. Did another shard of time take me away?

"No hurt you," Hades says in his small voice.

I look down at him, his eyes like sharpened steel, and then beyond him, and gasp. He has erected a covering of rock all around us. Black and glassy—obsidian.

My jaw drops as I stare at the child. Even this young, he can do this much.

Outside, through the translucent rock, I can see when the water recedes in a rush, like they're cocking it back to shoot again with better aim. But Hades plays his fingers over the obsidian, which shatters, turning into dagger-sharp shards at his silent will that hover in the air. I don't have to ask to know what he plans to do next—embed those jagged daggers into his uncle and grandfather. Before he can, something runs at us from the side in a blur of speed. It shoots between us and them.

The deadly daggers drop, and one embeds itself into Hades' forehead right at his hairline. He screams before that shard and all the rest abruptly dissolve into nothing.

But the obsidian already did its damage. Golden ichor gushes out of the wound.

I put my hand over it. "Shouldn't you be healing?"

Which is when it occurs to me where the injured spot is. Right where the streak of pale hair is for future Hades.

Zeus didn't do that to him?

Pushing my blood-soaked hand away, Hades points with a childish smile at a younger-looking Cronos, who stands between us and death. "Dada!" Utter trust shines in the child's eyes. He thinks we're safe now.

Lightning lifts from Cronos' clothes and his hair as if his entire being is charged. "I will not make my son a killer this young, but if you will not give this up, Father, then you leave me no choice but to do it for him."

For a split second, it's almost like Uranus shrinks, changing from the Primordial he is—one of the original sources of life and power and death—to something more human and frailer and broken. That lasts only the single beat of a hummingbird's wings before his features harden. "I showed you what he will do to the world if you let him live. Do not make me go through you."

"Do not do this," Cronos whispers harshly.

The depth of the Titan's despair and determination is like a living thing—a glacier of ice growing colder, gathering height and weight, crushing and destroying all in its wake.

For the tiniest second, I think Uranus might soften, but then his silver eyes—eyes just like Hades'—sharpen.

"Forgive me, Mother." Cronos' whisper is broken.

In the next blink, the Titan shoots across the water to where his father stands, so fast I don't even see him move. As he produces an obsidian scythe out of thin air, so like the weapons Hades just made, I vaguely hear Oceanus shout to stop him. But Cronos castrates his father and then slices through his gut, spilling his intestines and blood and semen into the ocean waves.

Then Cronos holds the blade out from his side like he can't stand to touch it. After a sickening second, he drops it into the now-still waters—like the ocean itself just died—and the Titan yells to the skies his rage and devastation.

Oceanus stares with a slackened jaw, turning a sickly shade before, while his brother is distracted, he slowly turns a gaze filled with blame and hatred on Hades. Once more, he raises his hands to wipe us out.

Before I can yell, Cronos rounds on Oceanus. "The scythe is the god killer, brother."

Holy shit. There's a weapon that kills gods? Primordials, too, apparently.

"If you do not want to meet the same fate," Cronos says, "I suggest you remove yourself from my sight. If I ever see you again, if you ever even think to come near my child, I shall do the same to you."

A stark shiver works its way down my spine and out to my extremities, and Hades pats my shoulder with a small hand, like he could feel it.

Cronos means it. Every single word.

Oceanus must see this, because after an excruciating moment in which the two brothers lock eyes, saying everything with a mere look, he disappears. And then, faster than even my goddess eyes can track,

Cronos is standing before me. Without a word, he takes Hades from my arms.

The boy goes eagerly but then seems to remember the moment earlier with the octopus, his bottom lip quivering. "Dada, I killed it."

And then they're gone, too, and I'm alone on the beach.

The sea gently washes up over my feet, and I look down only to gasp and stumble back. Because the waters are golden with the blood of Uranus.

Uranus, who predicted that Hades would do something terrible. Did the Primordial have the same vision that was given to Rima during the Crucible? Did he see Hades burning down the world? Destroying everything? A prophecy so powerful it would make a grandfather try to destroy his own grandson as a child.

What did I do? I just came from telling Hades that he would never do that.

But what if I was wrong? What if he does have that in him? My god of death has more secrets than stars in the sky. If I'm going to discover them all, I need to get back to him. I need to escape Tartarus.

I don't know how long I am here, backing up from the water a step at a time as the bloody tide rises higher and higher. I can't make myself care.

Not after what I just saw.

A father defending his son.

The gods were glamoured. The Titans are innocent. And Cronos has always loved his children.

*What kind of world is this?*

I should leave. Find my way back to the present. Except I know from past experience that I could be stuck here longer. What, exactly, I'm supposed to do if I'm stuck here for days—or years, like Iapetus once was—I don't know. Learn to sleep in trees, I guess. I may be able to understand and speak all the languages, but I have no money or goods. So basically, yeah, being stuck this far back in time, I'm screwed.

I don't need training to unseal the Locks. I need…history and ancient cultures lessons.

*You're a thief. Act like it, Lyra.*

I lift my gaze from the horizon and glance around me. I'll need to steal clothes that fit in here and find a place to hole up. It's not a great plan, but it's a plan.

I've made it about halfway up the beach when a sound like a burbling stream reaches my ears over the rhythmic roll of the waves, and I turn.

And stare.

Because the ocean is…*frothing*.

There's no other word for it.

The water churns gold and white above the blues of the Mediterranean. It's not the waves. This isn't natural. And I'm stuck out here on this damned beach like a sucker.

# 47

# EVERY BIRTH IS A NEW CHAPTER IN THE BOOK OF TIME

### LYRA

Checking over my shoulder frequently, I hurry across the last of the rocks to the safety of the larger boulder I hid behind before and stop there, peeking around. As soon as things calm down, I'll go somewhere safer to hide.

But the disturbance doesn't calm. It grows.

The waters bubble up higher and higher, reminding me of videos I've seen of a broken water pipe. But the water is still gold, stained with the father of the universe's blood and guts.

Then, with the force of a geyser, water explodes hundreds of feet into the air.

I duck down, throwing my arms over my head, ready to be scalded to death. But the water never hits me. I can still hear the violence of it, though, a mix between the sounds of steam, white-water rapids, and a dull roar.

Carefully, I peek back up to see the explosion is not frozen, exactly—the water is still moving upward and out, forming something like an umbrella, or...not an umbrella...a platform.

On the top of it, I can see the figure of a person.

It can't be Uranus, can it? Wouldn't he still exist in my present day if he'd survived? He died here. He must have died here, or the world would still know him.

The waters start to lower almost gently as the sun on the horizon dips and backlights the figure atop the fountain.

A woman.

Even thieves are taught the history of our gods. My memory finally kicks in—something that should have happened much sooner. I blame shock.

I *know* who this is.

Everyone knows her origin story.

Aphrodite.

Rather than lowering her into the waters, the gurgling platform on which she stands leans out and gently deposits her on the rocky beach, then eases away, almost as if it's slinking off in sorrow, leaving her there alone.

She stands perfectly still in all her natural glory, the most beautiful figure I've ever seen. And I've seen her up close.

She looks around almost dazed as if she's not quite sure where she is, and perhaps she's *not* sure. After all, babies cry as soon as they leave their mother's womb. It must be startling to come into the world not knowing anything about it other than the fact that it's different from where you have just been.

She takes a single, wobbly step, and almost like that movement knocks her out of her shock, she cries out a single word, which even I don't understand. Then she falls to her knees, seemingly uncaring about the rocks...and sobs.

She covers her face with her hands, rocking back and forth.

I have seen devastation like that. I've felt it.

Everything inside me cries out for her and pressures me to go to her. No matter how it happened, Aphrodite is my friend.

I only take one step around the rock toward her before Cronos suddenly shows up. He's not alone this time. Rhea, Iapetus, and Phoebe are with him.

"How is this possible?" I think I hear Rhea ask. Her voice is sweet, even this long ago, drifting to me on the winds.

I tuck back behind my rock and watch as they scoop up the brand-new goddess, born of the ichor blood and semen of their murdered father.

Though wouldn't that make her a Titaness rather than a goddess?

Iapetus scoops her up, Aphrodite still crying, and follows Cronos off the beach. Rhea puts her hand on her husband's arm, leaning into him.

And the winds stop in that moment, so I am able to catch her words. "We must bind her powers. She can't be allowed to finish what your father wanted to do to Hades."

When the Titans are gone, I slump to the ground, leaning against the rock and thinking through all I just witnessed.

Poor Aphrodite.

She feels emotions deeply. She cares about mortals' experiences of this life. She truly is the embodiment of love, even if she thinks of that power as weak. It's not. Apparently, her weakness isn't love. Her weakness is whatever they did to her.

But I can't blame them for that, either. Not after I saw a grandfather try to kill his innocent grandson.

I barely even notice when time returns me to Tartarus.

I just know that one second, I'm leaning against the boulder on the beach, and the next, I'm leaning against the pillar of the earth close to the obstacle course.

Cronos is here still, and Rhea is, too, now.

Looking at me like I'm a rabid dog that might turn and bite at any moment.

"The Pandemonium?" I ask.

Rhea shakes her head. "It's been days now."

Days?

Actually, that doesn't matter. Not after what I've witnessed.

In a rush, I'm across the stone floor to throw my arms around Cronos, burying my face in his chest. "You always loved your children," I whisper. "I'm sorry for what they were made to do to you."

I can feel the tension abandon him as he lets out a deep breath. Then, slowly, gently, his arms come around me, and he rests his chin on top of my head.

"She knows," I hear Rhea say from nearby.

And feel Cronos nod, then hear his whisper. "Things are going to be different."

## 48

# THE TRUE LABYRINTH DOWN HERE

### LYRA

Boone is still gone.

It's a truth that snags at me like the bare limbs of trees reaching for lost souls in a darkened winter wood.

The worst part is, there's nothing I can do but wait.

My internal thoughts must come out externally, because Iapetus suddenly says, "What was that, Lyra?"

I can't see him because of the blindfold over my eyes, but I tilt my head in his direction. Theia, Hyperion, and Koios have all been taking this time to help me memorize the paths and doors through the myriad tunnels carved throughout the rock prison of Tartarus. Tunnels that they apparently expanded on themselves, first while trying to escape, and later to hide from the Pandemonium. Which is also why they are helping me memorize everything—safety for when the Pandemonium come, so I have places to hide no matter where I am. Also, apparently, so I don't get lost if I have to run.

And, for whatever reason, Iapetus decided that he should be the one to test what I've learned.

He and I are in a better place than we were, after what I saw in the past, but I'm still pissed at him for dumping me down that Lock. "What was what?" I ask him.

"That noise you just made."

I guess I did make that out loud. "Just me thinking."

"And thinking requires noise?" he prods.

I turn my head in the direction of his voice. "*You* can feel free to think out loud less."

A laugh turned into a cough sounds behind us. Hyperion, I think. The other three, plus Cronos, all joined us to observe this test.

"Keep going," Iapetus grouses.

"You wanted to talk, not me." I keep walking, trailing my fingertips along the roughly carved tunnel walls, counting turns and doors.

Unfortunately, that doesn't shut him up. "I just am curious why you do that. The talking."

"And the humming," Theia tacks on.

Oh hells. Have I been humming? I swallow. I've been trying so hard not to.

As far as I can tell, the reason she, Koios, and Hyperion all are my teachers for this is because they all glow in different ways. They light the way through, and bringing multiple is a contingency if we have to split up.

I tap my finger against the handle of my axe strapped to my leg. "It relaxes me."

"So it's a tell." Iapetus is still harping.

"Yes."

He makes an annoyed sound at the back of his throat, and I smile, because making him annoyed is quickly becoming a favorite pastime. Immature? Yes. Satisfying? Very.

He makes the noise again, probably thanks to my smile. "So why don't you stop yourself—"

"Shut up, Iapetus," Theia and Hyperion say in unison. As usual, Koios stays quiet.

I don't join them. The thing is, he's right. I really need to stop.

"I was just curious," Iapetus grumbles.

The way he says that snags at my ears. I pause to lower my blindfold and blink in the glows coming off the Titans. The pinks and purples and oranges of Hyperion's sunrise blend with the greens and purples of Koios' northern lights, brighter in the total blackness of the tunnel. Theia has her fists closed around the light that comes from her hands.

I study Iapetus' face in the twinkling and blink. Am I reading him right? He's not being an asshole about this. "Wait. Have I made noises in the times I've been down here before this?"

The way he glances to Cronos, who shrugs, tells me the answer even before he says, "It's new."

Ah. I look down to my feet. A coping mechanism from the effects of my curse, maybe? Zeus and I really need to have a chat when I get out of here. I look back up. "It just comes out when my brain is working through things." Or when I'm nervous.

For once, Iapetus doesn't grumble or make a snarky comment. He just nods. Then gently pulls my blindfold back into place. "Where are we?"

That's easy. The groans coming from just ahead tell me exactly where.

"Two more doors down is Tantalus." The man who served his own son as a meal to the gods. His punishment is eternity without ever feeling satisfied by any meal. I think he got off easy. I would have given him much more pain—something like what Prometheus got for sharing fire with humanity. The whole eagle-eating-his-liver-every-day thing. "Then the next left takes us down the loop back to one of the exits to the pillars."

"Good," he says.

I very much ignore the feeling of pride trying to puff up inside me at the single word from the critical Titan.

"Keep going."

I force myself to move, hand trailing along the way, and we've already turned down the tunnel to the pillars when Theia suddenly gives a little chuckle. "Do you remember how Koios' and Pheobe's daughter, Asteria, used to stick her tongue out when she was thinking, and it would make her snort every time she breathed out?"

Theia doesn't tend to make conversation, as she's usually in a hurry to get back to Tethys, who doesn't like to have her sister out of her sight. The frail Titaness only seems at ease with Theia nearby. So Theia tends to rush these lessons.

"I think Koios actually smiled," she says a second later.

"She was...precious," Koios says in his even cadence.

Iapetus chuckles. "She was like the cutest little *piggy*. Snorting and snuffling."

"Are you calling my child a pig?" Koios snaps. No more smile, I guess.

"*Theia* brought it up," Iapetus insists. There's a rustle of clothing. I think he might be pointing at the Titaness.

A smack sounds close enough that I'm pretty sure she thumped him in the forehead. "But I didn't call her a pig," she says.

I duck my head to hide another smile. The second time in a few minutes. It feels weird on my face, but they sound like what I always pictured a family sounding like. And the thing is, I'm learning that this is how they always sound—like a squabbling, teasing, affectionate family.

The thieves were similar in some ways. Obviously, many made friends or at least allies within our ranks, but there was always a wedge of competition driven between us. And of course, thanks to my curse, I was always only looking in from the outside at moments like these.

*But now it doesn't feel like I'm on the outside. Even though I should be.*
I make a face at that thought.

Cronos clears his throat. "You can ignore them," he says softly, closer than I realized he was. He's been oddly quiet this whole time. "Especially Iapetus. But eventually, you get used to…them…"

The way he trails off makes me want to stop and look at his face, but I keep going. "We've done this before?"

There's a short pause. "Not exactly like this."

Iapetus sighs. "Cronos is always very grumpy until you figure out that you can trust us."

"I'm not the only one," Cronos grumbles. "Iapetus, you—"

I run into something that knocks my blindfold wonky, letting me see that the something is Iapetus, who is glaring over my head at his brother. "Don't bring me into this," he says as he sets me back from him, hands steadying at my shoulders.

Theia snickers.

I must be more like the two Titans than I realized, because the warmth that sparks in my chest is something I don't know how to deal with. So what I say next comes out just as grumpy-sounding as they are…and maybe a little out of left field. "I'm finding all the glamouring around here distracting."

# 49

## THIS IS HARDER THAN IT LOOKS

LYRA

Which has all the Titans staring at me. "Glamour?" Cronos asks slowly. "What do you see?"

I frown. "Should I not be seeing a glamour?"

"It's important," Iapetus insists. "What?"

I point at a door covered in a shimmery veil. "That."

"What are you talking about?" The confusion in their expressions would be comical if they weren't all so serious.

I glance from face to face. "The door. There have been several. You didn't glamour those?"

They go from confused to grim. A small arc of burnished fire streaks over one of Iapetus' arms before disappearing. "What fucking—"

Cronos cuts him off. "What door?"

I swallow. They can't even see that a door is there? That's... That doesn't seem good. "Here." I trace the frame with my hands.

"Is there a marking on it?" Koios asks.

"No. You really can't see it?"

"We really can't," Theia says.

"Why would the gods do that to you? Why hide doors down here?"

Koios is the one to answer. "Someone doesn't want us to know what's inside."

I raise my eyebrows. "That seems...sketchy?"

"I'm not sure what 'sketchy' is," Cronos murmurs, staring at the wall where the door is. "But it doesn't seem good."

"Should I open it?" I reach for the handle.

The Titan grabs my arm and tugs me behind him. "No."

"What? Why?" I wave at the door. "If someone is hiding this, it's for a reason. We should find out—"

"We will." He doesn't let go of me. "But not you." The last part comes out stern and gruff, and it gets my back up.

I twist out of his grip. "Is this some kind of alpha male thing? Because if it is—"

"I'm not risking you."

The rest of my argument dies a sudden, silent death. Because while I know that he means they need me to get them out of Tartarus, there's something in his voice, in the slant of his mouth, that makes me feel like he…cares. About me.

"Oh." I try to shake that feeling off, because of course he doesn't really care. They may not be evil, but to them, all I am is a tool. "But I'm the only one who can see it."

"We can teach you how to use your power so you can remove the glamour, and then one of us will check it."

Given how that didn't work when I tried to remove Persephone's glamour, and also how badly my goddess lessons with Hades were going before I got stuck down here… "That could take a while."

"It'll also mean you can turn your power on and off."

"I think I do that already. I don't see them most of the time."

"But you'll want to consciously control it. When you figure that out, then you should turn it off most of the time. Using your powers, even small ones, can be a drain. You don't want it on all the time. And if it alters your vision, that can also be distracting," Theia says. "Do you see Zeus zapping everything he touches all over Olympus these days?" Theia smiles when I shake my head. "He had to learn to turn it off."

"He had to learn that one young," Iapetus mutters.

Cronos' grin flashes in the dim corridor, but it's gone just as quickly as he studies me. "Ready?"

I nod, trying not to look too eager. Maybe, finally, I can be good at something other than throwing my axe.

Two hours later, I'm ready to throw a goddess-size tantrum. We've tried everything, and the Titans have not been quiet, either, offering all sorts of suggestions—arguing with one another, mostly. Cronos started by having me try to remove the glamour from the door. It involves picking up the veil itself, sort of like gently removing a cobweb. All fingertips and delicacy.

Not my wheelhouse.

When that didn't work, he tried having me glamour something, thinking it would be easier to remove my own magic. I did figure out how to make a rock look like a tomato, but only to me. Weak at best. And even then, I couldn't pull the glamour off.

I'm also starting to see why they don't glamour much down here to make their lives more comfortable. My stomach is starting to turn sour.

"My turn now." Koios shoos Cronos out of his way to stand in front of me. "Close your eyes."

The first thing he's said the entire time they've been trying to teach me.

"Really?" I ask.

"Just do it."

I sigh but close my eyes.

"Now I want you to picture something in your mind. Some way to turn things on and off."

"Flint to strike and make fire is what I imagine," I hear Theia offer.

Iapetus makes a sound like a hum. "I think of a dam that can be lowered and raised, letting water flow or holding it back."

Right. Turned on and off. The first thing that comes to mind is a light switch.

"Got it in your mind?" Koios asks.

I nod.

"Turn it off. Then open your eyes."

I flick my imaginary switch down, and the lights go out in my imaginary room…and then I open my eyes. The door in the wall is gone.

Completely gone. Not even a hint that it exists, that the rock is anything but solid.

"Oh my gods."

"Did it work?" Cronos asks hesitantly, like he doesn't entirely want to know that this was another failure.

"It worked."

Cronos straightens, then glowers at Koios. "That's all it took?"

Koios shrugs. "Simple is always better."

Iapetus barks a laugh. "Something Cronos will never learn."

"You, either," Koios points out.

Iapetus snaps his mouth shut.

Then Koios nods at the door. "Now turn your power back on. See if you can remove the glamour."

I turn it on fine, the shimmer of magic over the door becoming visible again with a blink. But I still can't pull it away. "I'm sorry."

He offers me a rare smile. The first I've seen from him. "It's all right. That door has been hidden for who knows how long. You have time to work on it."

His mention of time strikes me as off. "No I don't. Not really. We want to get out of here."

Koios considers that. "We can always return here after we leave and find out what's hidden then."

There is that. But it's brought up something I've been considering these days of waiting as more and more time has passed. "If Boone doesn't return today, I think I should unseal Demeter's Lock tomorrow."

No more waiting. I've done this without Boone before.

The bell goes off.

Cronos has me by the wrist, running us at a pace that even my goddess speed is struggling to keep up with. Just as I'm about to warn him, he skids to a stop in front of a door we can apparently both see and bundles us inside, with the others right behind us.

Just as they slam the door shut, someone else—one of the other Titans out in the tunnels—screams.

# 50

# COURAGE

### LYRA

I stand on the stone bridge overlooking the dark abyss that is the entrance to each of the Locks of Tartarus. Of course the gods would test courage with a leap into an abyss. Although, why that's a test for Titans and gods, I don't know. We're fairly indestructible. But it seems like one more roadblock to escaping this place.

Persephone is standing beside me, looking down as well.

After the Pandemonium were loosed again, we spent the rest of yesterday and last night in the tiny, empty room we'd hidden in. I woke up drooling on Cronos' shoulder. Something he was nice enough not to point out. When Koios went out to check that all was clear, he never came back. So we waited more. Waited and discussed Demeter's Lock.

Finally, this evening, Rhea found us.

Koios had been touched. So had Crius. They didn't let me see either of them. Something about staying focused on my task.

The Lock I'm about to enter. Right now.

Persephone sighs, gaze trained on the darkness, and slips her hand into mine. I tense at the contact but don't pull away.

"I wish I could go with you," she says. "Help you."

"No." I shake my head, still awkward with the hand-holding. "I wouldn't wish this on anyone."

Her lips tip up slightly. "Even me, you mean."

"I didn't say that."

She gives me a squeeze. "I'm not worried. Like I said, we become friends eventually."

I slide her a glance. "Every time?"

Her nod is definitive. "Every single time."

"Even if Boone thinks I shouldn't?" Now I'm watching her even more closely.

The goddess of spring can't quite hide the shadows that shade her features. "He is…" She pauses, thinking. "An unknown."

I think she also whispers, "Always has been," to herself.

"It seems like most of this time around is unknown," I say.

She gives another nod, this one slower. "But I also know you. You won't judge me based on someone else's opinion. You'll decide for yourself." Her sunshine smile isn't entirely out of the clouds yet, though. "And you'll decide you like me."

"Boone told me…about how he saw you on scores in his past, before all this."

All the sunshine disappears, and she lets go of my hand. It feels colder in here, as if she was warming me up from the inside. To get me ready for what I'm about to do? Or just because it's Persephone? "He did?" She blinks a little. "What did he say?"

I shake my head. "You'll need to talk to him about that."

"I've tried."

"Try harder. He's not an unreasonable guy. He just…" I make a face. Because his frustration with Persephone might have everything to do with the fact that she messed up his scores. And possibly, given how hard he tried to track her down, that he was interested in her because of that. A thief who could get the drop on him is a rare thing, and she is beautiful.

Persephone sighs. "Right now, you should focus on getting out of the Lock alive."

She's right.

I glance toward the massive carved doors at the end of this bridge. The ones Cronos pulled me through not all that long ago, and yet it feels like forever. I picture Hades on the other side, trying to figure out how to get in or how to get me out. Except he's not standing there still. My guess is that he's somewhere topside, probably in Olympus, and that he is using every manipulative trick he has to force his brothers and sisters to each unseal their own Locks.

If Rima's vision from during the Crucible is connected to this at all—and let's all fucking hope it's not—then he's not going to like his siblings' answers. The only person I could see being on his side is Demeter. She'll be desperate to get Persephone out, too.

"You can do this." Persephone pats my back before stepping away to stand with the Titans—all except Koios and Crius, who are still recovering—who are behind me in a line as I stare down into the darkness, working up the guts to hurl myself into the pit.

Cronos comes to stand beside me next. He doesn't say anything for a moment. Then he clears his throat and holds out his palm. Resting there is a small, carved butterfly, I think made of white quartz. It reminds me so much of Hades' butterfly, the only tattoo of his that wanted to stay with him when he gave those to me as one of his gifts for the Crucible, that I can't help but smile at it.

Cronos takes it in both his hands and snaps it in half.

"Hey!" I startle. "What was that for?"

"Hades made this for me and gave it to me on the anniversary of my... father's death."

The way he hesitates over those last two words, I can tell he's uncomfortable with describing that event. I don't blame him, after seeing exactly how that went down and why.

"My son told me that some things, no matter if they are destined to face imminent doom, are too precious not to be protected."

"Then why would you break it?"

He takes one half and puts it in my hand, curling my fingers around the broken piece. I can feel the smoothness of the carving as well as the jagged edge of the break against my skin. Then he holds up his half. "When you find yourself questioning anything in there, especially what you have to do, hold on to this. It will feel the same no matter what is happening. It will ground you to reality. And when you get out, I'll put the pieces back together."

His face is so familiar—Hades' face, only older. Except now, even just in these last few days, it's taken on a different shape for me, different peaks and valleys, different lines, different expressions. What I see in his expression now is also new...and surprising.

"You don't want me to go through this," I murmur. The words remain just between him and me.

"No," he admits.

"Is there something you're not telling me? About this particular Lock?"

He considers that. "It took a while for you to figure out how to get through this one the first time."

In other words, I died and set off several resets. In the last few days, it's become abundantly clear that time has reset a lot more than I realized. "So…my bad attitude in the past has…"

"A self-fulfilling prophecy is no laughing matter," Cronos says, all gruff.

I don't have a comeback for that. Because ever since the Crucible, I've wondered…in relation to my own curse. I didn't have a chance to ask Zeus how he worded that curse before I ended up down here. He's not exactly on speaking terms with us at the moment. But it seems to me that the way I eventually formed friendships with Zai and Meike and the others, as well as the way I was able to fall in love with and be loved by Hades, means that maybe my curse wasn't entirely what I was led to believe.

I know it was real. That, I don't doubt. There were too many little things about how my life played out for it not to be real.

But what if I made it worse?

What if knowing about it at all affected my own reactions, perceptions, and expectations, and because of that, I somehow made it worse? Kind of the same way Chance being an asshole to all the thieves around him basically guaranteed that no matter how good his skills were, he would never make Master Thief. He only focused on the competition side of our way of life and not the side that required periodic partnerships or even, at the very least, the ability to charm his way out of a bad situation. I always kind of thought that he made things harder for himself.

Wouldn't it be ironic if the same had always been true of me and I just didn't see it?

Again with the goddess of irony.

Oh my gods. What if that ends up being me?

But no. I'm already the goddess of glamouring. So disappointing.

*Focus, Lyra.*

"Okay. So I need to go into this one believing I can and will get out of the Lock," I say slowly.

Cronos opens his mouth, closes it, and then, instead of answering, he tucks his piece of butterfly into a pocket. "We'll be waiting for you on the other side."

I half turn as he leaves me there to return to Rhea's side. Persephone gives me another forced, sunny smile. And I realize that all these grim faces aren't helping. Neither is standing here trying to bolster my courage.

Sometimes courage is simply taking the leap.

So I jump.

# 51

# DEMETER'S LOCK

### LYRA

"You have entered the Lock of Demeter."

I stare at Demeter. Like Hestia, she is dressed in flowing traditional Grecian clothing, not white but deep blue, setting off the goldenness of her being—sun-dipped beige skin, coppery wheat-colored hair woven into a golden laurel crown. I now know, from the Crucible and days after, that her eyes appear golden from a distance but have specks of green in them up close.

Goddess of agriculture, harvest, fertility, and earth—she truly is like the fields she blesses or curses on a whim.

Like her daughter, too, now that I think of it.

Although Persephone is more tones of pink and greens, like her flowers. And it suddenly hits me that she's up there waiting while I get to visit a version of her mother, who she hasn't seen in *technically* a hundred and fifty years, but in reality for her, so much longer, thanks to the time resets. After I open this Lock, will Persephone visit the spirit of her mother? Will she seek comfort from her the way I want to with Hades' copy?

When I say nothing, waiting for Demeter to get to the instruction parts of this game, the goddess tilts her head, eyes glinting. "You do not seem curious, human."

I shrug. "This is the third Lock. I have a better idea of what to expect now."

Demeter doesn't glitch like Hestia's copy would have. More like Hades' lifelike replica, she gives a nod of understanding. Why was Hestia's different? Because the real goddess is dead?

"In that case," Demeter says, "I won't delay. This Lock will test your genuine kindness."

She pauses. Again, I wait. I'm pretty sure they just made up the reasons behind the tests as an excuse to cover for their bloodthirsty need to watch someone die in these Locks.

"Think of clothing that you can run in," Demeter says, "and I'll make sure that's what you wear."

*Wait. What?* I thought I was going to be harvesting grain down here. Grain that never ends. I've been practicing with a sickle. Why will I be running?

Demeter waves her hand, and the Lock's magic rips everything that is goddess from my bones, from my flesh, and from my soul. "Damn, that doesn't get easier," I mutter through clenched teeth, then squeeze my eyes shut, try to picture running clothes, and ride it out until the sensation eases.

When I open my eyes, still tossing and turning, I'm once again on my knees—knees covered in soft, stretchy yoga pants that match with a sports bra, a close-fitting running shirt, and the running shoes on my feet, all in black. Hopefully that's good enough for whatever I need to be running through…or from.

From would be worse.

Slipping my piece of the butterfly in my pocket, I force myself to focus on the change in my surroundings. Instead of standing in the round rock room at the bottom of the Labyrinth, I am standing in a field of wheat.

Golden wheat.

The stalks, which are maybe four feet in height, wave in rolling patterns, following the blowing wind. As they bend and shiver, their heads tip under the weight of the grains and a shooshing sound follows the flow. The sun, happily bobbing in a perfect blue sky, is warm on my face even as there's a slight nip in the air.

A perfect day.

Okay…this is what I was told to expect.

With another wave of Demeter's hand, a simple wooden table appears before me, and on it is a cup formed of hardened clay and filled with a thick-looking purple-hued liquid.

"This," Demeter says, "is my personal recipe for Kykeon."

I vaguely remember the term, only because it's known to still be used during the Eleusinian Mysteries, rites that initiates into the cult of Demeter go through. Most of what happens during those mortal rites is secret. All outsiders know is that something is recited, something is revealed, and acts are performed. And Kykeon, a drink made of barley, honey, and sometimes wine, herbs, and even cheese, is a part of it. For those rites, at least, the concoction is supposed to have hallucinogenic properties.

"To unseal my Lock, you must make it through three stages of a test. At the start of each stage, you must drink. When you drink, you will..." I'm not a fan of her smile. "See things."

So, yes to the hallucinating. Great. Awesome. Love this.

"And the things you see, you must save."

Save?

More things that need saving. *I need saving*, I want to yell. *What about me?*

"Right. Three stages. Save the things I hallucinate," I say instead. "I think I've got it."

Doesn't sound terribly hard. Except for the running.

"In that case, drink and start your test," Demeter offers.

Down the hatch. I chug the thick concoction, which has a consistency somewhere between porridge and a fruit smoothie and tastes of red wine and honey and beer all at the same time.

On my last swallow, Demeter smiles again. "Now to face your own hatred."

I almost drop the cup. "Wait. What?" This time, I say it out loud.

"You usually can't take it," she says.

I stare at the goddess. Oh my gods. Like Hades' copy in his Lock, this one also remembers.

Demeter points at the wheat fields. "Start walking that way."

With that final instruction, she fades away.

"I can't take it? Really?" I call into the skies. "That's information that would have been handy before I drank."

"You didn't have a choice." Her words float to me on the breeze.

Hands on my hips, I glare around me. But in the back of my head, Cronos' voice overrides everything. *Focus* is what he'd be telling me if he were here with me.

So I take a deep breath and look around. My vision isn't doing anything wonky. I'm not swaying or dizzy. Has the hallucinogen kicked in or not? I've been drunk before, so I know how that feels. But I've never taken a drug that would alter my perception, so I'm not entirely sure what to expect.

I feel...fine. Normal.

And nothing shows up in front of me.

"I guess I start walking." So I move my feet.

The instant I step into the field itself, the wheat shoots up all around me, well over my head, so I can't see the pathway out. This reminds me a *lot* of the fields I had to run through for Artemis' Labor. Not a pleasant memory. With every step, I expect a hand to reach out and grab flags I no longer carry, to cause me pain or confusion or worse. Or maybe a dragon to set it all on fire. *That* would definitely make me run.

A shiver that I swear sounds like a whisper of words cascades through the fields, and I spin to look behind me. But nothing is there. Just me and the wheat and the wind. Damn, these fields are creepy.

My fingers brush against something long and hard strapped to my leg, and I look down and gasp.

My axe!

She didn't take it away? "That's probably bad," I mutter.

But I keep going. What I don't do is let myself hum. Maybe I'm finally getting a handle on that habit.

"Take her," a voice whispers across the wheat, blending into the winds and the shoosh of the stalks.

I jerk to a halt, looking around me. I am positive I heard that this time, but there's nothing here. So I tilt my head back to shout at the sky and the goddess controlling this Lock. "If voices are all you've got, what am I supposed to save?"

Out of nowhere, a hand strikes me, flat-palmed, across the face.

The impact is hard enough that I go sprawling, flattening the wheat, and the bent spikes of it dig into my side and stomach. Holding a hand to my now-stinging face, I sit up only to stare into the cold eyes of my mother.

This Labyrinth of Locks seems determined to shove that woman in my face.

"Don't disrespect this man," she says to me. Or more like whisper-hisses at me like she's trying to keep this fight between the two of us and not let someone overhear. "He's going to be your mentor."

Man? What man? I realize that there's a vague feel of others being with us, too. Felix, my mind supplies. And my father. Except neither of them is visible...but they are here at the same time. I can *feel* them.

I remember them.

Oh gods...I remember *this*.

The familiarity of the moment is hazy but still impossible to deny—a memory I can't quite recall the details of. More like impressions. I was only three when it happened. But it doesn't take a genius to know that I'm now reliving the day my parents "donated" my services to the Order of Thieves.

The day they gave me away.

My parents, who never loved me, even when I wasn't cursed, according to Cronos.

I forgot that my mother had slapped me that day, that she seemed so angry with me for crying. Even when I saw my parents' faces on TV while I was in the Crucible, my father boasting how they loved me—even then, I didn't remember that she'd been just as hateful to me as he had.

My mother.

That's who I have to save.

"My mother again? Really?" I'm talking to Demeter, who I assume is watching all this. "You goddesses are an unimaginative group so far."

"What are you doing?" Mom claps her hand over my mouth, looking all around us as though my words will bring the skies down on our heads. "Do *not* anger the gods."

She's truly afraid, so much that she's trembling visibly.

Then, removing her hand, she leans over me. I *know* she's a hallucination—my logical mind knows that is true—but her hand felt real enough, the same way the replica of Hades' kiss did, and now I get a whiff of her perfume. Cheap, flowery. I'd forgotten that scent until this moment. Her expression is stiff. It's not hate, but I don't think it's guilt, either. Just... impatience. "You'll like it here."

I squint at her, trying to remember exactly what happened that day. Is this true? For a mother to be this uncaring, curse or not, makes her a monster in my eyes. Worse than the kraken. Worse than sirens or the minotaur.

The more the burn of anger stokes inside me, the smaller I feel, as if I'm shrinking, becoming the three-year-old girl they abandoned all over again.

"This isn't real," I say to myself.

But my voice comes out high and wavering, like I'm crying.

A darkly animalistic growl rumbles out of the fields to my right, and my neck prickles as fear-fed adrenaline spikes my blood. That was definitely not part of the day she gave me away. There's something in these fields with us. Something hunting us.

Another growl—closer this time—and instinct kicks in hard.

I grab my mother's hand and run.

## 52

# SAVE THE ONE WHO DIDN'T LOVE ME ENOUGH

### LYRA

"What are you doing?" My mother tugs on my grip as I drag her behind me through the fields.

"Running," I lob at her over my shoulder and tighten my grip. I only just bite back a *Duh*.

Wheat whips at us as we run, and I know we're making too much noise. But so would whatever is hunting us through the field. Right?

I can't hear it.

"Why?" Mom is whining now.

That's why I can't hear. She starts to claw at my hand, trying to get me to let go, pulling against me and slowing us both down.

I tighten my grip and plow ahead, dragging her. "Because of the monster."

"Lyra, I know you don't want to go with the thieves, but it will be all right. They'll take care of you." The tone in her voice is a sour combination of impatience, pity, and irritation.

"What?" I ask. "Like you took care of me? You don't know what you're talking about."

I keep dragging her in my wake even as she tries to slow me down.

"Of course I took care of you." She's wheedling now.

Gods, holding on to her is like trying to hold on to a wriggling worm. A heavy one.

"This is not how I'm going to die. Not for *you*."

"Don't be so dramatic," she says. "Thieves don't kill their pledges."

I scoff. "Only because we're worth too much to them," I mutter darkly under my breath.

Another growl sounds across the tops of the wheat, and I jerk to a stop. Because that sounded like it was in front of us now.

"Lyra—"

"Be quiet."

She tugs harder. "Let me go."

The last word comes out just as a shadow looms. I turn to clap a hand over her mouth and throw my other arm around her to hold her still.

But she doesn't want to be still.

Whatever is after us, it's big. I can hear the thuds of its footfalls on the ground, the way the wheat cracks under its weight. I manage to hold my mother still and quiet until its footsteps recede.

Just when I think we're safe, my mother whimpers.

The beast coming for us roars just as she jerks out of my grasp and tries to run away from me. I manage to stick a foot out and trip her, knocking her to the ground. In a flash, I'm on top of her, but she's all flailing hands and kicking feet, trying to get away.

"Get off me!" she shouts. "I can't wait to be rid of you!"

I go stock-still at those words.

Poison-arrow-tipped words.

Words no child should hear from the person who is supposed to love them most, protect them from the world, cherish them beyond all else.

Those words sink deep and true and…gods…I can't do it.

I can't… I can't do it.

Another blast of a roar shatters the quiet that fell between us, and I shove off her. "Fine," I force out between painful gasps. "I don't need you, either."

The second she jumps to her feet and turns her back on me, I have my axe out. With a sickening sort of thunk, I bring the bottom of the handle down on her head, and she collapses in a heap, out cold. Luckily, she's a tiny, bony woman, and I manage to heave her onto my shoulders in a fireman's carry.

Feeling like death is breathing down my neck, I run. Or clomp along awkwardly as fast as I can go with extra weight that is trying to shift and bounce with every step.

"You useless excuse for a parent," I whisper between heaving breaths.

Another roar is practically on top of me, followed by the pounding of feet or hooves or whatever it has, so close I can feel the ground shake.

Fear grabs hold of me by the throat, threatening to cut off my air, and the instinct to save myself screams through me, urges me to dump the piece of shit I got in the parent lottery and run.

But I won't. Damn her.

I won't.

Without warning, I burst from the wheat field into an open pasture that apparently has already been plowed.

In an instant, the roaring and pounding stop, and my mother disappears. It's so abrupt, I stumble under the sudden shift of weight.

Bending over, I put my hands on my knees, breathing so hard. "Fuck me."

Which is, of course, when another table appears with another round of hallucinogen in a shot, this one green in color.

"I take it back," I say to the absent goddess. "Not fuck me. Fuck you."

Then I down the drink, which tastes like grass, and toss the cup to the ground with a wooden thud in the dirt. Wiping a sleeve across my mouth, I glare at the field. "What's next? Psychedelic clowns? Eating my own liver? Talking about my feelings?"

Maybe I'm escalating things…and giving the goddess ideas.

Ancient-looking stone walls sprout up out of the ground, bracketing me on either side and running straight ahead for what looks like miles. Meanwhile, at my back, a very modern, very large piece of farm equipment appears. Do the replicas of the deities down here gather modern-day knowledge from their real-life gods or goddesses or something?

I'm a city girl, so I'm not sure what the tractor-like thing is called. *Combine* comes to mind. All I know is that it's huge, with a spike-covered cylinder across the front. Whatever demonic force is in the driver's seat— which is empty behind the plexiglass screen—sets those spiked blades to spinning.

I back up warily, looking from side to side for a way out. *Any* way out. But the walls are too tall to scale and exactly as wide as the spinning farm blades.

The combine doesn't move forward. Not yet.

"Who am I saving now?" I mutter.

"What in the fires of all the hells are you doing here, Keres?" a grinding voice demands.

I feel myself hunch over at the sound of that familiar, bullying tone. "I had to fucking ask."

# 53
# SAVE THE ONE WHO MADE MY LIFE A HELL

### LYRA

Chance was the only pledge who didn't ignore me. A flashing of memories unfolds in my mind like a flip book. Chance stuffing me in a closet so I couldn't go on a score. Chance arguing with me over the money he earned from another score. Chance being such a nuisance in the communal showers that I started showering at the local YMCA. Chance telling every pledge in hearing distance that I was pathetically in love with Boone.

If it didn't involve me dying in here, I'm pretty sure I would leave his ass behind.

*No choice. So start saving.*

"Can you see that?" I point at the combine or whatever that thing is.

With a sneer, Chance glances over his shoulder, then back at me. "What kind of question is that?"

Which tells me nothing. "Yes or no. Do you see it?"

He crosses his arms, feet planted wide. "Of course I see it, Keres."

That will at least make it easier to get him to run from it, unlike my mother and the field monster. "It's about to try to kill us." I'm still backing up, keeping an eye on the machine and on him. I need him to follow me. If he dies in the first few seconds, then I'm screwed.

He doesn't budge. "Gods in Olympus, what delusional bullshit are you spouting now?"

On that final word, the combine starts rolling.

"Holy shit," he yelps.

But at least, with nowhere else to go, he takes off running. Unfortunately, he also gives me a terrific rugby-style shoulder as he sprints past. Hard enough that I end up slamming into the stone wall, and it's lucky I don't fall over completely, but it means I'm behind him now as we both run.

That thing chasing us down is going just fast enough that nothing less than a hard run is going to keep us ahead of it. And it becomes patently obvious that Chance is so terrified, he's lost all sense of reason. Instead of running in a straight line, he starts ping-ponging back and forth between the walls, and I can hear him vaguely mumbling something about finding a door in frantic bursts of words.

"There are no doors in this wall," I yell ahead at him.

He ignores me, still going back and forth between the walls. It's slowed him down enough for me to catch up.

"Follow me," I call as I dash past him.

Out of the side of my eye, I catch that not only does he *not* follow, but instead he decides to try to climb the wall, and the combine is bearing down fast.

"Damn him." I double back.

At least he got high enough that his feet will be above the blades when the combine gets to him. With the sounds of the engines and the blades turning getting louder and louder in my ears, I scramble up after him as fast as I can.

I can feel the vibration of the metal on the air and am bracing for the blades to strike me down even as I keep going. I just barely get clear, pulling my dangling foot up at the last second, knee to my chest so that it doesn't slice it off.

But the combine backs up several feet and stops to raise the level of the churning blades.

"Keep climbing," I yell at Chance, shoving at him from underneath.

"It doesn't want me," he yells back. "Obviously it's here for you."

I look up just in time for his thick, booted foot to crash into my face. And I fall.

Arms windmilling, I manage to keep my gaze glued to Chance's face and the way he offers me a grin that is a caricature of evil. I don't even have that far to fall, but suddenly I'm remembering the moment Boone fell off the tower during Hephaestus' Labor. The way he dropped to his death.

Is it my turn?

I hit the tilled earth in a way that knocks the wind from me, but not nearly as much as it would have if the ground wasn't already churned up and softened. I jerk my head back and upside down to look for the combine.

Maybe the blades are locked into place before the machine can roll forward or something, but instead of bringing them down on top of me, the machine comes straight at me. I have only enough time to roll over, out of the way of the tank-like tracks that it has instead of wheels, and cover my head with my arms as it drives over.

The thing doesn't drive entirely past me before it stops and then backs up.

But I'd rather be on the back side of it than the front, so I start crawling as fast as I can, elbows and knees flying until I manage to get out from under it. I don't even remember thinking I should get to my feet before I'm up and wheeling to face it as it backs up at me.

I sprint to the side and the gap between the body of the vehicle and the wall. Thanks to the wider spinning bit, there's plenty of room for me not to get pinned between it and the rock wall. I run for the ladder that leads up into the cab.

The thing gives a shudder as I climb up the rungs, like it's not sure how to get me off. It really must be possessed, too, because it's trying to knock Chance off the wall with the blades, turning slightly so that it's whacking into the wall, and his foot slips so that he's dangling by both hands, screaming for his life.

When I try the handle to the door of the cab, it's locked. Immediately, I have my axe out and use the butt of it to break the window. I have to waste an extra few seconds to clear the glass as the machine jerks underneath me.

I finally get into the cab and start chopping with the pointy end this time. As it lurches and trembles, revving its engine like it's screaming in pain, I hack at every control I can see, every lever, every wire, and I don't stop until the combine gives a great, juddering shudder and a groan of defeat.

Then it stops and everything goes quiet.

"What in the name of Hades was that, Keres?" Chance yells from the wall where he's still dangling. "I've always known you were going to try to kill me. You bloodthirsty little bitch—"

Chance disappears a heartbeat before everything else does, too, and I find myself falling again. This time, when I land on my ass, it's on hard-packed earth. Not a field now but inside a large, round building that is perhaps twenty-five feet across in diameter. And tall. Really tall. Several stories. There is a door on my right, and I see a hatch up above in the roof that is open to the outside, blue skies taunting me with their happiness.

"What is this? A silo?"

Another table appears tucked up against the far wall.

"I'll take that as a yes," I grumble as I shove to my feet and make my way over to it.

This liquid is amber in color. It takes several gulps to chug it down, as it's thicker than the other two, and sweet but flavored more strongly, like beer. I don't get a chance to throw the cup on the ground because the table and cup disappear.

"Which horror of a human being am I supposed to save now?" I call to the goddess.

But instead of another person appearing, a bloodred crack of broken time bursts through the wall and swallows me whole.

## 54

# A STITCH IN TIME SAVES...NO ONE

### LYRA

When broken time deposits me in the past, it takes me a second to adjust to the disorienting move from trying to survive the Lock to being taken to only the gods know when and where. Or it could be Demeter's Kykeon kicking in. Does the hallucinogen work outside of her Lock?

The world isn't spinning, exactly, when I finally force myself to look around, but it feels weird. Fuzzy and oversaturated with color and sound and...sparkles. Sparkles? There weren't sparkles in the Lock, though. Or maybe it's just the way the roar of the crowds hits my ears like jackhammers.

Which is when *where* I am becomes horrifyingly clear.

I'm standing in the shadows of an archway looking out over the temporarily rebuilt Colosseum in Rome. And Dex is about to kill Meike.

Like staring at my own life through the lens of a movie, I can see past Lyra down there. Tiny from where I am now. In a haze of numbness, I watch as Dex takes advantage of Zai and Trinica and me pausing in our attack. Because it gives Dex time to lunge for Meike, who's still lying on the ground. Then he's back on his feet, holding her in the air by her neck with one hand. Eyes bulging, her face turns purple.

Past Lyra hurls her axe. I know what comes next.

"No!" I take off toward the stadium stairs that lead down to the floor of the Colosseum. To stop what happens next.

I've only made it two steps, still in the shadows of the arch, when arms wrap around me, jerking me to a stop. "Whoa, whoa, whoa!" Hades' voice sounds right in my ear. "I can't let you do that."

"He's going to kill her!" I scream.

Several heads of the gods and demigods filling the stadium seats nearby turn slightly, looking for the source. I kick out against his hold, but my powers are still stripped from Demeter's Lock. I'm mortal. I have no chance against him.

"Hades." His name escapes me on a whimper.

I can't look away as Dex jerks Meike down...and suddenly I'm not standing in the Colosseum with the roar of the crowds. I'm on the dock on the River Styx. Charon's pirate ship is tied up to it with a stream of dead souls entering the Underworld.

The harsh sound of my breathing feels like it only fills the air right around us. Hades is still holding me, arms wrapped around me, and I feel the tip of his chin as he sets it on top of my head, pulling me in closer.

Why did broken time do that to me? I didn't *have* to see it again. Meike's death.

I can still hear the crack when Dex broke her neck, still feel it in my own bones, in my heart. Still see the way her body landed all twisted up when he cast her aside.

Dead.

A second chance to stop it from happening, and I didn't. A second time to have the same thought. *I let Dex go.*

I could have stopped him before he ever got to her, but I didn't. I let him go. Then, in his glamour-crazed state, we killed him, too. We killed him, although we were only trying to stop him.

"Phi?" A new voice cracks through the air.

Hades spins me around, hand cupping the back of my head to bury my face in his chest, angling his body to block the rest of me. Does he not know that Charon has already seen me before? But maybe it's better if he doesn't now.

"What the fuck?" I hear Charon demand. "Did you interfere in the games again? The Daemones are going to do more than cut you this time—"

"Lyra's still up there." Hades cuts him off.

Charon's voice is all shades of confused. "Isn't that Lyra you're holding—"

I blink into Hades' shirt, still stuck on his words. She is. Past me is still up there, and she's about to unleash on Athena, and... I clutch at Hades. "She needs help. Right now. She needs to get out of there. Send Charon."

He doesn't even hesitate, popping off orders. "Get up to the Roman Colosseum and get Lyra away from there." I feel him glance down at me. "Not here. Olympus. My home. I'll come when I can."

A peek over Hades' shoulder shows Charon grim and not leaving. "What in the name of Tartarus is going on?"

"I can't tell you," Hades says. "Go. And do not tell Lyra who you saw me with. That's an order." This time, the words are that of the King of the Underworld, all authority and dire consequences for not being obeyed.

Immediately, Charon disappears. I don't know if it's the impact of living that moment again or the hallucinogen still in my system, but the world spins. I mean vomit-inducing spins, and I clamp a hand over my mouth.

"Lyra?" Hades takes me by the shoulders, and his face is in mine, swimming in my vision.

I lift my hand from my mouth only enough to ask, "Why didn't you save Meike? Why? The Labor was over. She won. It wouldn't have been interfering—"

He grimaces. "You didn't arrive soon enough. There's nothing I could do."

I shake my head, trying to clear it. "You were waiting for me in that archway already. Why?"

"You told me to."

The world sets to spinning faster. Why wouldn't I have told him to save Meike first? Why me? "When? When did I tell you that?"

"You came to me right after you gave yourself to me…in the water garden. After I took us back to your rooms in Olympus, late that night."

In his current timeline, that was days before this moment. Right before he went cold and broke my heart. In my own future, I haven't done that yet, but I must tell him how to put me through hell all over again. But wouldn't that be risking resetting everything? I know the Titans reset time to make sure I end up in Tartarus. But would I do that?

It has to be true. Otherwise, how would he have known to be waiting for me today?

But even through my fuzzy, swirling brain, it hits me that there's another explanation.

A worse one.

A more terrifying one.

"I think there's somebody else," I say, but now I'm slurring.

Hades' eyes narrow sharply. "What's wrong with you?" His face moves closer, silver eyes—several sets of them, now that I'm seeing him in double and triple—narrowed on my face. He scowls. "Are you drugged? Your pupils are blown wide open."

"Kykeon," I say, or try to with a thick tongue tripping over the syllables.

"You've got to be kidding me," he mutters.

"Not important." I shake my head.

"The fuck it's not—"

I reach forward, putting a finger to his lips. "Listen…" It comes out more like *litha*. I shake my head and smack my lips, which seem to be going numb. Then try again. "Listen. There is somebody powerful with the ability to glamour gods and make it stick for longer than short periods of time. What if they glamoured you? What if they're the ones lying to you? They could have told you—"

Something made of glittering red light shoots across the Styx, reflecting in the swirling blue waters. The damned fissure of broken time is coming for me. Fast this time. As if it doesn't want me to say more.

Hades is looking at me with the kind of impatient disbelief that you treat someone stoned with, not really listening to what they are saying, just figuring out how to get them somewhere safe to come down from the high.

"Listen to me," I insist. "Glamours. It's bad."

I know I sound wrong, but the words are true. *Hear what I'm saying*, I'm screaming in my head.

Hades sighs. "No one would be able to glamour me like that. I'd know it was you."

Because I think it would break him, I can't tell him that I know for certain that he and his siblings locked up their innocent parents in Tartarus, and that they are still glamoured to believe those lies centuries later. Millennia later.

That would definitely reset time.

"How would you know?"

I don't hear his answer. Time swallows me and spits me back out in the silo, in the middle of trying to unseal Demeter's Lock.

There is another figure trapped in the silo with me now. A girl. Splattered in bugs' green-and-yellow blood and guts. A hallucination of the same Lyra who just came out of Athena's Labor—who let Meike die and who was part of Dex's death. *I* was part of that.

The monster of a human being I have to save this time is…me.

# PART 5

# IS TIME ON MY SIDE...OR NOT?

Past, present, future. It's all a hot mess.

## 55

## SAVE...ME

### LYRA

Is the goddess watching? Is she taunting me now? Making me save the worst part of myself?

As if Demeter is answering that question I didn't voice with a definitive "yes," there's a thud overhead, and then, through the open hatch in the roof, grain pours down on top of me and past me in a forceful whoosh.

Demeter is filling the silo. The grain doesn't just pour, it *dumps* down on top of us. A wave of dust fills the air, and I pull my shirt up over my nose and mouth, coughing hard and eyes watering. The deluge comes so fast and hard that I'm quickly up to my ankles in the stuff, and a mound is forming in the center of the space.

Meanwhile, the hallucination of past me, standing around the curve of the wall from where I am, stares at me in horror. What I should do is run along the wall as fast as I can, trying to stay on top of the grains, grab her, and shove us both through the door opposite of where I am before the grain buries it.

But I don't move.

I can't.

Demeter knew well what she was doing.

I know what's holding my feet in place when I should be saving myself. Guilt.

Dex was glamoured that day in Athena's Labor. I know he would not have killed Meike if he hadn't been glamoured. He was a dick, but the way he competed in the Crucible Games was only to fight for his sister and nephew. He wasn't a murderer.

While I'm not the one who delivered the killing stroke, what if I'd made different choices? What if I'd stopped him in that glass labyrinth instead of letting him run by? What if I'd tried to help him, even after he killed Meike?

But I don't think I could have. Even now, anger at what he did burns like venom in my veins, scouring the guilt with something poisonous and awful.

I think the thing that's cementing my feet to this floor is that I'm pretty sure I don't deserve to be the one who lived through all of that.

Another realization slams through me like a thunderclap.

What if Phoebe's vision has always been wrong? What if everything they've done to get me down here to save them has never worked, not in hundreds or maybe even thousands of attempts, because I'm not the one who is going to save them?

Not really.

What if that vision was a glamour, too? Or, equally likely, what if the one they've really been waiting for isn't me...but Boone?

Since I've been in Tartarus this time around, the Titans have been surprised and even confounded over and over, in big ways and in small, by how differently this is going, all the changing parts. But what if what's changed this time around isn't *me*?

What's changed is *him*.

That thought is stuck on repeat in my head.

It's him.

It's Boone.

He's the one, and I'm just a distraction or, at best, a lure to get him here. Maybe it's time to stop fighting so hard and just let the real savior step up and do his job.

"Why in the name of Tartarus are you just standing there?"

I didn't even notice that I closed my eyes until the sound of my own voice yelling in my ear has me snapping them open. I have to squint to see my own face through the dust, but there I am.

"We need to get out of here!" past Lyra yells over the thunderous rush of pouring grain.

I shake my head. Because I'm convinced now of the truth. I should die down here.

The hallucination of my past self grabs me by the shoulders, shaking me hard. "Get your shit together! Run!"

I'm supposed to save her. If she gets out of the silo without me, would that count toward unsealing this Lock and save me, too? I can't take that risk. Luckily, I know myself. She's not going to leave someone else behind if it means she lives but I die. She'll die in here with me.

But she's just a hallucination. I can live with that.

Right to the end.

"I—" A violent cough seizes me, and it takes me several seconds to clear my lungs. "I'm not going."

All I can see is her green eyes over the shirt that she's also pulled over her mouth and nose. I see them go wide and then snap to narrow slits. Her black eyebrows, now covered in dust like the rest of her, draw together.

"We don't have time for this." She clamps a hand down on my wrist and starts dragging me. The grain is high enough now that she has to lift her knees to walk through it, and it feels like wading through wet cement, thick and sucking at us. Not that I've ever waded through wet cement, but now that I've accepted my fate, little details like that are filtering in.

Loss of fear is…peaceful. Lovely.

With a twisting motion, I jerk out of her hold, but she rounds on me, lunging to grab me again. "Come *on*!"

Still in my serene little bubble, I observe—almost like watching a movie—that she's turning frantic. Her pupils dilate beyond what the dim light in here would cause.

"This is Boone's story, not mine." I pause, reconsidering the wording because of who I'm talking to. "Not *ours*."

"What do you mean?" she lowers her shirt to yell. Then doesn't wait for my answer but tries even harder to get a grip on me.

"I was always a non-player character," I tell her.

She shakes her head. "No! That's not true!"

It is. She just can't see it yet.

"Cursed to be unlovable. Stuck down here time after time. My purpose was to get Boone here."

"What the hells are you talking about?" She ducks and jukes and manages to grab my arm hard, immediately dragging me through the grain. But now I'm fighting her. I'm not letting this hallucination of me keep me from my true purpose.

I fight so hard, I bite her.

The other me yelps. "What's wrong with you?"

Out of the dust and growing darkness, a dark figure steps between us, and she gasps, letting go of me so that I trip in the deep grain and fall on my ass.

"Hades," she calls to him.

"Go!" he yells at the other Lyra and points toward the door. "Wedge it open."

She looks at me, back to him, and then, without another word, she turns and runs—or, more accurately, plows her way through the heavy grains piled up in here.

"Hades?" His name slips from my lips as I stare at his face, waking up from the numbness that had me in its grip. "Did you open Tartarus? Is that how you're here?"

He freezes for a moment at my questions. "I'm not *him*, my star. I'm from down here."

# 56

## BETWEEN HELL & HIGH WATER

### LYRA

He's the Hades from his Lock?

The tiniest ray of relief that had fallen over me at his arrival is viciously cast aside by shadows too impenetrable to let light through. The disappointment that slams through my chest might as well be more of the grain burying me alive. It won't be much longer until that happens.

Hades is suddenly over me, in my face. "What's in your pocket, Lyra?"

"What?"

He gives a grim shake of his head. How is the dust in the air not bothering him? It's not even sticking to his hair and clothes. "Your *pocket*." Then he grabs my hand and places my palm flat over the compartment in yoga pants meant to hold a phone…where I stuffed my half of Cronos' butterfly.

The butterfly that Hades himself carved for his father as a child.

Does this version of him remember that? Probably not. He was made after Hades was glamoured to forget his parents loving him. So how does he know about it now? Unless Cronos has done this with me before and I told this copy of Hades about it.

I don't even have to reach inside the pocket and feel the full weight of the carving, the rough and smooth edges. Just the memory that it exists clears my mind of the fog the damned drink of Demeter's has no doubt caused.

By the time I drag my gaze from my hand to Hades' silver eyes, he's already positioned himself so that he's braced, leaning over with his fingers interlaced before him, and I know what he wants me to do.

No questions. No hesitation. I struggle to my feet, then lunge for him, shoving one foot into his hands, my palms going to his shoulders. He boosts me into the air, and I jump at the same time. The momentum takes me up and over the mound of grain in the center of the room, high enough that I'm able to get my feet under me before I come down on the other side. I hit on my ass and slide the rest of the way down feetfirst...

My momentum takes me right out the door that other version of me is forcing open with a rusted iron pole that she got from who knows where. I hit the clear air and whirl around just in time to see Hades buried by grain.

"No!" I shout just as the grain forces the door closed with an ominous and ringing clang.

I run to the door and bang on it with my fists. "Hades!"

"You *abandoned* him?" the other Lyra demands from behind me. Accuses, more like. Every single word strikes my back.

Before I can respond, though, everything disappears—Lyra, the silo, the farm and fields. All of it is gone, and I'm standing in a pie-shaped room made entirely of rock with only Demeter as my companion.

"Congratulations," the goddess says. "You have unsealed my Lock."

I hardly hear her. In my mind, I'm desperately trying to convince myself that I didn't just kill the apparition of Hades. He can't be killed, right? How was he even there?

Vaguely, I'm aware that Demeter waves a hand toward the now-open door and the Titans waiting in the chamber on the other side. But I'm already sprinting across the room, through the door, past all of them, and to the door to Hades' Lock.

"Hades!" I yell as I place my palm over his cold, dark emblem to open it.

Nothing happens.

A round of shushes barely penetrates my panic, but it's enough that I remember where we are and what sound could unleash. He's supposed to open it for me, right? "Please don't be dead," I whisper.

Which is when my powers slam back into me.

Icy pain feels like the cold hand of death trying to rip my spine right out of my body. By the time it recedes, I'm on the ground, leaning on Hades' door.

A door that's still closed.

"Lyra." A gentle hand lands on my shoulder. Cronos, I can tell. But I shrug him off as I push to my feet.

"Hades." I manage to keep my voice down, placing my hand over the etched symbols again. Still the Lock doesn't open. "So help me gods, if you don't open this door—"

"He's not alive or dead," Cronos says in a hushed voice, more gently than I ever thought him capable of being. "He is something that both does and doesn't exist at the same time."

"Then how was he in Demeter's Lock with me?" I demand softly without turning to face him.

There's a hollow ring of silence behind me. "That's not possible."

I know he's right. I *know* it. But how else did I get out of the silo? Hallucination Lyra saw him, too. But they can't ask her.

Oh my gods. If I'm relying on a hallucination's eyewitness account, I'm definitely losing it. And that's not the only indicator. I also was fully convinced, to the point of sacrificing myself, that Boone was the real savior in this story. Suddenly, I'm not trusting my own mind and my own logic. Not in this place where time is broken and immortals are chained, where invisible monsters appear when a bell sounds and the screams of the damned echo through the halls.

I slowly turn away from the stone door that remains silent and shut. I don't know what it is about Cronos' face in that moment—the sympathy in eyes that I have always expected to be hard and cold, maybe, or the fact that his face looks so much like the one I desperately need to see right now. On a swallowed sob, I step into him and bury my face in his chest, wrapping my arms around him.

"I don't deserve to be here," I say into his shirt.

He awkwardly pats my back. "None of us deserves to be down here."

I tighten my grip on the back of his shirt and shake my head. "No. I mean I don't deserve your faith. This isn't working for a reason."

I shouldn't have given up in that silo. That was a dick move on my part, Kykeon-driven or not. But when it comes down to it, my logic wasn't wrong.

Another awkward pat lands on my back. "We'll worry about that tomorrow." I'm guessing Cronos meant to use his most soothing voice, but it comes out all gruff and grumpy. These Titans really don't know how to deal with emotions any better than I do.

A watery laugh escapes me. "This entire thing just fucking sucks."

"*That* sounds more like my Lyra."

I don't know who gasps harder, me or Cronos, to find the replica of Hades standing on the other side of the open doorway to his Lock, looking none the worse for wear.

## 57

# BOMBSHELL

### LYRA

"You're okay?" I ask as I let go of Cronos to face Hades' copy.

He puts a finger to his lips, but the dimple on his left cheek flirts with me. "As you can see."

I give him an unamused look but do keep my voice down. "Playing it cool is not the right move here. You scared the shit out of me."

A scowl descends over his features. "*I* scared *you*? You were ready to die in there. You gave up." He flings an arm in the direction of Demeter's open Lock, barely visible around the bend.

My breath leaves me in a harsh burst because he's right. "I—"

"Don't ever do that again."

I tip my head, taking in his features, the way his face is pinched, brows puckered, eyes swirling. Is Hades' apparition…worried? "Thank you for saving me."

He grunts. Which I guess is pissed-off copy-god for *you're welcome*.

"Why did you?" I ask.

Hades' face does something super subtle, but the tension is real and tells me he's as confused as I am. "I'm not entirely sure."

He glances away only to look back just as fast, almost as if he can't stand not to look at me when I'm right here in front of him. "Perhaps the Fates have bound us together, and even separated by time and a corporeal form, I can feel that."

I swing around at a high-pitched whistle to see Boone crossing the chamber. A soaking wet Boone, trailing water from the tunnel that leads to the pillars and our practice obstacle course all the way across this cavern. When he reaches me, he steps between me and the open Lock, blocking my view of Hades. "What a load of bullshit," he snaps at the copy of my god.

Then Boone gives me a look that is an awful blend of accusing and worried. "Listening to ghosts is never a good idea, Keres."

"Oh my gods." For the second time in minutes, I'm hugging someone, and I am not a hugger. But the relief is too much. "You're back," I mumble into his shoulder. "Thank Olympus."

He pulls me back so I can see his answering grin. One that's gone too soon before he goes solemn, his eyes darkening with a kind of abandoned-puppy-dog hurt. "You opened Demeter's Lock? I thought you would at least wait for me."

"It's been days." I try to say it mildly, but the shock that hits his eyes makes me wince.

"Days." He says this more to himself than me.

"Where did you go? Or when?" I ask.

Boone blinks himself out of his thoughts, then shrugs. But it's too fast, like he's been waiting for the question and had a response planned, but his gaze seeks out Persephone. Only a quick glance. "I was just sort of stuck in a random place."

I peer at him closer, not buying it. "That's it?"

A nod. "What about you?"

I know he means when broken time took me when it grabbed him, but I've had a more recent trip since then. I haven't had even two seconds to process what just happened with the real Hades while I was in the middle of surviving Demeter's Lock.

The way I left Hades hanging on the possibility that someone glamoured him… Gods, he must've been in a panic after I disappeared. Of course, the Lyra going through the Crucible at that time was locked up in Olympus jail—to keep me safe from Athena's wrath after I called her a monster—and that Lyra was not allowed to see Hades at the time. So I have no clue how he handled the glamouring information.

I glance around Boone toward Hades' replica, who is watching me with intent, bright eyes from inside his still-open Lock.

"I guess we have a lot to catch up on," Boone says.

I open my mouth to say something like "later" or "not here," but a rumbling starts all around us. Soft at first.

Another earthquake.

They happen often enough that I've started tuning them out. Except the rumbling gets louder and moves closer, and suddenly the ground itself is shaking.

"Should we get in the doorway?" I'm looking overhead for any rocks that look like they might shake loose from high above. Too high for me to really see in here.

"We're immortal now," Boone reminds me. "Not sure the doorway matters."

On the last word, the shaking stops. "That was a bigger one," I say.

"Too big." Cronos' hushed voice does not match the direness edging the words.

I picture the cracks where the pillars of the cosmos feed into the earth itself. Someone should go check them.

"What does it mean?" I hear Mnemosyne murmur, and I look back over my shoulder in time to see Hyperion wrap his hand around Theia's even as she's holding Tethys' hand with her other.

"It means we're running out of time." Koios is the one to say it.

Oh gods. My stomach twists. What is it about a ticking clock that sucks so hard?

"Should we reset?" Eurybia asks, quietly dour.

Instead of dismissing her, they all look to Cronos and Rhea, but the King and Queen of the Titans are focused on Phoebe.

Phoebe, who turns her head and catches sight of us.

A tiny, choked sound escapes her, and—like what happened that day when I watched the gods attack the Titans—her entire body goes eerily rigid, head thrown back, and her face spasms into that contorted mask of what I'm pretty sure is pain. Her body lifts off the ground until only the tips of her toes touch.

Koios is quick to move behind her. He has to jump to reach her, wrapping around her and clamping a hand around her mouth to muffle the sounds of distress coming from her.

And almost as fast as it started, her feet drop back to the ground and her dazed eyes clear.

"Oh my heavens," she whispers, the blood draining from her face, leaving her visibly pale and shaken as she stares from me…to Boone.

"What?" Cronos asks. "What do you see?"

And I am expecting her to say that Boone is their savior. That I'm right about that and it's finally become clear.

But instead, she opens her mouth, and very different words come out.

"Lyra and Boone are bound by a fated line."

# 58

# TELL ME NO LIES

### LYRA

"What? That's not possible." I take a jerking step away from all of them, Boone included, and there's a distressed noise that I'm pretty sure comes from Persephone.

At the same time, a harsh, "Over my dead body," sounds from behind us.

Loud enough that the Titans all make shushing noises, and I should probably look toward the tunnel where the obelisk lies in wait. But I can't.

Because that protest came from the copy of Hades watching us from inside his Lock.

Boone turns and slaps a hand on the symbol. "Bye-bye," he says to Hades as solid stone slides down between us.

Which is when Persephone runs from the room.

"Shit." Boone spits the word but stays by my side.

"What do you mean?" Cronos asks Phoebe sharply. "Fated how?"

Wait. There are more fates than the lines linking lovers?

The Titaness glances around at the others. "Not lovers."

Thank the gods. Because no. I love Boone, but not like that. Nothing will ever make me turn from Hades, not even fated fucking lines, but I'm glad I don't have to make that choice.

Phoebe makes a face. "It's something else."

"Cosmos save us." Cronos mutters the words. "Can you see a new future?" Cronos demands of Phoebe, and Rhea sneaks another look at the tunnel the Pandemonium would come from if triggered.

But no bell goes off.

Phoebe shakes her head. "Other than their fated thread, I still can't see anything about Boone."

"It makes sense, though." Iapetus jumps in. "It's Aphrodite's Lock. It must have something to do with love and bonded hearts."

"And fire," I remind them all. "Fire doesn't sound like love to me, or all that promising, at least. And Phoebe said the fated line isn't lovers."

My gaze cuts across the Titans, and bile rises in my throat, because now all of them are staring at me with a new kind of hope. They've all, every single one of them, reached the same conclusion together—that things are different this time for a reason. They are all wondering if our fated bond means this is it, the final time. No more resets. All the stars aligned. All the right steps were taken. Escape is within their grasp.

I move several feet away, hard and fast. "It could be a lie. All of this could be lies. What if you're manipulating us so we let you out?"

Even as I'm saying it, I don't believe it. I know what I witnessed in the past. I *know* it was real. "We don't even know if time really resets down here. You keep telling us it does, but there's no way to prove it. There's no way to—"

"I can prove it," Mnemosyne says. "I can show you the memories of the past."

"No!" Cronos yells.

All of us freeze, dread tensing our bodies and contorting our faces as we wait for the bell to go off. It has to. He was so loud.

But it doesn't.

"Careful, my love," Rhea urges quietly.

"Seeing all of the past could reset her." Cronos slashes a hand through the air, and lightning crackles over his skin as he does. It's not exactly quiet, either. "The cracks in the walls, the differences this time, now Boone, and them being fated… All of it points to this being the last time. We're too close. We can't risk it. I forbid it—"

"You forbid it?" Mnemosyne murmurs. There's a sweetness to her voice that should be a warning.

One even Cronos recognizes, cutting himself off to glare at her.

"She can handle it," Mnemosyne insists. She is the Titaness of remembrance, but should I believe what she shows me? What if, like the gods, all her memories are made of glamours?

Keeping my gaze trained on her mask, I turn on my ability to see glamours with a flick of my will. No veil of light covers her face or eyes. I can't decide if I'm relieved or more worried, but I turn the power back off. "Show me."

"No!" Cronos and Iapetus both lunge for Mnemosyne as she takes a step, but she puts on a burst of speed, evading their reach to get to me.

She threads her hands into my hair on either side of my face, and she presses her forehead to mine, her owl mask feathers tickling my skin, and I close my eyes. "I'll only show you enough," she whispers.

"This is a bad idea—" I hear Cronos say. Or at least start to say before the sound of his voice cuts off abruptly, and in the same instant, my mind is filled with flashing images.

Not just images. Moments, like movies—all of my past lives.

I see different things as they happened. I discover what it would have been like if I hadn't been cursed, growing up with my parents. No matter the timeline, they treat me more as a burden than a beloved child. So many different ways my life would have turned out when the Greek gods had nothing to do with me. Or did turn out. I was a nurse. I was a teacher. I ran a little shop on the pier. I became an addict who died of an overdose in an alley.

With the images come the sensations I felt in those moments. The smells of my parents' home—slightly dank with a waft of unwashed socks. The damp of fog as I open the shop one morning. The dizzying high of the drugs hitting my blood before death claims me.

Then I get more versions of my life, different versions, now, with the thieves. And after that comes me in the Crucible.

All the ways I die.

Over, and over, and over. At least once on every single one of the Labors. More than once in Athena's and in Zeus'.

Worse than the sensations are the emotions. I feel what I felt in each and every one of those lives, especially in those ends—terror, pain, despair, a terrible kind of hope only to have it destroyed, regret, guilt, anger. All of it ripping through me like electric shocks.

And at the exact moment when my life would end in one timeline, a new life flashes before me. It's like I'm being yanked from the end of one story and shoved into the middle of another.

But they're all *my* story.

It's not just me, either. It's watching my friends die in the Crucible… or watching them live. There are versions where even Dex makes it to the end, although Meike never does.

The metallic taste of blood in my mouth. The horrible pain as I burn from the bite of the water dragon in Poseidon's Labor, consumed from the outside as Isabel watches in horror instead. Isabel lives. More than that, we would have been friends when we both lived.

I can save her. I could reset time and save Isabel.

Mnemosyne clearly follows the train of my thoughts, because she shows me how many times I tried, and there's not a single one where I end up in Tartarus with Isabel still alive.

Oh gods.

Hearing the dull thud of Zai's body as he hits the rocky ground in the cave during Dionysus' Labor, his eyes open and already sightless as the poison ivy combined with his allergies kills him quickly, because he didn't win Hermes' sandals that time.

Zai rarely makes it through the Crucible alive.

The scenes of all my lives changes again, moving on to Tartarus. Trying to get through different Locks and all the ways I died in those, too. Though she doesn't show me beyond Poseidon's Lock, which is next.

I would ask, but it's as if I've been paralyzed, unable to speak or move or do anything but experience.

Finally, she shows me different moments that caused the resets.

They're right.

My death is what triggers it maybe the most, but just as often, the resets are because of other moments. My mind not being able to take the truth of what they tell me. That does it a lot in the early years, until they learned. But also moments when one of us, not always me, is taken to the past and someone there discovers too much. Those minds also can't take it.

*Why does it matter, if they're in the past?* I want to ask.

But it matters.

Time resets.

It's real. It happens.

The feel of the memories is too much, as if they are physical things being filed into my brain and I can't expand enough to hold them, the pressure pushing outward on my skull.

A moan manages to escape from my paralyzed lips.

"Stop." I hear Cronos outside of myself. "Stop. You're hurting her."

Then there's a scuffle of running and more yells.

"Lyra, watch out!" Cronos' shout penetrates the memories that I'm drowning in.

The memories that are trying to *destroy* me. Already have destroyed me in previous lives, previous versions of me. Have destroyed my friends. Have destroyed Hades. Have destroyed the world.

I'm going to be sick.

Although I don't know if it's the past lives I've witnessed that send the surge of nausea rising up in me, or if it's the disorientation of being yanked out of Mnemosyne's memories and straight into the grim shimmer of broken time, followed by dead silence as it takes me wherever it's taking me.

# 59

# BETTER LUCK NEXT TIME

### LYRA

The broken cracks have taken me back to Hades so many times, the disappointment at not seeing his face when I land in the past is like a punch to the gut.

"What in the Underworld?" The words burst from me as I find myself in a place all too familiar. My bedroom in the den. The last time I thought I was here, I wasn't. Because Hestia's Lock glamoured me to believe that. To feel that.

Is this a glamour or not? But time took me here, not a Lock. It's not hazy here, either. No pink lighting. Even the smell—a familiar combination of rock, water, dirt, and stale air—feels more real. The air against my skin doesn't move. The way it always hasn't moved.

Still, just in case, I blink my power on, but nothing shimmers anywhere around me. So it's not a glamour. This…is real.

I flick it back off. Which is when my mind finally catches up. "Oh, shit." I think I know what happens right now.

So many things have been thrown at me, I'm not even sure what to process next. But one of those things was Hades insisting that I told him to do things—the Anaxian Wars, find me in the Colosseum, break my heart. If all of that is true, if that wasn't him being glamoured, then that means…

Am *I* doing things to make sure the past lands me right where I am now?

I slip my axe out of the strap on my leg that Demeter's replica let me keep.

This is how I test my theory, right? A small way that fits with my experience of life this time around?

This axe disappeared in my room about ten years before the Crucible, and later, I learned that he had no idea how or why it went missing. Now I know it's because *I* took it during my time travel experience while I was in Hestia's Lock. I glance at the mattress in front of me, covered in a moth-eaten blue blanket. The axe appeared on my bed.

Was it because *I* gave it to me?

Knowing I would need it. Or even just testing a theory. Does it matter?

So far, I've wondered at the way time seems to be determined to take me to specific moments—maybe it's future Cronos, maybe the Fates, maybe something else powerful. What if that influence is trying to give us chances to set ourselves up to succeed, to escape?

Am I the puppet master in my own story? The woman behind the curtain? Even if I'm a haphazard one bumbling between memories and uneasy coincidence.

The problem is, we don't have other weapons down in Tartarus. I might need this to finish the other Locks.

*Well…Tartarus take me now.*

Then I realize that epithet doesn't apply well to me anymore. Tartarus already took me.

Many, many, many times.

I sigh.

Hoping I'm doing this right, remembering Cronos' instructions as I try to glamour my own axe the way I made that rock into a tomato in the tunnels, I lift the axe and force my will into the object, whispering words, telling it to not leave past Lyra Keres' possession until she gives in and learns how to use it.

That bit is important.

Back then it was so annoying, the way I'd try to throw the axe away or stash it in the treasure room and it would keep appearing in my quarters. I smile as I lay the weapon down on the bed.

I close my eyes and picture flipping my ability to see glamours on like a light switch. When I open my eyes, I look at the axe on my bed. There's an opalescent sheen covering it. Which means I at least did something.

This is how it came to me in the first place. I'm sure of it.

I don't like giving up my only weapon, but it hasn't exactly been all that handy down in Tartarus in the first place. And future me…past me?…fuck. I'm going to need it in the Crucible.

Now…the question is, what else? I'm not sure how long I'll be stuck down here. Should I go steal some food to take back with me? Or find an empty room to hide in before past me comes back? Not that past me ever did. I definitely would remember seeing myself.

I reach for the door handle.

A red flash of light across my closed eyes is all the warning I have before silence engulfs me and I'm taken back to Tartarus.

When I reappear, Cronos is immediate with his demands. "Where is your weapon?"

A new suspicion creeps in as I stare at him, because I'm pretty sure I just proved my theory. But that also means…time *isn't* broken. Not the way we think. Maybe it's taking us exactly where we need to go to move forward until we escape this place.

I don't know why, or how, or who is driving it. Future Cronos makes the most sense. Maybe. But I am fairly confident that even if that's not true, *I* am the one making sure certain things in *my* past happen the exact way they did in my experience of this particular round of my life in order to get me to this moment. I should test it one more time, something bigger, before I really start to do foolish shit.

I let out a short, sharp breath, then hold out my half of the small butterfly that has been in my pocket since I got out of Demeter's Lock, hoping he'll take it for what it is—a silent entreaty to trust me. "The axe is exactly where it is supposed to be."

# 60

# POSEIDON'S LOCK

### LYRA

Evidently, the practice course paid off, because making it through Poseidon's Lock was easier than I anticipated. Not that it was easy. I may develop a phobia of water between the Labors and the Locks.

"Congratulations!" Poseidon's voice booms. "Your moral grounding helped you through the shaky foundation of my obstacle course."

I huff. That is what we were being tested for? "That is a weak connection at best."

"Well done, mortals," Poseidon says from somewhere behind me. "This Lock is unsealed."

Neither of us acknowledges the apparition of the god. "One more down," Boone says.

"Thank you." There was no way I could have done this one without him. He basically pushed me up the walls of the glass cage.

We finally figured that one out. I climbed in first and extended across, pressing my hands and feet against opposite sides, using the tension to stay in place above the eel-infested water.

Then I scooted up enough that Boone could do the same underneath me.

"Ready?" he asked. His voice didn't even sound strained while I was already sweating. "Don't forget to brace your toes on the backs of my boots."

"Right."

I had to feel and turn my feet sideways, so the arches caught the thick backs of his boots, but I eventually managed to get situated. This position kept my tension even when the top of the cage got too wide for me to fully stretch across on my own. It also added to Boone's leverage.

The trickiest part was going up in tandem like that. We moved on the diagonal. Right hand and left foot first. Painstakingly careful, with a few bobbles and slips, but we managed to catch them all. Or Boone did. Damn, the man is strong.

Everything else was cake after that. Even the hammers.

Oh my gods. It finally hits me. Four down. Only three to go.

Like it's ringing a creepy congrats, the damned bell goes off.

We swing to face the Titans, who are out in the chamber that surrounds the Locks. The doorway has parted the solid wall—the arch is intricately carved with a seahorse, a golden chariot, a bull, his sea castle, and a wave-crested mantle. All symbols of Poseidon. The Titans are scattered around the chamber beyond, where they wait for us. Some closer than others.

"Get in here!" I yell and run toward the door.

We stop at the threshold, ready to close it fast, when Boone suddenly mutters, "Oh gods. Persephone is out there."

I think for a second that I'm going to have to stop him from running off to find her, but that's when our powers decide to return. On a grunt of pain, I double over, breathing my way through the torture.

It takes long enough that, as soon as the sensation passes, I jerk upright in time to see that about half of the Titans have made it inside with us, but several of them are still outside.

"Come on," Hyperion calls, waving.

Suddenly, Iapetus spasms like something struck him in the back.

"No!" Mnemosyne shouts from where she stands inside the Lock. She lunges like she's going to run out to him, but Cronos grabs her around the waist, lifting her off her feet. The Titaness goes wild in his arms, clawing and fighting.

"You can't help him!" Cronos yells.

As fast as she fought, she goes limp and looks out of the Lock just in time to see Iapetus' face turn almost purple and his features contort with sudden rage.

Then he...changes.

I've only seen Theia this way once, and it was after she was struck. At the sight of the full transformation, horror crawls over my body, like a thousand of Athena's bugs. Iapetus' skin turns to flames encased in black crusts, like a lava flow. And he screams.

I clap my hands over my ears, trying to muffle the sounds of agony that rip from his throat. Iapetus is the Titan of pain. It's as if the Pandemonium turned his own power against him in a physical manifestation.

Rhea and Crius make it inside.

Just as Iapetus turns frenzied. I mean beating at anything and everything—his chest, the walls, the floor. And everything he touches erupts in flames.

Phoebe, meanwhile, is still running for us, and we all see the second Iapetus clocks her. He takes off at a dead sprint, running so fast he turns into a distortion of fire and ash.

She's not going to make it.

"Close it!" Cronos orders.

But Koios, Phoebe's husband, grabs Hyperion's hand. "No. Give her—"

"Protect Lyra and Boone!" Phoebe yells at him. Even as Iapetus bears down on her.

A yell comes from Koios that is guttural. Visceral. Then he shows us what two people bound by fate really look like. He steps outside the chamber. "Now!" he yells at Hyperion, who hits the symbol, sending the stone door shooting down.

As it reaches the ground, I hear Phoebe scream, and a splatter of golden blood hits the floor at Cronos' feet.

# 61

## WAITING & WISHING

### LYRA

There is nothing to do but wait it out.

After the initial shock, the Titans with us all sat down with their backs against the bare walls of Poseidon's Lock. The obstacle course disappeared from the pie-shaped room, leaving it just rock. Crius, the father of constellations with his star-pricked eyes, glamoured three tiny white stars that hover in midair, spinning around each other, giving us an extra amount of flickering light in addition to the glow coming off Hyperion and from Theia's palms.

I'm not sure I would have minded it being pitch black.

Seeing the worry etched in deep lines across the Titans' faces might be worse. Cronos, of all of them, seems to be taking this the hardest. "I knew we shouldn't all group together like that," he says to Rhea. He wipes at the blood on his leather-strapped shoe like Lady MacBeth trying to remove a spot that wasn't there. "I *knew* it."

"Iapetus can't kill Phoebe, can he?" I ask in a small voice. "Especially not with Koios there?"

Cronos' chin hits his chest as he drops his head forward.

Rhea is the one to lean around him. "Sometimes death isn't the worst thing that can happen."

A truth I already know.

"How long do we wait?" Boone asks. He's plucking at the Lycra of the shirt Poseidon dressed him in.

"She'll be fine," I tell him.

Boone stills, then lifts his gaze to me, and I shrug. He would definitely have gone after Persephone if getting our powers back hadn't stopped him.

"She's not my concern," he says in a voice gone void.

"Liar."

After a flat stare, he looks away from me to the Titans. "So...how long?"

At first, none seem to want to answer, or maybe they're so worried they can't.

"With Iapetus hit, longer is better," Hyperion finally says. "The Pandemonium might clear out, but he has to pass the worst of the rage, or we risk more of us being hurt trying to avoid him or stop him."

Right.

They weren't fucking around when they said rage. Titan-level rage is...

All I can think is the gods never would have been able to get the Titans locked in here if the Titans had truly fought back. I look around their strained faces again.

"I'd like to eat ice cream...real ice cream...every day," Theia says out of nowhere and out of context. "And hug my children every day, too."

Boone, who's sitting across the way, exchanges a raised-eyebrow look with me.

"I want to smell snow on the mountains," Hyperion offers, and Theia slips her hand into his.

Beside me, Cronos manages the tiniest of smiles. "I'll spend the first hundred years in our home on the beach, also with our children."

The place Boone and I saw? Does it even still exist? I strongly doubt it. I bump Cronos with my shoulder. "What is this?" I whisper.

He draws his knees up, draping his hands across them. "When the bell goes off and we know it's bad, sometimes we spend the wait talking about what we want to do most when we get out of Tartarus."

Oh.

Rhea smiles. "I want to meet each of my grandchildren."

I snort—mostly a dubious and sarcastic snort, because I've met several of those grandchildren—but cover it up with, "There are a lot of them."

Which makes her smile. "I know."

The others continue to play the game. A nice distraction. I wonder how many times they've shared the same things in all these thousands of years.

"Have you thought more about your fated bond?" Cronos leans over under the cover of the chatter to ask me, low-voiced.

I glance from him to Boone. "If it's not romantic…" Phoebe was sure of that. "What else is there?"

He hums in his throat. "Some fates are lifelong friendships."

"That could be it."

"Maybe…" He seems dubious.

"What do you think it is?"

He shrugs. "Some fates are bound to a specific event or action. Maybe that's you. Boone has made many things here different. Maybe the two of you together is the reason you get out."

I frown. That maybe makes more sense.

"Or he could be the sacrifice," I think I hear him murmur.

I stiffen. "Sacrifice?" I manage to keep my voice to a whisper, not wanting Boone to hear.

Cronos shakes his head. "I'm just thinking through different kinds of fates."

"Oh."

Still, the word rattles around inside my head.

He nods around the room. "We are all fated. Did you know that? Romantically, I mean. Soulmates, some would call us."

I straighten a little. My power to see glamours is off, but even when it was on, I didn't see any lines between them. "I never heard that. Titans were painted as simply evil, and that's about all we know."

He sighs.

"What does it feel like?" I ask.

His smile this time is warmer, sweeter, as he takes Rhea's hand and kisses her palm before curling her fingers around the gesture. "It's like you are only completely yourself when they are near you. Like filling a hollow place inside you."

The Titaness leans her head on his shoulder. "It's like everything just… fits. Even after eternity together."

Fits.

Filling something hollow.

That sounds like how I feel with Hades. At least the Titans are down here with their soulmates. Mine… I have to wait for broken time to see him again.

My gaze slides toward Tethys.

If I stay down here too long, is that how I'll end up? Broken without him?

Cronos must see I'm still spinning around what all this means. "Stop worrying about your fate. It will become clear enough with time."

"Damn," I mutter. "I'm really starting to hate time."

Which makes him chuckle. "Will it help if I tell you that fate isn't as unmovable as you think? It can be broken."

I stiffen. "What? That's possible?"

He grimaces. "I've only seen it happen three times in all my years, both with soulmate-type fates." He grimaces again. "Those are the most common."

"What happened?"

"It's worse for the one not choosing to break it. They never find love. They never feel whole. Their heart never heals."

That sounds awful. "Why did they break it?" I ask. "The ones you saw?"

"They simply chose a different path. One they believed was their true path."

I scrub a hand over my eyes. "They were in love with someone else?"

"Yes."

"Were they happy? Afterward?"

He's quiet for long enough that I drop my hand to look at him. "Cronos?"

"One was."

One out of three. After causing another misery. "Why did you tell me this?"

"So that you know that you always have choices. Always, Lyra."

"Choices? Rhea said I always end up down here, too. No matter what. How is that a choice?"

Cronos purses his lips, nodding. "True. But that's because you consistently choose the same paths. We may be able to reset time and manipulate a few things from down here to try to get you here, but we can't make those choices for you." The look in his pale-blue eyes feels... significant. Like he truly wants me to hear this. Like there is something bigger that he wants me to understand.

But then Cronos reaches over to pat my head. "I just want your happiness."

I swallow a wry chuckle. *Next time, leave me up there with Hades, then.* I think it but don't say it out loud, because that action feels…selfish now.

We fall into silence about the same time that the others stop talking as well. A quiet takes over the chamber, one that grows heavier by the second, each of us caught up in our own thoughts as we wait.

And wish things could be different.

# 62

# ALL ELSE CONFUSION

### LYRA

The door to Poseidon's Lock suddenly opens, and we all jump to our feet, ready to fight. But only Persephone stands in the chamber beyond.

Boone starts toward her in a jerk but seems to catch himself. I'm not sure if anyone noticed but me.

Definitely not Persephone, who holds a finger to her lips, which tells us enough. She's not sure where the others are or what state they are in. When we emerge, it's with a plan.

Spread out. Stay quiet. Know where we're going to run and hide at all times, until we reach safety. I have to say that stepping over copious amounts of gold blood that drags in a trail out of the room and down the tunnel we are going through doesn't make that plan feel like a good one. Neither do the melted spots where lava obviously hit, still glowing with heat all over the place.

Iapetus can do serious damage, it seems.

Cronos leads the way, and we spread out, with Boone in the middle of the pack and me at the very back with Rhea.

I'm vaguely aware that Persephone is up by Boone, talking to him too quietly for me to hear back where I am. Seems serious, though. The goddess doesn't offer him a single signature sweet smile. They pause just at the entrance to the tunnel itself.

My steps slow as I study them.

Are they arguing?

Just as that thought strikes, Boone grabs her by the wrist and drags her out of sight down the tunnel.

Of course, that's when the bell goes off. Again.

The tinkling, unearthly sound doesn't feel real, and my thoughts twist up under am onslaught of fear. It's too soon. It hasn't gone off again so fast before. We still don't even know where Iapetus might be or what state he's in. Phoebe or Koios, either.

The shock of it slows my mind.

Rhea, right at the entrance to the tunnel, spins toward me, but when she sees how far behind I am, terror seizes her features.

"You won't make it to me fast enough," she yells. "Run for the closest unsealed Lock."

I don't argue. I take off, and with every step, thoughts are firing like electric shocks. Last time the bell rang, Iapetus didn't make it to us. Neither did Phoebe. And they're faster than I am. Was he farther away? Is there any scenario where I don't end up a rage monster next?

Those invisible things, whatever they are, are silent.

Every single step, every breath, every thump of my heart, I'm expecting to be hit. To bend backward like Iapetus did and come up foaming at the mouth like a rabid dog. I'm not even sure how my powers can turn on me.

The closest Lock to me is Hades'. But the door is closed.

The doors are closed for all of them that I can see from here.

"Hades!" I yell.

It's a risk. The Pandemonium are drawn by sound, but I'm pretty damned sure I won't have time to escape them if I have to stop to try to open the door first.

The door that's still closed.

"Hades!" I'm screaming now, throat raw.

I flinch with every step I take. Waiting for the attack I know has to be coming.

Abruptly, the stone door of the archway flies open and he's there. He's there and looking beyond me, and the stark dread that crosses his features is worse than Rhea's a second ago.

Can he see them?

The Pandemonium?

"Run!" he yells.

I push my body faster than it's probably safe to go, risking losing control and stumbling. And I run.

For him.

Out of all the screaming terror trying to consume me, my mind reminds me of how this feels so much like Artemis' Labor when I was running from the dragon. Running to him.

Because Hades is, and always will be, my safe place.

"Faster." I see his lips form the words.

An answering burst of adrenaline sends me shooting forward, into his arms, which close around me, and the door slams down behind me so hard and fast, I feel the wind of it within an inch of my back.

The harsh sound of my breathing fills the empty room. Turns out even goddesses, at the speed I was going, get winded. Or maybe it's the fear making me struggle this way.

"You…" I have to pause to suck in again, and I back up, meaning to step out of his arms. Except the stone door is at my back and I can't move away, instead pinning his hands behind me. "You can see them?"

After only the slightest hesitation, Hades' copy nods.

Now I'm distracted. "What do they look like?"

"Hard to describe. Like a dark hole in the air. No one shape." He tilts his head. "With your new power, you should see them, too."

I frown. "Are they glamours?"

"No. But like the magic of a glamour, they exist in another realm, one that is layered over our reality."

"Oh."

He leans down, face in mine, serious as a heart attack. "The question is, why couldn't *you* see them just now?"

"I turned my power off."

"You turned—" His scowl is so deep, I think his dimples might have been buried forever. "Why the fuck would you do that?"

"It's distracting."

"It's *needed*," he insists, his fingers biting into my back as he grips me tighter. "It will keep you safe from them."

Them.

The Titans, he means.

Do I tell him that they aren't the evil in this place? Would he even believe me? Hades created this copy of himself when he was glamoured to believe lies. So this Hades only knows the lies. Except *this* Hades also knows other things. He's been watching. He's been around for all my past lives and remembers them.

Shouldn't he know the truth by now? "I don't need protection from them."

Hades frowns. "Of course you do. They're using you to get out of here, so they won't kill you. Not yet—"

"Not ever."

He cuts off, going scary silent as he stares at me. "Explain." A single, clipped word that is every inch an order.

Usually I'd push back, but he clearly doesn't know…and he should.

"You…or the you who put you down here to guard your Lock…you were deceived. Glamoured."

His eyes narrow, but he doesn't say anything.

So I keep going. "The Titans aren't monsters. They were loving parents who—"

Hades pushes away from me as if I carry a plague that could infect even him. "Lies." He spits the word. "You fell for their lies."

"They didn't tell me… I saw."

"Then *you* are the one who is glamoured."

I take a small step forward, shaking my head, but he's not interested in listening. Every inch of him screams furious denial, from the anger etched across his face, to the way his hands are so stiff they look like claws, to the smoke rising around him. Only a small amount of the real Hades' power, but it's nothing to sneer at.

"I should just kill you now." He takes a prowling step toward me.

I can't run. I can't go outside. It's just as dangerous out there. So I don't move. "I'm telling you the truth."

His head lowers in a way I've seen predators do in films, gaze tracking me like a lion tracks a baby gazelle.

*Fuck me.*

"I kill you, and I reset time. Erase these lies from your mind." Every step brings him closer, but I still don't run. I know I can't evade him, and it would only trigger a chase. One I'd lose.

"You would do that?" The words force their way out of my mouth, sounding small. "You could hurt me?"

He grabs me roughly by the shoulders, and the look in his eyes is so cold, so remote that I can't help the shiver that spears me like a harpoon. The true Hades has looked at me that way before—when he was trying to break my heart purposely. I've lived it twice now.

"I keep telling you," he snarls. "I'm not *him*. I'm a different beast entirely."

I don't know what I'm expecting. Maybe a quick snap of my neck, maybe a surge of power ending me, all before I wake up in a new timeline, oblivious to everything that has happened.

But it doesn't come.

I search his eyes—sharply silver and still so damned cold. "Then get it over with," I whisper.

His jaw works for several heartbeats before a new kind of anger flashes across his features. "Fuck," he snaps.

Then his mouth is on mine.

His mouth is on mine, but unlike the last kiss, this time, I *feel* it. I feel him. Hades.

*My* Hades.

It's like a piece of his soul is here with me, and the way he's kissing me—harsh and demanding, like he doesn't want to but can't help devouring me—that's my Hades, too.

On a sob of something dark and terrified and despairing that I think I've been trying to pretend I haven't been carrying around every second I'm down here, I wind my arms around his neck, going up on tiptoe to meet him kiss for kiss.

I'm not holding back.

I'm not thinking.

I'm just here, in this moment, with Hades.

Which is when the ground shakes. For a second I think it's me, that his kiss has hit me so hard I'm shaking. But then I realize…this is another earthquake.

We break the kiss to both glance up just in time for fine dirt to rain down on our faces, making us look away. And the ground continues shaking.

Still holding on to me with one hand, he places his palm flat against the door. "The Pandemonium—"

"No. An earthquake. It's probably making the cracks worse."

"What are you talking about, cracks?"

I glance around, realizing for the first time that there aren't any cracks in the Locks. Not that I've seen. Not even on the outside.

Then again, they are built to withstand everything the Titans can throw at them, to keep them imprisoned in Tartarus.

"We've been feeling these quakes in the cells that hold the Titans."

And whatever else they hold. "Cracks have appeared at the tops where the pillars of the cosmos feed into the Overworld."

Hades frowns. "We don't get quakes in Tartarus. This is the bottom of the world. The base. Nothing to shake."

I roll my eyes. "But you felt that, right?"

"Yes. But it's not possible. It has to be something else."

"I'm certain. I've felt them on and off ever since I arrived here, seen the cracks with my own eyes."

Hades steps back very deliberately, and I feel the space he's putting between us like an uncrossable void between universes. "The same way you saw the Titans' innocence?"

We're back to that now? "Haven't you felt the shaking? It's impossible to miss."

"If I'm not awake, I don't see much," he says.

"Awake?"

"There's a lot of time to do nothing. I often put myself in a... hibernation of sorts."

A nothing existence. I think that might be worse than a curse to be unlovable. Has he only ever known me, the entire time he's been down here? Themis died in Hestia's Lock. Has anyone else ever gotten this far?

Does it even mean anything?

He feels so real, and yet my mind tells me he's not. "I don't understand any of this."

Frustration flattens his lips. "I can't do this," he says quietly, almost like he's speaking to someone else not here. Then his shoulders pull back, body in a rigid state of rejection that hurts me to see. "You may stay here until it's safe to leave."

Then he disappears.

Not like smoke or even teleporting. It's like he was never here to begin with.

A hallucination.

The fact that he is, for all intents and purposes, exactly that, and yet is so real to me, scares me the most. What if I truly can't trust my own mind? What if none of us can? What if Tartarus is designed to break us, not just hold us?

I lean back against the stone door, sliding down until my ass hits the ground.

And I wait. Again.

# 63

# FRIENDS IN LOW PLACES

### LYRA

The door to the Lock slides open, and I fall back, smacking my head on the ground. "Ouch," I grumble, feeling the spot.

Cronos leans over, appearing upside-down to me. "That was a silly place to sit," he whispers.

Behind him, Rhea rolls her eyes but says nothing.

I guess it's not safe to make sound yet, or they're being extra cautious after the bell went off twice, since we're so close to the source here.

"Yeah, yeah," I whisper back as I get to my feet.

This time, when they lead me across the chamber and to the tunnels, I stick close to both Titans. Every sense is on screaming-level alert—my ears focused on every sound, my skin prickling.

Remembering Hades telling me my ability should allow me to see the Pandemonium, I squeeze my eyes closed and flip the mental switch. When I open them, nothing appears anywhere near us. No bell sounds. No raging Iapetus.

We make it all the way back to a different hidden cell than the one we've used to gather and sleep before, with Cronos silently pointing out the new turns and directions as we go. A safety measure to keep Iapetus from finding us—the Titans move where they all sleep any time someone gets hit. I guess they'll track him down after the effects wear off.

I turn off my glamour sensing as we cross safely through the doorway located down a very narrow, pitch-black passage with no sconces. With a door between us and the Pandemonium, I don't need my power for now.

We emerge into a cell that is not much more than a roughly cut cave with a door to it, and find all of the Titans, Boone, and Persephone asleep on the floor.

All except Iapetus, who isn't here.

I point at Phoebe, who is tucked into a corner, bandaged but not in pieces like I was worried about. "Is she okay?" I mouth the words.

We all need to rest after two rounds of bells.

They nod, then indicate we should also lie down.

Which I do…and then I just lie here.

I lie here like a useless lump and think through the thousand things that have happened, trying to piece it all together. Trying to get answers.

What I need is time. The broken kind.

Now that I've tested my theory once, in a small way with my axe, do I dare risk a reset to test it in a bigger way? I think I have to. I have to know.

So the next time one of those cracks appears, I'm going for it.

Making that decision feels…right. But now I'm stuck waiting again. So much down here is hurrying up to wait. So I shift, trying to get comfortable, trying to sleep, turning over. And yelp.

A hand clamps over my mouth, muffling the rest of my yelp, and Persephone, who is lying right beside me on the floor, lifts her finger to her lips.

I nod, and she takes her hand away, but then she doesn't say anything.

After a second of her staring at me with those big lavender-blue eyes and me staring back at her, I raise my eyebrows. "Can I…help you?" I whisper.

Hesitation steals over her features.

"If not, I'm going to sleep—"

"Have you ever lied to Hades?" she rushes to whisper.

I blink, then frown.

And she makes a face. "I mean when you time travel. Because you have to be careful what you tell him."

Oh. "I…try not to."

Persephone's perfect features pinch. "Oh."

"Why are you asking? Have *you* lied to him?"

She pauses, then shakes her head. "I've never gone to him when I've ended up in one of those broken chunks of time."

Which means Persephone was never Hades' source. He didn't arrange with her to use Pandora's Box to get her out. He arranged it with someone else. I'm not questioning it. I'm sure of it. And I'm starting to be sure of who.

"Who did you lie to, then?"

Her gaze slides away from mine, lashes dropping to hide her thoughts from me. She doesn't want to say.

"Boone?"

She'd be a terrible poker player, the way her gaze flies to mine. "No—"

"Now you're lying to *me*."

She goes quiet.

"Why did you lie to him?"

Her lips twist. "At least you bother to ask." She sighs when I say nothing to that. "I thought I had to. When I first met him, I had already caused a few resets and didn't want to do it again. I showed up where he was, in the middle of a museum, and I needed a reason for being there. So I pretended to be a thief and beat him to his score. But…"

I wait silently, studying her.

"Time kept taking me back to him."

Anxiety ties knots into my stomach. Time kept taking her to him. "Why?"

She shrugs. "But the last time it happened, I…"

"What? What did you do?"

"I kissed him," she whispers.

"You…" I deflate a little. Just a kiss? "That's it?"

"I shouldn't have. We'd had other moments. More than just me snatching scores from under his nose. Kissing him…was like coming home. It led to…" She blushes. The goddess actually blushes. "Other things. Except time never took me back to him again after that, and when I returned here, the item he'd been trying to steal was in my pocket. I forgot I'd already gotten it, meaning to give it to him. So he…"

So he thought she'd been toying with him just to get the score. Something a thief of the Order would take incredibly seriously. That's his freedom, one more score to pay off his debt. He thought she'd fucked him over. Literally.

No wonder he didn't trust her when we got down here.

"And this last time that he went to the past, I guess he saw me, the me before I ended up down here, with Hades. He must have misinterpreted something about that."

That tugs hard at the string of silly jealousy I've been trying to pretend I'm not all tied up in when it comes to her and Hades.

"But I can't think of anything I've ever done with Hades that would make Boone..."

"Make him what?" She's got me hooked now. I have to know.

"He seems determined to shut me out."

"Why are you telling me this?"

She stares for a moment, then sighs softly. "I thought, if you'd lied to Hades, maybe you could tell me how you..."

"Kept it up?"

Another shake. "Fixed it."

Oh. I think through the complicated relationship and timeline Hades and I have. And while I haven't lied to him exactly, I haven't been truthful every second, either. Same for him. Because neither of us had a choice in the moment. I can see that now.

"I wish I could help you. All I can say is, give Boone time, and never lie to him again."

After a beat, she offers me one of her trademark sunshine smiles. This one feels off, though, like it's dim behind clouds.

I eye her, sunny smile and all. "You say we always become friends?"

Persephone huffs a laugh. "Always. Eventually." Then she pouts a little. "You're taking longer this time."

"How, exactly?"

She tips her head, gaze turning inward as she purses perfect lips. "I think because we're opposites."

I blink because it's so in line with what I was just thinking. "Doesn't that make it harder?"

"No, silly. It means I lighten you up, and you make me..." She glances away, biting her lip.

"Heavy?" I say in a flat voice. "You were going to say I bring you down. Right?"

She rushes to grab my hand. "But in a good way."

"Uh-huh." I try to shake her off, but it's like getting rid of a barnacle that has goo-goo eyes.

"I mean it," she insists. "I think I ended up down here because I trusted the wrong person, even if I still don't know who it was." She makes a face.

"Hades was always warning me that trying to see the good in everyone around me opens me up to be hurt."

"That sounds like Hades."

Her smile draws me in, like we're sharing this thing in common. And part of me wants to let her. I could ask her if she thinks he ever really loved me.

But I don't.

Stuck down here, there's no way she'd know.

"So…there was never anything romantic between you and Hades?"

"Eww. No." She grimaces. "You've asked me that before, you know. In fact, you usually ask."

"Well…as his named queen, the entire world has a picture of you two as lovers. There's even a story of how he tricked you into marrying him with pomegranate seeds."

She sighs. "My mother put that story out there, actually. She needed some reasonable explanation to Zeus about why I'd ever want to be in the Underworld at all, let alone help rule it." She squeezes the hand she's still got a grip on. "You love Hades. That's why I loved you to start with."

I shift back. "That seems strange."

She scoots closer, clearly oblivious to my space needs. "He's one of my favorite people. He gave me a larger purpose than just flowers."

"Spring is important, too."

"Not when your mother can handle it without your help." Her voice turns dry. "And often does." Another sigh, and then she seems to cast off that small mood with a shake of her shoulders. "But Hades… Others are too afraid of him to love him. Except Charon and Cerberus, of course. And me. But you came along way before I did."

For a second, I think maybe she is going to say something else. Instead, she pins determined optimism on her face. "I wish I could tell you what to do about all of this, but I have faith you will work it out and we'll all gain our freedom."

My turn to huff a laugh. "Why in the name of the cosmos would you have faith in me that way?"

The sunshine is real this time. "I told you. Because you're my friend."

# 64

# FORTUNE FAVORS THE BOLD, OR THE COLOSSALLY FOOLISH

### LYRA

Persephone and I fall asleep with her hand clutching mine, and for the first time since I ended up down here, I relax enough to sleep well. Which is why the shimmer of light behind my eyelids is annoying as fuck.

"Go away," I murmur-slur. I'm only vaguely aware of speaking it in my sleep.

But the light frustrating me only grows brighter. And brighter. And drags me out of unconsciousness. I open my eyes to the sight of the underside of broken time directly overhead. It peeks through the cavern's solid rock ceiling, just a little, bobbing and dipping above me like it wants to play.

Rising up on one elbow, I check the room of sleeping Titans, but no one is stirring. No one else is even remotely awake as far as I can tell.

I check the crack again. It's still there. Still beckoning.

Persephone hasn't released my hand, so I try to slip out of her grip, but of course her eyes pop open immediately. My turn to put my fingers to my lips. Then I point overhead, and she looks, eyes widening before they drop back to me.

I point at myself and then time.

She frowns and shakes her head.

So I lean forward to whisper in her ear. "I learn too much from these not to."

Irritation on Persephone is just as adorable as every other emotion, squishing up her delicate features. But then she nods and lets go of her death grip on me.

Quietly and carefully, I get to my feet and reach up toward the shimmering prism of time. Like it was waiting for me all along, it lowers from the ceiling, swallowing me up.

When time releases its grip on me, I don't have the luxury of figuring out when or where I am—although the where is immediately clear and yet doesn't entirely penetrate.

Not around the silent gasp that chokes me.

Because Hades is on his knees in front of Persephone's altar in his Olympus home. "Forgive me," he says in a broken whisper. "There's nothing more I can do. You're just...gone."

Someone may as well have ripped open my chest and torn out my heart from seeing him so shattered. Never mind the twinge of jealousy.

In the same heartbeat, I have a terrible feeling I've gotten my answer to my own suspicions. I think I know what I'm supposed to do now. I was looking for proof when I entered this time loop. This might be it.

I scowl at the back of his head and make a decision.

This is probably a very bad idea.

But I also made a promise—to Rhea. I know where I ended up this time around. And I am 99.9 percent sure I'm right, that broken time is taking me to either where I learn something important or to where I can set certain wheels in motion. This is a big godsdamned wheel. So much bigger than giving myself the axe. And I'm trying really hard not to think about how many ways I could be wrong about that.

Or, for that matter, the world-ending paradoxes.

Because if I do this, there's one thing I become dead certain of...

*I'm* Hades' source.

It has to be me who told him all the things to do. It's the only thing that makes sense.

"She's not dead," I say quietly.

If I'm testing this shit out, I'm going all in. I wait for that weird sensation of a reset I experienced in the visions Mnemosyne gave me of my past, but none comes.

Instead, time marches forward and Hades is almost animalistic in the way he's on his feet and on me in less than a heartbeat, taking me roughly by the neck before he freezes...and stares at me with eyes wide and flashing silver daggers, a nerve ticking at the side of his mouth.

"Lyra?"

I'm right about this.

Please let me be right about this.

# 65
# EVERY TIME YOU GO AWAY

### HADES

I let up my hold on Lyra's throat, but my mind is so battle shocked that I don't let go when I know I should.

Or maybe I just want to hold on to her and keep her with me this time.

*No.*

Rejection of that idea slams through me hard. Not with pain, not with bitterness, but with cold, uncrossable distance.

I've had a long time, more than an era, to think about this. The last time I saw her, when I ended the Anaxian Wars, she used my power over the dead to make me confess my sins to her, then told me I could break my own fate and prophecy, and then, just before she left me again, confessed under my power to her love for me.

The sweetest words.

Words that made me rip her out of my heart.

I haven't seen Lyra's face in centuries. Not once. But that was for the best. It gave me the time I needed to harden my resolve. How I fell in love with her in what amounts to mere hours together, a day at most, spread across the ages…I can't remember anymore.

Gods damn her. I don't *want* to remember.

Even as I drink in every nuance, every curve and valley of a face I thought I had started to forget after all this time. I *made* myself forget.

For the sake of the world, I won't let her back in.

Because when she faded away that day, with more sweet words of truth still tumbling from lips I have yet to kiss, I saw in that moment a different truth. A hideous reality that I forced myself to face in order to break my fate, the way *she* told me I could.

*Lyra* will be the reason I burn down the world.

If I let her get close, if I gave her more of my heart than I already did, if anything ever happened to her, all the control I've fought so hard to gain… It would snap.

I know it would.

*She* is the catalyst to my prophecy.

The deep-seated truth became my base, and I cut her out of my heart with the precision of a surgeon with a scalpel. The extra time she gave me was exactly what I needed.

I feel *nothing* now.

Then her gaze shifts just past me and her eyes widen slightly, and I know whatever comes to take her away is already here. She's already leaving.

I bury the spark of reaction, the knee-jerk need to keep her. Keeping her would destroy more than me.

"She's alive." Lyra almost hurls the words at me. "Persephone."

My world tilts on its axis. That is so far from what I expected, I give my head a disbelieving shake, trying to rearrange the words she just said to make sense. It doesn't work.

Behind my confusion, anger rises like a striking snake. This woman truly is my torment, and I'm done with it. "Just go away, Lyra."

She blinks. The first one is surprise, and in the second, her green-and-gold eyes fill with hurt.

I almost take back the harsh words.

Almost.

It's much harder to be hard when she's right in front of me, looking at me like that, than I thought it would be.

But then she sticks out her stubborn jaw. "You have to listen to me—"

"No. I don't." I slash my hand through the air. "I'm tired of you showing up and telling me things you have no place telling me. Go back to whenever you came from. I'm done."

She flinches, green eyes going from hurt to so wounded, I have to take a step back, hands in fists to keep from reaching for her.

But then that stubborn little chin sticks out even more. "If you don't want to listen because it's me, I get it, after I've been so…flighty."

"That's not why—"

She cuts me off. "But for Persephone's sake, you will listen to me."

I snap my mouth closed so hard, my teeth click. Why can't she just leave me alone? "There is nothing you can tell me. I have searched for her *everywhere*."

"I know." She gives me a small smile. A *sad* smile. The knowing in her eyes is firm. "You won't find her because…" She takes a deep breath, wobbly, like she's afraid. I don't like wobbly from her. Or afraid.

"She's trapped in Tartarus," Lyra says.

Disbelief steals any other possible thought I could have. Disbelief followed by a flare of anger sharp enough that I can't contain it all, and Lyra stiffens, watching me carefully.

She's lying to me. There is no way that's true, and now I know for certain she's a liar. "That's not possible." The words come out in a growl.

She holds my gaze but takes several moments before she speaks, probably gathering more lies together. "I don't know how she got there, but she's there and she's safe. I promise you."

"Safe?" I bark a bitter laugh as all the hazy memories of being swallowed by my father, of fighting my parents and locking them up so that we and the world would be safe from them, bombard me with a mind-splitting pain. "You dare to tell me that she's safe stuck down there with those monsters?"

Another glance past me. What does she see when she comes and goes?

*You don't give a shit*, I tell myself. *You don't care anymore.*

But even with her spewing lies, having her standing here before me is…harder than I thought it would be.

"There's no possibility she could get down there, regardless," I tell her. "There are only two methods to get in and out of that place. One involves all seven gods who created the prison agreeing to something they won't, and Persephone doesn't have access to the other method. Neither do I. Only one person does."

Her face lights up like I just gave her all the answers.

"Pandora's Box," she says.

She might as well have punched me in the nose, the way my head snaps back. "How the fuck do you know about that?"

But she glances past me, shifting to her right like she's inching away from whatever's coming for her.

I start toward her, intending to shut her down in Phlegethon again, make sure she can't leave until I get answers. Again. After that, she can damn well disappear forever.

She doesn't back away as I stalk her, not that she can go anywhere with the wall at her back. My eyes narrow with every step until I invade her space, hands going to the wall on either side of her head, caging her in. Her scent, familiar now—vanilla and citrus tinged with smoke, which I've always wondered at—hits me hard in that second. I fight the urge to press my lips to her neck, to reach for her, to bury myself in her body before I send her away, work her from my system—

*No.*

Fuck, I'm losing it. She makes me lose it.

I'd never be able to let her go if I did that. If I touched her like that.

"Only the original seven who built that prison know about what Pandora's Box really does. It is impossible for you—"

"It's a jar. You put it in a keyhole that only you can see."

Zeus might as well have hit me with every thunderbolt in his vast arsenal. The effect would be the same. "How…"

"It doesn't matter how I know. I do."

Her frantic glance past my shoulder tempts me to turn and look, but I know nothing is there.

"The only way you're going to get Persephone out is with that key," she says. "And the only way you're going to get your hands on the box is if you become King of the Gods."

Rejection curls my mouth into a sneer. "I have no use for that title."

She gives me a look that is pure frustration, and I think she comes close to slapping me. "You do if you want to save her." She takes a gulping breath. "The only way to take the throne of Olympus is to compete."

I go deadly still, shaken to my core, unable to settle between rage, disbelief, and determination to send her away as fast as possible. Before I fucking claim her and punish her for these lies.

Before I believe her.

"You're telling me to compete in the Crucible Games?" The competition my siblings came up with after I ended the Anaxian Wars, games that my actions brought down on mortals' heads. Every soul lost to those games comes to me. "It's rigged. And barbaric. I refuse."

Her pulse at the base of her neck sets to fluttering like a trapped bird. I can see it.

Hells, I can't fucking look away. Just one taste.

"I've seen you win," she says.

That snaps my gaze back up to hers.

"There's only one way, though. On the night of the Selection Ceremony"—she pauses for a moment—"not this coming Crucible but the next, in the twenty-first century—that night, wait at the back of Zeus' temple in the city of San Francisco—"

"In the Americas?" I demand, mouth drawing down into a frown.

Why in the name of all my hells would she send me there? Why am I even listening to this?

She waves me off like I interrupted her, rushing her words more. "Yes. There. A young woman will appear and try to desecrate the temple. You must stop her, and then you must choose her as your champion and do everything you can to make sure she wins."

I could kill her for what she's doing to me right now. Does she even know the battle she's set raging inside me?

Believe her? Don't believe her?

Fuck her? Don't touch her because that will make walking away from her unbearable?

I rake a hand through my hair. "You're telling me to give up on Persephone for over a century. To wait. And then to throw some innocent human life to the horrors of those games."

She doesn't know what the gods make their human champions do. Just because my siblings can't control themselves if they fight, like toddlers. As out of control as I once was. It's pathetic. But that's not the worst thing.

I was right. Lyra is dangerous to me...because she makes me dangerous.

Maybe I burn the world down now to stop this chaos. Maybe it's already too late.

"I've seen it," she insists. And in her eyes, I can see how she's willing me to believe her. "Give your champion the rest of the pearls."

Persephone's pearls, she means. My eyes flare wide. "How do you know they aren't pomegranate seeds?"

She shakes her head, talking faster. "And as one of your gifts, give her a kiss that will protect her in the Underworld."

"Fuck me," I mutter. "That doesn't require a kiss. Any mark will do." This is too much to take in. Only…I'm starting to take it in. She's so damned…sure of herself. "How do I know that what you tell me is true?"

The lines of her start to blur, and I know she's leaving me.

"I have to go," she says.

I should take her to Phlegethon now. In the same instant, I reject that thought. Keeping her with me is worse.

I can't.

That damned prophecy is tied to her. I know it to the depths of my immortal soul.

"Damn it, Lyra." I grab her arms and pull her against me, holding on tight. I try to teleport, but nothing happens, as if the fire of my power was snuffed out as easily as a small candle. That realization brings with it a twist of fear.

"I don't have a choice," she says to the bottom of my chin.

"Fuck."

"I'm sorry."

My heart cracks as if those words squeeze inside without my permission, and I groan. What am I supposed to do? "I can't do this. How do I trust anything you have to say?"

She clutches onto me convulsively for half a beat before she goes up on tiptoe and places her lips softly to my cheek.

"Because I am yours," she whispers for me alone.

She turns even more hazy as she lowers to her heels, green-and-gold eyes tormented but still so damn certain.

She offers me a reassuring smile. Or tries to. It wobbles. "I have always been yours."

Then, like every other fucking time with her, she's gone.

# 66

## SALVATION...OR RUIN?

### LYRA

I'm enveloped in the terrible, endless silence I'm becoming so familiar with.

When I open my eyes, I'm standing in Tartarus among the sleeping Titans, and I've never felt so...alone.

He *hates* me.

I could see it in his eyes, the words he used, the way he held himself away from me like I was poison.

The only thing that kept me from total despair was knowing where our story ends, but... What if I'm wrong?

What if what I just did, what I told him changes everything? I didn't reset time. Gods, my heart was pounding so hard every second of that encounter, I'm surprised it didn't burst from my chest to land at my feet in a bloody pulp. But what if the future of us is different when I get out of here now?

What if I ruined us?

A hand slips into mine, and I look down into Persephone's questioning gaze. "Okay?" she asks softly.

And...I nod.

Not because it's okay. I don't know if it's okay.

But at least I know the truth now. If I'm certain of anything, it's this... I am the one pulling my own strings. Or trying to.

Our pasts...and our futures, whatever those might be now...are in my hands.

# PART 6

# PUPPET MASTER

What's done hasn't been done yet.
And all of it can be undone.

# 67

# BUT THE FUTURE KEEPS FUCKING UP THE PAST

## LYRA

After several days preparing with the Titans, when we go to the Locks this time, we don't risk all of us. Half of the Titans and Persephone hang back in our current safe room while Cronos, Rhea, Mnemosyne, and Iapetus escort Boone and me down to the next Lock.

I tried to get Persephone to come with us, actually. I don't know why that little conversation we had made a difference, but it did. She just shook her head, gaze sliding to Boone. I think maybe she's afraid to distract him or afraid to watch him go in Hera's Lock.

Honestly, of the two of us, Boone should be the most afraid, because apparently, for this Lock, we're going to experience the pain of childbirth. No idea how that's supposed to work for him at a biological level—me either, for that matter, given I'm not pregnant—but I'm sure the goddess will find a way.

Even knowing this, he insisted on going with me.

None of us speak as we make our way there, passing by doors that contain screaming, doors that rattle, and maybe the worst of all, silent doors, as we wind our way there. Is it terrible that after only the short time I've been here, I've stopped noticing? I'm pretty sure it is.

Meanwhile, with every step, instead of focusing on the Lock and what we'll face like I should be, I'm still hung up on what happened with Hades, what I did.

I haven't told anybody else about this yet, not even Persephone. I want to get all my mental ducks in a row before I drop this new fun fact on them.

But I'm so busy worrying over my thoughts, which are zooming around like bats inside the belfry of my head, that before I know it, we're past the ominous obelisk that the Pandemonium come from when they unleash and standing on the bridge overlooking the abyss that will lead Boone and me to Hera's Lock. I glance over my shoulder to find both Mnemosyne and Iapetus waiting at the entrance to the tunnel on the other end of the bridge from the doors.

Iapetus insisted on being one of those who came with us. I'm not sure if he insisted because he felt he has something to prove. That the last time the bell went off was a fluke. That this time, if that happens, the Pandemonium won't find him so slow again.

Honestly, I think it has less to do with pride and more to do with Phoebe. I've seen the way he flinches when Phoebe makes the slightest move or sound as she slowly heals from the injuries he inflicted on her in his rage state, or the way quiet, studious Koios, who hasn't left his wife's side, won't even look at Iapetus, let alone talk to him.

Maybe that's why I offer him a small smile now. One that gets a frown in return.

He really is a grumpy motherfucker.

Boone, standing to my left, whistles a question. *Ready?* Then nods at the pitch-black void we're about to toss ourselves into like human sacrifices.

I purse my lips to whistle back the signal for *let's go*, but the sound cuts off in my mouth as my eyes widen at the sight of a crack opening up out of nothing, like a scar in the air. It flickers oddly behind Boone.

In reaction to whatever my face does, he jerks around. "That's shit timing," he mutters. "We should jump now."

But the fissure stops.

Just…stops.

It doesn't disappear or go a different direction, but it doesn't move, either, almost as if broken time itself has been stopped. The way it's gone so unnervingly still reminds me a little bit of how it felt when Cronos stopped time long enough to yank me and Boone through the massive gates of Tartarus at the end of this bridge.

I check the Titan. "Is this you?"

He's staring at the rip of time. "I'm not the one—" He stumbles forward, hand flying out in front of him like he's trying to stop or catch something.

I whirl to face the crack only to back up rapidly at what's coming out. Boone grabs me by the wrist hard and keeps me from tumbling into the abyss, but neither of us takes our eyes off the horror we're looking at.

Me.

*I* am what comes out of the crystalline fissure, looking exactly like I do now except different clothing, and…

Someone or something has slit my throat.

Not a nice cut, either. Jagged, all the way across, and I suspect so deep they hit my spinal cord at the back.

"Oh my gods." Boone drops my arm and runs for the other me… future me?…as she takes one stumbling step forward. Her hand goes up to the slit in her throat, red blood—not golden because she's mortal in that moment—squirting and gurgling out between her fingers…*my* fingers… and down my arm to splatter and pool on the rock bridge at my feet.

I'm staring at me, feet frozen to the spot. And whatever future of me this is, she is looking only at me even when Boone reaches her, cupping his hand over hers, trying to stem the flow of blood.

She's mouthing something at me.

I shake my head. "What?"

She takes another unsteady step and, even with Boone trying to help her, goes down to one knee. Her wide eyes remain on mine, desperate for me to know what she's trying to communicate, and she's still mouthing. Two words, I think.

"Don't speak, Lyra," Boone tells her…tells the future version of me he's trying to save.

"Hera's Lock?" Cronos guesses.

She pushes Boone off her, visibly weakening and dropping to all fours, or threes, rather, as she keeps one hand still pressed across the wound in her throat. But she nods. Then forces her head up with her hand under her chin, opening the wound like a gaping hole down to her soul, allowing the blood to gush out faster as she mouths one more word.

"Monsters."

Then she collapses to the ground as her body tries to find some way to control the blood loss or get air down her windpipe, but she only gurgles as she sucks in the blood that's pouring out of the same hole.

"No!" Boone is on his knees beside her, trying to plug the wound, do anything.

But my future self shudders in slow jerks, and I know I'm watching my own death rattles.

That rip in time that dropped her here decides to move again, swallowing her body and taking it away from us, back to whenever or wherever that was.

Leaving Boone behind, on his knees and staring at his blood-soaked hands, looking like death himself. Meanwhile, my blood—the thick, bright-red liquid pooled on the bridge—drips over the sides and down into the abyss below.

Hades' undeniable voice cuts me off on a shout coming from far below. "Lyra!"

Then everything goes dead and silent.

At first, I think maybe shock has me in its grip so tightly, I'm not sure I'm still alive. I even try to cry out, but my vocal cords won't work. My body won't move, either, not even to blink. Not even to breathe. It's not time travel. I'm not caught in a broken crack.

This is something else.

Just as I think I'm about to follow my future into death, sound and sensation and breath return in the strangest kind of way. Not with a whoosh, but with a stutter, like a skipping record.

I think all of us must have been in the same frozen state, because we all come out of it shouting.

Boone is the loudest and directed at Cronos. "What the fuck just happened?"

# 68

# HARD RESET

### LYRA

At Boone's yell, all of us go still and quiet, trying to make like we don't exist as we wait for that fucking bell to ring.

But it doesn't.

I'm trying not to let the internal loop of my voice in my head repeating "oh my gods" over and over again drown out what's happening up here on the bridge.

We all look...*afraid* is not the right word.

Petrified.

Petrified is the word I'm looking for. I don't think I've ever seen Cronos like this. Not in this way. Not even the day his children attacked him.

"What happened?" I ask him softly. "Tell us."

He swallows so hard, the gulp of it is audible, bouncing off the rock walls. The sound of a Titan's terror is definitely one of the worst noises in the world. It sends a fresh wave of my own crushing fear ripping through me.

"Time just reset," he whispers.

It reset? But...I'm still here.

I'm vaguely aware of slipping back into a state of shock as Boone jumps to his feet with a squelch of his boots in my blood. "What?" I hear him demand. I'm still kneeling on the ground. "Then why are we still here?"

But the answer is on Cronos' face. In the tenor of his fear. All of their fear.

"The point we reset to moved forward," I say. It's not a question.

Out of the corner of my eye, I catch the way Boone cranks his head around to look at me. "So it's not a hundred and fifty years ago now?" he asks.

The memories Mnemosyne showed me—she showed them to me in patches but grouped and in chronological order, and suddenly it all makes more sense.

"The reset moved us forward in time. Am I right?" I ask Cronos. Seeing myself die wasn't what tipped me off. The weird feeling after clued me in.

The Titan shoves his hand through his hair in a gesture that is so patently like Hades, the tiniest corner of my mind wants to relent, wants to give the Titan a hug.

But we need to know. "Am I right?"

Blowing out a sharp breath, he drops his hand to his side, then nods. "Sometimes, when time resets, it doesn't go all the way back to the same moment it started from," he admits in a whisper.

"You didn't think you should tell us this once we knew about how things operate down here?" I swear Boone's close to taking Cronos by the throat.

Cronos doesn't look at him, though. He's still focused on me. "It's rare."

"How rare?" Boone demands in a harsh whisper.

By now Rhea has joined us on the bridge, slipping her hand in to her husband's. "We've had only four resets that started from a new point in time. The one we've been circling on lately started when Persephone ended up down here. Before that, there were hundreds of years between resets. Thousands."

Cronos stares at Rhea, exchanging so many thoughts with a single expression. "I didn't even think it was possible."

Boone looks at me, waving a hand at them. "Do you believe them?"

"Mnemosyne's memories," I remind him. "I've seen it. I just didn't know what I was looking at. They're telling the truth."

The look Cronos gives me is a combination of appreciation—I think for my believing him—and apology as well, as if he thinks all of this is his fault.

But it's not. Or not entirely.

He may have broken time, but I *just* told Hades things. Sure, it's been a few days down here since then, but…

What if this is because of me? What if this is my fault?

I've been dicking around with powers beyond my comprehension, assuming I was smart enough to figure it all out. Was I horribly wrong?

"Fine. I'll believe them because you tell me to, but one thing is for damn sure," Boone says. "Lyra's not going into Hera's Lock. Not if that's how she comes out."

Boone disappears from view entirely, using his thief's power to become invisible. Only the sound of his feet on the ground tells me that he takes a running leap right at the abyss.

Rhea, moving with the speed not even the gods possess, snatches him from the air and slams his invisible form down on the ground. He blinks back into visibility, hands going to her grip on his throat. She's kneeling on his legs, and Boone, no matter how he tries, can't dislodge her.

"I know you want to protect Lyra, but don't be rash," Rhea tells him with the utmost calm. "You are not simply jumping in there before we form a plan. We don't know if you're just as important as she is yet."

Boone's eyes bulge before he gives in, tapping her arm.

"You won't jump?" she asks, still sounding like she's chatting about the weather over tea in a library where she has to keep her voice down. "I have your word."

He nods, and when she lets go, he comes up coughing hard.

I'm glad she stopped him, though. Otherwise, I would have had to go over the ledge after him. And I really don't feel like going through the gruesome death that just happened to me a second ago.

Rhea leads the others away, but my feet are rooted to the spot, head spinning and guilt trying to induce a heart attack.

*Did I do this?*

# 69

# CONFESSIONS

### LYRA

The reset. Was it my fault? The question is echoing like the Ghost of Christmas Past.

Cronos pauses at the tunnel entrance to check over his shoulder, and I don't change my face fast enough. He takes a single look, and his features…harden.

Then he beckons me forward, and somehow, I manage to make my feet work. When I make it to him, all he says is, "Wait."

I frown. But I also wait.

I wait while our merry band of misbegotten gods and Titans makes our way back through the spiraling tunnels to the others. Cronos doesn't even walk with me, instead far ahead with Rhea, murmuring something in her ear that I can't catch. Which is probably why it surprises me when, as we're nearing one of the tunnel turn-offs to our latest safe room, he stops walking, hanging back until I draw even with him.

Boone notices and does the same so that the others continue on but the three of us are left.

"This is between Lyra and me," Cronos tells him.

I get in just ahead of Boone's protest. "I have something I need to tell him."

After all…Cronos saw it in my face. He is going to get it out of me anyway. No need to hide it.

When Boone doesn't relax even a tiny bit, I whistle a signal. *It's okay.* With a nod, he turns around and follows the others.

Cronos leads us a different way, eventually taking a tunnel that I haven't been in before. This tunnel has cells, like the others, but they're quiet, and I can't tell if they're empty or the inhabitants have reasons to be quiet.

Either way, my skin crawls a little more with every step we travel deeper into the mountainous rock base.

Cronos finally stops at one and passes his hand over the lock. The door gives with a quiet click before swinging open. He waves me ahead of him into a very small chamber, not even big enough to lie down on the floor and stretch out comfortably. The me who arrived in Tartarus not that long ago would have been terrified when the door closes and the lock turns with a loud, echoing snick.

But I'm not afraid. Not of Cronos. I glance around and then at him. "Privacy?"

He nods. "Also a safe place to do what I'm about to do."

Again, if I didn't know him like I do now, that would have come off as a threat, all dire-voiced and serious.

I can't help the way my lips twitch. "We've really got to do something about your delivery."

"My delivery?"

"The scary-as-shit Titan." I give an exaggerated shudder. "So ominous."

His expression flattens. "I was not ominous just now."

"You were."

"I was not—" He cuts off, giving me a closer look. "You're stalling. Why?"

Damn. Time to rip off this Band-Aid. "I...I think I'm the reason that things are so different and that time did a hard reset."

When he turns even more serious, it's not scary, it's formidable, and there's a part of me that squirms. The part of me that went unnoticed for so long, thanks to my curse. Which is when I realize that I don't want to disappoint him—any of them, really, but for some reason I can't pinpoint, especially him.

"Don't say more yet," he warns. Then Cronos—the god of time, the King of the Titans, son of Primordials Uranus and Gaia—sits on the ground crisscross applesauce.

There's something you don't see every day.

He beckons, and I sit on the ground facing him and wait for whatever he does next.

"I'm going to change what you are seeing right now. We're not moving locations. We'll still be safely locked in this room. Even if the bell goes off, the Pandemonium can't get to us. But it will feel like we leave. You and I are going to travel into my mind, where we can talk and only the two of us will ever know what was said."

"Damn. There are heads of state who really wish they had that power," I mumble.

Cronos huffs a laugh. "There are gods who wish they had this power," he says in a dry voice.

"I bet."

An amused chuckle follows me into darkness and silence.

Not scary or oppressive but warm and comfortable. Safe. Sound comes back to me first. Laughter. Children's laughter and… "Do I hear sea lions barking?" I ask.

# 70

# PUT YOUR HAND IN MINE

### LYRA

Cronos doesn't answer, but my vision clears, and I can see for myself. Definitely sea lions.

"What in the—" I take in where we are with wide eyes. "Seriously?"

Cronos chuckles. "Seriously."

We're standing on Pier 39 along the wharf in San Francisco. *My* city. The skies are crystal blue, no fog in sight, the temperature and the breeze both perfect. It might even be a weekend, given the swell of the crowds both here and walking the main street toward the food and shopping.

I can smell the slight salty tang of ocean air, popcorn, maybe even cotton candy. And for once I'm not here as part of a crew of thieves trying to steal from people, even if I'm just observing. I'm just…here. I don't have to worry about anyone thinking I look suspicious, or being caught, or the score.

I can just enjoy the moment. Even if I know the moment isn't real.

"Come with me," Cronos says.

I'm so busy looking around me that I follow him without question or comment all the way to an ice cream stand. One that miraculously has no line. "Is pralines and cream still your favorite flavor?" Cronos points.

"I told you that?" Must've been a past iteration of me.

"You've told me many things."

I wrinkle my nose. "I believe you. I'm just trying to figure out how ice cream came up."

He hands me a cone with a double scoop, taking his own plain vanilla and nodding toward an open bench in the sun. I like his version of San Francisco where we get so lucky.

"I would have thought you'd pick a more...flamboyant flavor," I say, eyeing his cone. "Cherries jubilee or mint chocolate chip, or one of those Ben and Jerry's flavors."

"Sometimes simple is better." He nods at my ice cream, indicating I should eat it before it melts. The sweet flavor on my tongue is perfect, too.

But I guess perfect is a problem for me, because before I know it, my eyes are stinging. I blink back tears.

The thing is...I used to lie awake in the den and fantasize about my parents coming to take me home and all the things we'd do together as a family. Thieves tend to do most of our thieving in heavily peopled areas, which means I saw a lot of the touristy spots in my city—and a lot of families doing those things. That's what I'd picture.

*This* is what I'd picture. "Are you being nice to me just because you need me to get you out?"

"Is there something wrong with nice?" Cronos meets my gaze. He's so different from the Titan who pulled me into Tartarus or who I thought he was. He's...steady...somehow. Has he always been steady and was meeting me where I was so I wouldn't reset?

I drop my gaze and study my ice cream, licking a drip off the top of the cone. "No," I finally say slowly.

"But you don't trust it." This, he doesn't ask, and I glance over to find him watching me with eyes that reflect curiosity rather than offense.

"I guess I don't." I frown a little. "Have we talked about this before, too?"

"Yes."

"That has to be so tedious for you." I can't imagine having to have the same conversations, or versions of them, over and over, maybe with different outcomes.

He gives a small shrug. "The reasons change depending on how you..."

"How my life went," I fill in.

He huffs a laugh. "I try to pretend those times haven't happened and let you tell me this time. Once you trust me."

That has to be so hard. I tip my head, looking at this Titan through a different lens. "Do I ever trust sooner?"

Another laugh, this one more a surprised bark, like the sea lions. "Come to think of it, no. You don't."

I lick my ice cream again. "So it's a basic personality flaw." I pause, still thinking. "I guess of the ones out there, that's not so bad."

"I'd even say it's helpful. Nothing wrong with self-preservation. It's how we survive."

His word choice makes me grin. "If Hades heard you say I have self-preservation, he'd probably strongly disagree."

Cronos grunts. "Well…yours does tend to be overridden by a stronger instinct to help others."

He does know me. "I have no idea why. It just…always works out that way."

"It is because, deep down, you have a good soul. Hades could see that, I'm sure."

"I guess." It's nice to thinks so, at least.

"So…" He hands me a napkin to wipe the lingering ice cream from my face. "Tell me what happened."

I open my mouth, then pause.

"Is it that bad?" he asks when I don't go on.

"I'm not sure," I mutter. Then side-eye him. "What have I told you before?"

"Uh-uh. Just get it off your chest."

Damn. I take a breath and start talking. I tell him my theories—that I'm the puppet master, that I'm setting up my own path before I'm even there, and that the way time comes for me, I have to wonder if someone is also making sure I go back to specific moments to be able to do that.

Cronos doesn't say a word. Not one. Not even a grunt. But his brows draw slowly together, lowering into a deeper frown the longer I talk.

Finally, I've laid everything out for him. "What do you think?"

He's still silent, gaze unfocused, or maybe focused internally, frown still heavy. This does not seem like something he's dealt with a thousand times already. That's probably not good.

"Cronos?" I whisper.

He lets out a heavy sigh. "You have used time to set certain things in motion during your past visits to us, but not at the level you're describing. It was little things in your previous lives. But if someone is manipulating my broken time"—he gives me a pointed look—"which is a new twist, that, at least, tells me that you should trust it."

I…should? "Without knowing who is sending me?"

"So far, it sounds like they are sending you to the moments you need."

True. "Do you think it's future you?"

He flattens his lips. "Hard to say."

"Right. I guess other gods have the ability to control time, too." I know Kali, in Hinduism, is the goddess of time, and in the Greek tradition, there are other gods who have an effect on time in different ways.

"Not like me," he muses. "But maybe Kairos."

"Zeus' youngest son?" I ask.

He nods. "Born after I was locked away. As far as I've been able to glean, his control of time is opportunistic, having to do with when actions must be taken to achieve certain results. So it fits."

"I've never even met him. And he'll have been raised to think of you as a monster. I can't see him wanting to help." Then I wince as my wording repeats itself in my head. "No offense."

Cronos shakes his head slowly. "No. I agree."

"Then…" Should I even mention this?

"What?"

I lean my elbows on my knees, suddenly chilly even in the sun. "I thought this last more permanent reset might have been my fault. Because I…pulled a pretty big string."

"Maybe…" He must see the way my face falls. "But I think we should trust it for now. If shattered time is taking you to opportune moments, do what you think is right. At the very least, think of this reset as positive. Maybe we've finally lined everything up just the way we need it to get out, without having to start so far in the past."

"Maybe," I murmur, sounding like him a moment ago.

"Come." He holds out his hand. "We should tell the others."

Even as I take his hand, I look around us, not wanting to leave this place.

He gives me a squeeze. "Fantasy is good, but staying in it to the detriment of your life in the real world is not."

"I know."

"I'll take you to the real place when we get out."

That warm and comfortable darkness and silence claims me again, and I close my eyes for a second, as if that helps. When I open them, we're both sitting on the floor of the tiny, locked room.

A new chill shudders through me. One of…loss. "You know," I say as we're getting to our feet, "I always imagined doing those things—the sea lions, the ice cream at the wharf—with my father." For some reason, that doesn't feel bitter to me now, and my smile for Cronos is sincere. "I never in a million years would have imagined that it would eventually be with you."

The Titan's gaze skates over my features, and I swear there's an affectionate light in his blue eyes. "I know. You told me once about wanting to do those things, so I…" He glances away like he's embarrassed.

The King of the Titans, whose release from this place is so feared, is embarrassed.

"Why?" I ask.

He seems to know what I'm asking, because a self-deprecating smile tugs one side of his mouth up. "I always loved being a father. I miss it. Miss my children sorely. I guess I just…wanted to give you those happy memories that you craved and remember myself what it felt like—being a father with his daughter—even for a second."

A glimmer off to the side draws our attention as a crack in the fabric of time forces itself through the thick rock wall.

"Actually…" Cronos puts a hand on my shoulder. "Before we go to the others, one more test wouldn't hurt."

I look at him with my eyebrows raised. "Seriously?"

He tips his head toward the time that is inching closer. "See where it takes you and go from there."

I consider the shimmering break, then take the few steps across the room to where it seems to be waiting. I pause to look over my shoulder, and Cronos waves me on. So I take that final step.

Just as the terrible silence grips me, I think I hear him say, "I trust you, daughter."

But I can't be sure.

…Where the fuck am I?

All I see are white columns. Some kind of temple to the Greek gods, obviously. But where?

Lightning sizzles overhead simultaneously with an ear-splitting crack of thunder. I slap my hands over my ears with a grimace. Then squeeze my eyes shut as familiarity and realization knock into me at the same time.

Oh no. Not here. Please not Zeus' temple. I hate that fucking place. When did broken time take me to now? It's one of only two options, because I've avoided this temple most of my life.

It's either the day I was born…or the day I first met Hades.

A quick look behind me shows no one else is in the inner temple. Given that my mother gave birth to me here on a day it was open to the public, I'm guessing when I am is option number two.

Carefully, I shift around the column, looking not inside the temple now but outside. I'm already positioned on the side of the building that I came at it from when I was determined to have it out with Zeus about my curse. So I'm watching for movement beyond the temple, up the hill among the trees.

But that's not what catches my eye first.

What catches my eye is the distinct form of a man leaning a shoulder against a column on the outside row, hidden in the shadows, the same as I am now.

Hades.

My heart feels like it both expands and contracts at the same time, even if that's physically impossible. Because he's here.

Hades *listened* to me. Despite how he was that day, despite how he hated me and didn't want to believe me…he still came here tonight.

And somehow, that makes what I'm about to put him through, as well as myself, even worse.

*I'm sorry*, my heart cries out to him. *Please forgive me.*

I barely stop myself from running to him, fighting every instinct that screams at me to. The problem is…I'd likely only make things worse by showing up now.

I don't know why time brought me here, but the smartest thing I can do is wait…and watch.

# 71

# ONCE UPON A TIME

### HADES

I shouldn't fucking be here.

I've waited a hundred and fifty years for this strange moment in time with not a lot to go on. A hundred and fifty years of trusting someone I'm actively trying to forget.

Lyra.

Maybe I should just leave? I almost didn't come in the first place.

Lightning zaps overhead with a thunderclap that rattles even the temple, and I shift against the column of my brother's house of worship in San Francisco. It's the first night of the current Crucible, and Zeus is putting on a show for the watching world. He's always cared more about humans' awe of him. That is the only reason he desires the throne of Olympus.

He's an asshole that way. Always has been. Maybe we should have locked him up in Tartarus with our parents.

I sigh, checking the skies. Why am I still standing here?

But I already know why.

I still don't have any proof that Persephone is in fucking Tartarus, but she hasn't shown up anywhere else in all this time. Neither has Lyra.

So here I fucking am.

At least, if this woman I'm supposed to name as my champion is a no-show, no one else will witness the classic fool I turn into for a woman I am actively trying to forget. Not that I've been able to do that successfully.

I should just leave.

But the last words Lyra said to me won't let me. They're what dragged my feet here tonight.

I asked her why I should trust her, and her answer slayed me— *Because I'm yours.*

Exactly what I thought. Both my heaven and my hell. The irony, given who I am, isn't lost on me. King of the Underworld, god of death, and sucker for five little words.

But my reaction to those three little words, the way they burrowed into my heart...that makes Lyra Keres just as dangerous for me as I thought.

Movement, a simple shifting of shadows, catches my gaze out in the trees that surround this temple on Zeus' mountain.

I narrow my eyes but otherwise don't move. Humans aren't usually so stealthy. It could just be an animal—

A woman steps into view, but she's at the farthest end of the temple, and I can only make out her profile.

Ignoring the way my heart thuds irrationally, I tip my head, studying what I can see of her in the moonlight and flashes of lightning overhead. Not short but not tall. Slender in a way that says she's healthy but has never known indulgence. Chin-length dark hair.

She stares at the pristine columns of the building, and I wish I could see her expression. The way she's holding her body so tensely, her hands clenching and unclenching at her sides, she looks like a brittle rubber band that could snap at any second.

Then she moves.

Jerky but fast, she bends over and snatches a rock off the ground.

And I move.

Teleporting is easy for gods. A whisper of my will, and I'm standing behind her just as she cocks her arm back to hurl her makeshift weapon. I clamp a hand around her wrist mid-throw and yank her backward, into me, so I can wrap my arms around her and pin her down. "I don't think so," I say in her ear.

She goes wild, thrashing against my hold like a feral thing. "Let me go!"

"I'm not going to hurt you," I tell her.

She goes still. Oddly still, but the way she's breathing hard, breasts pressing into my arm with each inhalation, she's not calm.

"I said"—she grits out each word—"Let. Me. Go."

I tighten my grip. This one will run if I give her the opportunity. "Not if you're going to hurl rocks at the temple. I don't feel like dealing with Zeus tonight."

Not until I'm ready, at least. If I decide to listen to Lyra and name this woman my champion.

"Well, *I* do!" She struggles to get away.

Something tells me that whatever issue she has with Zeus...with my brother, it's always well-deserved... But a strange thread of sympathy stitches through me. Humans aren't the only ones he ruins.

"He's an asshole, I get it. Trust me," I mutter in a low voice. "But if I thought throwing a tantrum would change that, I'd have brought that temple down with my bare hands years ago."

To my shock, not only does she calm slightly, but she leans back into me. Just for the smallest beat in time.

And I...relax.

Like we're in sync somehow. Did Lyra know this would happen? Maybe she sent me to someone I would work well together with because she doesn't fear me?

"If I let you go, do you promise not to attack a defenseless building again?" I ask softly.

"No."

I sigh. This one is stubborn, apparently. She reminds me of someone.

Then she says, "That fuckhead doesn't deserve *any* prayers."

I swallow back a bark of laughter, a strange warmth sparking in my chest. Mutual hatred is a heady bonding agent. "Careful."

"Why?" she asks. Is she smiling? It sounds like it in her voice. "You worried someone might want to hit me with a bolt of lightning while I'm in your arms?"

"Talk like that could win a few hearts," I whisper. Not mine, though. I gave it away a long time ago.

She goes as stiff as a corpse for long enough that I start to worry before her chin drops to her chest.

"Highly unlikely," she mutters. "Zeus made sure no one can *ever* love me."

The silence that drops between us might as well be a roar of dull sound. Zeus cursed her to be unlovable? It sounds like something my brother would do. But...why in the name of Tartarus would Lyra send me a cursed human as a champion?

Also...I like her. If she's cursed to be unlovable, shouldn't I feel... nothing?

I drop my arms and take a step away. Her back to me, the woman shoves her hands in her pockets.

"I...find that hard to believe."

My one small admission of doubt seems to turn her against me, her entire body going stiff. "Listen, I'm fine now. You can move on..."

She turns around.

If her admission a second ago was a roar of silence, the way my entire body takes the hit as I catch full sight of her face might as well be a thousand spears to my gut. It requires every ounce of my not insubstantial self-control to keep from doubling over or taking her by the shoulders to shake answers out of her.

Lyra.

This is *Lyra*.

My Lyra...only not. Same age as every other time I've seen her. Same green-and-gold eyes and stubborn chin. Shorter hair, though.

This can't be right. What in the name of the evils of Tartarus is she doing here? Is she just...fucking with me now or something?

And why is she staring at me with horror in her eyes, as still as a mouse staring at a lion?

"I'm afraid one of us shouldn't be here," she quips. Then, based on what her face does next, immediately regrets those words.

But I'm just...more confused.

So I say nothing. I need more. Anger—at her and myself—slowly builds like heaping fuel on a slowly growing fire, and I stand with my arms crossed, taking in every detail of her. She's dressed differently than before—jeans, black fitted shirt, and a jacket with lots of pockets. Basic current-day human garb.

When I've seen her any time before this, she's been almost relaxed with me. Like she knows me. But now, I get the feeling that she doesn't know if she should run...or bow.

I fucking hate being put on the back foot like this.

Because she sent me here. *Choose her as your champion*, Lyra said. But the girl is...her.

*Gods damn it, Lyra.*

"Do you know who I am?" I demand.

She pauses before answering. "Should I?"

My eyes narrow. I do not have time for her flippant bullshit. I need an answer to that question. A *real* answer. Now.

Playing on her nervousness of me, I deliberately take two long, slow strides directly into her space. "Do you *know* who I am?"

My Lyra would have snapped that yes, of course she does. But this Lyra… She goes pale. No way is she faking her fear, even as she refuses to back down from me.

"Hades." She swallows. "You are Hades."

A thousand thoughts hit me all at once.

Her physical response, more than her words, tells me that this woman in front of me is *not* the Lyra I've known for ages, but I'm starting to get a glimmering of an idea as to what she is.

I've always assumed my Lyra is a goddess who can manipulate time somehow, similar to my father's power, only maybe not very far along in her use of it, given that she doesn't seem to have control over much, including how long she stays in one place and time.

Is *this* Lyra's beginning?

Ages after my own beginning, and yet she's been sewn into the fabric of my life all this time. A glittering single thread that should have no bearing, and yet I suspect if I ever tried to pull it out, everything would unravel.

My Lyra must be from a future I still have yet to reach.

*This* Lyra's future, now, too.

How in the name of the Primordials did she go from this human form to the goddess I know? I add that as question one million and forty-two to my growing list of questions about Lyra and regroup. Lyra sent me to the human version of herself for a reason.

This is how we get Persephone out of Tartarus.

That's what she said.

By me making *Lyra* my champion. Lyra, who I'm trying not to love and need to stay away from. *Human* Lyra, who could die in those ridiculous games.

Fuck.

My gut rejects that so hard, it takes Herculean effort not to show it to her now. Right now…I need…

What do I need?

To figure out what to do with her. That's what I fucking need. And that's the trouble with messing around with time. Lyra told me to come here, choose her, for a reason.

Meanwhile, this human version of her I'm dealing with knows nothing. And if I learned anything from my father before we shut him up in Tartarus, it's not to mess with time. I'm pretty damn sure the wrong choice is telling her that a future version of herself sent me here to put her in the Crucible. I don't want to break her.

So what do I do with her?

The only option I see is to play into her obvious assumption that bad luck landed her with me catching her here about to throw a rock at Zeus' temple. As far as she's concerned, I'm just another asshole god like my brother.

And all of this hits me in the blink after she said my name.

*My* fucking name. On her lips.

Underworld give me strength.

I offer her a condescending smile. "Was that so hard?"

Immediately, her expression makes me want to laugh. She thinks I'm a dick. It's adorable.

No, damn her. Not adorable. Nothing is adorable.

"Now," I say, more for distraction than anything. "Let's talk about what you think you were doing."

She gives me a confused frown. "I thought you already—"

"And with the Crucible starting tonight, even." I deliberately suffuse disappointment in my voice, only stopping short of tsking. That might be too much.

She sighs. "Do you want an apology before you smite me or something?"

There's the mouth on her I've come to know. I draw arrogance around me like armor. "Most would fall to their knees before me. Beg for my mercy."

She swallows hard but still meets my gaze. Even as a human, this woman is fearless. Or foolish. I haven't decided which. "I'm pretty sure I'm dead either way," she says. "Would kneeling help?"

Fuck. If she keeps this up, naming her my champion is the worst possible thing I could do.

"Is that why you're here?" she asks. "The Crucible?"

*You, my star. You're the reason.* "I have my own reasons for being here tonight." I mean it to be a warning. To cut off any more questions.

She ignores the hint in my tone.

"Why did you stop me?" She glances at the temple.

I'm done with question-and-answer time and tap my thumb against my chin. "The question is, what do I do with you now?"

"I assume you're going to send me to the Underworld," she says.

An option that appeals, but for an entirely different reason. One that has no place in the here and now.

I hum vaguely. "I can do worse than that." I'm focused more on whether or not I should name her my champion.

Walking away is what I should do, *because* it's Lyra. I've had over a century to think about this, and I still don't know, swinging wildly between options and reactions.

Godsdamn.

I am not an indecisive god, but this is fucking impossible.

"Oh?" She tips her head. "I do hear you are creative with your punishments."

Right. I'll let her go for now and figure out my next step when she's not standing so temptingly close.

"I'm flattered." I give her a tiny, mocking bow. "I could make you roll a rock up a hill and never make it to the top, only to start back over every single day for the rest of eternity."

"I'm pretty sure Zeus came up with that."

The hells he did. "Were you there?"

She shrugs. "Either way, it sounds like a vacation. Peaceful, undisturbed labor. When do I start?"

I shake my head. "I'm not going to kill you. Yet."

It's a tease, but the wariness that clouds her eyes… I don't like it. "Relax, my star."

Her eyes flare slightly.

Shit. Should not have called her that. Not yet. But I'm not taking it back, and I don't explain myself. Ever.

In the silence that falls between us, she takes in what I'm wearing. I didn't think much of the worn boots and jeans, the blue button-down shirt rolled up at the sleeves, or the vintage 1800s leather holster that most mistake for suspenders, custom made to hold the axes that Odin once gifted me.

"Do I pass inspection?" I drawl.

Her gaze swings back up to meet my eyes. "You look different than I thought."

I can't help it, twitching my eyebrows up in question. Because even my Lyra hasn't shared something like this before. "And what did you expect? All-black clothing? Perhaps a full leather getup?"

"Don't forget the horns. And maybe a tail," she says.

Never knows when to stop talking. Even now.

"That's a different god of death." I scoff, then mutter under my breath, "Damn, I abhor expectations."

"Your home in the Underworld is Erebus," she points out.

"And?"

"It's called… Wait for it." She holds up a hand, suddenly reminding me so much more of the Lyra I know. "The Land of *Shadows*."

I've fantasized about what it would be like to kiss those lips since I was still a young god of nineteen. But that's out of the question. She needs to stop talking.

I slip my hands in my pockets so I don't reach for her. "I always thought that naming was unoriginal. It's the Underworld. Of course there are shadows."

She always does this to me—gets me off topic and takes me down murky paths.

"I guess," she says slowly. Then, after a beat, "I mean, technically, you're not the god of shadows or even the goddess of night. And if the fire-and-brimstone thing is true, then it seems like it would be quite well lit down there."

She should know. She's seen it. But not yet. This Lyra hasn't seen shit. Fuck, I hate all things time travel.

"You have a perception issue, if you think about it," she says next.

I rock back on my heels. "*I* have a perception issue."

"Yes, you do. If they can't see for themselves, mortals will believe what they are told. I was always told that Hades is shrouded in darkness, smells of fire, and is covered in tattoos that can come alive at his will."

The tattoos are real enough, not that that's the point. I get the sense that I'm losing control of this conversation. Time to take it back.

I trail my gaze down her body with slow deliberation and wait for her cheeks to turn pink. Which they do. Deliciously. "And yet you're the one dressed in black and with tattoos, my star."

She glances down at her clothes, then tugs the sleeve of her shirt down, hiding her star tattoos from me. I manage to stop myself from frowning at the gesture, but it's a close thing.

"So…" I straighten to step closer. Close enough to breathe her in. She smells of oranges and vanilla and the faintest hint of lightning, thanks to standing this close to my brother's temple. No brimstone, though.

I despise even that much of him on her.

"What's your name?" I ask to buy myself time to calm down.

"Felix Argos."

Liar.

"So…" She glances to the side of the temple and the way down the mountain toward the bridge and the city across the bay. "What happens now?"

My entire world narrows to her face. Cosmos, what a question. *What happens now*. She's real. She won't disappear on me. That wasn't an option I considered when I made my "Lyra is off fucking limits" rules. What I want to do is take her and run…and spend an inordinate amount of time making sure she smells like *me* and not like my damnable brother.

But real Lyra, present-day Lyra, a Lyra who doesn't leave me for ages—she's even more dangerous to me than future Lyra. If I'm struggling this much already, within minutes of being around her, maybe I don't name her my champion. I walk away, find another way to get Persephone out.

"What did you mean about being cursed?" That scent of lightning on her skin reminded me, and I need a distraction.

Her eyes get shifty. "You don't know?"

"Tell me like I don't."

"What if I don't want to?"

I lift a single eyebrow and see the resignation in the droop of her shoulders before she takes a visible breath.

Her words come out in a hurry. "Twenty-three years ago, when I was still in my mother's womb, she and my father came here to make an offering and pray for blessings on the birth. Her water broke, and your brother apparently took offense at her defiling his sacred sanctuary. As punishment, he cursed her baby—me, as it happens—that no one would ever love me. There. End of story."

The. Fuck. He. Did.

I'm going to destroy him. Strangle him with his own dick and hope he chokes on that ego of his.

But that curse makes no sense. Not with the feelings even this human version of Lyra stirs in me. I've been trying hard to feel nothing for her. With the added curse, shouldn't I truly feel nothing? It's not fucking working if that's the case.

"He made you unlovable?" I ask slowly.

She gives a jerking nod. I can see in her eyes that she believes that with her entire being. A history is there, lived experiences that dull their green color and pale her cheeks.

It's real. I think. I'm going to have to try to find out more, but I won't have time before the Crucible starts. Selection is tonight.

I need to think. I can't do that with her here.

So I wave a hand at her. "You may go."

She startles. "I can…go? Really—"

I lift my eyebrows slowly, taunting her. "You wish to argue?"

"No."

"This way," I say.

Why in the names of all my hells am I offering to walk her down? She got up here without being caught just fine.

Pathetic excuse for self-control.

Thankfully, she doesn't break the silence. Which means I'm not expecting it when Lyra suddenly stops walking.

I stop, too, glancing back. "Problem?"

"Um…" She stares past me, and I follow her gaze. Ah…she's worried about the crowds on the main street we've reached seeing her with me.

"Don't worry about them," I say. "Only you can see who I truly am. Everyone else just sees a regular mortal man."

She still looks doubtful.

"Come on."

She finally gets moving again. We emerge onto the teeming sidewalk, and she pauses, then offers me a small salute. "I appreciate you not smiting me."

Every single part of my body clenches at even a hint of her leaving by choice. Before, she was very clear that she wasn't controlling when she came and left me. But right now…it's a choice. She's still in the world, in this time, with me…and even though I told her to go, I also want to keep her by my side, find out what makes her laugh, find out how she tastes when I kiss her, and I can't do any of that.

*If* I name her my champion, she's going to *hate* me. But worst of all, I need to stay the hells away from her. How am I supposed to do that as I get her through those games alive?

She's watching me, waiting.

"Be more careful with your words, my star," I say in a voice as out of my control as the rest of me, and rough with it. "You never know when the gods might take up the gauntlet you just threw down... And any other day, I probably would have."

I mean to scare her away.

Instead, her eyes flare with interest. "Smiting is a quick death," she whispers. "There are worse things."

My chest tightens as I search her expression. Does she feel it, too? This Lyra doesn't know me beyond my roles as god of death and King of the Underworld. The bogeyman as far as she's concerned. And yet the way she looks at me...

Fuck my life.

My control shreds a little more, and I can't help myself. I lift a hand to draw a fingertip from her temple to her jaw, just the barest touch. She's so soft, and the quiver I invoke in her isn't fear...it's *for* me. I stare at her, and she stares at me.

"You're right, my star," I murmur, dropping my gaze to her lips. Just a taste. Before she hates me. Before I put her through the games. Before I have to walk away from her at the end of it. But I won't do that to her. If I name her champion, I need her to focus on surviving. And only surviving. "There are worse things."

I'm so fucked.

I straighten abruptly, spin her around before I can give in and kiss her until she moans my name, and give her a little push into the crowd.

She walks away.

It hits me that technically we met around the same age. Although now that she's a goddess, who knows how far into the future she was when she traveled back in time to me?

*Don't do this to her.*

I promised myself that I would never drag her into my world, into my hells. We're too dangerous together. Tinder and fire, set to go off and take the world down with us.

I can't do it.

I fucking won't do it to her or to me. Even if future her told me to.

I'll find another way to get Persephone out.

When she disappears around the curve, I turn away only to pull up short at the sight of my Lyra high on the hill. Long hair twisted up haphazardly, dressed in some kind of tracksuit that I think I've seen before.

She's already turning hazy around the edges.

I think maybe she calls to me. Her lips form my name and then only two words. "Trust me."

Then she's gone. Again.

I was right before. I'm so fucked.

# 72

# TIME THIEF

### LYRA

Time brings me back to Cronos in the small room, and the Titan searches my face. "Did you pull a string?"

I frown. "More like…confirmed that the string I pulled worked."

"And you came back to now, rather than resetting." He passes a shaky hand over his face. "I think you might be—"

His eyes go wide on something behind me.

I don't even have time to turn before crystal light flickers around me. "Already?"

And then I'm in Hades' water garden.

In all the celestial, peaceful beauty I remember from my time. The sounds of water all around me are soothing.

"Lyra, I don't know if I can take much more of this."

Hades is standing behind me with his arms crossed, and it's impossible to deny the familiarity of this moment from the very first time I was swallowed up by broken time.

"Um…" I glance around. "Did I just kiss you?"

He stalks toward me, expression taking on a dark cast. "My mark on you alerted me that you'd shown up in the Underworld. But that's impossible because you're fighting for your life in Poseidon's fucking Labor right this instant."

That's right. He mentioned that the first time. She's in the Labor right now. I am.

Oh gods.

*Isabel.*

I couldn't save Meike, but maybe Isabel. Mnemosyne showed me all the ways I could save them, save her, but I don't remember seeing a version where I sent Hades to fix it. I have to try.

I grab Hades' wrist. "You need to go back to her...to me—"

"Damn you, Lyra." He shakes me off. "The girl you told me a hundred and fifty years ago to enter in the Crucible is *you*. Only she has no bloody clue that we've ever known each other."

"I know, but right now—"

He takes me by both arms, fingers curling around me like he wants to shake me but is barely holding back. "You show up here, kiss me like you're desperately relieved to see me, and then disappear like usual."

"There's something more import—"

"And now you're back an instant later..." His gaze narrows on my clothes. "Only different."

How can he tell?

"Isabel," I snap. "She's going to die in this Labor if I don't stop it. You have to—"

His grip tightens before we blink out of existence. We arrive in the hallway just outside his rooms in his Underworld home, and he waves me inside.

"If you don't want to be seen, I suggest you don't leave." Hades shuts the door in my face.

I run to the door. "The water dragon bites her," I yell through the door. "Don't let it bite her...or me!" I definitely died that way a couple of times.

No response.

Is he even still there?

A snap of fingers sounds on the other side, and then Hades is giving someone a gruff command. "Guard her. Do not talk to her. Ever."

I don't know what Cerberus says in return, but I know it's him because of the smell of sulfur. Also, who else would Hades get to guard me? Especially down here?

My arms drop to my sides as I stare at the door. I don't dare speak aloud. Cerberus probably shouldn't hear my voice. "Please," I mouth, then kick at the heavy wood.

A trio of warning growls comes from the other side.

The sound is so... Gods, I've missed that three-headed mutt, even more than I let myself think about until this moment.

I put my hand against the door, like he can feel me. Then my forehead. "Damn," I whisper.

I think I'm already too late.

But I know Hades comes back to me here. After Poseidon's Labor, after he holds me when I'm upset about Isabel, he leaves me to come down here. He left me up there to let me wander Olympus alone to come back down to…me.

And then everything goes dead and silent. Not with time travel. It's the same gut-kicking, petrifying experience I've already felt once today. I try to cry out, but my vocal cords won't work. My body won't move, not even to blink. Not even to breathe.

Time is resetting. Again.

I made it reset. How? By sending Hades to save Isabel?

Just as panic starts to set in, that same strange skipping-record effect brings back sound and sensation.

And I'm not in Hades' bedroom.

I'm in Tartarus just above the abyss to the Locks, looking at the crimson bloodstain where I died.

"What the fuck just happened?" Boone demands. "Why do I remember other things? Doing stuff before this?"

"It was me," I whisper. I'm shaking so hard I have to sit down. "I reset us. Again."

I guess because we're down here with the others, inside Tartarus, for this new reset, Boone and I now remember everything from the previous life, too.

Boone squats down in front of me. "What did you do?"

I look at him, pleading with my eyes for him to understand. "I tried to save Isabel."

# 73

# THE UMPTEENTH TIME

LYRA

"Lyra, I don't know if I can take much more of this."

"You and me both," I mutter too softly for Hades to catch.

I'm back in the Underworld, with him in the water garden. Again.

I've heard those words so many times, I've lost count. A hundred, maybe. After all, it's only resetting a few hours of my time, personally.

By now, my heart is so heavy I can hardly breathe, hardly move.

In a hundred times revisiting him here, that part always stays the same, and yet I've never saved Isabel. Not once.

Timing truly is everything.

I've tried giving him specific instructions on how to fix it. He's even tried interfering directly. Any time he interferes results in a reset. We've tried having Boone come with me, but the fissure of time never picks him up, or at least it never takes him to the same place. Any instances I've interfered—yes, I tried going up there myself—it resets. My more subtle attempts might change *how* she dies, but she dies in Fingal's Cave every single time.

Fifty attempts in, the Titans gave me only another fifty tries.

Seventy-five in, I knew the truth deep down—that sometimes it's just a person's time to go—but I wasn't ready to quit.

But it's over now.

My choice. Cronos didn't have to convince me. I've realized that with where time now resets to, it's not going to let me fix anything before this.

At least that's what Cronos said after I shared that conclusion.

When I asked him why he didn't tell me that sooner, he said that some truths have to be felt so deeply to sink in as truth that the only way to learn them is through our own experience.

He was right about that.

But that also means I can't save the others, either. Meike, Neve, Dex, Dae's grandmother…

Their deaths are part of the larger tapestry that makes up this story of life. At least in this timeline we're now stuck with.

"Lyra?"

Hades is still behind me.

There's a huge difference between acknowledging a harsh reality and going through with it.

"Lyra?" He puts a hand on my shoulder.

I take a deep breath and face him. "I know I'm in the middle of Poseidon's Lock. You should go back to her. She's going to need you when it's…over."

He takes in the set to my features. I can only imagine how I look. How I feel is…empty. Numb. No…not numb. Guilty.

"You're sure?" he asks slowly. "You don't look well."

"Something bad is about to happen for her. You'll find out soon enough." My only consolation is that I know where Isabel is in Elysium. She's told me herself that she's happy there, waiting for her partner, Estephany, and other members of their family to join her.

Hades makes a noise in the back of his throat. "I can help—"

"No. Not this time. I promise. I've tried." Gods, I sound so…cold. Heartless.

"Lyra—"

I hold my hand out to him. "Take me to your rooms. I'll wait for you there."

Maybe he sees that I'm beyond arguing with. A small spark of grateful warmth that he doesn't push me further settles in my chest as he takes my hand, and we're instantly standing in his rooms.

Like every other time, he sets Cerberus to guard me.

Only this time, Hades is reluctant to leave.

"Go," I tell him when he hesitates.

I'm not sure how long I stand here staring at the fancy rug, the patterns swirling around my feet until they distort. It's a while. Honestly, I'm waiting for time to take me away again.

After so many resets, that feels like my new normal.

I sit down on the edge of the bed, not really taking in my surroundings. I've been here before. Hells, this is my room, too, now, minus a few photographs I've added to all our homes.

And I wait.

I wait for time or Hades. Whichever returns for me first.

Not that I sit still while I do. I move from the bed to the closet to the bathroom, pacing across the floor, splashing my face with cold water. I forgot what water feels like—the kind that doesn't shock the shit out of me, at least—just in the short time I've been stuck in the bowels of the hells.

Looking out the wide windows over the "sunny" version of our Underworld home, I try to pause and soak up the beauty here. What if I never come back?

The mountains that the castle is built into are shrouded in deep purples and phosphorescent blues, leading to clouds hanging around their peaks in the distance, which are cast in brilliant oranges and yellows. The mountainous "sky" overhead is so high, all I can see are the deep blues broken by bright-blue specks that could be stars but aren't. They're not bugs, either, but crystals. The yellows and oranges of the clouds make the distant mountains look like they are on fire, but a fire of such beauty I would gladly burn in it.

The Labor didn't take this long, did it? I had already started it when he came down here for me.

I sink to the bed with wobbly knees that won't support me any longer. Isabel dies today. Holding my hand. In agony.

And I'm sitting here wishing for it to go faster. To get it over with.

The lock clicks in the door loud enough that I jump as Hades steps inside. There's no sign of Cerberus in the hallway. My god of death is… grim.

"Isabel died?" I ask.

He gives a jerking nod. I can't look him in the eyes as I also nod.

Hades doesn't come inside. He leans against the doorjamb, arms crossed, one foot casually over the other. But there's nothing casual about the vibe coming off him. His eyes glint. "So you are the future of her?"

Who cares if I reset now? "Yes."

"Then why in the name of Tartarus would you do this to yourself?" He's still posed so casually, but I swear a stiff breeze would shatter him, he's holding himself so fiercely tight.

"It's what has to happen," I tell him. Sounding cryptic as fuck, I'm well aware.

"Has to happen," he murmurs. "Why?"

"I can't tell you."

His lips flatten. Damn, he can look so ominous, even just leaning in a doorway. "You could have warned me."

I've warned him so many times. About so many parts. "If I had, would you have entered the Crucible? Would you have picked me?"

"I almost damn well didn't this time, Lyra. I debated it after I found you at Zeus' temple, tried to come up with any other way. But you told me to do it, to trust you, and…" He looks away, jaw working.

Is this why I'm here now? To make sure he follows through? "You have to trust me, Hades. This is the only way."

"The *only* way?" His gaze snaps back to me. "Like when I destroyed Olympus? Was that the only way, too?"

During the Anaxian Wars. "You're blaming me for that?"

My head is spinning. Maybe I suck at this time-twisting bullshit. I couldn't even save Isabel. Maybe I'm making it worse. Except…

"I am Lyra's future." I point up toward the Overworld, where past me is probably in Dionysus' bar by now. "*I* am proof that things go the way they should for her. I will win the Crucible, even if at times it looks as though I won't. Even when it hurts. You will be King of the Gods and get Pandora's Box. This is what has to happen."

Hopefully, a future version of Cronos is sending this version of me back to his son over and over…and that future Cronos is out of Tartarus. He must be. It's the last shred of hope that I hold on to.

The tension doesn't leave Hades. Even without moving, without changing the set of his features, his growing anger can be felt across the room all the same. "How long do I wait for you?" he asks. "Until you stop disappearing on me?"

I can't answer that, either.

When I say nothing, he looks away.

"Do you wish you'd never met me?" The entirely unfair question comes out as small as I feel.

"Damn you, Lyra." He spins away, hand running through his hair, leaving it standing in spikes. "I just left you up there, and you're devastated. And blaming me."

"I know."

He shoots a glare at me over his shoulder. "I'm committed now, but all I care about is you surviving. Forget winning."

I'm stepping toward him, hand up like I can stop him, before I know what I'm doing. "Don't do that. She has to win. I have to—"

But he's gone again. Door locked behind him, as if that could stop me.

I close my eyes, dropping my hand to my side. I could just teleport out of here. Go topside. Try to warn Meike. Or Zai. Any of them.

But I've tried that, too. So many times.

So I stay where I am. And wait.

# 74

# FROM TIME TO TIME

### LYRA

I'm pretty sure I haven't slept all night. Hermes' Labor is coming for past me in the morning.

Food showed up on its own around lunch and dinner time. Food I couldn't stomach but made myself. Even goddesses can use a boost. Then I tucked myself between the sheets, and I've lain here, alone in our bed, staring out the window at night in the Underworld, aglow in the beautiful, phosphorescent colors of blues and purples and deep pinks.

I was sad. Now I'm irritated. Why am I being left to marinate in my own sorrow in this room? I've got shit to do. Getting us out of Tartarus. Boone and I have three more Locks to unseal, and we don't know what changed in Hera's to kill me.

Wasted hours without a single sighting of cracked time or Hades are not my idea of productivity. Not that I'm surprised about him, I guess.

He has…me…oddly.

Past me.

But it still hurts. I only get these glimpses of him. So not taking advantage is just…

I kick out a leg from underneath the blanket, trying to get comfortable enough to sleep. I can hear one of Cerberus' heads snoring, the rumble of it rolling down the hallway outside.

A pale-yellow shimmering catches my eye, and I turn over to watch the Underworld "sunrise." The morning light hits the far mountains first, almost making them look frosted, and then deepens and brightens, appearing to melt and turn to liquid gold that flares to red.

Maybe it's because of that sunrise that I don't catch the shimmer of time until silence and darkness consume me and I'm deposited in a cave.

Not Tartarus.

Bonus fun, it took me with the sheets wrapped around me. I untangle myself and get to my feet, my bare toes pricking against the uneven rock floor.

"A sea cave?"

The rhythmically swelling water, crystal clear down to the sandy seafloor, is my first clue. The smell of salt in the air, my next. But it's the Grecian columns that hold a massive stone lintel, illuminated by torchlight flickering from sconces around the small space, that are my biggest clue.

I have no idea where I am, or when, or why. But I know I'm meant to find out.

I look to the heavens. "A road map would be nice. Maybe an app with details about my next stop."

Of course no one answers.

Or…no one from up there.

From the entranceway, I catch a faint voice. "Enter if you dare…"

I cautiously check the corners as I make my way through the door into a single hallway. I don't know what I expect when I get to a room that looks like ancient Greece vomited in here. The furniture. The decor. More columns.

And sitting on a beat-up-looking chaise longue is a man.

Or…a god?

Blond, maybe with silver mixed in, he has a beard down to mid-chest and hair almost as long that hangs in tangled locks. He wears a Grecian tunic that, like the furniture, has clearly seen better days. It also falls only to his mid-thigh, and he's flashing way more than I want to be seeing, since he's lying on one side with one knee jacked up in the air.

"Who are you?" He shoves a bite of charred fish in his mouth. I assume he just finished cooking it over the firepit in the corner.

"Who are you?" I ask back. I already know. I've seen him once before this, when Uranus tried to kill Hades as a child.

"Oceanus," he says. Titan of the oceans and waters.

Oceanus. Tethys' husband. The traitor. "You're still alive?"

He lifts an unimpressed eyebrow, then waves around his domain. "Living like a king."

"While your siblings are fighting to escape Tartarus."

His indolent posture stills, and though he doesn't sit up, I can tell I have more of his attention than I did a second ago. "Don't make me ask again. You won't like it if I do."

"I am Lyra Keres. Queen of the Underworld. Goddess of glamours. And I've seen your siblings recently. They miss you."

He barks a laugh. "You should have stopped while you were ahead. I don't believe you now. I know they curse my name."

"They try to do it less when Tethys is around."

He stills again, but not for long enough to get a read on his reaction. "Don't speak her name," is all he says.

Is that guilt, disinterest, or something else? I can't tell. "How would you know they curse you, being up here?"

Oceanus eyes me narrowly. "Watch your tone, little goddess."

Maybe it's knowing I can deal with a reset if I have to, or maybe I'm just tired, but my mouth is in charge. "At least I didn't call you a traitor," I say sweetly. "This is me being courteous."

He takes another bite of his fish, chewing thoughtfully as he considers me. "I have my sources," he finally says.

I frown. What is he talking about…

Ohhhhh.

I asked how he knew that his siblings curse his name. Which they do. Often.

"What source?" I'm really tired of cryptic sources. The last one turned out to be me. It had better not be me again. Or what if he has no source? What if Oceanus is the one… "Have you been there?" I ask slowly. "In Tartarus?"

Another bite of fish. I'm getting ready to slap it out of his hand if he does that again.

Then he looks behind me. "Time's up, little goddess."

I whirl around, expecting to be attacked, only to be swallowed by a fissure of broken time and spit back out again—not in Tartarus but in Hades' bedroom.

"Fuck me." I don't bother to say it quietly for Cerberus.

Because I need him to go get Hades. I'm pretty sure Hermes' Labor is over, and this is when past me meets the three-headed hellhound. He came to Olympus to fetch Hades, but neither would tell me who Hades had to go see.

It was me.

I knock on the door and deliberately raise my voice to something squeakier and hopefully unrecognizable. "Excuse me?"

No answer.

"Hello?"

Still no answer.

"I know he said you can't talk to me. But I need you to go get him. Now."

I maybe could wait until Hades comes down later, but I have a feeling this is what time is waiting for. I can tell by the strong sulfur smell that the three-headed hound is still outside the door. He hasn't gone yet.

"I know he's in the middle of the Crucible Labor, but I promise by the time you get up there, his champion will be done."

There's a sound like a harrumph on the other side of the door. Ber, probably, his grumpy head scoffing at the idea that I'd know that.

The damned dog is giving me no choice.

"Fine. If you won't go, I will. I'm teleporting out of here in five seconds, and if Hades sees me up there, he's going to be pissed at you, not me."

There's another harrumph. Only with less conviction.

"Five. Four. Three... Are you sure you want to test me? Two. One—"

There's a sharp bark, and then the scent of sulfur lessens.

I grin. He's a loyal beast, that's for sure. I would love to have opened the door and buried my face in his fur, but I can't do that.

Knowing this is going to take more than a second, I sit on the end of the bed and wait.

And wait.

Why does everything feel like it takes so much longer than the first time around? Did we really chat for this much time?

Finally, there's a bark outside the door, letting me know Cerberus has returned. Would he talk to me if he knew it was me now that he's met Lyra up there? Probably not against Hades' wishes.

More waiting.

Come on.

"You summoned?"

I jump and have to shift on the bed to face where he's arrived behind me. And right behind him is another shard of broken time, coming for me.

"Gods damn it all to hell." I'm on my feet.

"What?" He whips around, looking but not seeing what I do.

I don't answer as I cross the room to him. "I don't have long, but you need to listen. I think the person who has been glamouring everything is Oceanus."

Hades frowns. "What are you talking about?"

Oh gods. I haven't told him about the glamouring yet. I tell him that after Athena's Labor.

"I—" I stare at him, but I've got nothing. What do I tell him? "The day of Athena's Labor, wait in the southernmost arches of the Colosseum for me to show up. I tell you more then."

It's not much, but more now will probably reset us.

"What are you talking about?" he demands.

I shift my weight from foot to foot, then start to draw him across the room, away from the crack. "Oceanus can get into Tartarus."

"That's not possible. He doesn't have enough power—"

"Are you sure of that?"

"Dead sure. I'd bet my life on it."

I shake my head. "Then he's fooled a lot of people. He says he's..." Oh shit. I almost just gave away that I'm stuck in Tartarus. I quickly revise my wording. "He said he has a source inside there."

Hades slashes a hand through the air. "Also impossible."

The jagged gash of time starts moving faster. I guess I've said what I have to. "Just promise me you'll check into him. If you do and find you're correct, no harm, no foul. Right?"

"Lyra, I don't know how you think I have time to run the Underworld, keep you alive, and also track down Oceanus, but—"

"After the Crucible, then. Promise."

"Fine. I promise—"

Silence.

## 75

## SOULS

### LYRA

Time doesn't drop me off in the same room as Cronos. It carries me all the way to the arched door of Hades' Lock. Hades' copy still doesn't know whether I'm injured or not after my blood dripped down to him. I raise my hand to the glowing symbol in the center of the wall, not sure if he's even going to let me in. Not after the last time we talked.

I place my hand over his symbol.

Nothing.

"Hades?" His name comes out soft. Tentative.

The door opens so fast I can feel the movement of it in the rush of air against my skin.

Then he's there.

Standing on the other side, looking enigmatic. Cold.

"So," he drawls in a bored voice. "You're alive."

I open my mouth to say yes, then realize that's not entirely true.

He must see the way I pause, because the cold drops away to reveal something I might once have mistaken as anger. But because I know Hades, the real Hades, I see the worry behind it, even in this replica's eyes.

"What happened?" he asks.

"I… Well…" How to explain? "A future version of me—now a past version, I guess—died." Was that technically still today? I've lived over a hundred days since then, with extra days in the Underworld sometimes.

"What?" He takes the tiniest jerking step forward, and the toe of his boot crosses the threshold. Hades grunts, expression twisting in what might be pain before he disappears entirely, and the door slams closed again. His symbol goes dark. Like the lights are off. No one at home.

I'm left standing with my jaw hanging open, staring at the carved symbols on the rock face.

"That was quite careless of him." I jump at the sound of a female voice echoing through the chamber. A familiar voice. "He won't return for some time, I'm afraid."

After a terrified glance at the Pandemonium tunnel, I back up slowly and scoot right until I can see Demeter standing in her own doorway. I was busy when I unsealed her Lock, and I don't think I've looked at the symbols on her archway until now—a cornucopia, a plow, a torch, poppy flowers, and snakes. I'm guessing the symbol in the center is a sheaf of wheat, but with the door open, I can't see it.

"Sorry," I say. "But what?"

She cants her head in the direction of Hades' door. "If we cross the barrier, we have to regenerate. It takes time."

I frown, looking between her and the closed Lock. I have so many questions. "Regenerate from what?" I ask. "What are you, exactly?"

Demeter tosses her coppery golden hair over her shoulder. "When we made this place, we left small pieces of our souls—our essences, I guess you could call it—in these Locks. As guardians." She peers closer at me. "Didn't they tell you?"

I shake my head slowly. Pieces of their souls?

I glance again at Hades' Lock, heart turning over even while my mind twists to make it make sense. It's him in here. Not *him* him, the real him, but still a piece of him, in a way I don't really understand, and yet something inside me is telling me that this means more than I thought. He's not just a recording or a trick, but a piece of Hades' own soul.

I open my mouth, then close it again, thinking. "But Hestia..."

How do I say that she wasn't really there?

It turns out I don't have to. At the sound of her sister's name, Demeter appears to shrink in on herself, her eyes gaining shadows that seem to come from within her. "Our sister died in the Overworld, and it affected the remaining piece of her down here. We are like shadows and draw our existence from the souls we were cut from."

In other words, if Hades dies up there, then he dies down here, too, leaving behind a glitching version of himself that can only repeat basic instructions. The way Hestia's replica did. "Is that true the other way around?" I have to ask.

If Hades dies down here, is the real Hades above affected?

She shakes her head. "We're from them, not them from us."

"I see." Not really, but close enough. My heart isn't quite sure how to handle that truth. "If you can't leave the Locks, then what good are you as guardians?"

Another toss of her hair, but this time in irritation. "It's better than no eyes down here at all."

Trapping their own souls in the worst part of the hells doesn't seem like all that great a solution to me.

"Can you feel them?" I ask next. Then take an eager step forward. "Talk to them?"

"We can feel them sometimes." Now Demeter's just toying with me. "When their emotions are high."

I deflate. "That's it?"

Although…it seems to me that Hades' emotions must be pretty high at the moment where he is. Is that why the Hades down here seems more and more like my Hades with each interaction? Because he can feel what my Hades feels?

I'm hating the idea of this more and more. Hades trapped himself, or part of himself, down here. Forever. Alone.

They all did.

They were that desperate. A desperation built on lies, but still, no wonder his replica was so pissed at me.

"At least you can move between the Locks." So they aren't lonely.

Demeter's perfectly curved eyebrows shoot up. "How do you know about that?"

"Hades helped me during your Lock—"

Her eyebrows go from high to low in a fierce frown. "He did *what*?" Her face contorts with fury. "That squirrelly cheater."

"Didn't you see?"

Without so much as a "see you later," she's gone, and the door to her Lock closes. The wheat sheaf that is Demeter's symbol glows golden in the center of the archway.

"Hey—" I cut off whatever I was going to say in my throat. No point in arguing now. Then I lift my gaze to the ceiling and past it—past the

Underworld, past the Overworld, all the way to Olympus. "When I get back up there," I tell all the gods who can't hear me, "we're going to do seminars on better communication."

No wonder Hermes is so grumpy, being that he's the messenger god in charge of communication and all. His family must drive him to distraction. His job must be like a game of adolescent giggling girls at a sleepover playing telephone.

Not that I ever played the game, but that's neither here nor there.

The sound of boots coming down the tunnel toward me has me turning around. Because whoever is coming—and it's not the Pandemonium because those fuckers are silent—is not walking. They're running.

Boone bursts from the tunnel, only to skid to a halt at the sight of me, followed by a fierce glower. "What in the name of the Underworld are you doing down here?"

# 76

# WHAT DID I MISS?

### LYRA

"Did Cronos send you for me?"

Boone gives me a funny look as we close the gap between us. "No. We've been waiting for you to come back."

He turns to walk beside me back toward the tunnel.

Waiting? "How long?"

"You've been gone a week—"

I stop walking, staring at the darkened tunnel entrance. "A week?"

No wonder time didn't bother dropping me back where Cronos was. He's not there anymore and hasn't been for a while.

But a week?

Boone touches my shoulder lightly and whistles. *Are you okay?*

"I'm fine." I clear my throat and start walking again. "I'm just surprised. Did anything happen while I was gone?"

"No." He sounds grumpy about it, too. "What happened in this one?"

We've already been through the me-being-the-puppet-master stuff before. Boone remembers all those other times, just like I do. When I'm done, he just gives a grim nod. He knows how hard letting go of saving Isabel was for me.

"So, Oceanus is the bad guy?" he asks.

I shrug. "Maybe."

When I try to go straight at a juncture, he tugs my elbow and draws me down a different path. "We had to move again."

There's only one reason they would have done that. The Pandemonium. "Who?"

"Hyperion, this time. It turns out his light consumes him when he goes feral. We're lucky none of us is permanently blinded."

"Is he okay now?"

"Yeah."

That's something, at least. "What else have you been doing while I was gone?"

Boone glances at me. "I wanted to try to figure out what was going on in Hera's Lock so we can plan, but they wouldn't let me enter alone."

"If you reset us, we just start over on that bridge," I point out.

His turn to shrug. "We'll figure it out when you're ready."

They've been waiting on me. A new layer of guilt grows over the first one like mold.

Boone's quiet as we take a few more turns. "Lyra…did you feel it? When the other you died?"

"I didn't feel her pain or her end if that's what you're asking." I felt pretty damned sick.

"Yeah. Me too." We both keep walking.

I want to ask him how things are with Persephone. I even open my mouth to do that, right before the bell tingling makes us both jump.

"Fuck," we mutter at the same time.

I don't know if they trained him on this part of the tunnels, but I know exactly where we are, and doors are few and far between.

Except…

I grab his hand and try to run, but he pulls me up sharply. "Not that way. The closest door is this way."

So he does know, but not about what I do.

"There's a hidden door closer, this way." I grab him and drag. "No time to argue."

"Hells," he mutters. But he stops resisting, and we both run.

We run as fast as I can go—I know that Boone is holding back on his full level of speed—and it takes two curves before I remember to turn on my damned power.

Thank the gods I remembered, because I blink just as we flash by the veil-covered door. "Stop!"

Boone stops so fast that, even though I was slowing, I slam into him. He absorbs the impact like I'm a feather, but I'm already reaching for the handle.

"Wait—"

"It's glamoured. I can see it."

That doesn't so much as make him pause. "Do you know what's in this one?"

"No. But it's our best option."

His grim gaze skates over the wall I'm reaching for.

"Whatever's in there can't be as bad as what's coming out here." I glance over my shoulder. Hades' copy said I could see them coming with my ability. Is that true in the darkness not penetrated by our light, though?

"Do it," he says.

It's as I'm reaching for the handle that I think about the fact that the door may be locked. But it's not, and we rush inside, closing it behind us. Then both breathe a sigh of relief, because the small room is empty. We whirl back around to press our ears to the door, listening not for the Pandemonium but for anyone else who might be trying to find safety.

"My, my." A voice that is somewhere between a song and a hiss sounds from behind us. "Visitors. I'm honored."

Boone and I both spin, hands coming up to face whatever or whoever is in here with us. Just as fast, though, we both spin back to face the door.

"Holy shit!" My exclamation drowns out Boone's, which is along the same lines.

We both speak at the same time in fits and starts, talking over each other. "Is that…"

"It can't be…"

"I definitely saw snakes…"

"Don't look her in the eyes…"

"I am right here," that sweet slither of a voice breaks in. "You could simply ask."

Except what I saw wasn't a woman with a snake's tail for a body. It didn't have a body at all. Just a head stuck in a single alcove in the wall.

We're lucky we're not stone statues right now.

"Medusa?" I finally ask.

There's a smile in her voice when she answers. "I would clap if I still had my hands."

*Oh. My. Gods.*

# 77

## GORGON

### LYRA

"Do not fret," she says. "I can no longer shoot my bow and arrow. Stay."

Boone and I glance at each other. "We're stuck here anyway," he whispers.

"Yeah."

We both lower to sit on the ground, our backs still to her.

She hisses. Or maybe it's the snakes that make up her hair. Either way, I can't help but shiver.

"You can face me, little goddess. I would never hurt a woman who has not personally wronged me. But *him*—"

The snarled word hangs in the air. I don't remember learning that women are safe from Medusa's eyes or rage over what was done to her. "I don't think I'll chance it. No offense."

Her chuckle is a low rasp. "I am not lying, but you're smart. Smart is good. Smart will keep you alive, if that is what you want."

I glance at Boone again, and he shrugs.

The thing is, curiosity has always been my Achilles' heel—pun totally intended. We're here for a bit, and I have questions.

Boone beats me to it. "How are you—"

"*You* may not speak to me," she says. "Only her."

Yup. She definitely hates men. Given what Poseidon did to her, I don't blame her.

"How are you even alive? I mean... You're just..." I make a slicing motion across my neck.

Beside me, Boone drops his head in his hands. "You didn't just do that."

"What?" I ask him. "Is it indelicate to point out that she's only a head? I mean, obviously she's fully aware of that fact."

"It is true that I am not entirely myself," she agrees cheerfully.

Medusa is…cheerful.

Not like Persephone's brand of eternal sunshine. There's still an edge in her voice that is like the handle of a gun glinting in its holster, fury ready to unleash, and yet cheerful all the same.

"A gorgon is not so easy to kill." Her tone changes, turning into a true hiss. "That bitch Athena should have thought of that before she fucking cursed me into one." She scoffs. "Best friend, my ass."

I blink, eyebrows crawling up.

That was a whole lot to unpack, but I think I get the gist. Gorgons can survive even without their heads attached to bodies. Not sure how that's physically or anatomically possible, but it's not like I can argue with the alive head in the wall. But that last bit was possibly the most interesting part.

"You and Athena were best friends?" When Medusa was the goddess's acolyte? "How did that work—"

"I have no wish to speak about her."

"You brought her up," I mutter. Only to get a nudge from Boone's elbow. I wrinkle my nose at him but drop it. "How did you end up down here? It's rumored that after Perseus used you to kill a kraken, he threw your head into the ocean. Others say that Athena put your head into the shield Aegis to use as a weapon. But I've seen that shield." Samuel used it during the Crucible. "Obviously, that didn't happen."

"It did, actually. I pretended to be dead for Athena and Zeus. They both used that damnable shield. I am not certain how I was removed from that and put in here," she says. "I woke up in this wall. Rhea found me. She visits regularly."

"What?" I move to turn around to stare at her, but Boone's grip on my arm stops me.

Stone statue. Right.

I settle, facing the door. The door the Titans couldn't see…except Rhea seems to be able to see Boone when he does his disappearing thing. Is she the one who glamoured the door?

"Rhea visits?" I try for more casual than a second ago.

"Yes. But even Titans can be turned to stone, so she doesn't want to risk moving me out of this space and accidentally making eye contact."

"Gaia bless," Boone murmurs. "I thought the Titans had it bad."

Seriously.

Medusa doesn't respond. Not to Boone, anyway.

"What's the last thing you remember?" I ask. Because what she said about waking up in here sounds eerily familiar. Just like Persephone.

"I remember being carried in the shield," she says. "I do not know by whom, because they were careful to keep Aegis turned away. I remember vague words in a muffled voice about helping me…and then nothing. I remember nothing."

Boone and I frown at each other. That's not exactly a lot to go on. But Oceanus' words are bouncing around in my head. What if Rhea is his source down here? Only…I saw her face when Hades came to take her to Tartarus. She was devastated. Does she have a part in all this that I just can't see?

Boone's eyes widen slightly. "What if we can bring things here from the future, when we are in the broken time?"

He's thinking about how the Titans have also traveled through those cracks, too. Except, Hades was holding me the last time I was brought back, and he's not here. "I don't think so."

"Your axe."

Right. I blink.

Oh my gods. *Is* that possible? Did someone inside Tartarus bring Oceanus here? Or Persephone? Or Medusa's head? Was it Rhea? "Why?"

Medusa gives a hiss-like snort. "Don't ask me. I've known only these walls for centuries now."

Centuries.

I sigh.

Maybe Boone understood the undertone of it, because he slowly angles his head to peer closer at my face. "No."

"I didn't say anything."

He leans in, practically nose to nose. "No to whatever you're thinking."

"Are you going to let him speak to you that way?" Medusa murmurs from behind us.

"Do you want my help or not?" I toss over my shoulder.

"Your *help*?" She sounds suspicious now. "In exchange for what?"

"For nothing," I say. "Someone should have helped you more than this a long time ago."

That's greeted with silence. Since I can't turn around, I have no idea if it's suspicious or otherwise.

I give Boone an imploring look. "You know what happened to her was not only *not* her fault, it was wrong on too many levels to count."

"Even the Titans try not to look at her."

"So we don't look."

"She's *dangerous*."

"We can work around that."

"And," Medusa inserts, "I can be very helpful to those I consider friends." Her hiss lingers over the last letter.

Boone scowls, but I know that's a point in my favor. "We have enough troubles," he insists.

That's not a good enough reason to not do the right thing here. "If that bitch of a goddess, Athena—"

"Only *I* am allowed to call her that," Medusa snaps.

"Oh, good grief," I snap back. "Do you want out of that wall or not? Work with me here, woman."

Hissing fills the room, almost as though the snakes are speaking to her. Then, calmly, "I am listening."

"What are you suggesting?" Boone asks. "Carting her head around in a cloth sack like Perseus, hoping her acid blood doesn't eat through it and create monsters?"

"You've seen too many movies—"

"I no longer bleed," Medusa says.

It's so hard not to turn around to stare at her. "See," I say to Boone.

"If possible, I would prefer a box," the gorgon adds. "Perseus' sack rubbed my face raw."

It's Boone's turn to give me a look. "Other than having a powerful weapon in our possession—"

"I am no one's possession," she snarls. "Even like this."

Boone ignores her. "Why, Lyra?"

"Because she deserves more than this room. And who knows, she could become a possible powerful ally. But I won't make that part of the deal. This is just the right thing to do."

His jaw works, dark eyes worried. "We'd have to carry her around everywhere."

Relief leaves me in a puff, and I smile at him. "Maybe Asclepius could regenerate her body?" Although I doubt it. Asclepius is a healer, not a creator. "Or at the very least, Hephaestus could create her a new automaton body."

"I do miss my snake tail," she murmurs.

"You aren't helping," I shoot over my shoulder.

Medusa huffs.

Boone looks up toward Olympus, not that any help can come from that direction when we're stuck down here.

"If what happened to her happened to me…" I nudge him with my knee.

Everyone knows Medusa's story—pledged to purity as Athena's acolyte, raped by Poseidon in the goddess's temple, wrongly blamed and cursed by the same goddess, who'd apparently once been her best friend, and then exiled to a cave on Sarpedon, where she was constantly hunted by humans, turning them to stone with her gaze one by one, until Perseus cut off her head to use that gaze to stop the kraken.

Boone takes a deep breath. "Fine. But she stays here until we can figure out a box situation that will be easy and safe to cart."

"What did he say?" Medusa asks me overloudly. "I have trouble listening to men."

Which earns me a glare from Boone as I swallow a laugh. "If we can help you get out of here, we will," I tell the gorgon most feared above all other monsters, but who I have only ever felt sorrow for.

"That's assuming you can unseal all the Locks," she says.

We both straighten. "You know about the Locks?"

"Rhea keeps me informed."

Oh.

Boone leans toward me. "And we still don't know how Hera's Lock has changed to become so deadly."

I don't think I'll ever not see my future self with my throat slit when I close my eyes to sleep. "Then we should get going on that."

# 78

# HERA'S LOCK

### LYRA

"You have entered the Lock of Hera—"

"We already know the rules." I cut off the goddess standing before us. "Testing our sense of optimism by pitting us against monsters while steering by stars we can't see." That's what's changed. No more childbirth as an optimism test. "Let's get this over with."

Twenty-two.

Boone and I have been through this Lock twenty-two fucking times already. This makes attempt number twenty-three. And let me just say that between not remembering and remembering all the past iterations of my life...I'll take *not* remembering.

Because for the last twenty-two attempts, one or the other of us always dies and resets time. Although at least that doesn't mean repeating our entire lives, or for the Titans, the last hundred and fifty years. There is something handy about resetting in the middle of the game instead of the beginning. Kind of like a superpower.

The problem is, death hurts like a son of a bitch most of the time. Or at least a dozen times from this particular Lock. Now we get the fun of remembering *all* of those moments. Each and every gruesome end—by fire, drowning, gutting, beheading. Honestly, I should stop keeping lists. Worse, watching Boone die. Over and over and over. Watching him fall to his death in the Crucible was the most awful thing, and now I have more of those memories. The only thing saving my sanity is that I know the reset will save him. Even so, I think those moments, those real memories, will haunt me forever.

Irritation flashes across Hera's beautiful features. Like all the other pieces of the gods' and goddesses' souls down here, except Hestia, she's entirely cognizant and lifelike. "Very well," is all she says.

With a wave of her hand, I'm back in the same sports clothing Demeter dressed me in, with Boone dressed to match, and we are now standing on the flat deck—really more of a roof than a deck—of a trireme. I have learned way more than I ever wanted to know about these ancient warships, which are operated by three tiers of oars under this flat, rooflike cover we stand on. The oars can drive us faster or slow us down and operate on their own in this Lock, so at least I don't have to deal with the guilt of using people, even if they're not real.

I have just enough time to remind myself not to hum before a wave crests over the side and slams into both of us, tilting the ship at an angle that makes me lose my footing and sends me sliding across the railless deck with a yelp.

But before I drop into the pit in the middle that leads down to the tiered levels of oars, an arm comes around my middle and drags me to a jarring stop. Even over the violence of the storm raging above and the waves churning the sea around us, I hear Boone's grunt and look up to find that he's managed to grab a piece of rope dangling off the center mast.

"That had to hurt!" I call as both of us jump to our feet.

"I'll worry about it later," he says before running off.

We both know the jobs we have to do. The plan.

Boone heads for the helm at the stern of the ship, where he drops down a half level under the flat deck. Only his head and torso are visible as he grabs hold of the tiller to try to steer us. We've tried it with me operating that, but I'm not strong enough in this kind of weather.

That's why I run to the bow of the ship and stand just behind the figurehead, which is a thick, curving, intricately carved peacock head—I know because I've seen it from the water. One of the ways I died was taking a peacock beak to the temple.

I lash myself to the figurehead, with enough give in the rope to allow me to move side to side to see around it when I need to. But I don't look to the water. Not yet. Instead, I tilt my head back, staring at the clouds, waiting for any break to see the stars.

"Why couldn't the test for this Lock have been identifying a new constellation?" I mutter to myself. Not for the first time, by the way.

I missed that particular Crucible Labor while I was healing after Hephaestus' automaton almost killed me, but it was Hera's and seemed the least violent. *That* would have been nice. Even childbirth might have been nicer than this. Maybe. Instead, the on-again, off-again Queen of the Gods redesigned her Lock to be brutal this time around. Clearly. Or we would be done with this thing by now.

There.

A tiny break in the clouds, just enough for me to see stars shaped in a lazy W that makes up the constellation Cassiopeia. The modern version, by the way—no idea how, and I don't care.

All I care about is that Hera has shown me the direction we must travel by.

Keep Cassiopeia dead ahead.

As long as we do that…no monsters.

And we're already off course.

"Right!" I yell back at Boone. Because he probably can't hear over the storm, I also make a gesture with my whole arm, pointing the blade of my flattened hand at the exact angle we need to go.

What I don't do is turn to look and make sure he saw me. Not even when it takes the boat too long to make the maneuver. It's not exactly fast when we're having to fight against the crashing swells of waves churned by a goddess's rage. I'm not sure if Hera has abilities to manipulate seas and storms that no one ever knew about or if she got both Zeus and Poseidon to chip in for this new Lock. Doesn't matter. I've already made the mistake of turning my gaze away from the sea once. Instead, I keep my eyes on the water in front and to the sides of us.

"Which monster is it going to be this time?" I say to myself, or maybe to the watching ghost of the goddess.

Hera's Lock hasn't given us the same stars, destination, or monsters every time. Some have repeated, some haven't.

Always an adventure with her Lock. Almost impossible to plan around.

In the depths, I catch it—almost a blur, everything is so fast, but I'm pretty sure I see tentacles.

"Drop!" I yell.

At the same moment, I hit the deck flat on my stomach, just in time for one of those tentacles to whip by overhead.

The Lock sent us the giant squid again.

Hera seems to like this monster. Jules Verne must've been a follower of Hera's, because while this squid is covered in glittering green scales that I swear are made of actual emeralds, it's straight from the pages of *Twenty Thousand Leagues Under the Sea*. Plus a few other...modifications.

I don't see the fingerlike appendages at the tips, but I know they're there. For grabbing. And strangling. And dragging into the water so deep even if it lets me go, I'll never make it to the top before I run out of air. All with one tentacle while it uses the others to propel itself ridiculously fast through the waters.

I can't see Boone. He has to be in the small well in the deck, hopefully not leaving the tiller to do as it will. If we get back on course, the monster leaves. Stay off course, and more will come.

There's a reason why every single ancient civilization feared their own monsters of the oceans and seas.

Hera has to be borrowing a few of those horrors.

Once the tentacles don't pass overhead again, I get cautiously to my feet and catch sight of Boone doing the same. We both peek over the starboard side, and that's when I see more of the thing attacking us. Just a glimpse before it shoots away, off into the raging of the seas, although I swear its beak mouth smiles at me.

I jerk my head up, but the stars are obscured.

Did it leave us alone? Or did it run off to fetch a friend?

"A new one!" Boone yells. At least that's what I think he yells.

I don't answer as I focus on the skies. How off track are we at this point? Hopefully Boone managed to keep us at least on a path close to what we should be.

I gasp in relief at another break in the clouds. Cassiopeia... We're headed dead at her. I whistle and shove a thumbs-up high into the sky where Boone can see. *Stay on course.* That's our signal.

A piercing answering whistle, louder than mine, is our version of *understood* from our thieving days.

I don't see the rogue wave coming until it broadsides us, and I have to hold on tight or be washed over. Even with my ropes, it would take a lot of physical effort to pull myself back on board, and now that we're off course again, another monster is coming. I've already been bait, dangling on a line to get chomped up by more than one set of teeth in this hellhole.

Not planning to do that again.

When the vessel finally settles, I can feel how the oars on one side are working to turn us back toward the constellation. At least Hera gave us one advantage—the boat works for us, not against us.

I don't stand all the way straight, just enough to glance over the edge of the deck, waiting for the next thing to come our way, hoping to see a very specific feature.

A single horn.

# 79

# GET IT RIGHT

LYRA

Boone is not a huge fan of this plan, but I argued that there's got to be a reason why the horned monster is the only one we've seen every time we've been in here.

I don't think the stars are the key to this Lock. I think the stars are a distraction, a decoy, Hera's way of making sure whoever comes in here is going to fail. Because it's impossible to guide this boat by those stars. The monsters don't attack as long as we stay on course, but there is no way to stay on course.

And I know this goddess well enough to be certain of how wily she is and that she's never unfair without a specific purpose. Look at the protection she provided her champion in the Crucible, Amir, with one of her gifts. Anyone who messed with him would have that karma revisited on them a hundredfold. Was it brutal, and did it end up killing Dae-hyeon's grandmother? Yes. Was there a purpose and not just brutality for the sake of violence? Also yes.

Eventually, we'll land on the right purpose in this Lock, too.

"There!"

This time, I do look to see Boone pointing aft. Is it sad that my first reaction when I see what's coming is a burst of relief? Because we've encountered this one a few times and figured it out.

A kappa.

Usually found in rivers and lakes in Japan.

Both Boone and I scramble up to the deck cover and formally bow at the waist. The turtle-like creature also bows, which spills the water from the bowl on its head—an act that seems to weaken it, but the resulting swell of water pushes us away, and I jump back down to the slightly lower platform.

Which is when I see it.

Seriously, did all the classics writers follow Hera? Melville must've seen one of these in his nightmares when he wrote *Moby Dick*. A massive, white beast breaches the water ahead. From its forehead protrudes a spiraled horn with a nasty pointed tip that I know firsthand feels like fire when it's shoved into my belly before it cleaves me in half.

Basically, a demonic, gargantuan narwhal.

I have to try to whistle twice, because fear is messing with the muscles of my lips. The second one comes out extra loud out of desperation, and I point.

Then hold on as the ship starts to turn straight toward the monster. Hopefully I'm about to be smarter than Ahab was with his white whale.

At ungodly speeds, the monster heads for us, cutting a frothing swath through the churning waters. And Boone, following my pointing, keeps us dead on to it as much as possible. I keep losing sight of it with the swells and the masthead between us, but we are on a collision course.

On purpose.

"Hold," I say through clenched teeth, keeping it in sight and my hand pointed right at the creature coming for us. "Hold."

Then, focusing on the swells instead, hoping I'm right about how fast the boat will turn with the direction of the water, I drop my hand, whistling the signal for *Now!*

And we turn.

The oars get into it. One side stops while the other rotates backward. The Fates must be on my side for once today, because the waves give us an added push, and the ship lists hard.

Right into the oncoming path of the monster.

It's coming at us so fast, planning to do what it's done before and ram us head-on. Twice, it's essentially split our boat in half. It doesn't realize the problem until it's too late, and when it rams us, instead of splitting the boat, it impales us. The horn goes through the oar holes, in one side and out the other.

The boat doesn't shatter like before. It lodges on that long horn.

Holy shit. That worked.

Boone and I immediately jump down into the galley, lashing its horn to the ship with whatever ropes we can get our hands on quickly.

Water pours in from above and the sides as the beast thrashes and bellows, and I gasp as I'm almost thrown deeper into the tiered levels below deck. But for the second time, a grim-faced Boone grabs me around the waist to keep me from falling.

"This was a bad idea," he shouts into the side of my head.

He's probably right. "We had to try it."

Another gush of water surges in through the oar holes, hitting hard enough that we're both thrown back. Luckily, we're shoved toward the wall, not the drop.

"Swim!" Boone yells.

We start fighting through the torrent toward the somewhat protected spot by the tiller. More than once, Boone has to hold us both in place, wrapping around me and holding on to whatever he can. But we eventually drag ourselves up there and manage to peer over the deck cover.

I grin. And maybe laugh slightly maniacally. "It's working."

The massive creature can't rid itself of us easily, and the boat is so large that unless it breaks—which is a possibility—it's too much to drag under. And all of this is on purpose, because I'm pretty sure this briny bastard is going to ram us into—

I gasp and point. "There! The lighthouse."

Our destination. If we reach land, we win.

"I'll be damned." Boone grins, looking entirely like the pirate I've always pictured him as.

We stay where we are for as long as we dare, but we can't be in the boat when it hits. Our currently frail mortal forms won't survive it.

"Let's go," Boone says. He holds on tight to me as we make our way topsides.

When we're in position to jump, clinging to the edge, we both look back at the lighthouse growing larger and larger and larger in our sights.

*Not yet*, I think to myself.

"Not yet," Boone says a second later, echoing my thoughts.

He also tightens his grip on me like he's worried I'm not going to listen.

He's taller and can see better, so of course I plan to listen. Even as my heart pounds so hard and fast against the underside of my ribs that I worry it might punch its way out.

"Go!" Boone yells.

But before I can take the leap, he wraps his entire body around me, hefting me off the deck, and jumps for both of us. Then he rolls us so that he hits the hardest, taking the brunt of our impact against the water. It must feel like hitting cement.

All I know is that I'm thrown out of his grasp, and I skip like a rock across the surface of the water.

Right to the base of the lighthouse, somehow.

A huge crash sounds off to my left, and the ship explodes into the land with a horrific sound of rending timber. I don't look. I swim.

I swim for the shore so close to me. Boulders piled up. Please don't mean that I have to get my feet on dry land. Just touch it.

Which is when I see him.

The child.

When the Titans showed us the map of the seven Locks, the icon etched in Hera's was a creepy kid, and here he is. White-blond hair curling on his head and lightning whispering over his skin.

Zeus?

She put a childlike version of Zeus in here?

The child raises his hands over his head, lightning jumping from palm to palm, and I realize what he intends to do.

I swim harder, pushing my way through the water, fighting with everything I have, waiting for the instant he shocks me to death or another monster rises out of the waves behind me to kill me another way.

When my hand touches rock below the surface, I don't even realize at first what I'm touching. Suddenly, I'm not in a churning ocean but lying on a smooth rock floor, dripping wet and spreading water everywhere.

"Fuck me, Lyra-Loo-Hoo," Boone groans beside me, using my old nickname for once. "That plan sucked."

I turn my head to find him lying down, too, knees bent and hands on his stomach, which is moving with every harsh gulp of air he sucks in as he stares up at the nothingness overhead.

Breathing hard, I frown, looking around. "Did it work?"

The resets have never returned us here before.

"Very smart." Hera's voice slices through the labored sounds of our breathing. "Congratulations," the goddess says. "You have unsealed my Lock."

The door at one end opens on a rush of air, letting in the heat of Tartarus. The cheer that hits us from the Titans waiting on the other side is whispered because of the damned Pandemonium, but even so, I feel it down to my toes. The fact that even Tethys smiles, the emotion bringing color to her cheeks, says it all.

We did it!

We damned well did it. I honestly thought it would take us another hundred and fifty years of painful deaths to figure that one out.

I look at Boone, and we laugh, trying to swallow the sound as we do. We're both too exhausted to do more than that.

"Thank the gods," I say between breaths.

"About fucking time," Iapetus says.

And, maybe for the first time ever, I grin at the jerk.

# 80
# WAKE UP

## LYRA

"Lyra." Someone is shaking my shoulder. "Lyra," they whisper in my ear.

"Go away," I think I mumble.

Despite my goddess healing, Hera's Lock really took it out of me. More mentally than physically, but still.

"Lyra." This person is not going to let me sleep.

I crack a bleary eye to find Phoebe leaning over me, holding her long, silky hair out of the way. Her anxious face eases when I stir. "Oh good, you're awake."

"I am now," I say pointedly.

She doesn't seem to notice my grumpiness. "Come with me." She's still whispering.

I drag myself off the floor, through the room of sleeping Titans, and out into the hallway. I roll my stiff right shoulder and crack my neck.

Phoebe leaves me there to go back in, and when she returns, it's with Boone. I think I know what this is about now. But I still try to ask. "What—"

She holds a finger to her lip, then waves at us to follow. We don't go far, only around the bend, and we stop at the sight of a new crack in time hovering there as if it's been waiting for me.

I look from it to Phoebe, who shifts on her feet. "How did you know?"

She shrugs. "I can feel them sometimes."

Interesting.

I share a glance with a sleep-rumpled Boone, who is now wide awake. Thief ready. "Are you sure you want to—"

"You're not talking me out of going," he insists.

"Me neither." We all spin at the sound of Persephone's voice to find her at the bend in the tunnel. She must've followed us out.

Boone's scowl could strip rust off a bucket that's been rained on every day for a decade. "Go back to bed."

Her chin sticks out stubbornly, suddenly reminding me of me. "No. You're not the only ones who need answers."

Boone isn't giving in. "No—"

"You can't tell me what to do."

He crosses his arms. "You've visited enough past lives."

I sigh. "I'm getting really tired of you two not talking whatever this is out."

They both turn to me like their heads are on swivels. Then Boone shoots Persephone a considering look, which she returns with raised eyebrows.

"Later," he says.

"Yeah, right," Persephone mutters. Spring-and-sunshine woman knows how to mutter.

I like her a little better for that. Perfection is hard to trust.

Meanwhile, that fracture of time doesn't move, like it's waiting for us to decide. No way is that thing *not* being controlled by someone or something.

"I'm coming," Persephone insists. "I can help."

"You weren't there," I tell the goddess gently. "In my past. Not that I ever saw. And I think if Hades had ever caught sight of you, things would have turned out differently."

She looks from me to Boone and then back again. "I thought you'd be on my side," she whispers at me. She's quiet another second, and I see when the truth wins and she deflates just the tiniest bit. "Okay," she says softly.

Like he can't get away from her fast enough, Boone grabs my hand, tugging me toward the waiting break. "Let's get this over with."

I go first.

But just as I step inside, I hear Boone grunt, and then he's gone. Not holding on to me at all. The silence and pressure clamp down, and when sound returns and my vision clears, he's not with me.

I have to swallow my gasp at where I am. Somehow, I manage to not make a single sound as I stare in dawning horror through the barely-open door in front of me.

I'm outside my bedroom in Hades' home in Olympus. Past Lyra is in her bed, asleep in Hades' arms.

I don't have to question when this is, but I never remembered him being there with me. I remember making love in the water garden in Erebos. I remember waking up the next morning alone in my cold bed. But not this part. Not him.

The last piece of my puzzle falls into place.

He once told me that I instructed him to break my heart. That early trip through time to the night after Athena's Labor when I yelled at him before I knew what was going on.

He told me. I'm the one who told him to break my heart.

It's got to be now that I do that.

I scowl at the black-painted wood door, debating exactly how to handle this, since past me is involved.

I'm no astrophysicist or time travel expert, so I have no idea if seeing future me is going to make past me lose her shit, or if it will create world-ending paradoxes or maybe some kind of time wormhole. But at the very least, I'm pretty sure it will make time reset, because after Mnemosyne showed me how that works, now I don't think anybody could mentally handle that.

However…

I do happen to know that I never saw myself wandering around my bedroom. That's the only reason I'm trying this. I'm assuming future me did this to past me then, too.

Pushing the door open wider is easy enough. Hades keeps his house well oiled. Or maybe it's that any house of a god is not going to do what mortal houses do and age or deteriorate. They wouldn't dare. That's something I'll have to find out later, hopefully when I figure out how to get out of Tartarus. In the meantime, I do have a few thief skills still in my back pocket, and getting in and out of rooms quietly is one of them.

*Why did I have to find out this information so late?*

I could have told Hades sooner and not be hanging my life and future on this bad rom-com, comedy-of-errors maneuver.

As soon as I have the door open just wide enough, I go from my knees to all fours and slink my way into the room and along the side of the bed where I know Hades is lying. Holding my breath, and as careful as I can be, I poke my head up to make sure that it's him.

He's sleeping on his side, facing away from me, I think maybe with an arm possessively wrapped around past Lyra's stomach. I seem to remember the weight of him, the comfort of that sensation that night. His entire body is curled around me protectively…possessively…in a way that I think past me would have liked to have felt before he shredded her heart.

He's so…relaxed. I can tell from the lines of his body, the pattern of his deep breathing. And I don't think it's just because of slumber. The way he's holding past me, it's like the only way he can sleep is with me in his arms.

I can't help how my gaze softens on his back, and my belly turns a little squishy at the sight.

*Move your ass, Lyra.*

I need to wake him up in such a way that he doesn't jerk or, worse, leap into some kind of defensive move. Because that will definitely wake Lyra up.

Can't have that.

But I don't think gently whispering in his ear is going to make him all that much less defensive. I bite my lip, debating my options, but there's only one thing I can think to do. The question is, will the god of death allow himself to be teleported by anyone with no warning or permission? I mean, the fact that I've managed to sneak in here at all without him noticing is a bloody miracle.

I'm pretty sure I'm about to piss him off royally. Hopefully he doesn't kill me before figuring out who I am.

Right. Teleporting.

I study the way he's lying, searching for a body part to hold on to. I don't want to lose him in the process of taking us away. Unfortunately, turned away from me as he is, all he's presenting is his broad back. It'd be better if I could grab him by the hand or the wrist. I'd even take an ankle, but that's under the sheets.

*Damn.*

The flaws of this plan are growing by the second.

*So get moving, Lyra.*

The longer I stay here, the worse it gets for all three of us. My best bet is to try to wrap my hand around the scruff of his neck and hold on. Maybe I should grab him with two hands, just so I don't accidentally lose him.

To get close enough, I have to stand, looming over our sleeping forms in the dark. Slowly and silently, I reach for the back of his neck, and I'm focusing so hard on not making a sound or disturbing the bed in any way that I don't see it coming when a big hand suddenly grabs my wrist and we teleport instantly away.

When we blink back into existence, I'm immediately spun and yanked hard against him, my back against his chest. The hand holding my wrist crosses my shoulders, and his other arm comes around my waist and pins me tight. "You dare come anywhere near what is mine?"

# 81

## DESPERATE TIMES, BATSHIT MEASURES

### HADES

The woman trying to sneak into Lyra's room while she slept in my arms shudders against me.

"I *am* yours," she says. "Your queen."

That's Lyra's voice.

I grunt with shock before spinning her around to face me, hands on both her shoulders. My gaze skates over her, but it's the long hair, rather than short, that tells me who I'm dealing with.

Something catches hold in my mind, the words she used finally penetrating the shock like darts, and everything around us sharpens and then goes hot.

Because I took her to my bed—present-day Lyra. I'd promised myself I wouldn't. So much easier to stick to that edict when she wasn't in touching distance all the damn time.

I failed at that.

But it's done. I'm not going to hurt her, pushing her away again.

Aphrodite once told me that there's balance in the universe. That the prophecy I carry, my powers over death and that grave responsibility, would balance out with something equally sweet one day.

I'm hoping like hells that Lyra is the sweet.

Hope is a fool's errand, but I held out as long as I could.

And I must've been right to, because of the word this Lyra just used.

"You're my…queen." The words come out both as a harsh demand and as a confused question, my voice wavering over it.

She hesitates.

I see her hesitate.

"I will be."

Fuck. She scared me. My heart was already thudding, but that one pause made it drop.

Then she tips her head and lets everything she feel show in her eyes, the green and gold both seeming to turn brighter and warmer. "I *will* be, and I am now, but only if you break my heart first."

Rejection of that is so violent I stop breathing for a moment. When I finally take a breath, my brows snap together. "Break your heart. I wouldn't do that."

"That's why I'm here. I'm telling you that you have to."

I let her go, dropping my hands to my sides, swimming through my confusion to figure out why she would tell me that. She never gives me reasons, just cryptic warnings or directions. I'm so fucking sick of it. "You're here to tell me to break your heart?"

She inhales slowly. "Yes. I've seen too many versions of what happens next in the games to count or to tell you about. But there's only one way we end up together at the end of the Crucible with both of us alive." She's holding back. I can tell she is.

"Why?" I demand. "For once, tell me *why*, Lyra."

She considers me like she's trying to decide if I can take it. "If you don't break my heart now, and keep it broken until the end of Zeus' Labor, then the sirens that are part of it will be able to see me. There's no version of that future that doesn't end with one or both of us dead if my heart is whole. Because I have to be broken and feeling unloved for the curse to hide me from them. I have to *believe* that you don't love me. That you used me."

I look away, jaw clenching and unclenching. "There has to be another way. What if I break you too much and you don't even make it to Zeus' Labor? There's still Athena's—"

She puts her hand on my arm, giving me a reassuring squeeze. "This is me telling you to do it now. Be harsh with me. Be cold with me. Keep your distance from me. I'll make it through both, but I need my curse intact."

"Fuck." I spin away from her, running an agitated hand through my hair. "How am I supposed to do that after what we just shared?" I fling an arm out.

Does she remember?

I can't do this. If I thought going through with naming Lyra my champion was bad...

Gods damn it. If I'd known this was how it would be, I wouldn't have followed her into that grotto last night. Did I do something in a previous life to be tormented like this? It's as if the Fates have teased me with her all my life, forced me to fall in love with her only to live without her, then to have to break her over and over again in this sadistic contest.

All because she told me to herself.

What a mind fuck.

"Look at me," she says softly.

I pause with one hand in my hair, which I hadn't even realized I'd been raking it through. I slowly lower it and face her.

"I am telling you that the version of me standing before you is the future of the girl in your bed right now. I'm telling you that if you do this, as hard as it will be for both you and for her, you will still win my heart in the end. But more importantly, she'll live through the games, and we will both be exactly where we need to be when they're over."

"Together?" I demand.

She better fucking say together.

Her smile doesn't waver. "Eventually, everything will work out the way it's supposed to."

Relief is like falling only to be caught before hitting the ground.

I didn't know love could be like this. Or maybe I've always known, because I fell for her so long ago. Agony and ecstasy, trust and too many doubts to count, and all of it tied to someone who, despite my being King of the Underworld, has always had all the power over me.

I've never loved anything or anyone like I love her. Spending this time with her every day has made that clearer. "I will hold you to that, Lyra."

She bites her lip.

Damned if I don't go instantly hard at the sight, sucking in sharply, gaze pinned to her mouth. "I think I've been in love with you since I was a teenager, when you showed up at my family's home in the Overworld and told me that you had faith that I'd learn to control my powers, that I wasn't dangerous. And for whatever reason, I believed you."

I can't believe I admitted that to her. But the way she glows at the words, like she can't decide if she should smile or cry, makes it worth it.

And more sappy words come pouring out.

"The god of death and future King of the Underworld struck down by love at first sight." I huff a self-deprecating laugh. "Aphrodite would be ecstatic if she knew."

Lyra chuckles. "Yes. She would."

My gaze lingers on her smile before I sober. "But now you're telling me to risk *all* of that, after waiting for you for *thousands* of years, after having been so patient and damn well terrified through the Crucible Games—an ordeal that I didn't want to put you through in the first place and only did because you told me to." I shove a hand through my hair again. "Now you're telling me to break it all."

She takes a step forward, and I take a step back. Hurt flashes in her eyes, but she stops pushing. "I need you to trust me. I *will* be your queen. But this is the only way."

I shut my eyes, because I can't think when I'm looking at her. And for maybe the second time in my life, I wish I had a higher power than me to pray to.

What do I do?

"If I do this," I finally say slowly as I open my eyes again, "I need you to stay here. I need something of you to hold on to."

She swallows hard, giving a tiny shake of her head. "You know I can't promise that. I don't control when I come and go."

"Fuck," I mutter. "I don't think I can do this. The Crucible is bad enough. But this… You're asking too much."

I can see the way her eyes darken, the gold almost disappearing into the green. Is it hurting her to do this as much as it is me? Does she even think about it after she flits off to wherever she goes?

She clears her throat. "I've already survived this, and I know where we end up. You just have to trust me that this is the right thing to do."

"Fuck." I repeat the swear word several more times, tension vibrating off me the same way my bident vibrates when it hits metal, not absorbing the strike but reflecting it back outward.

Like she's determined that I won't push her away, she takes a step toward me, and I go rigid.

But she keeps coming, taking one step, then another and another until she's close enough to cup my jaw. "What will help you hold on?" she asks softly.

"Why won't you let go?" I demand, pushed beyond my limits. "You're the reason there's a prophecy, because I'd burn the world for *you*."

Shock reverberates through me as the last word passes my lips. I didn't mean to admit that. I never wanted to put that on her shoulders. Or maybe I was terrified that she'd look at me like the monster I'm supposed to become.

Like she looks at me lately as I push her away over and over.

But she doesn't. This Lyra only gives me a smile. "I know you wouldn't."

"You can't know that," I snarl. "You scare the shit out of me, Lyra."

"I know you wouldn't, *because* I wouldn't want that."

Not what I expected her to say. "You think I would?"

"What I mean is, you know that burning down the world would hurt me."

I'm shaking my head. "I don't understand—"

"I know you, Hades. You can't burn down the world, because you love me, and that would hurt me. You would *never* hurt *me*. Not if you could help it. That's why you hate what you're doing to...her...me...for the Crucible."

The mountains of Olympus may as well shake under my feet the way that hits. Have I been so busy protecting her from myself, worried about my reactions, that I *never* considered that?

Could she be right?

The longer we've spent in the Crucible, the more my feelings for her have grown, until I couldn't help myself and took her to my bed.

I've been so scared all this time of what she could do to me. Her power over me. The craving I have for her. "What if something happens to you, and the world takes you away from me? What if I can't help myself? What if they deserve to be punished? What if I do it for you?"

A shadow passes over her features, but she pins a smile to her lips, surety scaring away whatever dark thoughts she just had. "Life is never without problems," she says slowly. "Whatever trouble I get into, I promise you I can get *myself* out. I don't need you for that. I just need you to wait and hold me afterward."

"I've waited for you this long." The whisper tears from my throat, even as my heart is thudding painfully hard against my ribs. I believed I should stay away from her for so long, but then I realized that I just...couldn't. But this...this hope...she's giving me.

Can I believe in it? In her.

"What's a few more seconds," she whispers.

A few more seconds, I could handle. But after having her permanently in my life, without being taken away from me over and over, I don't know if I could go back to years...centuries.

I shudder.

"Just...think about it. And maybe one day you can make me a promise that you'll fight it, if the prophecy does come for you. Fight it for me."

"Fuck, Lyra. You ask the world."

"Only because I know you can give it," she says. Then lays her lips to mine.

She doesn't do more than press sweet, heartbreaking kisses against me. Soft kisses. Kisses I accept reluctantly, trying so damn hard to hold myself still. And I almost outlast her. But when, with a sigh, she goes to draw away, I can't stand it, and my hands move of their own volition to cup the back of her head, threading in her hair.

With a groan of desperation and need, I take over.

I bypass gentle and sweet, replacing them with a feverish need in every brush of my tongue against hers, the way I nip at her lower lip. The way I control every second and yet am so completely out of control myself.

On a deep sigh, I slow until we stand mouth to mouth, breath to breath, just absorbing each other.

"You can do this," she whispers against my lips. "I promise. I'm *telling* you the way through. I need you to have faith in us. In the *us* I promise we become."

Why does it feel like she's still not telling me something important? But I can't fight her any more. I don't want to. I press my lips to hers one last time before gentling and putting my forehead to hers, wrapped tightly around each other, eyes closed, breathing her in.

Then there's a terrible, endless emptiness I've become so familiar with over millennia.

When I open my eyes, I'm alone.

# PART 7

# THE QUEEN'S GAMBIT

Fuck the Fates. I'm in charge now.

## 82

## ZEUS' LOCK

### LYRA

When I open my eyes, I'm standing in Tartarus…and my arms are empty. I guess I was dumped in some random room, because it's pitch-black in here. With a snap of my fingers, the sconce lights the way it's supposed to, and I get my bearings.

It's another tiny room. One I'm not sure I've seen before. The second I open the door, a scream rips through the bowels of the tunnels.

The sound of it has me bolting out of the room, but the doors in this tunnel have no carvings, which means I have no clue where I am and no way to orient. So I go right, running in what I hope is the direction the sound is coming from. They can't be too far away, since I'm able to hear them through the thick rock.

Another scream racks through the corridors, and I pull up short. The sound is getting softer. So I flip around and go back the way I came, passing not only the room I was in but several other doors. As I run past one, something hits it from the inside so hard I swear the stone cracks, and I put on a spurt of extra speed, getting past it, then checking over my shoulder as I run.

Nothing bursts out to follow me.

Three different times, I come to a point where I have to choose a direction, but I only have to double back once when the screaming again gets softer the farther I go. I'm so busy running that I almost shoot past the source. But the movement of bodies beyond an open door catches my attention.

Shocked, I screech to a halt between the door posts and try to make sense of the chaos of the room. My mind takes way too long to catch up and sort out the jumble of limbs and people and words and screaming. And then my gaze finally lands on Boone.

*He's* the one screaming.

My heart slams around the cavity of my chest, and not from running. I've never heard Boone make sounds like that.

No one notices as I shove my way into the room, trying to get a better look. I'm almost sorry I did when I see the problem. Both of Boone's legs have been snapped at the femur, the bones sticking out like jagged broken blades, the lower parts of his legs limp, and all of him just…wrong.

I clap a hand over my mouth as I gag, breathing through my mouth instead of my nose, trying not to smell the golden blood of the gods. It's everywhere. Cronos is on the ground at Boone's head, gripping him by the shoulders. Hyperion and Koios are on either side of him at his grotesquely twisted legs.

I know what they're doing—trying to reset the bones before Boone's god healing can get too far. I've seen a real-life example of why they have to move fast—Hephaestus. The god of forges and invention's feet are backward because he healed too fast after being thrown down to the Overworld from Olympus as a baby.

"Ready?" Cronos asks.

"Do it!" Boone yells.

Cronos looks at Hyperion and Koios. "On three." Then he mouths the word "two." They both nod their understanding.

"One," he counts. "Two—" All three Titans pull. Hard.

A new sound pours out of Boone, high-pitched but garbled, as if his throat can't decide if he should scream or groan or vomit.

I go to clap my hands over my ears but stop halfway when I see Persephone take Boone's hand and, with her other palm, sprinkle something over his eyes, some kind of dust. The terrible sounds cut off abruptly as Boone passes out, his head flopping back loosely on his neck even as the Titans continue to strain his body.

The room goes much quieter, filled only with the sounds of our breathing and the muttered instructions passed between Cronos, Hyperion, and Koios as they work as fast as they can, against immortality. Every so often, Persephone murmurs softly in Boone's ear. I can't make out the words but imagine they're something along the lines of how they'll take care of him.

Finally, twin cracks of sound explode in the room. I'm not the only one who flinches, but at least Boone's legs don't look so…wrong. Koios leans over first one leg and the other, literally digging into the open wounds with his fingers to check that the bones are aligned. He looks up at Cronos and nods.

Iapetus stands over Boone's head, first passing a hand over his eyes and whispering more words I can't hear. Then he moves to the damaged flesh, and the fire of molten lava drips from his fingertips over the wounds, cauterizing them.

They're not done. As Iapetus works, the others are shoving the meat of Boone's flesh back together, trying to line up everything as well as they can before they take strips of cloth to bind him. I didn't even see Rhea pulling apart sheets in the corner. Glamoured sheets. The Titans start tying him up tightly. When they're finally finished, everybody in the room just kind of goes still and quiet, all of us taking a collective breath after that awfulness.

I realize my hands are still hovering somewhere between my mouth and my ears, so I drop them limp to my sides. "What happened? Did the Pandemonium attack again?"

Iapetus jumps. "Holy shit, Lyra."

The entire room kind of freezes before they swing to face me with varying expressions that aren't entirely penetrating my shock after what I just witnessed. Even Tethys and Mnemosyne, who are behind me, seem surprised that I'm here.

"When the fuck did you come from?" Iapetus asks as he swipes his hands down his shirt, gold blending with the yellows in the pattern and yet still leaving streaks across the other patches of color.

Before I can answer, Persephone's on her feet, pushing the others away to get to me. "I'll tell you what happened. Boone decided to open Zeus' Lock on his own."

What? My gaze shoots past her to Boone, whose chest is moving rhythmically, but he's still out cold. "Why didn't he wait for me?"

"Because you…" She flings her arms out wide, coming close to hitting me. "Decided to stay gone for a week. We didn't know how long it would take you."

A week? It was one night at most. How has it been a week down here? "That's not fair."

It's not like I had a choice of when time would bring me back.

"Fair?" She shoves a pointed finger in my chest. "You want to talk about fair? He almost died because he was alone."

Because it's coming from her—from sunshine on a stick who keeps insisting I'm a beloved friend—I flinch. Hard. "I told him not to go without me…"

The Titans had already started preparing us for that Lock. A test of wonder and curiosity, apparently—another loose connection. Zeus' Lock is about throwing us in the middle of the power of nature by outrunning four elements—a volcanic eruption, a tornado, a tsunami, and an earthquake. But there is a trick to each—as there always is with Zeus—a safe place to hide if you look hard enough. Ones that tend to move around and change.

I look at Boone's broken body. He did that alone.

Persephone's not finished. "He had to drag himself through the rest of it like *this*." She points an accusing finger at his still body.

You'd think after so many shocks in a row, I'd get used to it. Inured. Inoculated. Something along those lines. But nope. My ears start ringing, low and disorienting. When it finally goes away, Persephone is still glaring at me. What happened to the sweet spring goddess?

"I didn't mean for him to—"

"He did anyway." She pokes me again. Anger on her is almost scarier than anger on Athena. "Where were you? With Hades?"

"Persephone…" Rhea murmurs. "She didn't know."

"Didn't know?" Persephone scoffs. "She wouldn't stop messing with things. She never believed she could get us out, and now a good man is *broken*."

Her voice cracks on that last word, and she whirls away from me only to spin back around and shove me in the chest, pushing me back toward the door. "Get out."

Another shove. And I don't know if it's the shock or guilt, but I let her. I let her push me again, right out the door into the tunnel.

"Unless Boone asks for you, you are barred from entering this room," she snaps. "Even then, I'm not sure I'll say yes."

Despite being made of stone, the door clangs when she slams it in my face, and I'm left completely and utterly alone in the hallway.

I know this.

I've been here before. The outsider—ignored or ostracized by those who I need to work with to survive.

In the time I've been here, I've learned that this is not in Persephone's nature, so hopefully she'll cool off soon. Although yelling and blaming are also not in her nature. Maybe that's why there's an ache growing tentacles inside my chest.

She's right about one thing. I should have been here.

Boone has been working on our escape while I've been mucking about with trying to be the puppet master of broken time. Not that time really gave me the choice to come back here sooner.

But would I have if I could?

Boone will always be one of my most important and cherished friends. He shouldn't have had to go through that alone.

"Damn," I mutter.

I lean back against the rock of the wall opposite the door and slide down until I'm sitting with my hands draped across my propped-up knees, and I prepare to wait.

For as long as it takes.

# 83

# A SNAKE IN THE GRASS

LYRA

The Titans trickle out of the room over the course of the next hour or two. I'm not really sure how long, because it's not like I'm able to tell time down here.

The first out is Mnemosyne, who crouches down in front of me. "You should get some rest. I'm sure you've been dealing with…things."

It says something that I've gotten used to her owl mask mouthing along with her, I guess. She's trying to be kind, but the way she said that, I know she thinks the same thing as Persephone. That I've been wasting my time hopping around the past—first trying to save Isabel and then doing anything at all with Hades.

Other than Cronos, the others aren't exactly convinced of my puppet master theory.

"I'm comfortable here," I say.

I'm not leaving Boone. Not when I have the choice to stay. Even if it looks like too little, too late to them, he's my friend. I have similar conversations with the others as they emerge. Iapetus tells me that sitting around outside Boone's door isn't going to solve anything. When that doesn't budge me, he asks what I'm going to do if the Pandemonium are unleashed.

I point to the door. "I'm pretty sure Persephone's not going to keep her rule up if it means I go wild and hurt somebody else."

He gives me a closed-lipped stare, visibly debating the worth of arguing with someone so stubborn. Then shrugs and leaves me there.

Phoebe, meanwhile, can't even bring herself to look at me. Koios is with her, and he glances between us. At least he offers me a nod before they leave me alone without a word. Eventually, the only ones left with Persephone and Boone are Rhea and Cronos.

Given that they weren't exactly fans of Boone's when he first arrived with me, I'm surprised they linger as long as they do. At the same time, though, with me having disappeared for chunks of time and Boone using that time to work toward and fight for releasing us all, I guess I get it. Besides which, Boone is just that guy. The guy everybody likes. He wins over even the hardest of hearts when he wants to.

The door squeaks on its hinges, and I raise my head to find Rhea and Cronos finally coming out together. I get the briefest glimpse of Boone, still wrapped up on the bed, white cloths soaked with his blood, and Persephone with her back to me, holding his hand.

The Titans both stop once the door is closed behind them, and I drag my gaze from the door to their faces.

"Are you unharmed?" Rhea asks.

The outer edges of the emotional walls I've been sitting here rebuilding around my heart, familiar from all my cursed days, develop cracks. She's the first one to ask me that. Forcing back a chin wobble, I nod. "Thank you for asking."

She nods in turn. Then glances at Cronos when he takes her hand.

"I'm going to stay with Lyra," he tells his wife. "What do you want to do?"

She doesn't even blink. "I think I'll go with the others."

He kisses her cheek, and the two share a soft smile of understanding before she squeezes his hand and walks away.

After he watches Rhea disappear around the bend in the tunnel, Cronos proceeds to sit next to me against the wall. He sticks his feet out in front of him, leather-sandalled. I don't know why I have to fight down the sudden urge to laugh at the sight of a Titan's toes.

We stay here in silence for some time, and I don't know if he's expecting me to start a conversation. There's a lot I could tell him right now, but the quiet between us feels…easy. I don't want to break it.

The longer we sit here like this, the more I can feel my shoulders coming down from where they've hiked up around my ears without my even noticing. As if by just sitting here with me, Cronos is telling me that he's here for me, that he's not going to abandon me or keep me on the outside, no matter how badly I fuck up. At the same time, he leaves enough space between us so that I can fill it with words if I want to.

"I've been thinking about Oceanus," I finally say.

I'm not sure why that is the thing I choose to discuss first. It just came out. Cronos already knows about my visit with his brother. I told him before the first time we went to Hera's Lock, but I've had a little more time to think since then.

I glance over to find his eyebrows rising slowly. "What about him?"

"I should have mentioned this before, but I was too focused on getting us out of here sooner. I told him that you miss him—"

Cronos cuts me off with a sharp bark of a laugh. "That bloody traitor? I curse his name."

Exactly what I expected to hear.

"That's the thing. He knew that all of you curse his name every time it's mentioned." I let out a long sigh. "But how could *he* know that?"

Cronos' lips purse as he stares at the door across the way, gaze going distant. "I assume you asked him."

I nod. "He said he has his sources."

Cronos makes a thoughtful humming in the back of his throat. "You're thinking he might be the one who glamoured all our children?"

"It makes sense." I shrug. "He's a Titan, more powerful than the gods, and the only one of you not to be locked away in here, and it seems to me that the only way to keep glamours of that magnitude going this long is for someone to be out there feeding the power that keeps them in place. Maybe even checking the fence lines and repairing any holes so the cows don't get out."

"You lost me with cows."

"Forget the cows." I wave a hand. "After all this time, and for that many gods… The more I think about it, Boone was right when we talked about this. They had to glamour other pantheons of gods as well. You were friends with Odin, right? And Osiris."

"We were never friends," he says slowly. "But yes. We know each other."

"Wouldn't they have spoken up, though? The reasons for imprisoning you are widely shared and believed all over the world. If those gods remembered you correctly, they would have challenged those stories."

Cronos sighs. "I've had much longer to think about this then you have," he muses. "The only conclusion I've reached is that it would take multiple people banding together against us to accomplish what they have with the glamours you saw. Unless Oceanus—curse that traitor's name—has a much greater power than I know him to possess—in which case I think he would have used it to protect my father from me—then he doesn't have enough power to do what you're talking of. Not on his own."

I drop my head back against the rock. "But he *knew* things. I'm getting very tired of never having the full picture."

Cronos chuckles. "You have many millennia of history to catch up on, Alani. Millennia of knowledge I have at my fingertips, and yet I still don't have the answers to the riddles you pose."

"You're right. You should be much better at this than I am." I shake my head in mock disgust. "I feel so disappointed with my Titan experience down here in Tartarus."

"I'm afraid we don't offer refunds."

"I demand to speak to management." I pound a fist on my knee.

We share a grin, though they quickly fade from our faces, and we sit in silence again. Without consciously realizing what I'm doing, I lay my head on Cronos' shoulder. He tenses a little at the contact but then eases on a soft huff that might be a laugh.

I think that maybe he pats the top of my head before resting his cheek on it. "Don't worry, Alani. We will find the answers together."

"If there are answers," I mutter.

# 84

# THIRD TIME'S THE CHARM

### LYRA

I guess I fell asleep on Cronos' shoulder, because a yelp surprises me awake. Me *and* Cronos. "Did you hear that?" I ask.

"I did." He nods. "It came from in there."

In a blink, we're both on our feet, and he's reaching for the door handle when it's jerked open and Persephone is standing there.

Persephone…only…

"What the fuck—"

She grabs my hand, drags me into the room, and points at a crack of time hovering, almost threateningly, directly over Boone. "Do something about that," she commands, the finger she's pointing shaking hard.

"Persephone…"

"Don't argue." She twitches away. "Fix it before it takes him."

"Persephone—" I grab her arm and turn her roughly toward me. "Who got to you?"

Her perfect brows, already pulled together in concern, snap down over her eyes. "New lies, Lyra?"

"I'm not lying. I see it."

"What are you talking about?" Cronos demands.

"I'm talking about glamours." My power is still on from before. "I'm talking about how she—"

I'm spun around and shoved hard in the chest. Hard enough to send me stumbling backward. Right into the fractured piece of time, which closes around me as Persephone says, "It's better without you around anyway."

And I'm just in time to see…well…me.

I'm on the mountain in Olympus by Hera's observatory again.

For the third time.

And the me I'm looking at is not the Lyra fighting in the Crucible who came up here after Athena's Labor. She's already been taken away by the Daemones. This is the Tartarus version of me who time traveled here once already. The me who asked Hades why he'd been so cruel.

And as soon as my mind absorbs all these things and centers me on where and when I am, that past version of me disappears, too.

I know where she went—sucked back into broken time to return to Tartarus. But it's very different to see it from out here. No crack. No crystalline flashes. It's almost as if she turns into mist and floats away—fairy dust on the wind—turning into nothing as she goes.

*So that's what that looks like.*

As soon as she's gone, Hades pitches forward, hands to his head like he's trying to hold his skull together, and the mountain beneath my feet shakes.

Hard.

I'm across the space between us and on my knees in front of him faster than a Titan can run. Hades doesn't seem to notice, eyes shut tight as he breathes. I put my hands over his, bracketing his face. "I'm here. I'm—"

I don't know if what sets him off is me touching him or my voice, but Hades explodes away from me.

"You." Rage descends over his features. "Damn it, Lyra. Why do you keep doing that?"

I glare right back. "I've told you, *I'm* not controlling it. I have as much choice in the matter as you do."

He's not listening. I can tell because his eyes narrow to glittering, silvery slits. Again, the mountain underneath me shifts with the force of his emotions, and a trickle of fear creeps down my spine. "Hades?"

"You blame me for hurting you when you *told* me to after a different you just told me that somebody can glamour the gods. That someone could have made me do things to you that I am—"

I cut him off. "I was wrong."

Maybe *wrong* isn't the best word choice. There *is* somebody who can manipulate the gods in that way. But after what I've experienced now, I know they weren't responsible for what Hades did to me. That has been me all along. "I know more now than I did when I visited you a…second ago."

Okay. That sounded as ridiculous out loud as it did in my head.

There's no give in him. "How do I know this is the real you now and not a glamour?"

An impossible thing to prove. "What does your gut say? You *know* that was me, and this is, too."

Another tremble of the mountain. "Fuck," he snarls as he throws his hands down and turns his back on me.

What I desperately want to do is wrap my arms around him and tell him to believe me, tell him that everything will be all right, but I don't know that for sure. Either of those things. Besides, I'm pretty certain if I move at all from my current position kneeling on the ground that Hades might smite me before I even gain my feet.

"Ask me something only Lyra would know," I offer.

"That doesn't help," he snaps back. "Because I don't know which versions of Lyra I've seen throughout my life are really her or not."

Right. "Good point," I mutter.

There's got to be a way to prove I'm me. But honestly, I'm so tired of fighting and thinking and scheming that my head feels like it might explode from all the things.

I've got nothing.

He runs a hand through his hair in an agitated gesture, then pauses and slowly lowers it to his side. Though his back is still to me, I can practically see the transition from raw emotion to cold calculation simply in the way his shoulders change their angle. "Let's pretend for a second I believe this is you," he tosses over his shoulder at me. "Tell me what you need me to do, then."

"Who says I need to tell you to do anything?"

"Lyra…" He's at the edge of snapping. It's in his voice.

I sigh. Apparently, I get to tell it to his back.

I stay where I am, still kneeling on the hard ground. "I know I've been confusing you these past two visits." Past two for him, at least. I think. "And I'm sorry. So I'm here now to tell you to stay the course. Get me through Zeus' Labor by keeping my curse intact. After that, why you had to do any of this will become clearer. And will be…"

I bite off the words *worth it*.

I know he catches the hesitation. But I won't finish it, leaving the hole of silence empty. I can't tell him it's all going to end happily, and I can't tell him it will be worth it. I still have hope to hold on to that Phoebe's vision will eventually come true and we'll get out of Tartarus. After all, the Titans have had their own hope wrapped around that truth for ages.

But I can't tell him any of that.

I stare at his back, waiting for any sign that he believes even a smidge of what I'm saying.

Although now that time reset to after all of the Crucible Games, maybe it doesn't matter? But somehow, I feel like how we get there is just as important as getting there. Gods, my head hurts from trying to wrap itself around these riddles. I have to move forward the way we've planned. I'll act as Hades' source and make sure I end up where I am now. Boone, too. No choice about him after the reset.

"When are you from?" Hades asks abruptly.

When I don't answer immediately, he finally turns slowly to look at me with eyes still narrowed, the silver so pale they look like glittering, freezing ice chips.

I sigh. "I can't tell you that."

"But you will be my queen?"

He needs reassurance when I've told him so before? Relief at being able to finally answer one question is sharp in my chest. "Yes. I will be your queen." But the tremulous smile that starts on my lips freezes at his next question.

"Forever?"

Damn his sharp mind. "I don't…" I almost tell him that I don't see the future, only the past, but that's too much information, too. "I haven't seen that far out yet."

"Then we still have nothing."

I know. That's what hurts the most, the ache of it always there. Right where my heart should be. Because if we can't trust in each other, we have…nothing. And if I never return to him, we have nothing.

Maybe Hades and I had nothing all along.

But part of me refuses to believe that, and I take a deep breath. "There *is* a being out there who can glamour the gods the way that I told you. That's still true. But now that I've seen more, I am convinced that whoever that is doesn't know what I...can do." Not yet, at least. And regardless of who is sending me through time, I still have to be the one to set the gears and cogs in motion when I get where they send me. "They don't know that they need to pretend to be me to get to you."

Hades glances away, the emotional walls he's erected between us still skyscraper-high and solid steel.

I swallow. "I know trust doesn't come easily to you, after what you've seen humans do over the eons that you have guarded their eternal souls. Or, for that matter, what you've seen your own family do, corrupted by power, jealousy, or worse." I lean forward, appealing to him with every part of me. "And I'm not telling you to trust me blindly. You should check that it's me every time. The problem is, I don't know how to make that easy for you."

There's got to be something about me that is so essential that only he would know it. But I don't know what it is. Nothing that couldn't be mimicked if witnessed.

I drop my gaze to the ground as I scour my mind for something, *anything* that could help both of us. And I don't know if he's just a damned silent predator or if he teleports closer, but suddenly Hades is crouched before me, a finger under my chin to tilt my gaze to his.

"What is the first thing you said to me that night when I stopped you from throwing a rock at Zeus' temple? Not before you realized it was me. The first thing right after."

I blink at him, running through that night, and then can't help the way my lips twitch. "'I'm afraid one of us shouldn't be here.'" I roll my eyes. "As true today as it was that night."

If there's even a hint of give in him, I'm not seeing it.

I let loose another sigh. "But you saw me there watching you—future me, I mean, not..."

"I get it."

"What if someone *else* was there that night, too, and overheard?" I ask. "That doesn't seem like a very good test—"

With speed only an immortal could demonstrate, Hades closes the distance between us and presses his lips to mine in a demanding, harsh kiss.

Immediately, we go up in metaphorical fire.

That fire might as well be real, the way this feels, and I gasp and whimper at the same time against him even as I kiss him back.

Heavens of Olympus, he tastes of *him*—that delicious scent of bitter, dark chocolate winds around me as our tongues tangle and more whimpers pour from me. I'm practically crawling to get closer to him.

A groan escapes Hades, coming from deep in his throat, and he's gathering me against him, lifting me off my knees and into his lap. Hazily, I realize that's almost impossible, given the way he was crouching, but I don't care. My entire world, my entire existence, is centered on his lips, his tongue, and every shattering touch.

Although I do have the vague impression that we've moved locations, sitting on the side of a bed somewhere. I don't care.

I only care that I can add one more memory like this to the ones I have of him. Of us.

How did I ever—*ever*—doubt him? No way could he fake this just to continue using me.

Hades breaks the kiss to bury his face in my neck, breathing hard and harsh and erratic. "Lyra," he groans into my skin. "It is you."

# 85

# ABOUT DAMN TIME

### HADES

Lyra winds her arms around my neck, holding on to me tight. "How do you know?"

I groan, still so relieved I don't know which way is up. "Because, my star… I know your taste, your feel under my hands, the sounds you make. Not even Aphrodite herself could imitate those elements that are so completely, elementally you. Not to me."

"Oh." She burrows into me.

"Shy?" I chuckle into her hair. "You've already given yourself to me once."

"More than once," she murmurs.

I suck in, my arms tightening around her compulsively. More than once. Because we have a future together. All this gods-cursed time holding back and breaking Lyra so she can survive the Crucible bursts like a damn giving way.

I *need* her.

I need to know that I don't lose her.

"Then…your body knows my hands," I say. Soft.

She shivers as I slide one hand under the bottom of her shirt, smoothing over the bare skin of her back. I tease her with the tips of my fingers, relishing the difference between us—rough and silky soft—lightly brushing around her waist to tease at the sensitive flesh of her stomach. To trail upward, though not as high as she wants, and dip down, but not as low as she wants.

And all I can think is how much I need this.

To lose myself in her. In us.

"Hades." My name escapes her on a breathy whimper.

She feels it, too. She knows all the parts of us, all the moments before the Crucible, the connection built over time. "I know, my star. I know."

Holding on to her with one arm around her waist and my hand still teasing her belly, I stand us both up. Capturing her gaze, I walk us backward. Still teasing, unable to stop smiling. Unwilling to stop.

And she looks right back at me with green-gold eyes so full of trust, but also a hint of something else. It's as if she's trying to absorb every nuance of my face, of the feel of my hands, of…me.

She gasps when I press her up against the wall.

Then slowly—agonizingly slowly, because I love the way her breath increases to needy little pants—I draw her shirt up. I stop just at the top, with her arms trapped inside, pinned above her head, and half her face covered.

Mine.

Fucking *mine*.

For the longest moment I just keep her there, my gaze tracing over everything I see, and she shivers, but her full lips are smiling.

I lay my cheek against hers. So godsdamned soft. So godsdamned mine.

"Your lips know my lips," I murmur in her ear.

But I don't kiss her. Not yet.

Instead, I suck on the lobe of her ear, and she whimpers, tilting her head to give me more access. But I don't accept the invitation. Instead, I trail slow, tantalizing kisses across her jaw, only to hover just barely out of reach of her lips.

"Kiss me," she whispers. Demands.

I grin.

She will be mine. My queen.

I slip the shirt the rest of the way off only to capture both her wrists in one hand, pinning them above her head, curling my other hand into her waist.

"Do you know how long I've waited for you?" I ask her.

Millennia. Ages. A fucking eternity.

She lifts her gaze from my lips to my eyes. The gold has nearly swallowed the green now as if her very blood has heated to boiling, to overflowing.

She doesn't hide a single emotion from me, and I let her see mine—all of me—in my own eyes.

Wanting. Of course wanting. I could turn to ash in a blink at the heat stoking inside me. But the unguarded emotions that reach between us, ones I couldn't let her see yet in any time…those I give to her freely now, knowing our future together is close, even with what she still has to endure. If she didn't survive it, she wouldn't be here now.

So I show her. Tethering me to her in all new ways. I show her *all* of what I feel.

Craving. Longing. Desperation.

Promises. The world.

But also wariness, because I can't quite believe it's real, this future where I can keep her by my side. Somehow.

And underneath all that is the patience, the wild kind of faith in her, that it took to get us this far.

"I've wanted you all my life," I say. "Loved you for I think at least half as long. I'm not even sure when the loving started. It crept up on me between your sporadic, confusing-as-fuck visits. And I think your curse doesn't work on me, because I was already half in love with you the day you tried to throw a rock at Zeus' temple."

She sucks in sharply, eyes widening.

"And now you're *here*, in the present and not disappearing for centuries at a time. But I can't—" My voice breaks, and I swallow hard. "I can't have you."

The words are a growl, laden with my need, frustration, and pain.

Her gold-and-green eyes turn glassy, and even though I have her pinned, because I'm suddenly fucking terrified to let go, she still manages to press a soft kiss against the corner of my mouth. "I'm sorry," she whispers.

Sorry.

She's sorry.

And I can see that she is. Feel it.

All that time I've spent just…waiting. But I don't know what she was doing. I tried to stop myself from imagining it. From worrying over it. If I wasn't already a god, I'd pray. Hells, I'd get down on my knees to even Zeus if it meant that the waiting was over.

Especially since she reminded me that how I react to the prophecy is still my choice. The biggest reason I've been pushing her away. It didn't take away the problem, but the different perspective gave me… permission. Hope.

She presses another kiss to the corner of my mouth. "Thank you."

I tilt my head, wanting to kiss her, chasing that contact, until the words sink in, and I pause.

"Thank you?" My voice is a rasp now. "For what?"

"All of it," she says. "For waiting. For falling in love with me. For trusting me. Enduring me. All of it."

*Heavens save me.*

I lean into her, pinning her harder against the wall with my entire body, pressing the ridge of my arousal into her belly. Even then, I still hold back.

"I don't want your thanks, Lyra," I snarl.

But the way she always does when she should fear me, she smiles instead. "What do you want, then?"

Everything. "Your fucking eternity."

Her smile falters. Just the tiniest bit, but I see it.

"I've *earned* eternity with you." I'm still snarling. "With the time I've already paid."

She doesn't speak. She doesn't say the words I want to hear. Make me promises.

"Can you even give me eternity?" I demand. Accuse.

I slip the hand at her waist past the band of her pants, past her panties, and twist to slip inside her.

"Fuck me." She's already slick.

I pump that finger once, slowly, before going still.

Her hips chase more, but I don't allow her to move. "You can't promise me eternity. Can you, Lyra?"

She looks me in the eyes. "No one can promise that."

What does that even mean? Obviously, she survives the Crucible, or she couldn't be here now. But does she leave me after? What the fuck happens that would make me let her go?

The way I've pinned her, I've left her with only one way to reach me. She takes it, dropping her head forward so we're cheek to cheek. "What I can promise is my heart, no matter where or when I am. And nothing—not time, not death, not the heavens or the hells, not even the Fates—can take it away from you."

Fear and fucking feral possession war within me, and I go rigid against her, fighting both. The only movement is my chest, pressing into Lyra with the rapid rise and fall of my breathing. She lifts her head slowly, meeting my gaze.

She doesn't shy away from what she sees in it. In me. She never has. If anything, she's always run straight for it.

"You can promise me this?" I demand through stiff lips.

She offers me a smile, letting her heart shine through. All of her—the teasing, the faith in me, the trust, the need. All those words she said to me after I stopped the Anaxian Wars, words I was too afraid to hear then—still am, if I'm honest—those words settle inside me in a way that I will never turn my back on again.

"I promise," she whispers.

Mine. Only because she gifted herself to me. Mine. Only because I'm going to give myself back to her. Every part of me. Holding nothing back ever again.

"Leave your hands above your head," I command.

A flush of pink warms her skin, and she nods. Then doesn't move as I slowly lower the hand holding hers above her head.

"Toe off your shoes." Another command.

She obeys.

Fuck if I don't love it. Maybe especially because she usually doesn't obey a damn thing I say.

I strip her of her pants and panties, rising to reach behind her and untangle her from her bra.

Then, gaze devouring every inch of her body stretched out on display for my eyes alone, I take several steps back. I reach one hand overhead, and my shirt comes off in one tug. And I love the way her eyes greedily trail over my body.

I remove the rest of my clothes, and the instant the last item hits the floor, I teleport, and when I return, I am on my knees in front of her. I grin, throwing all my fears and questions aside. This moment is for us alone.

"Every queen should be worshiped," I murmur. "Now…spread your legs, my star."

Despite the way her limbs are visibly trembling, she eagerly obeys me in this, too. Fuck if having her submit to me, because she's as desperate for me as I am for her, isn't the sexiest godsdamned thing I've ever seen. I'm so damn hard, every pulse of my blood through my cock is on the edge of pain.

The instant she parts her legs, my mouth is on her. My tongue. The taste of her my own sweet heaven. I slide a finger deep, even harder because of the sound she makes. One finger. Then two.

She drops her hands to either side of her hips for balance as she gives herself over to me.

I torture her with my tongue. Lash at her before gentling, then pressure. I drink in her taste but also every moan, every shudder, every buck of her hips, every tremble.

Her orgasm comes hard and fast, catching us both by surprise.

She cries out and then tumbles forward, as if she can no longer hold herself up. But so fast that I have to use my god speed to catch her against my chest.

She looks up at me with pleasure-hazed eyes, the pupils blown out wide so that only the gold glitters at me from them, cheeks flushed and her body replete against me.

I can't help the laugh that rumbles through me.

To make her look like this.

How long I have dreamed of it.

"So that's what stars look like when they collapse," I tease.

But before she can smile or grumble in return—either response is possible—I pin her back against the wall, hands above her head again. Only this time, with my other hand, I lift one of her legs and wrap it around my waist. "Hold on."

Keeping her upright with one hand holding her wrists as she stares back at me with so much desire, I feel heat flush through my body at her look alone. I almost fumble positioning myself with my other hand.

Then I'm gripping her leg, under her fucking perfect ass, lifting, and…

Her head drops back as I enter her in one long, lazy stroke, taking my damn time as I lower her agonizingly slowly, as if we're both moving toward each other and what we can bring each other.

I don't stop until I am as deep as she can take me, slick and hot and tight, her eyes on me.

I groan and drop my forehead to her shoulder. "Paradise," I whisper. "And madness."

Maybe that's why I love her so much. Because she reflects my kingdom—heavens and hells—and my kingdom reflects me.

She is my mirror.

Made for me.

And me alone.

Then I lift my head to stare into those beautiful eyes that adore me even as her hips press into me in an unconscious physical plea for more.

"I want more." I echo that need aloud. But I'm not just talking about pleasure. "I want your heart. Your soul. Your fate. Your future. All of it."

There's a desperation in that demand. I can hear it in my voice. I don't care. I'd strip my soul bare if it meant I'd never lose her again.

"Only in exchange for you," she whispers. And my heart stops dead in my chest. "All of you for all of me."

My heart goes from dead to exploding with elation.

"Done."

I snap my fingers, and a glittering golden ribbon made entirely of light winds around us, playing between our bodies, all as I start to move, sliding in and out of Lyra.

Then I start to speak, timing my words to what I'm doing to her with my body. "I, Hades, King of the Underworld and god of death, bind myself to you, Lyra Keres. All of me. For eternity."

The ribbon tightens, as if the fabric of the cosmos is tying us to each other.

And my heart is near to bursting with the moment.

It doesn't feel heavy, or wrong, or as if I'm trapping her, tying her to the monster that lurks under the surface. She's right. I will find a way to beat that fucking prophecy. *Because* of her. Because of her faith in me. But also for her.

I'm *making* a faith. Pledging myself to the woman who has loved me across time, despite who I am fated to be.

Will she give me this, too? This magical bond I'm asking her for?

I continue to move my body. I will bring her to that peak of pleasure again, follow her into that abyss gladly, even if she doesn't choose to say those words back to me.

"Only if you wish it," I whisper. She needs to know this is her choice.

"I, Lyra Keres," she murmurs.

And I didn't think it was possible, but my heart explodes again.

She's absorbing every stroke, every thrust, surge after agonizingly beautiful surge, and staring down into my eyes as she says the words.

"Queen of the Underworld and goddess of things still unrevealed, bind myself to you. Give myself to you. Vow myself to you, Hades. All of me. For eternity..." She swallows. "Even should we be parted."

Parted?

I dislike that word intensely.

She presses her hand to my face. "Don't worry," she whispers. "We'll find a way."

The ribbon of power and energy around us tightens even more, cinching down.

"I believe you." Everything she's told me to do has been true. Not always easy. In fact, most of the time, they've been the hardest challenges of my life. But true.

I lower her enough that she's clinging to my shoulders so I can take her hips in both my hands. "Hold on, my star."

And then the ribbon turns from sparkling bands of light to...fire.

It starts at the tips, the blaze eating along the trail it's made over our skin, and heat follows. Heat and Lyra. I move inside her with the speed of a god, claiming her body as our bond burns into our very flesh.

And the pleasure that builds in the wake of both heats extinguishes everything except for her...and us.

Until it ignites inside.

When she comes undone, I swallow her cries with a kiss, groaning into her mouth as I follow her over the edge—incandescent, indescribable, ineffable.

Rapture.

She's *mine*.

# 86

# A TIME WHEN IT WAS MAGIC

### LYRA

When I come back to myself, I'm wrapped in Hades' arms, in his bed—our bed—in the Underworld. My lips part on a soft gasp.

"What?" Hades' voice is an amused rumble against my back.

"I can see the bond."

"What?" He shifts against me, propping up on an elbow to see my face. "You can see it?"

I nod. "I can see glamours."

I guess my power turned back on while we were wrapped up in each other.

"That's not a glamour, though," he says.

Oh. "I suppose I can see invisible things, too, then."

"You don't know?" he asks slowly.

I still, my gaze caught by our discarded clothes on the floor. He doesn't know when I am from, and he can't know that he loses me in Tartarus. I need to be careful. "It's…new…and still evolving."

Silence to that.

I trace a finger over the glittering golden lines around my arm. I think maybe I thought the celestial ribbon had been more for show, but I'd never wish it away.

I turn over, fascinated, and trace the lines across his arm, his neck, his chest. Until Hades captures my hand with a grunt, then kisses the tips of my fingers. "I'd love to continue that, but first…"

When he doesn't keep going, I raise my eyebrows at him. "First?"

He opens his mouth, pauses, then says, "Don't go."

The fascination fades. Don't leave him again, he means. I don't think that's what he meant to say, and I feel every part of that down in my deepest heart. "I—"

He shakes his head. "Never mind. I know."

Will it make a difference that past Hades created this bond with future Lyra, though? I bite my lip. It's a worry that will have to answer itself.

Hades seems to gather in on himself and goes back to what he originally meant to say. "First, I think you need to give me more. What else should I know?"

"I have to be careful *when* I tell you things as much as *what*," I say slowly. Reluctantly.

"I understand."

"Do you?" I ask his clavicle.

He gathers me closer, face to face, heart to heart. "I think so. I know you are a future version of yourself. That you are helping make sure things go the way you need them to. Me too, I assume. Right so far?"

"Yes."

"And you're sure that this is the right way?"

A thousand different witnessed pasts tell me so. "As sure as I can be."

He nods. "I also have to assume that my father is dead."

His words might as well be Poseidon's electric eels shocking me to stiffness. "What?"

Hades frowns at the way I said that, and I have to reel myself in. He has no idea about the truth when it comes to the Titans.

"Why would you say that?" I ask in a calmer tone.

"Because only he has control over time in this way. Now you do, even if you're still learning it. He'd never give it up willingly. That power of his is the most important thing to him. Always has been."

His bitter words are like a snakebite. Meanwhile, though, I try not to let myself visibly relax. Hades thinks I have power over time. If he figured out that some version of Cronos from a future I haven't reached yet is the one sending me to him, he'd stop doing anything I tell him. Stop trusting me entirely.

The veil over his face is there. Not even a hint that it's weakened over time. It's so hard not to try to remove it, to pull it away from his face, to relieve him of that burden.

But I haven't figured out how to do that yet.

"I told you that when I win, you have to get Pandora's Box." It's the only thing my brain comes up with to redirect the conversation.

He gives me a look. "You told me that a long time ago now, but yes. I remember."

Clearly, given where past me is right now. "Persephone will be waiting at the gates of Tartarus. Bring a few helpers with you. Charon. Cerberus, me."

"No." The word is a snarl. "Not you. It's too dangerous."

I press my hand over his heart, finding it thudding, and melt a little. "This is the only way. At least give me the choice."

Wince. It's not entirely a lie. I may still be down there, but I've gotten as far as I have. I will get out of there, damn it. Back to him.

Hades' jaw works as he grinds his teeth. "Anyone else?"

I hesitate over the other two. Boone hasn't been saved yet in his timeline, is still a soul in the Underworld. And I haven't tried to tell Demeter about her daughter yet. Neither would make sense to him.

I shake my head. "Others might join. That's up to you and…me…when the time comes. But those three are important."

I'll have to trust that I'll bring Boone again.

"Anything else?"

I burrow into Hades and think. Hard. Is there anything else I can tell him at this point? "Oceanus?" I wrinkle my nose. "You probably haven't had time—"

"I looked into him. He hasn't left that cave since the day the Titanomachy started."

He hasn't. Then… "How does he know things he shouldn't?"

Hades leans in, nose to nose. "How do you?"

I wrinkle my nose at him.

"Can't tell me?"

I shake my head, my long hair rustling against the pillowcase with the movement.

After a second, Hades relaxes against me and touches my hair, winding one long tress around his finger. "This is why I know you'll be safe after all this is over."

"My hair?" It grew instantly in Hestia's Lock and didn't go back, but why—

"You must be from far ahead in the future to have grown it this long by the time you come to me. Even when I was younger, millennia ago, you looked like this when you came to me."

It takes everything I have to control my reaction, my expression.

"And now you've made me promises in the bonds under our skin." He tips my chin up and kisses me softly. Sweetly. "I'll believe in that and get you through the rest of the Crucible, no matter what it takes."

"Don't forget. You can't show me you love me. You have to keep my heart broken."

His arms curl tighter around me. "You ask the worst things of me, my star."

He's going to hate me.

When I disappear into Tartarus.

He's going to believe I lied. That I broke the bonds of these promises. My heart wants to crack, shatter for him, for the future I make him endure.

"Lyra?" he murmurs into my hair.

"Hmmm?"

"When we marry in the future, don't ever leave me again."

I squeeze my eyes shut tight. Oh gods. What have I done to him?

# 87

# HERE I GO AGAIN

### LYRA

Those terrible nightmares where you wake up somewhere totally unexpected and unwanted always suck. That's what it feels like to be taken by time in the middle of the night. Snatched right out of Hades' arms and shoved back into hell.

Or the worst part of the hells, at least.

Time travel can also be like bad déjà vu.

I land back in Boone's room to the tune of Titans arguing with each other over his body, no longer bloody but still out cold.

I don't give a shit what they're yelling about.

I'm staring at Persephone. She's sitting by Boone, holding his hand but staring straight at me with a face gone pale. Which is when I remember what I saw just before Persephone shoved me into the shard of time and sent me away.

Bringing my power forward, I grunt at the sight of the veil contoured to her features. Not just her eyes—over her entire face.

A glamour.

She's been glamoured. Again.

Taking a note from Hades, I prowl through the room, directly to her, parting the Titans with the force of my determination to get to her fast.

Persephone jumps up, backpedaling until she hits the wall. "What are you going to do to me?" She throws her hands up.

I grab her wrists, yanking them down, and then I pluck the mesh of light right off her face.

This time, unlike when I've tried before, it slides right off. Like film formed over cooling melted cheese. There's the second glamour under it, the one I originally saw. But that one doesn't budge when I try it. Persephone sways a little, eyes rolling back in her head, and I grab her by the shoulders. She sucks in a sharp breath, coming back to herself.

Then she stares at me with eyes growing wider and wider. Her hands fly up to cover her mouth, blue eyes welling with tears. "What did I do? On Olympus, I never meant to hurt you, Lyra. I—"

"It's okay." I squeeze her arms, then swing around to face the rest of the room.

The Titans have all gone dead silent, watching us.

I hold up the mesh they can't see, then throw it on the ground, where the magic hisses and fizzes until it turns black and the ash blows away. "She was glamoured."

"I *knew* she wasn't acting like herself," Mnemosyne murmurs.

But it's Iapetus who whirls on the others. "Which one of you motherfuckers is a traitor?"

"She's not the only one," I say.

Then I kneel beside Boone and remove his. It's so easy for me now. Maybe learning one power—like teleporting or seeing the glamours—makes figuring out the next one easier. Or maybe the intensity of the need to do it helps bolster my ability. Because removing the door's glamour or the rabbit's wouldn't make a difference, really, but this is important. I've also had a lot of time down here now, what with all the resets. So maybe time sitting with a power plays a role. I don't care which it is, just that I can do this now.

Just like with Persephone's, the glamour dies a quick death.

Boone doesn't wake up, but the frown of pain immediately eases and a bruise on his cheek starts to visibly change colors. His healing is restored.

"Boone, too?" I hear Koios say.

I don't answer as I'm back on my feet and crossing to Phoebe. The goddess's eyes flick from me to Koios and back. "It's not me," she says. "I would never—"

I pull the mesh from her face, too, tossing it away to the sound of more hissing and fizzing, and she stumbles back a little. Koios is instantly there, propping her up. When the Titaness recovers, tears suddenly spill from her eyes. "I… I was wrong."

"You were all glamoured to believe I was awful," I say. "It's okay. I—"

"No." She shakes her head hard, silky hair streaming around her too-pale face. "I mean the prophecy. It was a glamour."

"What?" I take a small, stumbling step back. "We can't get you out?"

"I don't know about that. But you and Boone... You're not fated in any way. It was all a lie."

# 88

# WHAT'S THE QUESTION

### LYRA

Silence, I'm starting to learn, is not good.

Not around the Titans. Silence means bad things.

"What does this mean?" Eurybia's dire question drops into the room like a small explosive device, setting all of them off in arguments and discussion.

But Koios' answer drags them all back under the silence. "It means we were wrong that the key to Aphrodite's Lock is Boone and Lyra together."

I happen to glance at Cronos' face then, and shock ricochets through me at the set lines. He truly believed that fate had sent him two saviors, I think.

"Whoever is doing this, they must not want us to get out," Phoebe says in a strangled voice.

As if all of Tartarus sucks in a shocked breath at the Titaness's revelation, the ground under our feet starts shaking violently.

Persephone throws herself over Boone as cracks appear in the ceiling, starting in one corner and sweeping across it, growing longer and wider in fast bursts.

Again. The damned rock ceiling is trying to come down on top of my head again.

That's my only inane thought before Cronos is grabbing me by the arm and pulling me up against the wall, shielding me with his body.

I peek around him, squinting my eyes against the dust and rock coming down on top of us to see Hyperion, Koios, Crius, and Iapetus all standing in a circle, holding up the ceiling that makes up the floor of the tunnels and cells above us, like the pillars at the corners of the earth they originally were, protecting us from being buried now.

When the shaking stops, none of us move for a shocked second.

"Is the hallway whole?" Koios demands.

In seconds, Cronos is opening the door, though he's hardly able to because the partially dropped ceiling is blocking the way. He has to punch up to pulverize a hole big enough before he can swing it wide to step out. Then there's the sound of more pounding.

There's a groan from Boone. "What happened—"

His eyes blink open, still heavy-lidded, but he takes one look at Persephone leaning over him and his eyes grow wide. With memories or the realization of his glamour, I'm not sure which, because he doesn't say anything. He just threads his fingers in her hair and pulls her down to kiss her like she's the air he breathes.

"It's clear," Cronos pokes his head in to say. "Get him out of here."

He means Boone.

Persephone groans, then pulls away. "Later," she whispers. Then points at the ceiling.

"Fuck," Boone says. "I was out for a second, and the world fell apart?"

Quickly, Rhea and Persephone drag the pallet he's lying on out the door, Boone holding Persephone's hand and complaining all the way. I'm not sure he even sees that I'm back, but now is not the time to be pointing that out.

The rest of us follow.

I don't see how the four Titans holding up the ceiling get out. All I know is there's a massive rumble and crash, blowing debris out the door and all over us. But when it clears enough to see, the four of them are standing in the hall with us.

"Why is this happening?" Phoebe asks through a bout of coughing.

Koios wraps an arm around her.

The others don't even seem to notice the question, but I'm frowning. Persephone said the cracks in Tartarus were new. They started the first time I was sucked in here.

It can't be coincidence, can it? Is someone trying to bring down all of Tartarus on my head to stop me? Or was Hades unable to keep from burning down the world when I disappeared in here?

The Titans clearly don't have answers.

"We need a new safe room." Koios breaks into my thoughts.

As the others discuss where to go and how to get Boone there, I tug on Cronos' arm. "I need to talk to Hades."

His frown is slow to come on. "How—"

"The Hades in the Lock." I rush to catch him up with my thinking. "He tends to have a lot of answers."

A grim sort of amusement steals across the Titan's features. "It appears my son can't resist you even down here."

Warmth spreads through my cheeks unexpectedly. "That's not the reason—"

"I'm teasing, Alani." Before I can respond, he turns to Rhea and murmurs in her ear. The Titaness glances over her shoulder at me before she nods at him.

"Come with me."

I can hear Rhea softly explaining to the others as I follow Cronos down the hall. Which is when I remember that I'm not sure exactly where I am in this place. I ran through hallways that I didn't recognize, more focused on getting to the screaming than where I was going.

Sure enough, we pass doorways I know I haven't seen yet, all marked with Xs—one marked with bottles of poison, another with a sheaf of wheat, and the creepiest of all looks like a sea of children's faces frozen in screams. Definitely not going through that door.

Eventually, I recognize the doors we pass as we make our way down to the Locks. When we get to Hades' archway, I raise my hand to press my palm against the symbol, only to pause and look at Cronos. "What if another earthquake happens?"

"I'm coming in with you."

"Oh."

His small smirk tells me he caught the thread of disappointment in my voice. Am I really so desperate for time with Hades that even a few seconds alone with his replica is like a gift? I never pegged myself for the pathetic type, but maybe twenty-three years of feeling unloved made me that way.

I press my palm to the sigil. "Hades—"

I don't even finish speaking his name before the door slides open and he's standing on the other side.

He stares at me with eyes that shimmer with an emotion I can't pin down and yet sends a spark of heat through me all the same. Heat that cools instantly when his gaze slides over my shoulder to Cronos, and whatever emotion he was letting me see disappears behind narrowed eyes. "Why is he with you?"

"To keep me safe."

The silver of Hades' eyes glints dagger-bright as his gaze flashes back to me. "Don't you believe it," he says. "He must have some other plan."

I ignore that. "If he comes in this way, will it kill him?"

Hades' eyes sharpen to silver edges. "Not after a Lock has been unsealed, but he's not welcome—"

"I don't have time to argue about this right now," I say. "I need to know something, and I hope you have the answer."

"If you think I'm helping you let him out—"

The sound of the bell going off sends an immediate shiver violently ricocheting up my spine.

If we didn't have time a second ago, we really don't now. Cronos and I both go to step inside the Lock, but Hades blocks our way, arms raised to ward us off. "*You* can come in," he says to me. "But not him."

I take two rapid steps backward until Cronos stands between me and Hades. "If he doesn't come in, I don't come in."

It's a gamble. Hades could just leave me to become the feral monster the Pandemonium will create if they get to me out here in this round room with no place to run or hide. In my head, I'm making a plan to run to Demeter's Lock next if he doesn't budge on this. But I'm pretty sure she's not going to let Cronos in, either. I think neither of us was thinking that the damn bell would go off so quickly after the earthquake. Someone really is determined to keep the Titans from getting out.

At least that's how it feels.

Slaps of running feet sound, coming from the tunnel that winds up past the obelisk to the bridge over the abyss. Too many to count, all coming in our direction.

I glance over my shoulder and yelp. Because it's not the Titans running at us. It's…

I can *see* them.

The Pandemonium.

My glamour-seeing is still on. I don't know what I was picturing when there was just nothing and silence—monsters, maybe, with terrible faces or fangs and claws, or holes with no shape like Hades' copy described.

Instead, the glowing outlines are human shaped.

And yet the way that they move is anything but. Unbelievably fast but also jerking. Like stop motion animation, or maybe like their limbs don't quite work right and they have to keep aligning them to move forward, and their mouths are open in silent screams.

"Damn it, Lyra." I'm vaguely aware of Hades snapping, "Get in here. *Both* of you."

Somebody's grabbing me and dragging me into the Lock a second before the door streaks closed past my nose.

"You stay here by the door," Hades orders.

Part of my mind processes that I heard him, and even then, I'm not sure if he's telling both of us or just Cronos. But most of my brain is still occupied with what I just saw. I'm still staring at the door, unseeing, unable to get the vision of the Pandemonium out of my head.

What are they? Does Hades, the one reigning in the Underworld above, know about them? Does he know what they do to us down here?

"Lyra?"

Maybe because Hades' voice is soft when he calls my name, it gets through, and at the touch of his hand on my shoulder, I turn around to stare at him.

His eyes widen slightly.

Do I look as shaken as I feel? Pale, even? I feel pale. I feel like all the blood abandoned my head, leaving me woozy. I can't even force my lips, which are pressed together tightly, holding in a scream, to unlock and speak.

"You saw them?" he asks, again gently.

Out of the corner of my eye, I catch how Cronos looks at me more closely. "The Pandemonium?" he asks.

I manage a nod, answering both of them at the same time. Finally, my jaw seems to unhinge a little. "You told me to…" I stop to clear my throat, trying to force my voice to be something other than reedy. "You told me I needed to see them."

Hades nods once—hesitantly, almost.

I stare at him with a thousand questions. "I know you want me to protect myself…"

"What did you see?"

The way he asks that... "What do *you* see?" I ask.

"Just...light. Energy, I think you'd call it these days. A glow."

Oh.

"Lyra." His voice drops into a command. "What did you see?"

I take in a shaky breath. "Tormented souls."

"Not souls." Cronos' correction is quiet. "Soul. Only one."

Hades and I both look at the Titan.

"I thought you couldn't see them?" Hades demands. He's only asking exactly what I'm thinking.

Cronos grimaces. "I can't. But I've seen where they come from. I once happened to be standing right at the source when that damned bell went off. They come from the obelisk that marks my mother's tomb. I think they are manifestations of her grief at the death of my father. Like her soul shattered and the shards want everyone else in the world to feel her pain."

Hades jerks forward, fists clenched at his sides. "You mean her grief from when you, her son, murdered his father, her husband."

Then he's grabbing me by the wrist and tugging me behind him as if he, a fraction of Hades' soul himself, could protect me from the Titan. "I told you that you can't trust him."

"I can," I insist.

Hades rounds on me. "You are too trusting—"

I cover his mouth with my hand to stop the words. "Someday, you're going to learn to trust me. But until then, we will get nowhere arguing about this."

Hades' eyes swirl with anger and something else. Another unidentifiable emotion. Even as a copy, the man is an enigma. A fact proved by the way his eyes change again, turn warm as they trace the lines of my face before he presses a kiss in the center of my palm.

I gasp, yanking back my hand to curl my fingers around that tingling spot. "What was that for?"

"It seemed a better option than biting you to make you take your hand away," he drawls. Then glances from Cronos to me and back. "*You* remain here by the door, or I kill you," he commands the Titan.

With the grip he still has on my wrist, Hades leads me away. I look back over my shoulder to Cronos, who, surprisingly, stays where he is. He points at the ground and crosses his arms, and I nod my understanding. He's going to wait for me there.

Not that there are many places to go. It's a pie-shaped rock room.

Except when we cross the center, my vision blurs, different colors forming shapes that I can't make out properly. Just as I'm about to protest, my surroundings sharpen again, and I'm not standing in the Lock anymore. Instead, I find myself on a rocky beach dotted with boulders and surrounded by cliffs. It feels so real—the sea air against my skin forming a fine sheen of salt, the smell of the brine, and the rhythmic roll of the waves against the shore. It's gentle today.

"This is where we met," Hades says. "Do you remember?"

Where we met when he was not much more than a baby and I protected him from his grandfather, but also where we met on the bluff above when he was nineteen. He must not remember either time the same way, though, or he wouldn't be so angry with Cronos now. Unlike with the real Hades, I don't see mesh over his apparition's face. How am I supposed to take the glamour away from him if he is only a single piece of soul, not much more than a memory, to begin with?

"I remember."

He turns to face the sea. "I formed this place from my memories and come here sometimes." His lips quirk disparagingly. "More than sometimes."

Then he glances at me. "You haven't changed since that day. Exactly the same as you are now, except for the clothes."

I smile. "You've changed a little."

A peek of what I am pretty sure is very real amusement has his dimples winking out at me, but only for a second before he sobers. "You had a question?"

"Not about getting out of here," I assure him. "It's one I think you can answer."

He crosses his arms. "Ask it, and we'll see."

Not exactly promising, but it's better than *no*. "Do you know what's causing the earthquakes?" I know he can feel them now.

I'm not sure what I expected, but it's not for him to go so grim that I shiver and have to force my heart not to run away from me.

"Me," he says.

# 89

# THE WORST THING YOU CAN DO IS NOTHING

### LYRA

*Me.*

I stare at Hades, and the single word he uttered rattles around in my skull, which empties of its brain entirely—shocked away to nonexistence—giving the sound lots of places to rattle. "What? Why would you try to destroy this place? Do you think—"

"Not me." He points an impatient finger at the skies over the beach. *"Me."*

My thinking capacity is only just now booting back up, so it takes longer than it should for me to realize what he means. I feel the way my eyes widen, even as I'm hoping that the answer I've reached isn't right. "My Hades?"

The replica of him winces. "Yes. I draw power from the god who made me. I think you already know that's why the Hestia down here doesn't work so well. We can feel them. I can feel him, my maker. The stronger the emotion or the closer he is to me in the Underworld, the more I get from him. Flashes." His eyes trace over my features again. "Even after I was placed down here, I've seen you. I used to think it was dreams."

A shaved-off piece of a soul can dream? "That's…" I shake my head. "I don't know what that is. It seems…wrong, somehow."

He scowls. "I don't need your pity."

I bark a sharp laugh. "Never that."

He slowly closes his mouth, considering me. "You filled a long existence with something…new…every so often," he says. "I thank you for that."

I don't know what to say to that, either. Or maybe I do, as I mentally flip through the flashes of me he might have gotten and a snort escapes. "I'm sure it was quite entertaining."

I think maybe he's going to grin, or even laugh, but he doesn't. "He's trying to help you."

We both go still like we're both surprised at the words that came out of his mouth. "Hades?"

The copy of him shrugs. "Apparently, you are quite important to him. I don't know everything, but it's obvious to me since you've been down here that the other gods who created these Locks have refused to open their Locks and let you out."

I wrinkle my nose. "So he's trying to bury me?"

"No." He gives me a patient look. "Something else. I'm not sure what."

My chest expands on a sharp inhale. Hades is trying to help me. "Is he burning down the world?"

This Hades' eyes narrow. "The prophecy?"

"Yes."

"I'm not sure." His vision goes hazy, like he's looking beyond. "He's… gone dark now. Like I can't feel him."

I close my eyes.

"Lyra?"

"I believed," I whisper, then lift my lashes to look at him. "I truly believed he could choose not to give in to it."

Getting out of here and back to him was already at a near-panic level inside me every second of every day, but now…

"I have to help him." I swallow. "Is there any way to help him while I'm still down here?"

Hades hesitates. "I don't think so."

Olympus be damned.

"But you shouldn't stop him."

I frown. "What?"

"Some destinies are fated for a purpose. He is what he is—I am what I am—for a purpose. If I were in his place right now, I would find another way."

I have to bite my lip to keep it from wobbling and only release it when I'm sure that it won't. "Would you try to get me out?"

He doesn't have to answer aloud. Because I already know. He would if he was up there and I was down here.

"Even if it let out the Titans?"

His face goes hard, and he takes a measured step away.

I don't need him to answer out loud. He already did.

"Boone and I are not fated in any way. It was a lie." I don't know why I tell him that.

Maybe it's to see the way he takes the tiniest inhale like that means something important to him.

"How long do you think I have before this place collapses?" I ask, glancing around. The cracks here aren't as bad as above the pillars, but they're visible now when they weren't before.

When he doesn't answer, I pull my gaze back to him to find him watching me like he's not sure I can handle the answer.

"Hades?" I prompt.

His eyes narrow slightly. "Given the size of that last earthquake, not long."

Urgency is like an immediate burst of blood-boiling need inside me. We have to get out of here. Now.

"What is the secret to Aphrodite's Lock?"

Disbelief clouds Hades' eyes a heartbeat before his eyebrows snap low over them and the silver turns a flat, gunmetal gray. Instantly, the illusion of the beach we are standing on dissolves, and we are back in the round rock room of his Lock. "You would ask me to go against what I was made for? I am a guardian. That is my *only* reason for existence."

"You would ask me to stay down here, trapped?" I demand right back.

"If it means not unleashing them—" He flings a hand in the direction of where Cronos is. "Then, yes."

And that's the difference between the guardian and the god above. My Hades would get me out of here either way. Even if it meant I left him behind. Apparently even if it unleashes evil.

"I'll be buried alive," I say.

"When that happens, time will simply reset—"

My turn to take a jerking step away from him. "Then you expect me to go through this over and over, including the pain, just so that I won't let them out?"

"You'll be with me—"

I take another step. "Except that you aren't him. Not all of him. And I need—"

The way his face spasms, I don't keep going, swallowing the words back.

"Don't you see? I can't leave him up there thinking he did this to me, blaming himself for all eternity."

Something in his eyes dies. "But you can leave me down here for an eternity, getting only glimpses of you?"

"I…" I shake my head. I know that he's not a fully formed person, but he is so real. And he is a piece of Hades. Hades, who I love every part of. *Can* I just leave him? "You could come with me."

The sadness and truth that stares back at me is too much. Too big. Too hard.

My eyes well with tears that threaten to spill over, and I can't blink them away fast enough. He sees.

"Lyra," he whispers. "Don't—"

Then he's across the space I put between us, mouth crashing down on mine before I can take another breath.

He kisses me like he'll never again have the chance. Like he's willing me to stay and saying goodbye all at the same time.

I whimper against his mouth.

Hades whirls us around at the rock-on-rock slide of the Lock door opening. He tucks me behind him as he faces whatever just opened that door, an animalistic growl unleashing from his throat.

Boone stands on the other side. Or, more accurately, is propped up between Hyperion and Iapetus, with Persephone hovering behind him, face pinched with worry. That didn't take Boone long. He's visibly in much better shape, even if he can't quite stand on his own.

He ignores Hades, his gaze locking on me.

I lay a hand on the guardian's back, feeling him tense under my touch. I also feel the way he surrenders in the next breath, hunching slightly even as he straightens to face the small gathered crowd. "I should keep you here with me," he murmurs for me alone.

"I—"

He looks me right in the eyes. "I won't, Lyra. I wouldn't do that to you. Even if it means we end up enemies."

My hand, still resting on his back, curls into his shirt. "Hades." His name comes out as a whisper.

And he closes his eyes against it. "Go, my star. Before I change my mind."

Even knowing that I'm not walking away from my Hades, it still takes every ounce of willpower to make my legs work, to make them take me away from him.

He's leaving me no choice. We can't stay down here.

When I cross the threshold of the door, the last to step out, it whooshes closed behind me. Those doors close the same way every time, and yet this time, it feels…final.

"Thank the gods you made it back," Boone says. "They told me…that we aren't actually fated."

It takes me a second to switch from what just happened in there to what came before. The glamours. His healing.

"I'm…" I make a face. "I'm not sure if I should say I'm sorry or not." We didn't know what it meant…but it gave us hope to get out.

Now that hope is gone.

"We'll find a way through Aphrodite's Lock," he says. Back to cocksure. "I know we will. Thieves don't need fate for that."

I glance past him to the Titans and Persephone. "Who could do such a thing, make a glamour of that effect?"

Koios' scowl tells me everything. They don't know. And worse… "How did they do it down here?" he asks.

I glance past him to Persephone, who won't look at me, and finally, it sinks in. All the implications. Because someone might have glamoured Boone while we were still outside of Tartarus, but Persephone has been here over a century, and her new glamour was about me. The person who cast it had to be down here to do it.

I swallow around my fear, the bile of it stinging my throat. "The earthquakes are Hades trying to help me in some way—I don't know if it's to dig me out or protect me."

"Fuck," Cronos mutters. "If that's the case, then he's not thinking of how that might collapse Tartarus and the possible effect on the Overworld."

"Exactly." I look at Boone, who stares back at me.

He shrugs off Hyperion and Iapetus' help, straightening to his full height. "Only one more Lock," he says, already on my page. "We go now."

One more because he already unsealed Zeus' without me.

I give him an off-kilter grin. "Let's hope it doesn't take as many tries as Hera's. That really sucked."

# 90

# APHRODITE'S LOCK

### LYRA

I wait at the edge of the bridge over the abyss, watching as Boone and Persephone whisper to each other.

She's not coming with us. She wanted to, but Boone said he couldn't handle it if she did. She has hardly left his side since he woke from being healed and I removed their glamours. As I watch, he leans over and kisses the tip of her nose. Color rises in her cheeks, and he grins, but even I can see it's full of worry.

Then he walks away.

Over to where I wait. He still looks like shit, but we waited an entire day, through more and more quakes, through the worry that the next one would bring everything crashing down on us. But he had to heal.

"Last time," he says.

*We hope.*

I don't say it out loud. I just nod. I'm not sure I have that kind of optimism in me right now.

"Are you sure?" I ask for the thousandth time. "Whoever glamoured us wanted us to go in there together. What if—"

"We already talked about this. There are too many what-ifs to count," he says.

Arguing with him is only going to delay the inevitable, so I nod.

"One," he begins. And we both half crouch, ready to jump. "Two—"

Someone shoves me hard in the back, and I pitch into the darkness in a flail of arms and legs. I hear Boone yell, but can't see, already too far down.

Godsdamned darkness of the abyss, and there's nothing I can do but fall. And fall. And fall.

And then I'm not.

The heat is what hits my senses before anything else. Heat and…

"Fire," I whisper.

Cronos said all they know about this Lock is that it involves fire, but this is… What is this?

I stand in the center of a pristine room. Circular. Cut from marble—gray marble that appears sheared and polished to a dull metal sheen. I am in the center of a round platform with stairs that lead to the walls. No, not walls…to a red, glowing pit, like a moat that follows along the walls. From the tops of the ceiling around the circumference, fire falls in a curtain to be contained by the pit in the floor.

While the heat is manageable, I have yet to be stripped of my powers, so it's about to get much more uncomfortable.

If I didn't know better, I'd say Hephaestus created this room for Aphrodite. It looks exactly like the volcanic forger god's taste. But he didn't exist yet when the Titans were trapped down here. Did Aphrodite have the original power over fire?

Bigger question…what is she going to do with it?

"Boone!" I call out.

He's not here with me. I'm completely alone—

I whirl at the sudden movement behind me…and then gasp at the face looking back.

Not Boone, but…

"It's okay," Cronos says. "This was my choice."

"No!" The cry comes from my soul because I know what this means.

"You have entered the Lock of Aphrodite," a familiar, husky feminine voice rings out.

Panic manifests as physical pain that rips through my heart and then sears along my veins to every nerve. "You can't be down here!"

Ignoring Aphrodite's replica, I run across the platform to grab his arm, hard, searching overhead frantically with the half-baked idea that I can throw Cronos back to the bridge or something.

But Hestia told me in that first Lock. The only way out is forward. There is *no* forward for Cronos. Not in a sealed Lock. Not when our powers get stripped. I return to human, but he…

"No, no, no, no," I mutter.

"Lyra." His voice is entirely calm. Not like mine.

I'm not listening. Checking the room for any exits, still holding on to him.

He says my name again, and I round on him, fury following hot on the heels of the panic. "What have you done?"

I'm yelling, but he fucking smiles at me. The damned Titan actually smiles. "This is the only way."

Only way. I'm shaking my head. "No," I snap. "It's not. It can't be." He'll *die* down here.

"Opening my Lock," Aphrodite's guardian says behind us, "takes sacrifice to test the purity of your intent."

Sacrifice.

The word flays me as I meet Cronos' eyes. Blue like Zeus', but his face, while I used to think he looked like Hades—now Cronos is just… him. The Titan father who frightened and annoyed me to start has become something more. Something I didn't want to name until we got out of here. Something I thought we had time to grow…

*Oh gods.*

His gaze is trained on my face with patience. With knowing. With utter, terrifying acceptance.

"Sacrifice." The whisper tears from my lips. "Please don't do this. Please don't—"

"Two hearts must enter," Aphrodite continues. "One for the fire. One to be set free by that ultimate act of pure love."

One for the fire. That's the sacrifice. One of us must die, and since this place will kill him anyway, I already know who he intends that to be.

"You can't." I desperately claw at him, trying to hold on to him hard enough to keep this from happening. "There has to be another way. I'll kill myself. I'll reset time—"

"I won't be there if you do," Cronos says. "We learned that with Themis."

Because Titans are *only* made of powers. When he's stripped completely, there will be nothing left.

*Hades, help me. How can I go to you without your father, who loves you?*

"Please," I choke out, shaking him a little.

His expression gentles, turning tender. "This is what love looks like, Alani."

My chin wobbles, tears blurring his face. I dash my arm over my eyes. "But I *need* you—" I cut off the plaintive wail in my throat.

Cronos puts his hands to my face, wiping my hot tears away. "I have always thought of you as a daughter."

A heavy coldness takes me over, freezing the heat out of my veins and leaving in its wake an ache so deep that I can't breathe. Can't think.

"One day, you'll understand." He glances past me to Aphrodite, who stands at my back. "I am the sacrifice."

"No!" I try to pull away. To whirl on the goddess and take his place. But he holds me fast, and behind me, I hear her end it.

"So be it." I'm vaguely aware that she sounds…resigned. "Your test starts now."

I grip Cronos by the wrists and try to yank him away, drag him to a safety that doesn't exist. Not down here. But he's as immovable as always. "You can't leave us—"

There's a zap of pain down my spine as my power is stripped from me. I feel Cronos slip something into my hand and manage to look down at the little carved butterfly. He put the pieces back together. I force my head back up only for my eyes to go wide, my agony turning to panic because Cronos is glowing.

Glowing and…disintegrating.

Horror steals any of the breath left in my body, and I choke.

Even dying, he's stronger than me. Holding me steady, he leans forward and places a soft kiss on my forehead, like a blessing, and whispers words I don't hear. Then he releases me and, before I can stop him, takes a step down the platform toward the circling wall of flame, still dissolving.

Already dead.

I follow with some unhinged thought of dragging him back, but my hand immediately blisters, and I hiss, jerking away. I'm too human now to get that close to those hellfires.

Then I whimper my distress. It's like an invisible barrier I can't cross, and he knew it would be.

"Cronos!" I scream his name, throat raw as I pace the line of heat like a feral animal.

He turns his head to meet my eyes. More of him continues to

disintegrate, like his body is turning to dust and blowing away, becoming nothing as it floats off.

"Don't cry," he says, taking another step. "I've known for a long time now that this was the only way." His skin, what's left of it, starts to blister. He doesn't stop. "Like you did with Isabel, I've tried ten thousand ways, but in the end…" Another step, and his clothes catch fire. He hardly seems to notice as he tips his head to one side, his eyes in a face already losing shape taking in my features with a look so full of his heart it makes mine shatter. "A father should always be the one who sacrifices for his child."

My knees give out, unable to hold the weight of my heartbreak any longer, and I fall to the ground. "No! Please, no."

"Tell Rhea that I will love her even in the ether." One more step down. "Tell my children that their faces are the images I held on to when I died. That I always loved them."

I wrap my arms around my middle, rocking, hardly able to see him through my tears. "Cronos…"

"When you're ready…when you need me…come find me…in our cell."

The next step brings him to the edge of the pit, and I'm not sure which is worse, the burning or the disintegrating.

I reach out for him like the incredibly powerful Titan could still take my hand and stop this. "Father," I whisper brokenly. "Don't go."

The trace of his smile is the last thing I see before he pitches himself into the flames, gone too fast for me to comprehend.

I've learned the hard way—when Boone died, when Meike died, when Isabel died over and over in these time resets—that there is always this moment when, no matter how loud it is around me, the world goes silent with the dreadfulness of what just happened. It's too horrible for the mind to comprehend quickly, and even in the next few moments, it feels like it can't be real. Like it can be fixed.

But I can't fix this. I can't reset. I can't put him back together.

Gone.

Cronos is just…gone.

"Congratulations." Aphrodite's voice rings hollow.

That terrible word hits me so wrong, I feel like the goddess took a spear and drove it through my heart just to be cruel.

"You have unsealed my Lock," she says. "You have been tested and proven worthy."

Now she's just twisting the spear. I'm not the worthy one here. Cronos is. *Cronos* should be here for this.

I bury my face in my hands, and my shoulders heave through sobs so deep, they can't even crawl out of my throat.

"You are free of the prison of Tartarus," Aphrodite announces.

Not like this. It shouldn't have been like this.

The icy sensation of my powers returning rips through my body so fast that I feel myself spasm around it, but the pain shocks me into a new stillness and silence. When it's over, I shakily lower my hands from my face to find that the room has changed.

At opposite ends of a familiar, blank, rock-hewn room, two doors burst open. The one behind me, in the wider curve of the pie piece, I know leads to the Titans waiting in the chamber around the Locks. The one before me defies physics. Because through that door is the bridge across the abyss, leading to the way out.

At my back, Rhea screams her husband's name.

I clap my hands over my ears, unable to bear her pain.

A muffled clanking noise sounds outside the chamber I am sprawled in, and I raise my tear-blurred gaze to the double doors at the end of the bridge—the massive gates of Tartarus with their swirling carved designs. More distinct clanks follow, echoing through the chamber, and even Rhea goes quiet by the seventh.

There is a small silence, and then...the gates that have held the Titans at bay for thousands of years swing open soundlessly

So easy. Like a breeze could have pushed them wide all along.

We are *free*.

## 91
# INHERITANCE

### LYRA

Smoke and fire.

Thick, curling smoke seems to writhe like the bodies of a thousand twisting snakes entwining one another. Only it's not just smoke. It's more like the smoke is a casing around in an inner body of brilliant blue fire. Those flames flash and sizzle between cracks in the outer sheath of smoke. It is all I can see outside the gates of Tartarus.

I bow my head, my chin hitting my chest, unable to stand looking at it. To fathom passing through those doors now. Not after Cronos…

He knew.

He knew he would never leave this place. He knew he would never see his children again. Based on the now-quiet sobs coming from behind me… Was he the only one who knew? Did he not even tell his wife?

Of course he didn't. He would spare Rhea all the pain in the world if he could.

Hands are suddenly on my shoulders, and I squeeze my eyes shut.

Boone.

"He pushed you," he says quietly. "And held me back until he could jump in after you."

"Why?" The question breaks in my throat.

Why didn't he let Boone die in his place? Or at least try? This is the first time Boone has been down here. Cronos said he'd tried all the options, but he hasn't tried that one. Why didn't he…

The answer is so clear.

Because of me.

Because the choice would have been impossible for me. That choice would have broken me. Is that why?

"It should have been me," Boone whispers.

I shake my head. "Don't... Don't take the choice away from him. He knew what he was doing—"

Light hits me.

Like a physical thing, it slams into my body, and I feel myself propelled up into the air, flipping and spinning with the force of an explosion.

Only to come to a dead halt in midair, my body stretched out, hands and legs wide.

Another explosion of light, coming from gods know where, makes it impossible to see and slams into me again. Into my chest.

My mouth opens wide on a silent scream, because it feels as though that light is drilling through my bones, through my sternum and ribs, to crack me wide open.

Red light, brilliant and bloody, even.

Vaguely, I'm aware of Boone shouting below me. The other Titans yelling. Someone tries to tug on my feet, like they are trying to get me down, but the light won't let me go.

Then a crack in the fabric of time appears in front of me, crimson, jagged, gaping. A whimper manages to escape my throat. How can Cronos in the future be controlling the broken shards he created if he's dead?

Another crack of time appears before me. Then another, and another, until hundreds of them fill the line of my vision. I'm unable to turn my head, but I think they must be circling me. Are they going to rip me apart? Is time vindictive? I'm the reason Cronos is gone. Is time going wild without its ruler?

The shards start to glow.

Faint at first, but brighter and brighter, new colors join the red, coming out to play in the form of rainbows that seem to shimmer and leap and play between the ragged breaks. Brighter and brighter still, and I would close my eyes against the brilliance except that, just as I think to, one of the breaks is absorbed into the one directly before me.

What in the name of Hades?

Another joins those two. Then another. And with each one, the crack itself doesn't grow. It gets...smaller.

Like broken time is...

*It's repairing.*

The speed with which time is mending itself, blending and shrinking, appears to speed up, going too fast for even my goddess eyes to track, until there is a single, tiny ray of light left.

I stare at it. Fear and awe thunder away in the beat of my heart.

It comes closer and closer, glittering and glowing in pulses that seem to have no rhythm or meaning. Not slamming into me like the light that holds me still, though. Instead, it stops just in front of my chest.

And my heart...calms.

No more fear.

It's like I know this light. Like we are friends.

This time, when it pulses, it stays lit, and the light that is holding me lets go. I don't drop, remaining suspended in the air, but I'm no longer bound, either.

I float there, watching as the light that was holding me is absorbed into the tiny orb before me.

It turns impossibly brighter and yet doesn't hurt. I don't turn away.

The awe now is soft, is reverent, as it absorbs every ray, every drop of the light coming from outside this place, and then it moves into me.

As soft as butterfly wings and as warm as a gentle sun on my skin.

And I absorb it.

I become it.

It is *my* light now. To wield however I see fit.

I don't even realize I'm lowering until my toes touch the ground, and the glow recedes to show me Boone and Persephone and all the Titans gathered before me, staring in jaw-dropped wonder.

Rhea, her cheeks still wet with tears, moves forward to frame my face with her hands, looking deep into my eyes.

"There you are," she whispers.

Then she smiles, and the endless sadness in the weight of it makes my heart ache.

"Behold," she announces to the others without turning away from me. "The new goddess of time."

# 92

## GODS OF DEATH

### LYRA

The goddess of time.

Me.

I'm still too stricken to take it in. My first, gut-level reaction is that I don't want it. I can't do this. Not this way. Not ever.

Rhea must see it, because a small sob wells out of her, but she swallows the next one down. "It's his gift to you," she whispers.

My face crumples as my shoulders heave even while I'm trying to hold it in for her sake. She has even more reason to grieve than I do. "I don't want it," I whisper. "Not like this."

"I know." Her lips tremble so hard she has to press them together as she moves her hands from my face to my shoulders. "But you need to be strong now. Honor his sacrifice."

Guilt piles onto the heaviness already trying to crush my heart to a bloody pulp. She's right. I owe him that much. I try to take a deep breath but only finally manage it on the third try.

A gift. This is a gift from him.

Forcing air into my lungs, I reach for the strength Cronos would want me to have, and I nod. I find strength in her eyes and gather calm around me like a dome of shields, then nod again. "It's not over," I say.

We still have to face a world full of gods glamoured to believe the Titans are evil.

Determination narrows Rhea's eyes. "Not yet."

Which is when a violent explosion of light knocks us all to the ground.

Shielding my eyes, I duck as a column of pure energy—beams of light of different colors wrapped around one another into one giant thing—pounds into and through the room we are in and into Tartarus, and before we can get up, the ground starts to shake. It shakes so hard, my brain rattles in my skull.

The quake doesn't stop as I surge to standing. It just gets worse, making it hard to stay upright.

There's a sharp, groaning *crack* from under my feet, a sound that sends dread rippling through me. The bridge is going to collapse. That's followed immediately by an ear-splitting bang overhead, and the ceiling falls.

Instinct kicks in hard.

One second, I'm on the ground inside Aphrodite's Lock. The next, I teleport so I'm standing outside the double gates of Tartarus, looking in.

And I'm looking at Hades' guardian, who is holding up the ceiling in Aphrodite's Lock as the other Titans get out.

Because I beat them all out here.

"Run!" I shout to him as Koios, the last one through, clears the doorway.

Through the smoke and debris, I see Hades' face, and I know…

The guardian can't leave. He exists only in Tartarus and within the Locks themselves.

His lips form words. Three simple words that I don't have to hear to know what he says.

*"Go to him."*

My heart screams a denial an instant before the guardian lets go, and Tartarus implodes, collapsing down on top of him.

Debris blasts out toward where we are, and someone drags me over the bridge, away from the abyss on this side. Pure power continues to explode into the ground. Then a scream of sound that makes my bones shudder fills the entire cavern, and a new power slams into the column of light. Three streams made of fire and billowing smoke go after the light. They pulverize it, like they're beating it to dust.

Even through the chaos, I can see that the fire is still attacking the light, trying to dig and drill its way through it into what is now rubble.

We emerge on the other side of that war of powers into clear air, all of us coughing, but my heart wants me to run back. To dig Hades' guardian out. To dig the others still trapped in their cells out. Medusa is down there. Some, I don't give a shit about, but her… I promised her.

"Fuck!" Iapetus whispers.

I stop struggling against Boone's hold to jerk around and gasp.

Because we're not alone.

Facing us here in the pits of the Underworld are…gods.

Close to a dozen of them—and the light is coming from *them*. Each of them combining their powers to attack Tartarus.

Were they…*trying* to kill us?

I glance behind me. The smoke and fire is from Hades. It has to be. He wasn't burning down the world. He was trying to stop them from killing me.

Slowly, I face them, death rising in my heart.

They get one look at us and stop, power shutting off so fast that the cavern dims suddenly. I blink through the dimness, trying to determine who my new enemies are.

Not Charon. Not Cerberus, either.

Hermes is here, though, slighter in build than the other gods but no less dangerous. He's hovering above the others with his sandals flapping like hummingbird wings. The woman below him, hiding a pale face behind flowing black hair, is Hecate, a goddess of many things, including a small corner of the Underworld. We haven't formally met yet.

But there are other gods with them who are not of the Greek pantheon. A red-blood-spattered skeleton with eyeballs floating in black eye sockets has to be Mictlāntēcutli of the Aztecs. I think the woman beside him is Hel, of the Norse, with half blue and half pale-oak-colored flesh and dark hair cropped close to her head. There's a two-faced god beside her who flicks his forked tongue in my direction. And the Egyptian god Anubis, with his black-furred jackal head, is also kind of hard to miss.

Who they all are is also impossible to ignore.

The gods and goddesses of the Underworlds. Of Death.

They're here for *us*. For the Titans.

I know this because of both the fine veils of glamour over their faces and the way each slowly assumes a stance of battle, weapons and hands raised, ready to fight.

The Titans all tense around me.

They don't assume fighting positions, but…they are all wearing armor now, with weapons in their hands. Gleaming, plain armor. Not the fancy decorated shit their children wear. Armor and weapons they didn't have inside Tartarus. No more loud print shirt for Iapetus. Instead, in his hand is his famous spear.

I look down to find I'm back in the clothes I wore the day I was pulled into Tartarus, including my vest and, judging by the weight of them, *both* my axes.

Then the strangest sound, somewhere between a roar and a cat's yowl, bursts from just behind them, and two of the death gods have to duck as a pair of massive male lions—one with a dark-black mane and one with no mane at all—leaps over them to run to Rhea, who kneels to take the impact of their ecstatic greeting. They curl and rub all over her, making frantic sounds.

"My babies," she coos. "You waited for me?"

My eyebrows shoot up. Did Hades know they were down here? Have they been waiting for their mistress all these ages?

Across the way, the gods facing us shift on their feet, glancing at one another in question.

"Are you Lyra?" Anubis calls out to me. His jackal-mouth moving as he speaks is weird as fuck.

I glance at Boone. "Why does the Egyptian god of the Underworld know my name?" I whisper.

He whistles the signal for *no idea*.

"Yes," I call back.

"You are needed urgently in Olympus. Hades sits on the throne." His gaze moves past me to the crumbled remains of Tartarus and the arms of smoke still hitting the rubble. Trying to get to me now? Dig me out?

He must not know that I got out first.

Doesn't he feel it?

Is he so far gone? Shit. I can't leave yet, though.

"He will kill us all," Hermes yells at me when I don't respond. "Already, Zeus—"

He can't finish the sentence, and the implication hits me like one of the thunder god's bolts of lightning, straight to the chest. Is Zeus dead?

"We were here to stop the Titans from being released," Anubis says. "It seems as though we are too late. We now must fight on two fronts."

Fighting no matter what. No listening to arguments first. That damned glamour.

"Titans of Tartarus." Anubis addresses the others around me. "We cannot let you live outside your prison."

Yeah. It's a no-matter-what situation.

I take three purposeful strides to stand before my family, and Boone joins me on one side, Persephone on the other.

A serious-faced god dressed in a traditional Korean hanbok of beautiful reds and purples—Yeomra, I think he is called—beckons me to cross the unmanned divide between us and them. "Come, young goddess. You are safe now. Go stop your lover."

I will. But I won't abandon the Titans.

I skate my gaze across the gods before us, trying to catalog who we are facing.

Hades was just starting to familiarize me with all the other gods of death and the Underworlds when I got stuck down here. I almost sigh in relief when I realize there is no woman with talons for feet. Ereshkigal isn't here. Hades told me that the powerful Sumerian goddess of death was the only Underworld deity who he feared could destroy him. Someone was smart enough not to invite her.

"Lyra." Hel's voice is gentle, flowing like water, like the sweetest music, at direct odds with her downcast face. "Come to us."

The effect drifts over me, soothing and yet disturbing at the same time, and I have to close my eyes, giving my head a shake to dislodge her. Only when I don't feel the urge to obey do I open my eyes again to find her staring at me with her own narrowed into angry slits.

I give her a pointed half smile. *I'm a goddess of the Underworld, too*, I silently remind her.

"You misunderstand," I say. "We will stay here to protect the Titans... from you."

# PART 8

## BURN IT ALL DOWN

I promise we'll never do that again.

## 93

## THE DEPARTED

### LYRA

Shock turns the bristling gods across from us immobile for several breaths.

Then Hermes' face twists into something so riddled with fury, I can no longer recognize him. All focused on…me. Hecate opens her mouth in a hiss even as Hermes, black eyes flashing, snarls a single word. "Traitor."

The messenger god, the former god of thieves, bolts across the space between us with a guttural shout. His winged sandals lift him a few feet off the ground, shooting him through the air at impossible speeds until a gust of wind catapults him backward. I jerk around to find Eurybia with her hands up. She only stops when Hermes' angry yell grows distant and he's far from us.

The Titaness drops her hands.

As if the sudden cease of wind is like the lowering of a flag, the gods of death unleash.

"Try not to hurt them!" I yell over my shoulder at the Titans.

They're glamoured. This isn't their fault.

Then I brace to take a hit from Anubis.

But he doesn't slam into me. Hyperion shows up out of nothing and teleports him away.

I grunt like the Egyptian god did hit me but reset to face the next threat, only, as if I am the Moses of the Bible, the other gods part around me like the Red Sea. Chaos reigns with the clash of bodies and weapons everywhere, the shouts and groans of pain or impact. It rages all around me, but nothing and no one comes straight for me.

I drop my arms to my sides as I straighten and look around in jerking turns. "What in the name of Hades?"

Why aren't they coming for me?

Because they need me.

Hades needs me.

"Oh my gods!" My tattoos. I was given back my vest and axes—why not them, too? I draw a line down my arm, and immediately they come to glittering life. The tarantula waves her two front legs at me, while the owl fluffs his wings and the fox and panther both leap around. Happy to see me, I think.

I wish I had more time to join them in the joy.

"Get to Hades," I order them. "Tell him I've escaped Tartarus. Quickly."

All four animals leap from my skin, becoming life-size. Only instead of turning to flesh and blood, they remain in their glittering forms. I cock my head, but before I can ask, they disappear. Teleported, maybe?

Please let them get to him. At least I'm sending him some hope while I deal with the mess down here.

That done, I look around me.

The only battle of gods I've ever witnessed, and then only a few moments of it, was the fight to imprison the Titans. I don't know why I was expecting anything that could look remotely like a human war. But that's not what this is.

Gods don't just fight on the ground. They don't only do hand-to-hand or weapon-to-weapon combat. The massive cavern is filled with gods and Titans disappearing and reappearing, still fighting, and with powers being thrown around—winds, waters, darkness, fire. The deep, black cavern lights up in strobes and flashes.

The two-faced orisha, who has to be Eshu, the messenger spirit of the Yoruba, shifts swiftly into a hippopotamus and charges Rhea's lions with a shocking speed. The damned animal is like a tank.

But before it can hurt her babies, Rhea appears on Eshu's back. She puts her hands to either side of his ears, and the hippo starts to slow and even calm. But not soon enough. The lions realize it, too, chasing the hippo and its rider down.

"No!" I only have time to reach out before all of them tumble over the edge of the abyss.

Rhea can teleport. I have to have faith she'll get herself and both her newly reunited pets out of there.

Which… The Titans can all teleport now that we're out of Tartarus. They can hide. No need to fight.

"Teleport and hide!" I yell out. I cup my hands around my mouth and yell it again, louder.

Now to figure out what I need to do. I don't think my axes are going to be much help in this situation. When I cross them, they create a defensive shield that can keep out even a kraken, but no one is coming at me, and I'm not sure how to use it as an offensive tool.

"Not so fast, Mnemosyne."

I whirl at the twisted words. Across the room from where I stand, partially blocked from view by a stalagmite, Hecate splits into three versions of herself, standing back-to back so that no one can approach from any direction. Her long black hair flows from one form to the next, the only thing connecting her. All three of her forms hurl fire from the torches in all her hands.

The guide of the dead hurls a ball of fire at Mnemosyne. But the Titaness merely lifts a hand, absorbing the blast and dousing the fire with no effort. With an animalistic snarl, Hecate starts to spin. As she does, she hurls ball after ball of fire from her six torches, and the Titaness absorbs blow after blow. Not fighting back. Not getting closer. Just keeping her occupied and away from me.

I take Hecate's distraction as a chance to run toward her. There is only one way to stop this fighting. I need to take away their glamours, or they'll never stop coming until we kill them.

Killing is out of the question.

There's no way to sneak up on Hecate, though. Two of her three heads turn abruptly to face me, and while she's busy throwing fire at Mnemosyne, darkness hits me right in the chest from the other two.

I don't even see it coming.

I'm running, and then I'm suffocating.

I can't see. Can't breathe. Can't move.

Until a shaft of light splits through the blanket of night Hecate buried me under. It grows closer and closer until suddenly a hand is reaching through the dark and drawing me out of it.

The same way the dark came on so fast, I'm instantly back in the chamber. Hecate's heads, all three of them, glare at Hyperion, who releases my hand. The father of the sun, moon, and dawn shows us exactly why as he glows brighter and brighter by the second, filling the cavern with pure light.

Light so radiant I have to throw a hand over my eyes or risk losing my sight.

I hear a scream, and then the light winks out.

I drop my arm, blinking spots out of my vision. Hecate is gone. "Did you hurt her?"

He shakes his head. "She ran away. Though she won't cower for long."

Hyperion's gaze jerks over my head, and I catch a *whomp, whomp, whomp* of sound just before he shoves me to the ground. The blade passes close enough that I feel the disturbance in the air over my back. I follow the trajectory of the scythe until it unexpectedly stops midair in front of Theia, who merely stands in its way.

A scythe.

It could belong to so many of the gods and goddesses here.

Theia looks at the weapon, then tips her head, and with the blink of her long lashes, the precious metals that comprise the weapon all melt, falling to the ground in a puddle. The jewels that had dotted the staff hit the rock with glassy tinks, scattering at her feet.

As the jewels bounce around, two gods appear on either side of her. Moccasins and caribou coats are the only indicators of what part of the world they might come from. Twins, maybe. Brother and sister, surely, they look so much alike. And that's what gives them away…

Tia and Ta'xet. The Haida goddess of peaceful death and god of violent death.

Theia's cry of alarm cuts off as they all disappear together.

I jump to my feet, looking for anything I can do to help stop them.

*Get closer. I need to get closer.*

Hermes returns with a war cry, sprinting across the room at speeds that make him near invisible, thanks to those sandals. I set my feet and focus on the hint of a blur that is the god. If I can snatch at the mesh of glamour when he's close enough…

Boone appears directly in front of Hermes, taking his speed with a slam of bodies and grunts from both. The two of them disappear. No idea who teleported whom.

To my right, Iapetus is using his spear—the famous Spear of Mortal

Life. He's going head-to-head with Anubis and his crook.

"I always knew you wanted a piece of me, Piercer," Anubis taunts.

Typical Iapetus—the Titan grins. "What gave it away, mutt?"

Anubis bares his teeth, the hackles on the back of his jackal neck rising. The two gods thrust, parry, spin, maneuver, weapons flashing and neither gaining ground on the other. Equally matched.

I won't get closer while they're doing that, and I don't want to risk getting the sharp end of that deadly spear.

Mictlāntēcutli appears out of nowhere, directly in front of me. Instinct has me jumping back when I should be reaching for his face.

"You are needed in Olympus, little one," the Aztec god says in a voice that is so otherworldly it sends chills all over me.

Those eyeballs floating in empty eye sockets are unnerving as fuck.

I need to get closer, though, so I force myself to smile. "Why don't you—"

Vines explode out of the ground and wrap around Mictlāntēcutli, who unhinges his bone jaw to show an endless dark void inside. It's the last thing I see before he's covered in them.

"Run, Lyra!" Persephone shouts at me.

Before I can take more than two steps, a hiss of sound comes from within the vines and a black circle of darkness cuts through the thick vegetation as if it doesn't even exist. The circle of darkness disappears, taking Mictlāntēcutli with it and leaving a hole where it was, and the parts of the vines that had touched it turn instantly black in a horrifying display of immediate death. That necrosis creeps farther and farther out until Persephone's creation is rotting ashes on the ground.

Mictlāntēcutli appears before me again, but in the next instant Crius and Koios are here, too, and once again, they all disappear.

"Someone better fucking fight me," I mutter.

Like a good little god, Hermes appears in front of me once again, taking me by the throat. We shoot up into the air, my legs flailing while I try to peel his fingers away from my neck with one hand and reach for his face with my other.

"I knew from the day you joined the Order of Thieves that you'd be trouble," he snarls.

"Bullshit," I manage to croak around his grip. "You didn't even notice I existed."

His veil-covered face descends into a glower of blame. "I lost my position as the god of thieves, and you're the reason."

"No, motherfucker. I'm the reason," Boone growls.

Hermes' gaze snaps over my shoulder. He drops me to go after Boone, and as I fall away from them, flailing—I'm definitely doing too much flailing as I fall into voids lately—I watch as Boone gets in at least two good punches that stun the messenger god, who maybe has never taken a hit before.

Boone lets go, falling away from Hermes, but the god grabs him by the ankle and they both disappear again.

"Gods damn it!" How are the Titans supposed to get out of here and hide if they can't leave because they need to defend one another?

Someone is going to die—on either side—if we don't stop this now.

If *I* don't stop this now. Given the way both sides seem determined to keep me alive—even Hermes wasn't trying to kill—I might be the only one safe down here.

And I need to get those glamours off their damn faces.

That will stop all of this.

I teleport, landing on the ground when I reappear.

Just in time to see Hel swallowed up in a bubble of water that forms around her, moving with her attempts to swim out.

Tethys, I realize.

Phoebe is right there, too, as close to the water as she can get with her hands held up like she wants to press her face against glass. "Don't you remember me?" she calls at trapped Hel in a voice that sounds lost and heartbroken. "We used to be friends—"

Hel's expression is so full of disgust it turns her beautiful face ugly as she vehemently shakes her head.

"Let me go, you bitch!" she screams at Phoebe. Or I think she does. I can only see her lips moving from here.

The water ripples, and Hel goes red in the face as if she's being squeezed.

"Don't hurt her, Tethys," Phoebe cries out.

Which is when I start running for them, the rock walls blurring with my speed. "Can you pull just her head out of the water?" I yell ahead of me.

The water moves so that when Hel swims again, her head breaks the surface, but the rest of her remains trapped in the water.

And I'm so close. I'm reaching for her face when Hel looks at Phoebe. "Oh, I see now. You aren't the one doing this," the Norse goddess says to her. "This is…"

In the water, her hand splays wide, and just as I brush a fingertip over her cheek, the bubble of water breaks with a splash. Immediately, the water cascades across the floor, then starts drawing back in, gathering until it forms into a body.

A body that doesn't move.

"Tethys!" Phoebe drops to her knees beside her sister and leans over her before jerking away with a gasp, her hands over her mouth.

She stares at Hel in horror. "What did you do?"

Hel lies there, breathing hard, then shoots a maddening grin at Phoebe.

"You didn't," Phoebe whispers.

"Hand of Glory."

I feel the blood drain from my face as nausea rises up to greet it. Oh gods. Hel can kill any living being she wants with her touch alone.

Tethys is…

I stare hard at her form, lying on her side, her back to me. She's not moving. Not breathing.

She's…she's dead.

## 94

## NIGHTMARES

### LYRA

"No!" Theia's scream pierces the void of nothingness as the Titaness hurls herself out of a teleport and straight at Hel.

The Norse goddess is on her feet and manifests her famous Nightsword in an instant, slicing through Theia's leg. But the Titaness heals as fast as the sword cuts. And by the look on her face, she's going to kill Hel.

We can't lose more.

It's not Hel's fault. The glamour made her believe that she was right to do this.

With only one thought in my head, I teleport closer. When I rematerialize, Anubis is there now, facing Theia with Hel. He backhands me, sending me flying across the room.

I teleport again to avoid crashing into the rock wall of the chamber, then instantly try again, aiming for Hel's other side. And go flying yet again. The hit comes from her this time. They must feel me approaching when I teleport.

Now they're facing three Titans—Theia, Phoebe, and Iapetus.

Wait. Neither Anubis nor Hel used a weapon on me when they both possess them.

"They can't kill me," I say to myself. "They need me to stop Hades."

If I end up dead, I don't know what he'll do. Not when he's already so out of control he doesn't know I've escaped Tartarus already. Not when the violent tunneling smoke-and-fire tentacles behind me are still ripping into the remains of the prison, trying to dig me out.

I wince. What I'm about to try is probably going to hurt.

I teleport again, and this time I aim for right where Hel is thrusting her sword. I reappear in the world just as it slices straight into me.

Hel's eyes go wide. So do Anubis', and I swear even his black fur pales when I cough and golden blood comes spurting out of my mouth, blade still lodged deep in my chest.

"No," the jackal god whispers.

Feeling every slice, every scrape against my flesh and nerves and insides, I push my body into the blade, closer and closer to Hel, until the point pierces through my back.

"You're the only one who can stop him." Her voice is laden with disbelief. "What are you doing?"

Bonus—Anubis comes in closer, too, maybe to stop me, or maybe to keep Theia from getting to Hel.

I don't care. I just need him within reach.

"I'm the only one who can stop *you*." I grip at the veils covering both of their faces and tear the glamours away, tossing them onto the ground where, just like with Phoebe and Persephone, they burn up in a fit of hissing until they turn to ash, joining the ash raining down on us from the fire and smoke Hades is still drilling into the ground.

Anubis stares at me with dawning horror darkening the browns and golds of his jackal eyes.

"It's not possible," he whispers in a voice turned feral.

But it's Hel's response that I can't look away from. With a cry, the goddess lets go of her sword, still buried in me, backing away and turning to look at Tethys' body on the ground.

"No." The word is a moan. "Please, no."

Her back is to me, but it's impossible to miss the way her shoulders shake and heave. She knows what she's done. She knows she can't take it back. Even if it wasn't truly her fault, she'll have to carry that with her always.

I look at Anubis. "You have all been glamoured to believe something that is not true."

The Egyptian god of the Underworld bares his sharp canine teeth at me. I don't know what I think will happen next, but it's not for him to grab the hilt of the blade still buried in me and yank the weapon out.

I pitch forward, trying very hard not to vomit or pass out. On a gurgle of pain, the intensity of it drops me to my knees. And then Anubis is beside me, his hands cupping the entrance and exit wounds. A glow emanates from his hands, and warmth grows inside the wound, passing all the way through me as if it's traveling down the hole left by the sword and knitting me back together. Because when he stops, all the pain is gone and I'm able to rise to my feet, I peel back the tear in my clothes to find my flesh perfect again. A thousand times faster than even my goddess healing. I look up at the god.

He shrugs. "Some gods of death aren't only about death."

"How is it possible?" Hel asks from behind him.

The others are still fighting all around us, I realize. I'm not even sure they know what's happened.

"I don't have time to explain. Protect the Titans and get me to the others so I can remove their glamours."

Anubis nods, then disappears, only to reappear again holding Hermes by the arms.

"What the fuck are you doing?" Hermes jerks against the jackal god's hold but can't break it.

I reach for Hermes' face yet again.

Hermes engages his sandals, dragging him and Anubis out of my reach. In the same instant, someone tackles Hyperion.

Shit. This is going to take too long, even with help. We're risking even more losses.

*"What the fuck is going on here?"* A gruff and grumpy voice sounds in my head, followed by the echo of two very different voices saying the exact same thing.

"Cerberus!" I'm across the room and burying my face in what's basically the three-headed hellhound's armpit, my arms splayed wide as I try to hug the big oaf.

*"Lyra—"* The three voices of Cer, Ber, and Rus all break on my name, and the dog is suddenly curling around me, heads cuddling me as he makes squeaky doggy noises of relief.

I grin and laugh into his sulfur-smelling fur. "You're here."

*"I'm here,"* Cer assures me.

*"I felt you reenter the Underworld."* Ber's snarl is almost accusatory, and a small flame shoots from his nostrils.

Rus nuzzles me. *"But I have felt that before—"*

He suddenly breaks off, and all three heads growl. A sound that is scary as hells on a good day, but with my ear squashed against his chest and his heads down by me, the hair-raising noise surrounds me like the rumble of thunder.

I don't have to pull my face out of his fur to know what he's looking at, though.

"Wait." I push back, intending to remove the veil from all three of his faces, but… "There's no glamour?" The words pop out of my mouth.

Rus tips his head to the side in dog for *what?*

*"What does this mean?"* Cer demands, his gaze still fixed on the Titans and fighting all around us.

I swallow, then explain as fast as I can. I'll fill him in on details later.

*"This can't be right, tiny immortal,"* Ber snarls. *"Hades would not have been fooled—"*

"I've seen the glamour on his face. He has been."

All three heads shake at that, their jowls flapping. *"No."*

"It's true," Anubis says. The Egyptian god has stayed right where he was, daring to come no closer to us. "I wouldn't believe it if she hadn't removed the veil from my own eyes."

One of the heads—Ber, I think—huffs. A hellhound version of a grunt of acceptance. At least I hope so.

"That explains it," a voice says from the other side of Cerberus, and the hellhound rounds with another hair-raising growl.

"For soul's sake," Hel mutters, unsheathing her sword.

But neither attacks.

I duck to look under his belly and see the bottom of Yeomra's hanbok. When Cerberus remains unmoving, hackles raised, I work my way around him to find the Korean god, the fifth king of their Underworld, gazing over the open pages of a massive leather-bound book in his hand and staring not at Hel or Anubis but at the Titans.

"My mind is trying to tell me that the Titans are evil incarnate and deserve imprisonment and every punishment they get. But the book is showing something else."

The book of judgment.

Heavens above, whoever glamoured the world missed something.

"I trust the book," he says.

Patting Cerberus to let him know it's all right, I move out from under him to approach Yeomra. "I can remove the glamour that is clouding your eyes, if you like."

He glances from me to Hel and Anubis and back, then nods. With a flick of my fingers, I pull the spiderweb-fine netting away.

While Yeomra is blinking and readjusting to real memories, I turn back to Cerberus. "Can you protect the Titans without hurting the other gods until I can remove the glamours from the rest of them?"

Cer lowers his head to peer at me closely. *"Hades needs you more than they do, my queen."*

My heart cracks. "I know. But I can't go to him until I know they won't be harmed, and we can't let this fighting continue. No more deaths. Not for a lie."

As if the Fates heard me, a boom ricochets even over the roar of Hades' smoke and fire, and out of the rubble of Tartarus burst familiar winged creatures.

"Nightmares!" I hear Eshu, I think, yell.

I grin. The Nightmares pledged their loyalty to me.

I put two fingers to my lips and let out a high-pitched whistle. Like a flock of birds, the Nightmares wheel in the air toward me. I don't want them to be attacked, and we don't have time.

"Stop the gods from attacking us!" I yell to them. "Do not harm them, but be careful. Bring them to me."

At my command, the Nightmares disappear. All except one. Like a lone arrow, he arcs through the air, then plunges to the ground, barely flaring his bat-like wings before he lands directly in front of me.

*"This will take only moments, Mistress."*

Really? That would be impressive. I nod, then blink, because before me stand all the gods and Titans, a Nightmare at the side of each one. Each powerful being stares into space, glassy-eyed.

"That is…"

The head Nightmare at my side sounds amused. *"I know."*

Mental note to make sure to give them rules before I loose them on the world. "You can let the Titans go."

Those who were influenced immediately blink, then inhale sharply as if they've been underwater a little too long. "That is quite unpleasant," Mnemosyne murmurs as she glares at the Nightmare who had her. She also takes a small step away from it. It might smile. Hard to tell with those blank faces.

*"We can't hold on to gods' minds for long, though,"* the one beside me warns.

Right. With them all still, it doesn't take me long to remove all the glamours, each Nightmare releasing their captive from whatever hallucination they had them in as I do. The same blinking-and-sudden-breaths reaction happens with every single one, followed by the shock and confusion.

Rhea moves to my side. "We're safe now and can explain everything to them. You need to go to Hades."

Safe. I can't look toward the Titaness on the ground. "Tethys…"

"We'll honor her when the time is right," Rhea assures me.

She's lost a husband and a sister today. How is she still standing?

"We can't go with you." Rhea glances around the others. "We shouldn't be seen yet. Not until you can remove the rest of the glamours."

She's right about that. I nod.

Then Rhea leans down and kisses my forehead, the same way Cronos did before sacrificing himself, and I squeeze my eyes shut. How can she bear to look at me? I'm the cause of her greatest loss.

Then she folds me into her arms, squeezing long enough that I get the sense she doesn't want to let go. Thieves don't like touch, but what I want to do is lean into her, draw this out—but I can't. Not yet.

With a sigh, she releases me. "Go, daughter."

My eyes flash open at the words to find her looking at me with a mother's love. I can't hold back the tears, letting them slide silently down my cheeks even as I'm shaking my head. How can she call me that?

But she brushes them away with the pads of her fingers and offers me the softest smile. "Don't let Cronos' sacrifice be in vain. Time can't reset now that it's been healed and is yours. Go show Hades you're safe. Stop him before he does more than try to dig your body out of the rubble."

I glance away, toward Boone, seeking him out. We've been through this together. He meets my gaze steadily and gives a single, low whistle. *Go.*

With a swallow, I return my focus to Rhea. "I don't know how."

"Just let him see you. Truly see you."

## 95

# BURNING DOWN THE HOUSE

### LYRA

Let Hades see me.

That, I already figured out. Hopefully he believes it's the current-day me who escaped and not the future me who disappears on him all the time.

"I don't know how to get out of here." When Hades brought me down, it took him three teleports.

*"He cannot see me,"* Cer says in his serious way. *"He thinks I am attempting to stop him. Already took several swipes at me, and he was not joking around."*

Urgency shoots up my spine. It's *that* bad? I mean, Zeus is one thing, but Hades loves his dog. I can't picture Hades going after Cerberus like that.

"I'll take you," Hermes says, moving to stand in my line of sight.

I blink at him. "Seriously? You're not going to try to dump me in a pit somewhere or—"

"This is more important." Hermes doesn't love it any more than I do, but at least he's being less of an asshole. "We don't need anyone else stopping us. Hecate can't leave the Underworld anymore, and the others are supposed to be down here guarding Tartarus. But no one will question me coming back topside. They'll think I have news."

Right.

I look at Rhea, who raises her eyebrows back at me. The decision is mine.

I hold my hand out to Hermes. "Please take me to Hades."

Hermes makes a face at my palm and clasps me by the forearm instead. "Hold on tight. I'm not as smooth at this down here as Hades is."

Honestly, with the first teleport, I'm still expecting something nefarious, but he truly is taking me up to Olympus. It takes Hermes closer to nine teleports to navigate our way out of the Underworld. The god is breathing hard with sweat trickling down his temples by the time he says, "Last one. Prepare yourself."

"What's that supposed to mean—"

My question gets cut off by us blinking out of existence. When we blink back in, all it takes is one quick glance around before I'm blindsided with a whopping dose of terror.

"Holy mother goddess Gaia." The words rip from my mouth in a harsh whisper as shock closes my throat around them and cuts them off.

Hermes has brought us to the top of the mountain in Olympus where he held his Crucible Labor. Not the very top, but to the path just underneath where our planks were. From this vantage point, I can look out over most of Olympus.

And what greets my eyes is a shitshow of horror. Apocalyptic proportions.

The three waterfalls that pour from the carved statues of Zeus, Poseidon, and Hades are decimated, water bursting into the sky in white, blue, and black plumes that rain down on the buildings below. The source of the tentacles digging through Tartarus is clearly the main temple that sits up high. Black-smoke-encased arms of bright-blue flame have blown the roof off, and they wave around like the heads of a hydra.

One tentacle is shoved down the statue of Hades' throat, and the waterfall is making less of a plume in the air, instead spraying out in all directions. That must be what Hades is using to dig down to Tartarus, forcing the fire through the bowels to the gates of Tartarus and now into that hell.

Three more waving tentacles have wound their way through the streets of Olympus, leveling everything and setting it all ablaze. All I can make out under the smoke and flames is ruins and rubble. He set the entire mountainside ablaze with that blue fire, leaving a trail of bleak annihilation across one of the most beautiful places in existence. A scar. Given how he cried in my arms after destroying it the first time, he's going to hate himself after we stop him this time.

Meanwhile, at least five other tentacles of flame wave wildly in the air around the temple as gods attack the fortress of smoke that Hades has built around himself. They are making zero headway as the tentacles keep knocking them back and flinging them away.

No wonder they need me.

No one—none of the gods, even with all their power—can get near him.

"Teleporting is useless. None of us can get beyond the outside of the temple, and his smoke finds us immediately that way. So don't try that." Hermes gives me the side-eye. "You better fucking be able to get to him," he mutters.

"Yeah," I whisper. I don't even care that he's back to being a dick and that that was basically a threat.

No teleporting? Of course my god of death wouldn't make it that easy.

Hades is doing this *for* me, though. To protect me from the gods trying to destroy the Titans and me with them. So if anyone has a chance…

At least I'll keep telling myself that.

"See if you can get the others to stand down," I say to Hermes.

I ignore the affronted look he tosses my way because that came out as an order, but I don't have time to coddle his ego. I'm already teleporting away. I land on the paths just below the main temple and, with epically bad aim, within feet of one of the fiery barriers that encircle it.

"Shit!"

Before I can pull out my axes to cross them and put up the invisible defensive shield they create, I'm tackled from the side by something hard and moving fast. If arms didn't wrap around me to take the brunt of the impact as we both plow into the rocky mountainside, rolling over and over, I'd have thought Hades' tentacles had gotten me.

It's not until we finally roll to a stop and he jumps up to loom over me that I realize it's Ares.

For a minute, I picture him shattering my token in the pre-game challenge during the Crucible when we all had to earn our gifts. But he's not the vindictive, competitive god he was in that moment. This Ares isn't worried about winning. He is still in full armor, but his helm is missing a portion of the face plate, and golden blood drips down one arm.

His one remaining eye grows wide as recognition sinks in. "Lyra?"

Even the god of war sounds shaken.

"How are you here?" he demands.

"I got out." I don't tell him that we all did. That won't help yet.

Ares scrubs a hand over his jaw. "Thank the gods." He glances back up the incline we rolled down, toward the temple. "Can you stop him?"

"That's why I'm here." I hold out a hand, and he pulls me to my feet. "He needs to see me. I don't think he knows I'm out yet."

Ares' jaw goes hard. "It's impenetrable. We've tried attacking in force, in waves, sneaking in one at a time. He's battered us all away."

"You shouldn't have been fucking attacking at all." The snarl that comes out of me fast and hard is pure Hades, and I swear Ares blanches.

"We'll deal with that later," I say. Definitely a threat.

He glances over me. "Your weapons will do no good, and teleporting doesn't work."

The teleporting, Hermes already told me. "I don't plan to need weapons."

The god frowns. "I can't let you go in unarmed."

"Hades is fighting to protect *me*. As soon as he sees I'm out, he'll stop."

Ares blows out a sharp breath. "Maybe. I've never seen him like this. Wild. Unhinged. Even when he leveled Olympus before."

*Because that was a controlled burn.* I don't say it out loud. "He'll stop." I believe that with all my heart. "But first he needs to feel safe from attack. I need all of you to stop fighting. Hermes is telling the others. Go help him."

"I can't leave you defenseless."

I've always thought of Ares as one of the most handsome of the gods. Rugged in the way one would expect, but leanly muscled rather than bulky. Right now, he's not the god of war, but the protector that many mortals forget he is.

"I'm not defenseless."

"Lyra—"

He's not letting this go.

Fine. "Can you send me Aphrodite, then? I need you out here if it doesn't work."

Indecision ripples over his face for only a heartbeat before his expression settles into determination. "Don't get too close until she finds you."

Then he's gone.

"Right," I say under my breath as I think through my next steps. "Don't forget not to hum."

I'm just about to teleport closer to the temple when a sound like a whimper comes from the bushes, followed by a rustle.

I crouch, axes ready, prepared to defend myself.

But when my panther tattoo emerges, limping hard, keeping her visibly broken left front paw off the ground, I run to her in an instant. She butts her head into my hand with a tiny chuff.

"Poor baby. Hades wouldn't let you near?"

She shakes her head.

The others?

She turns, limping away, and I follow her, not too far down the mountain, to find the fox unconscious. I run to him, dropping my axes on the ground to check him over, then let out a gusty sigh of relief when I find his chest moving. The owl hoots, and I look up to find him in a tree, one wing also broken. The tarantula, sitting on the owl's good shoulder, at least looks unharmed.

I can't risk Hades' defensive system of fire and smoke hurting them further. "Thank you," I say. I want to say more. Assure them that he wouldn't have hurt them himself, that he had to be unaware of what was happening outside of where he's trapped himself in the temple.

Instead, I recall them to my arm, where they can rest and heal.

Picking up my axes again, I make my way toward the temple path where Ares tackled me, stopping farther back. "Hades," I call out. "It's Lyra."

A tentacle comes for me, making the air whistle it zeroes in so fast. I cross my axes in front of me, and the tentacle bounces off the invisible shield. This time, though—unlike during Zeus' Labor in the Crucible—I'm a goddess. While I have to dig my feet in as I'm propelled backward, I'm not thrown to the ground.

"I guess you didn't believe me," I mutter under my breath.

Okay. He's not going to just let me walk through. I kind of guessed that when he didn't stop trying to dig me out of Tartarus.

I wrestle with panic that wants to take over. A thousand fears are shouting in my mind over the roar of my slamming heart. Is he this far gone? Can he be stopped? I have to get to him.

"Lyra! Thank the mother goddess!"

Two hands on my shoulders spin me around, and then I'm in Aphrodite's embrace. Even in this moment, despite the fear that is trying to paralyze me, warmth infiltrates my heart and soul, and I lean into her. Just for a second.

But we don't have time, and we both know it, drawing away in unison. I stare. Aphrodite does not look like herself.

No longer the glamorous goddess, she's dressed in armor that is so silver it hurts to look at. It's not her fancy armor that she wore during the opening of the Crucible, though. No bodies contorting in hedonistic pleasure. This armor is plain and simple. This armor is for *war*.

Her dark, luxurious hair hangs around her in a knotted mass, and dirt is smeared with golden blood over the underclothes and spattered across the metal. There's blood on her face, too, though I can't tell where from.

Aphrodite's expression is near frantic. "I didn't know…" She swallows around her trembling voice. "I never thought he'd… Zeus, Lyra. He killed him."

Bleak horror tries to wrest rational thought from me. Even for Zeus, Hades is going to hate himself for that. Not only will he carry the guilt for eternity, but he'll have their souls to care for afterward. I can't let him kill more. He may never recover from what he's already done.

I frame her face with my hands, focusing her on me. "Can you help me stop him without anyone else getting hurt? Or do you need to hide?"

Of all the gods and goddesses Hades is targeting, he likes Aphrodite. Maybe he wouldn't harm her.

"I—" Her gaze jerks above my head, and then she grabs me by the arms. We teleport away, only to reappear nearby. Despite the nothingness of teleporting, I still feel the vibration of the air where the tentacle of fire just blasted through exactly where we were standing.

"He won't let me in," I tell her. "How do I stop him if I can't get to him?"

Aphrodite shakes her head, her hair falling over her shoulders in a tangled riot. "He doesn't know it's you. It's like he's turned off all reason."

"What have you tried?"

She grimaces. "All of us have tried every power we have in our arsenal. Not just us, but other gods—Norse, Egyptian, Celtic, Aztec, Cherokee, Kushite, Dravidian. You name it. Nothing gets through—"

"No." I squeeze her arm to stop her. "Not everybody… *you*. What have you tried?"

"Me?" Her smoldering brown eyes go wide with confusion. "I'm not a warrior—"

"I mean love."

Aphrodite blinks. Then shakes her head. "That's the first thing I tried." The glance she casts toward the temple is one so full of fear, her lips turn white. "He couldn't knock me away, but I also couldn't push through the fire and smoke. A stalemate. Useless." She drops her gaze to the ground. "Just like everyone says."

I don't have time to argue with this goddess's beat-up self-image. I tuck my axes into the back straps of my vest, adjusted for two. "What about *my* love?"

Aphrodite blinks again several times before her mouth opens in a silent gasp. "I don't... I don't know."

"Is that something you can do? Tap into my love? Project it somehow? Make him feel that I'm here?"

The smile that tips up her lips isn't a sexy smirk or the knowing moue she often uses. It's real and just the tiniest bit hopeful. "It's worth a try."

She spins me around and pulls me into her so that my back is to her front. Except I can feel her, not armor. She wraps one arm around my stomach and the other around my arms to press her hand over my heart.

"What do I do now?" I ask. "Think a happy thought?"

"I'm all out of pixie dust," she mutters. "But happy thoughts couldn't hurt."

She's scared. I can feel her trembling against me.

Maybe I should be more afraid for myself right now, but I'm holding all my fear for Hades and the others. He would never hurt me. Not intentionally. He just needs to be pulled out of his despair-fueled, protective rage long enough to see.

"We move together," she says. "If he can sense me anywhere as part of this, he'll become suspicious, and he's not exactly in the mood to be reasonable."

"Sounds about right."

She whispers something then that I don't quite catch. Maybe something like, "Please let this work." Except more like a prayer. If ever a goddess was praying to herself, this is it.

I don't know what I expect—a glowing red aura to surround us, perhaps, or a pink floaty bubble, or maybe even little hearts shooting out of Aphrodite's hand. It's not for us to walk forward without anything—no armor, weapons, or visible magic. Just...flesh and bone and beating hearts.

Exposed.

Vulnerable.

The way every heart is when desperately asking another heart to love them.

Our first few steps are out of sync and awkward, making us trip a little, but then we get the rhythm of it.

Step. Pause. Step. Pause.

Like a bride walking down the aisle to her waiting groom. We get maybe ten steps before fire comes at us so hard and fast that I flinch.

"Keep moving," she whisper-hisses.

Despite my heart trying to crawl out of my throat to escape, we both keep walking.

The tentacle stops inches from my nose, smoke billowing toward me only to curl back under before it touches my skin. If a column of blue fire sheathed in smoke could be confused, this one is. It cocks back, giving us room to take several quick steps, then slams forward but doesn't manage to come any closer.

So we keep walking. A little at a time, backing Hades' defenses up. It's slow going. Agonizingly slow. Overhead, I can still see other tentacles waving wildly.

"We need to move faster," I murmur.

Aphrodite puts her lips right by my ear and says in the softest whisper, "Talk to him."

Talk to him? We're not exactly the lovey-dovey type of couple who offer each other sweet nothings. "Other than letting him know I'm here, what should I say?"

"Just let him hear your voice," she whispers.

I give a tiny nod as we keep walking with slow, mincing steps. "Hades."

The smoke and fire before me instantly ripples as if my words are stones dropped into a still lake, sending waves outward. Then the smoke around the flames grows darker, blacker...pretty sure angrier.

"It's not working," I murmur over my shoulder. Any second, that thing is going to figure out how to stop us for good.

"Keep trying. It didn't do that before."

"It didn't get angry before?"

"It didn't ripple." She sighs. "*Make* him hear you."

# 96

# FOR THE LOVE OF HADES

### LYRA

Make him hear me? How?

"Hades," I call out. "It's Lyra." The smoke ripples again. "I escaped from Tartarus—"

The tip of the smoke tentacle rears up over us like the mouth of a giant snake trying to swallow us whole. But it isn't able to move us or eat us… or even touch us. As if an invisible wall won't let it near. After a second, it settles back to being a barrier.

I get the message. *Don't talk about Tartarus or Titans, Lyra.*

"I'm safe," I call out instead. "I'm here."

More ripples, but it doesn't move.

My frustration echoes its movement, rippling through me, tightening my muscles until my hands fist. "So damned stubborn, as always," I mutter.

This time when the smoke ripples, it also turns clearer. Just for a second. "Did you see that?" I whisper at Aphrodite.

"Yes. Keep talking."

But that reaction has me wondering…

I eye the smoke, which is still keeping pace with us, remaining between us and my fury-locked god of death. And I picture Hades—the clench of his jaw, his eyes cutting metallic silver and narrowed in rage, his bident in his hand.

I picture every beloved detail, because that's who I'm talking to. Not this extension of him. "You've spent a fucking lifetime listening to me, and now, when you need to the most, you're going to ignore me?"

Even as the smoke ripples and turns clearer again, Aphrodite's inhale is sharp in my ear. "What are you doing?"

I pat her hand, telling her silently to trust me. I know that this is the way. Keep talking. But not only to make him stop. This is me and him. That's all it comes down to.

Our communication is built on sharp honesty.

"I've been fighting to get out," I call, my voice steady now. Sure. "I told you I could get myself out of anything, and I made it. I got myself the hells out of that hole, and the only face I want to see is yours."

The tentacle rears again, not to attack but to writhe, as if it's in pain, the fire pulsing under the smoke in flashes of blue that become more and more white. Hotter.

I pray to every god and goddess of love and hope that he's hearing me. I just have to push a little harder.

"Now. Move this fucking thing out of my way, Hades. I need to hold you."

The tentacle goes so still, even the smoke does not move.

"Please," I whisper. "Please hear me. I need you."

The fire and smoke blow away, splitting into feathery tufts on either side of a single, narrow path, until I can see the temple up ahead.

Aphrodite lets me go. "It's all you now, darling. Go."

I'm already gone, stumbling and tripping as I run. To get to Hades. I might as well be wearing Hermes' winged sandals I fly so fast up the mountain, past the crumbling, blackened outer columns of the temple and toward the inner sanctum, where my steps slow to a halt.

Because it's pitch-black in here.

Not just from the smoke blocking out the light, but the walls of the temple itself are midnight black. No longer brilliant white marble but, instead, obsidian. The flicker of what I think is firelight coming from farther down reflects off the glassy black walls, and I make my careful way toward the source of light.

The smaller temple in the center of the building is also columned, like the larger outer shell. Also turned obsidian. I step inside, and a thousand impressions bombard me all at once.

The only thing in the room is the throne at the other end with Hades seated on it.

Owning it, even as his posture is…indolent.

Like he doesn't give a shit who he has to kill or what he has to destroy.

Death is child's play to this god.

It shouldn't be this way, but a stark shiver of fascination slithers through my fear for him.

I can't pull my gaze away from him, but I somehow still absorb the rest of the details. The blocky, deep-seated throne, like the temple itself, is now made of obsidian, the seat padded with black leather, and instead of carvings of all the gods of the Greek pantheon, there is only the symbol of the bident and scepter carved into the ends of the arms. It is repeated again in the tops of the posts on either side of the seat back. And at the crest of the seat above his head, a curved bident is carved out of the obsidian, honed to fine points at the top of the circle, looking like devil's horns and a halo at the same time.

All around the throne, coming out of it like wings of darkness, is the source of the fire and smoke. And the way the flames move and thrash and flow, they seem to be living things, forming into nightmarish images in the darkness behind him—creatures, burned husks of trees, wings, screaming faces. Above the throne, the tentacles disappear upward, obscuring the hole where a ceiling used to be. The fire comes from a single source—lava so hot it is a bluish-purple shade, cooling to reds and yellows at the edges. The lava sparks and flows in a ceaseless waterfall from behind Hades' throne, only to rise into the pillars of flame and smoke.

None of that matters.

Because the most terrifying part is Hades.

Hades as I've never seen him before.

He's dressed not in his modern liquid metal armor. Instead, he's in something that's a cross between a medieval outlaw and a video game assassin. Thick steel-toed leather boots come up to just below his knees, and it's hard to make out what he's wearing underneath a cloak that shrouds him, the hood pulled up over his head and low over his face so that all I can see is shadows instead of his features. The top of his hood looks to be embroidered with metallic thread in an intricate depiction of the same bident and scepter, like he's wearing a crown.

His hands are fisted on the flat arms of his throne, and he's wearing gauntlets of leather and metal that go all the way up his forearms. Thick chains drip across his chest—holding the cloak in place, maybe.

Except... I peer closer... Maybe not.

Because, even in the dimness of the room, I'm pretty sure I see thinner chains attached to his gauntlets and boots, bolted into the floor between his feet and into the arms of his throne—tying him down. My heart aches as I take in this tortured man who has chained himself to his throne in an effort to believe in me and not unleash himself completely on the world.

The energy that is coming off him is…palpable.

It fills the room with power and wrath.

But I feel no fear. Not for me. Just for him. I wish to Elysium that I could still sense his emotions like I did after he gave me some of his blood to save my life during the Crucible, but that effect is gone now. He seems so distant, so far away, separated by all available darkness that cloaks his very soul. But even through that terror, I still feel my body react.

Like Hades is my true north, magnetic, imposing, furious, and…fucking hot.

My erratic heart settles, warmth floods my cheeks, and a familiar pulse of pleasure takes up an elemental beat in my core.

"Your hair is long." His voice seems to come not from him but from all around me, deep and echoing.

And cold.

What I want to do is throw myself into his arms and sob. That, or straddle his lap and kiss him until he wakes up. Such polar opposite reactions, and I can't do either one.

He's not himself. Too self-contained. Too unpredictable. And…I know what that question means. I was given my clothes and weapons and tattoos back when I escaped Tartarus, but my hair is still long, hanging around my shoulders and to my waist.

Hair he associates with the Lyra who abandons him.

I take a slow step toward him, then another, the way one might approach a feral animal caught in a trap, needing to be rescued.

"My hair grew when I was in Hestia's Lock in Tartarus." I finger a strand that shook out over my shoulders at some point in the fight with the other gods of death and the Underworld.

"Long hair." His echoey voice is more a murmur now, but it still rings around me. "So you won't be staying long."

I shake my head. "I won't be leaving ever again. This is me. This is current-day me."

"I don't believe you." His voice goes quieter. Deadlier. But he must also tense somewhat, because the chains around his wrists rattle and sparks peek out from under his boots. "You've lied to me before."

"Bullshit." I keep walking.

"What?" he snarls.

"Name one lie."

"Stop," he demands.

I don't listen. I continue to take my slow steps toward Hades. Only about ten more, and I'll be at his knees.

"Stop."

I shiver hard at the command in his voice—how am I so turned on in this moment—but take another step. Nine more.

"I said *stop*."

The final word reverberates around us as thin ropes of smoke shoot out from the mass behind him and snake around my wrists and ankles like shackles holding me in place.

My heart stutters as hope flickers to pathetic sparks inside me. Only eight more steps. So close. I can't let him stop me here.

His next words come out even colder, quieter. Brutally so. "*You* are the reason Lyra is trapped down there."

"I didn't lie to you to make that happen." I lean against my bonds, trying to get closer to him, my gaze on what I hope is his, trying to let him see all of me. "Think about it. Did I ever lie?"

The smoke bonds loosen enough for me to take one more step. Seven to go. Just a few more. Please the cosmos.

I try to take another, but the bonds clamp down on me again.

"You told me to trust you," he says.

"You were right to trust me." I offer him a patient smile. One I know will irritate him, but that's how we are. We get under each other's skin. "You kept trusting me even when I ended up in that prison because you listened to what I told you in your past. You didn't burn down the world. You just protected me until I could figure it out… I figured it out."

He jerks forward, the chains at his feet clanking through the metal loops as he widens his stance, elbows on his knees. Okay. Probably shouldn't have mentioned that last bit, because it could have been a lie. That was something I did not know for certain.

"No one would willingly enter that place."

Forget patience.

"I did. For a reason." I strain against the bindings around me, using all the strength he gave me as a goddess to take one more jaw-clenching, muscle-shaking step. "How do you think I've come to you in the past?" I grind out one more step. If I can just *touch* him.

What he says next comes out as a menacing growl so dark it rattles the teeth in my head. "Cronos sent you. That's how."

He can't handle the entire story now. All the reasons. What will get through to him?

"Cronos..." I choke as I continue to strain against his bonds. "Is dead." The sound of the Titan's name on my lips so soon is like a dagger to my heart "...*I* am the goddess of time, now."

Hades' entire being goes rigid. "More lies."

"It's the truth. He died as we...as I was escaping Tartarus, and his power passed to me."

"Prove it."

Prove it? Shit. It took me forever just to get the teleporting and glamouring stuff. Even then, it's more like I had to wait for those to settle in versus learning by practice. Can I prove it? "Release me and I will."

The smoke suddenly lets go, fading away in a puff of nonexistent wind.

"Go ahead," Hades says.

I was planning to run to him the instant I gained the ability, but he let me go so fast I wasn't ready. I wasn't ready and...I realize now that just touching me won't help. He's touched future me in his past as well. That didn't make her stay. That didn't make her words true.

So instead, I take a deep breath and close my eyes. I call on the part inside me that isn't mine, that incandescent light that belongs only to the King of the Titans.

To my shock, the light rushes to my bidding, illuminating the backs of my eyelids, and my lips part in a silent gasp. And then, like I've learned to do with teleporting and glamours, I simply whisper my will to the light.

In an instant, everything goes dead still. I open my eyes to find all things frozen—even sound ceases, and the smoke stops moving, as does the lava flow at his back—because time itself has stopped.

*I* stopped time.

And it was so...easy.

I take the final few steps and drop to my knees at Hades' feet. I briefly consider ripping the veil of glamour from his eyes now, but no. Too much too soon. He needs to calm down first before I break that to him.

So I simply release time.

Sound and movement resume, and Hades slams back in the throne at my sudden appearance.

The tears that came unbidden at the mere sound of Cronos' name on my lips continue to fall as I lay my chin on his knee, on top of my hands. "It's me. I got myself out of that place. I'm here with you. You have always been able to feel the truth of us. Let go of your fury and fear and *look* at me, Hades. Really look at me."

I know I'm begging. Pleading with him.

Even as the words come out of my mouth, I'm also praying to him. *Please don't send me away. I'm not lying. Please see me. I'm here. I love you, and I'm really here. I'm never going away—*

A shudder rips through Hades from head to toe so violently, it shakes me loose from his knee, and I sit back, watching him warily.

Waiting for the death strike.

Except he bolts forward, his hands coming up to cup my cheeks, and his hood falls away to reveal his face, his mercurial eyes a true silver searching my gaze, my features, my body like he still isn't sure I'm real.

"Lyra?" he asks unevenly. "It's you?" He frowns, silver eyes turning slightly stormy. "Not you from your future or my past or whatever the bloody hell you've been doing to torment me my entire life. But from *now*. The one I made into my queen."

I cover his hands with mine. The tears are slipping down my cheeks faster, but I blink them away because I don't want them to blur his face. I want to see everything.

"I'll never leave you again," I whisper.

"Thank the heavens." His voice breaks, and Hades crumples around me, holding me so tight I can't breathe, and I don't care.

# 97

# STARS, HIDE YOUR FIRES

### LYRA

I don't want to take the time to breathe if it means one second without him. I can't… I don't think I could do that again. Lose him. Be separated from him. I don't know how he became so integral, so necessary to my happiness, so fast.

But he is.

Hades goes to drag me onto his lap, but the chains at his wrists and feet clank and strain. With an impatient sound, he breaks them in an instant.

"Those weren't exactly useful, were they?" I tease with a grin.

Only to have his mouth crash down on mine. He kisses me like I'm the oxygen he needs to breathe. "It really is you," he groans against my lips.

But he doesn't stop kissing me, so I can't ask how he knows.

He makes desperate sounds in the back of his throat as he successfully drags me onto his lap, and then cool air hits my skin, and I open my eyes to find we're in his room in Erebos.

Closing my eyes again with a smile, I kiss him back. Just as frantic. Just as desperate.

This coming together isn't like our first time, which was all slow touches and Hades in total control. Or like any of the times before I went to Tartarus, which were like love songs, excited about our future together. Or even the time while I was in Tartarus, which was like a dream in the middle of a nightmare.

This is…deliverance.

Relief so stark, so wild, so acute that our bodies can't hold it in, and so we are sharing it together in a violent unburdening.

I can't get enough of his mouth on mine. Gods, he tastes like the bitter dark chocolate that I smell on him. And when he sucks on my lower lip, I whimper as pleasure draws through me with each suck.

For me, our love has been a whirlwind, even with my extra time in Tartarus.

For Hades…our love has been thousands of years of waiting.

He's loved me for his whole life. And now I'll love him for the whole of my immortality.

Eager fingers aren't gentle as he hurries me out of my clothes. The rasp of fabric tearing comes with the tiniest bite of pain at my hip. Pain that I welcome as he rips my panties off and lays me bare.

He doesn't pause to look his fill like usual, though.

He's too far gone. Too over the edge.

Hades scoops me up and pins me against the wall, and I'm vaguely aware of something falling to the floor. A weapon, probably, knowing this room.

But who gives a shit when he lines himself up at my entrance, grunting when he finds me already slick for him, then drives into me.

We both moan hard.

Then his hands are at my hips in a punishing grip that, if I was still human, would definitely leave marks for weeks.

I welcome that bite of pain, too. Because his hands are also shaking.

He was this terrified for me, that I'd be trapped down there forever, separated from him forever.

My god of death, my King of the Underworld, who has never needed anyone. Not really.

He needs me this much.

As much as I need him. I think it's the first time I've truly seen that. That my need is not, and has never been, more intense or impactful than his.

*Gods, I need him. Everything about him.*

I take every brutal, rough, out-of-control thrust of his body into mine. This isn't punishment. It's a reclaiming.

It's what savage joy feels like.

I spear my fingers through his hair and tug hard, and he throws his head back to look at me, his pupils blown out black so that the silver is a mere sliver around the circumference, like an eclipse.

"You told me you'd get yourself out of any trouble."

"And I did." I smile.

"They wanted to bury you."

I hold on to him tighter. "I figured out what you were doing. I knew you'd resist the prophecy."

"I wasn't okay without you," he groans to the rhythm of his thrusts.

He says it with such stark honesty, such shock in his face, that I finally let myself feel all the emotions that I stuffed way down deep in order to survive.

"Me, either."

A sob tears loose inside my throat, and he grabs me by the back of the head, crashing our mouths together, taking my sorrow and fears and loss, replacing them with incandescent elation in the knowledge that those fears and that loss weren't for forever.

"We're together now," he snarls against my lips as he grinds his cock into me.

"Yes. Gods yes."

He lifts me and flings us both around to land in the bed, still connected. And as soon as we settle, he's thrusting again. Pounding.

He lifts up on his elbow so that he can see my face, bending my knees around his waist and adjusting the depth he reaches inside me. Then he's lacing our fingers together, his grip so hard it hurts.

And I love it.

I take in the beauty that is my god of death, the form of him, the power of him, the intensity of him. I take it into myself.

I'll give him everything he needs. Even if it kills me.

"Harder," I whisper harshly. "Punish me."

He jerks still for a single, harsh breath, eyes flaring, and then something wicked—something menacing, even—crosses his features before he rears back and slams in hard, hard enough it hurts. A pain I welcome.

Then again. And again. Slower now, though not slow.

Who the fuck knew I'd get off on this kind of sex? But because it's him, because it's us, because of what we've gone through, what I had to put him through, my body responds as if each thrust is flint and I am tinder ready to combust. The tension inside me builds and heats and writhes with every slam of our bodies.

"I can take it," I tell him. "Harder."

"Gods damn it." His hand comes up around my throat and squeezes. "You *left* me."

"I know." I'm not afraid. I know he won't hurt me. If anything, I love it. Except for the way my heart breaks for him. Maybe we both need this.

He squeezes harder, enough that my vision narrows, but my pleasure takes on a new edge.

"You knew exactly what you were doing, going to Tartarus, and you fucking *left* me, Lyra."

Only once I was in there, but I wouldn't change it. Not after I promised Rhea.

"I know. You're right." I can hardly get the words out.

I'll tell him everything later.

His face spasms. "You made me put you through that farce of deadly trials, and then you let me lose you inside the worst hell. You told me to—"

He chokes on the next word and slams me even harder before grinding his hips, hitting every fucking nerve ending I have.

"It was my fault," I whisper, the sound hardly a rasp through the cage of his fingers on my throat.

His grip tightens. "Yes, my star," he snarls. "It was."

I start to see those very stars thanks to lack of oxygen, but I also feel release coming. Like his smoke and fire that slammed its way into Tartarus, gathering heat and barreling at me.

He leans down, mouth to my ear. "And now you're going to scream for me."

Then he bites into the curve of my neck. Hard.

And I scream.

I scream as my orgasm explodes through me in a rush of violence. I thrash and moan as he sucks on that bite mark through every obliterating pulse of pleasure so intense I think I might black out.

Not for long.

Because when I come back to myself, it's to the feel of his lips pressing to that spot—so soft that a fresh round of tears wells in my eyes.

"Mother goddess, Lyra, you scared the shit out of me." His voice breaks.

Then he gathers me in his arms and showers kisses over my eyes, my cheeks, before returning to my lips.

He's still hard inside me, still unfinished, and he starts to move, but now it's like our first time. As if now that he's punished me, the tenor can change to something heartbreakingly tender.

No more thunderstorm. No lightning. Instead, a gentle rain that might be my undoing.

I trail my fingertips over every part of him that I can reach, tracing every ridge, every dip, and returning when a particular spot makes him moan or shiver. I smile every time he does. Contentment is a funny sort of place to be when he's loving my body, when he's moving his hips and building the pleasure for me again.

But that's what this is.

This hazy, cloudy, perfect place with Hades.

In his arms, I'll always find contentment. I hope I am the same escape for him.

I keep touching him, kissing him, moving under him, giving him back pleasure for pleasure. Feeling him swell within me, feeling as the urgency starts to grip him tighter, make him move with resolve and then abandoning control.

We're both breathing hard, and he tears his mouth from mine to bury his face in my neck even as he continues to move. Faster. Faster. He groans and swells even thicker, stretching me. "Fuck, Lyra."

A second release starts to gather in my core, tingling in the base of my spine and pulling in tighter and tighter with every stroke. But I can also feel him holding back, straining to wait for me.

But I'm already here. I'll always be here with him.

"I'll always be your star," I whisper in his ear, then press a soft kiss to the spot just under it. "I love you too damned much to be anything else. And I'm never leaving you again."

It's like the relief of hearing those words unleashes something inside him.

Hades rears up and grinds his hips into mine, and we both leap into the abyss together, holding on to our sweat-slicked, trembling, shuddering bodies as we find each other in a different kind of oblivion. The closest thing to Elysium outside of that heaven.

And we don't come back until we're both spent.

Wrapped up and in and around each other. I'm tracing lazy circles over his back as he runs his hand through my now-long hair.

"Say it again," he whispers.

## 98

## GIVE SORROW WORDS

### LYRA

*Say it again.* I know what Hades is asking.

"I love you," I say, then giggle.

Hades rolls us a little so he's not crushing me and smiles, dimples in full view, although they disappear again as his face clouds. "I never thought I'd hear that sound again. I thought the end of us was Tartarus."

I trace the white streak through his hair. "I'm sorry."

He scowls. "I should be the one apologizing, Lyra. If I'd known, then I never would have—"

I put my finger to his lips. "That's why I couldn't tell you."

His expression ripples with something I think might be pain. "How could you do that to yourself? Knowing what you would go through?"

"I was always only ever trying to get home to you," I whisper.

Hades stares at me, searching my gaze long and hard, then kisses the tip of my finger. "You're right. I should have trusted that you'd find a way. That you'd get out." He offers a self-deprecating half smile. "I think we both always knew you'd be my undoing, my star."

"I never wanted that." I'm waiting for the other truths to drop. The brother he killed. The havoc he wrought.

"I know." He drops a swift kiss on my lips. "But love isn't always fair or reasonable. Since you're in my arms now, I forgive you."

I sigh. "I have so many questions for you now. Although I think I know the answers to most of them."

With a smile, he tucks a strand of my hair behind my ear. "Like what?"

"Well…" I think. "The first time we made love, in the pool, you said that you couldn't give me a future or care for me the way mortals need. But you also knew a future goddess-powered version of me had already visited you in the past, so…"

Hades groans, wincing a little. "You had me so twisted up, I had no idea what the right thing to do was. I had no idea how or when you would become a goddess. And the way future you was so careful to the point of fear about what you told me, I worried I'd fuck something up by telling you too much. And I didn't want to make you promises I didn't know for certain I could keep."

"I thought that might be it," I murmur as I melt a little. Because Hades has a reason for *everything* he does and says.

A frown slowly draws his brows together. "How in the hells *did* you get out?"

I blow out a long breath. I wish we could stay here forever, in the paradise that we create when we're like this, but there are too many things that need to be done first. That need to be said. And he still doesn't seem to remember what he did in his wrath.

"I'll tell you the entire story later, but I'm afraid that first, I have to bring you…more pain."

Hades goes eerily still, his face losing color so fast I gasp. "You… You're not going to disappear again. You said—"

"No!" Oh gods, I'm a fool. I wrap my arms around him tight. "I won't leave."

Hades takes a deep, shuddering breath against me. "As long as you stay, then I can deal with any blow you land me."

I wish that was true. I wish I could wait. Give him time to recover. But the Titans are waiting, and he won't be able to understand unless I hurt him first.

I loosen my hold on him to look him in the face. "Do you remember when I said that someone was out there glamouring the gods?"

He scowls. "Hard to forget. It made me question every single moment with you. Was it a glamour? Was it a lie? Was it real?"

"I'm sorry." I choke on the whisper.

He shakes his head. "No more apologies. Agreed?"

After a minute, I get a handle on my guilt and nod. "Agreed."

"So…" He tucks my hair behind one ear again. "What about this mysterious glamourer?"

"They got to more people than we realized at first." I swallow. "I need you to trust me."

His lips tilt. "As long as you don't put me through the hell of thinking I'd got you trapped in Tartarus again…" He trails off at the sight of my face. "Too soon?"

I swallow again. "I'm sorry."

Then I pull the veil of the glamour off his face and throw it behind me, its dying hiss filling my ears.

Hades' grip on me tightens to the point of pain as he stares at my face. I can practically see the race of real memories replacing the fake ones, of the dawning realization of who the Titans truly are and how they were wronged…as well as his part in that.

Then he inhales sharply. "What have I done?"

To his parents? To his siblings and gods of death in trying to protect me? Or both?

I don't have time to ask before he buries his face in my hair…and sobs.

It's a thousand times worse than when I held him after he leveled Olympus. To know that this god who is the strongest, best man I know, who can take the emotional beating of caring for dead souls for ages without turning numb or hard-hearted or cynical…to know he hurts this badly burns my heart to ashes.

When he cried last time, it was silent, but this time, it's like he can't swallow the depth of the pain. I feel every sob like a dagger, and every heave of his shoulders slays me.

All I can do is hold him through it.

"Lyra?" He has to take two short breaths. "My father is dead…"

My own grief sideswipes me.

I didn't even see it coming. But I haven't had time to grieve for Cronos myself.

I think of giving him Cronos' butterfly—the one Hades carved for his father long ago. It sits in my pocket. But it's too soon. After the worst of his grief has passed, maybe.

Instead, I just hold him through it. We hold each other.

# 99

# IT ALL COMES TUMBLING DOWN

### LYRA

Hades is the one to break the silence. "I'm going to find this person or people who did this to my parents."

His voice is so dark, so cold, I glance around, expecting shadows to form from him like dark angel wings, expecting him to return to the dark king of fury that I only just pulled him out of. But no fire or smoke is visible anywhere.

"I'm going to put them in a *new* Tartarus." His words are a vow, a dark promise.

Still no fire forms, and I don't hide my sigh of relief.

His arms tighten around me as he jerks his gaze to mine, realization turning the gray of his irises to a swirling thunderstorm. "I'm fine." He presses a kiss to my temple. "As long as you're with me, no one has to worry."

I see the instant what he did sinks in.

The full weight of his actions strikes, and he goes as still and cold as a glacier. Then his eyes go almost black. "Fuck," he snarls. "Fuck."

He's out of bed in a rush and snaps his fingers to be clothed instantly. Not in the cloak and chains from earlier, but in the black suit that he chooses only when he has business with the other gods to deal with.

And he *will* have to deal with them.

"I have to fix it."

"Don't go without me." I crawl out of bed and hurry over to my drawers. I haven't mastered the snap-and-dress quite yet.

What? No. They went through the river from Olympus down to the Styx. Then it hits me. Three tentacles were down there. I thought one had split, but there must've been more.

Hades shudders as a fresh wave of guilt passes through him, but he pulls back his shoulders, determined. "With me," he orders Charon. "Now."

I start after them. "What about—"

Hades spins on his heel and crosses the room to grab me by the arms. "Stay in here—"

"No."

"I can't fix this if—"

"The Titans," I rush to say. "I left them down there. I guarantee they're already working to fix it."

I see him take that in, realize the implications, then take a step back. I step toward him. "Take me down to them. I can help."

He gives his head a sharp shake. "I only just got you back—"

"You did all this to protect me until I could get out. Let me help fix it."

He searches my face. I stare steadily back. "No more doing this apart," I say. "Please."

"Fuck."

Then he looks at Charon. "Get to Olympus. Tell Poseidon to do what he can."

Hades and I blink out. Getting down to Tartarus with him is impossibly fast.

The sight that greets my eyes when my vision returns is straight from a nightmare. With a violent roar, water pours into the chamber and down into a hole that used to be Tartarus. Hyperion, Koios, Crius, and Iapetus are standing around it, each at a corner. The four Titan pillars that once held up the skies now contain the waters. Their powers spread out from each individual Titan to blur and mesh together, forming a container of sorts, keeping the water directed.

Then I see the figure inside the deluge. Eurybia. Titaness of the seas. Though her arms raised, it's impossible to tell what the quiet Titaness is doing, but I think she's trying to stop it or redirect it back up.

Before I can blink or take in more, Rhea is standing before us.

"Mother—" Hades' voice breaks.

The look she gives her son... For a second, I think she means to hug him, to hold on to her baby and never let go again. But just as fast, she looks to me. "You removed his glamour?"

I nod.

She swallows. "I wish we had time," she says to Hades. "But you need to be somewhere else. We'll take it down here. You coordinate with your brothers and sisters in Olympus and in the upper levels of the Underworld. Stem the flow if you can."

"Understood."

He reaches for my hand, but Rhea beats him to it, tugging me out of his reach. "I need Lyra."

Immediately, he shakes his head. "I'm not leaving her ever again—"

"We don't have time," Rhea says. How is she still calm in the face of world-collapsing chaos? "I'll keep her safe," she promises Hades.

"It's okay," I say. "Still together in this with you."

The indecision that racks his features is torture to watch. Not that I'm not feeling every horrible thing he is. Every fear that we only just found each other and that the Fates seem determined to make sure we don't get happiness together for long.

"Fuck." That single word from him contains every second of the ages he's had to wait for me. Then he kisses me, hard and fast. "Don't fucking die."

He looks at his mother, the two exchanging a silent moment that makes my heart crack and crumble.

In an instant, he's gone again.

Rhea wastes no time, grabbing me by the shoulders. "You need to use Cronos' power," she says. "Now."

## 100

## FATHER TIME

### LYRA

I rear back. "What? No. I only just got it—"

"That"—she points at the water the five Titans are containing—"can't be fixed."

"You just told Hades—"

"Because he'll never let you do what you need to right now if he's here watching."

Oh. I try not to panic. I try to breathe. Oh gods.

"I don't know how—"

"Go to Cronos. He'll help you with the rest."

Go to Cronos? I almost laugh in her face. Sure. It's so godsdamned easy to just time travel to Cronos in the past the very first time I manipulate my power to do more than walk a few steps. Under the gun, clock ticking, and with Hades unaware of the batshit thing I'm about to try.

Sure.

Simple.

This will be cake.

"Try it," she urges. "You're our only hope."

"I'm getting pretty damned sick of being the only hope around here," I mutter.

Then I squeeze my eyes shut, hearing Cronos' last words echoing in my mind. *When you're ready...when you need me...come find me...in our cell.*

I picture the exact moment, the room. I try to recall the scents, the feel, where Cronos was sitting, and where I was when time took previous me away somewhere else.

Is it working? I don't think it is. Because, unlike those broken cracks that would drag me into pressure and silence, nothing happens. I feel no change.

"You can look now, Lyra."

My eyes spring open at the sound of a voice I heard so very recently and yet thought I'd never hear again. Tears spring to my eyes. Again, damn it. And I throw myself against Cronos' chest. I feel the way I surprised him, the way it takes a second for him to accept the embrace and wrap me up in his arms.

"What is this?" he asks, amused, into my hair.

I swallow and pull back to look into brilliant blue eyes that haven't faded in ages of time, even if there are laugh lines deep in the skin around them. "I don't even know where to start to explain."

He considers me thoughtfully. "I died just recently for you, didn't I?"

I flinch with a whimper, staring at him. "How…?" I shake my head. "How did you know?"

His smile is resigned in the most horrible way. "This isn't the you trapped down here with me in current time. You got out."

Oh gods. A shaking takes hold of me that comes from my very core. Did I make him believe his death was the only way just by coming here? But he told me to.

"What happens?" he asks.

I shake my head. "Maybe there's another way."

"There's not."

"You don't know that!" I jerk to my feet, backing up in the tiny room where he once took me to San Francisco. I keep going until I hit the door, hands over my mouth, holding back my horror.

"I do know it," he says. "I've been manipulating time far longer than you, sweet girl."

"No!" I shout the word through my fingers. "You sacrificed yourself for me. You didn't have to—"

"I've known for a long time what my end would be."

The rest of my words cut off on another choking noise between a whimper and a protest. "How long?"

He doesn't answer that. "Why did you come now?" he asks instead. "To tell me that? Warn me?"

All of those things. "You told me to come."

"I did?" He glances away, thinking that through. "Sounds like something I would do."

"And Rhea did, too. After…"

He sobers at that, then opens his mouth like he's going to tell me something, but with a shake of his head, he closes it again. Then, "Ah."

"Ah?"

"My power." He nods. "It's new for you?"

"Yes."

"What do you need to do with it?"

"Reverse what Hades did to the world without reversing our escape from Tartarus."

Cronos' eyebrows shoot up into his silver-shot dark hair. "And what did my son do? Be precise."

I describe it. All of it. Olympus. Zeus. The temple. Tartarus. The oceans.

When I finish, Cronos rocks back on his heels. "That is…complicated."

Disappointment is a sensation I should be getting familiar with, have been familiar with all my life. But this time…Hades has been through so much. I put him through so much. I thought maybe I could help with this one thing…

He places a gentle hand on my shoulder.

"I can teach you."

"We don't have time."

Cronos smiles at that, eyes crinkling, truly amused. "You are not bound by the wards of Tartarus. You can go anywhere in the past you want, for as long as you want, and return to the exact moment you want. And I can teach you, for as long as it takes, before you return to where you started."

I stare at the Titan who sacrificed himself for me. For Rhea. For all of us. Who now knows that his future ends in this place. I have to bite my lip to stop it from wobbling.

He sees it anyway, eyes turning both sad and understanding. "It will be okay, Lyra."

No. It won't.

He tugs me back into a hug. "We have all the time in the world now."

Even if that's true, I want to hurry. I want to rush back to them. To Hades. "Let's get started, then."

He huffs a laugh. "That's the Alani worthy of my Hades." Then he pulls back. "We start simple."

# 101

# RIGHT TIME, RIGHT PLACE

### LYRA

"What first?" I ask Cronos.

He purses his lips, considering. "You've already managed to come to me. So you can get where and when you want. Next, something small but impactful. A moment in your own past. The first time you go there, don't interact, just watch. The second time, your goal is to manipulate something there. Understood?"

I nod. "How?"

He smiles. "That's the easy part. The same way you came here." Then he talks me through it anyway. "Ready?" he asks.

*No.* I nod.

"Then close your eyes. I'll talk you through it again."

I'm reluctant to do the first part, not wanting to shut out his face, knowing I won't have much longer seeing it, even if this takes a thousand years to learn. But I close my eyes, and Cronos starts talking. Listening to his steady instructions, I picture the place I want to go. I imagine the moment and what it looked like, where everyone was standing.

"Now," I whisper.

Did that work? I peek and sigh.

Because I'm still in Tartarus. Cronos squeezes my shoulder. "That's okay. We have time."

So I try again.

And again.

Until I lose count.

Until finally, I feel the air against my skin change. Is it working?

I crack one eye open, probably making a ridiculous face, and then gasp and open the other wide. I did it. I time traveled. I'm in my past.

I'm standing inside Zeus' temple in San Francisco, in all its modern-day, white-marbled, gold-gilded, lightning-topped glory. The sizzle in the air tells me I'm right.

"Holy shit."

I think.

I frown and look around for the one person I'm here for.

My gaze lands on a man in a ridiculously expensive bespoke suit topped with a shock of white-blond hair.

There he is.

Zeus.

The man-size, tantrum-throwing god baby. Hades killed him. My heart aches a little, even for Zeus.

He is standing just outside his inner sanctum in the temple in San Francisco.

Through two sets of columns, I can see the glitter of the famous bridge with its Corinthian columns spanning over a night-blackened bay. Then I move my focus to where Zeus is looking.

To a couple in the outer temple, the woman's belly swollen with child.

I guess I timed it right, because she abruptly stops walking. Her eyes go wide as a small puddle forms around her feet, unimpeded, since she's wearing a loose dress. My mother.

This is the moment.

Only...Zeus doesn't move. He clearly sees what happens, but all he does is wrinkle his nose in visible distaste.

I look between them and him, and still the god doesn't so much as move in their direction. No anger. No cursing. What the—

*Oh. My. Gods.*

The universe has got to be shitting me. Am *I* the reason I was cursed?

Cronos said I was supposed to watch the first time, manipulate the second time. But I already know what I'm supposed to do here. Now. The rightness of it settles in the center of my chest. The same feeling I get when I'm with Hades.

So instead of returning to the Titan, I move silently behind Zeus. From the side, I can see the mesh of the glamoured veil still in place. As I lean closer, Zeus doesn't even twitch, not even a hint that he realizes I'm right beside him. I frown. Then reach out and wave a hand in front of his face. Nothing. Not a blink. Not a frown. Not a sneeze. He does nothing.

Wait a minute.

"Can you see me?" I ask, my voice feeling overloud in the space.

No reaction. From him or anyone else in here.

Am I invisible when I time travel now? That would have been handy before.

"Shit," I mutter. That better not mean that I'm wrong about this.

I step closer to the god of thunder, and using the technique Cronos tried to teach me about glamouring, I go to whisper in Zeus' ear and send my will into his mind, only to jerk back before I say a single word.

Because his mind is already…shredded.

The dark hallways are lit by the race of neurons firing, and they are… twisted and knotted. A labyrinth of memories cut off, buried, burned, destroyed. Of pathways reformed, burrowed inside his head like the tunnels of Tartarus.

Someone else has been controlling Zeus. Glamouring him.

Controlling him a lot and for a very long time, it seems.

Why?

Fuck. That is a problem for another time. First…

I reach back into his mind with my power and whisper in his ear. "You will heed my command, Zeus."

The previous King of the Gods' face goes slack, eyes focused on some distance only he can see.

That was easy.

Too easy.

Whoever has been messing around in his head, they've done a bang-up job.

I point at the couple as my mother moans around a contraction and my father is on the phone to get help. "You are *offended*. They dared to desecrate your temple. Curse the child in her womb to be unlovable."

I pause, thinking of Hades. Of how he fell in love with me. I think maybe he's loved me since before I was cursed, or after the curse was broken, depending on how you look at it. Regardless, that explains how my curse didn't affect *him*.

But the others…Aphrodite, Zai, Meike, even Boone, since I brought him to Olympus during the games—my friends who love me—and it suddenly seems so simple.

I whisper an extra instruction. "The curse will only work in the Overworld. In Olympus or the Underworld, it loses its power. And once someone starts to care even the tiniest bit for that child, no matter when that starts, the curse will no longer work, even in the Overworld."

I think that covers most of the scenarios. The only possible exception is Boone.

I know that Boone once told me, just before he died in Hephaestus' Labor, that he'd always wanted to partner with me, that he admired me, that I put him and all the thieves at a distance, making friendship impossible. He brought me tools and my vest to compete in the Crucible. I'm not sure when friendship for him started, or how, but I know it did. I just will have to have faith that either the exception to the rule I created now or something else in our futures or our pasts will make it possible.

"Go," I whisper to Zeus. "Do my bidding."

I silently apologize to baby me as the god storms over to my mother and seals my fate, then disappears in a swirl of clouds and lightning bolts, leaving my parents stunned. My life, even the worst of it, really has been in my control all along. And this is the way I ended up where I am now. The only way the Titans get out.

I'm the bitch who made my own life hell.

Awesome.

I'm about to close my eyes and return to Rhea when glittering red light catches my attention. My mouth parts around shock as a familiar crack of time appears in the room and a man steps out just before it disappears again.

Boone looks around, confused, and then his gaze lands on something off to the left that I can't see. I ease forward until I clear one of the columns and catch sight of…him.

Of Boone, only younger. Maybe seventeen or eighteen.

He's not alone, leaning over a girl, caging her in with his hands on the column on either side of her. At first glance, I don't recognize her—a petite brunette who gazes at him with wide eyes—but then the glamour I can see over her shimmers and shifts, and I suck in a strangled gasp.

Persephone.

He recognized her in Tartarus, though. Immediately. Was he in love with her then? Is that how he knew?

Time-travelling Boone watching the couple jerks his gaze away, turning his back on them, bitterness twisting his features into something unrecognizable.

Which is when he sees my parents.

I can see his recognition of them cross his features and stiffen his shoulders.

Hestia's Lock. He's seen my parents' faces. He knows who they are.

Then he's leaning forward, eyes narrowed on them, and a new emotion flashes.

Decision.

He approaches them, kneeling in front of my mother, who is now bent over. He talks to her in hushed tones, and I don't know what he asks or what she answers, but he startles.

"Fuck." His lips form the word. And then I think he says my name.

Just like I did moments ago with Zeus, he leans in and whispers something in my mother's ear. With my ability to perceive glamours, I see the veil fall into place over her face. Not iridescent but green. Like the color of his power.

He rises and gives my father a hard stare, and I start hurrying toward him.

What is he doing to them?

I get to his side in time to hear his words. "When she is three years old, you will deliver your daughter to the Order of Thieves."

A sound of shock tears from my throat.

But Boone doesn't hear. Doesn't even know I'm watching.

He steps back, giving them both a glare. "You don't deserve her," he tells them. "She'll be better off with us thieves than she ever would have been with you."

He's saving me from them? Because he knows they aren't good people. Damn. I should have thought of that myself.

But Boone...

I know I wasn't the only one broken time in Tartarus was taking to the past. Boone disappeared several times, going other places. What I didn't know was that I'm not the only one whose been affecting *my* past. Although, unlike me, Boone has been trying to make my life better.

I stare at his face—the familiar lines of it, the scruff, the crooked mouth that, when he smiles, reminds me of a pirate. "You're a good man, Boone Runar."

A sparkling, jagged rip in time appears behind him, and he turns his head, then, with one last glance at my mother, steps inside and disappears.

I stare at where he just was for a long beat, even as my father helps my mother hobble away. "We're going to have a chat later," I promise future Boone.

I still have a world to fix.

So I close my eyes and return to Cronos.

To continue my learning. For as long as it takes, because time is finally on my side. I seriously need to meet the goddess of irony someday. Maybe if we become friends, she'll stop fucking with me.

# 102
# A BAD PLAN IS BETTER THAN NO PLAN

### LYRA

I make sure that when I return to Rhea exactly when I left her, it's with my back to her. I have to, so I have a second to compose myself. To wipe the pain of saying goodbye to Cronos again from my features. I refuse to make her see that.

"Well?" she asks from behind me.

I turn to face her. "It worked."

Her eyes darken with sadness, and yet I see warmth there at the same time. "Cronos must be so proud."

She has no idea. Or maybe she does.

"Do you know what to do?"

I know what to try. Even after teaching me everything he could, making me practice over and over, Cronos couldn't hide his doubt. What I'm doing is dangerous and extremely tricky.

"We need everyone who was in Tartarus with us," I say. "And Hades. Fast."

She shakes her head. "We don't have time to explain to him—"

"I'm not doing something this huge without him knowing first." Period. Not after what I've put him through. If it goes sideways…

Rhea must see the strength of my conviction, because she nods. They have to send Boone and Persephone to get Hades. I can't risk anyone remembering seeing the Titans.

While they get him, we figure out the plan. If this is going to work, we can't be seen, especially by the Underworld gods who were in here before.

But we also need the four pillar Titans to keep the water off of us at the beginning. Luckily, they are spaced in a way that the rest of us can stand between, forming a circle of linked hands. They *all* need to be physically connected to me to do this.

"What the fuck do you think you are doing?" Hades thunders, the sound preceding him into the cavern.

In an instant, he has me by the wrist, trying to drag me away.

And I freeze time.

A blink of my will, and everything goes silent and motionless, the column of water weirdly suspended mid-deluge. Except for him and me.

Hades' eyes go wide as he looks around. I know the instant he figures out what's happening because his jaw goes steel hard as he cranks a blazing gaze down to my face. "You're—"

"The goddess of time," I say. He already knows. He's seen me freeze time before, but then he was trapped in the shell of his own rage. This time, he's entirely here with me.

He shakes his head once. Twice. "It's not possible."

"I'll tell you everything, all of it, but first we have to save the world."

His shoulders go rigid. "You mean *you* have to save the world, don't you?"

"Yes—"

"I won't allow it." His hand snaps out—ready to teleport me away, no doubt.

I freeze that hand and give him a patient look. "I'm doing this," I tell him. "You saved me during Zeus' Labor in the Crucible. Now it's my turn."

Smoke lashes out at me from his body, but I freeze that, too. I can see in the blaze that turns blue in his eyes that he wants to unleash everything he has to stop me.

So I step into him, lift my hands to his face, and press a kiss to his lips. "You know I have to do this," I whisper.

The sound he makes is between a rage-filled grunt and a terror-filled whimper. A sound I never thought I'd hear from my imposing, all-powerful god. "I *can't*," he says in a tortured voice. "I can't lose you again."

I take a deep breath. "I can't promise that you won't, but your father has taught me well."

His eyes flare with more fire, but they're a normal, silvery color this time, not quite so hot. "What did you do, Lyra?"

"I'm ready," is all I tell him. "But I couldn't do this without you knowing. I put you through millennia of hell with my secrets. I won't do it again. Not unless you force me to. I can start back before I sent them for you. You'll never know."

A tiny crack, like glass starting to slowly shatter, appears across his arm. He's fighting me? Fighting the hold my frozen time has on his body.

"Hades," I whisper, smoothing my thumbs over his features, memorizing every detail of his face. "Please. I need you on my side if I have any chance of succeeding."

I can feel the tensing of his finer muscles under my palms a heartbeat before his head drops forward...and I know he's going to allow this. He's not going to stop me.

His gaze holds a thousand emotions in a roiling flame. "I'm here," he says. "Do it."

I release him and position us where I need us with the others, explaining what's about to happen as fast as I can.

Hades *hates* everything about this plan.

I can see it in the way he's so tense that he moves like a robot, his hand clamped down painfully around mine.

"I'm ready," I say.

Hades' gaze flares with blue fire yet again but then, at my pleading look to not make this harder for me, softens, and he leans forward, putting his forehead to mine. "I should be here to help you. Protect you. Do... fucking...something."

"You've already done enough, nephew," Iapetus pipes up from his corner, where he's still working to funnel the water.

"Shut up," we both snap at him along with all the others.

Hades' arms tighten around me, and I feel him inhale silently.

"I think I'm going to throw up," Iapetus mutters.

"I never liked you, uncle," Hades tosses at him.

But he also lets go of me. Only instead of stepping back, he kisses me. Not fast. Not soft. It's long and hard and desperate all over again.

Then he lifts his head, and the public mask of my arrogant god of death is fully in place. "Fuck this up, and I'll find you somehow."

"Rude." I step away and take Rhea's hand. "If I fuck this up, I'm the one who'll have to come find *you*."

His eyes narrow, and I smile. Forced. Because I'm more scared than I've ever been in my life. But I don't want him to see that.

"You always find me," he says.

My heart cracks and sings at the same time. "Always."

Then his gaze moves to his mother's face, and behind her, to Persephone. They haven't had time for anything more than the briefest reunion. And what I'm about to try...

*Please the cosmos, let this work.*

"You understand," Rhea says to him, "that while mortals may forget anything they witnessed, the gods will not. The few times Cronos did anything like this, immortals could remember. They still won't be happy with you."

Hades gives a curt nod.

I also nod. Cronos already told me that much. It's not like the way broken time resetting could only be remembered by those of us stuck in Tartarus. He and I came up with a plan, a web of stories to weave. I've already told the others.

Cronos also told me something else. A plan to protect Rhea. Her heart is visibly breaking even as she stands beside me with the others. His request is a kind of protection I understand very well now.

"We may lose any allies among the gods of death," Iapetus warns.

We've already been over this, but I say it again. "If they remember the glamour being removed, then they'll come asking. And I have many more people to remove that glamour from anyway."

He makes a disgruntled face. "You three had better have your story straight, then."

I exchange a look with Boone and Persephone, who gaze back with less confidence than I think any of us would like. But Cronos and I thought through this, too.

Power over time does have its advantages.

I have bigger problems to tackle first. "Let's just see if I can even do this," I say. "Is everybody ready?"

We all stand in a line, hands clasped. Theia is holding Tethys' hand as the Titaness's corpse lies on the ground beside her at the end.

Hades is separate. The only people connected to me are the ones who were in Tartarus with me all this time.

He's not one.

I look at him, and he looks at me. And then…he smiles. No dimples. No teasing. Just…*this* is what trust looks like.

It's taken us a lot to get here. "If I don't manage to protect the things I need to protect, I already know I can pull you out of it again." I mean if I don't manage to hold Tartarus open and end up locked down there again and he loses control and goes all *burn down the world.*

"If that happens again, I'll know it, too. I'll have faith in you. Always."

I nod, then drag my gaze from him to the remains of Tartarus, which is quickly drowning. "Let this work." I don't know who I'm praying to at this point. All of us, maybe.

I call Cronos' power forward. It's so easy now. Like an eager puppy that just wants to play fetch.

*Don't kill me*, I silently tell it. Hades can't handle that.

I didn't warn him about that little risk. About the part where the magnitude of what I'm about to do could drain me dry, first of my immortal powers, and then my immortality, and then my mortality, leaving only a dry husk of a corpse.

Hopefully that doesn't happen.

The trick is to keep it as simple as possible.

I can't Superman this shit and fly around the world, reversing time. Because that would reverse everything that's been done. Those kids in the bus would fall off that bridge if he's saving Lois on the second time around. There are things that I need to stay as they are now, and separate things that need to change.

Even Rhea agreed, though I think another small piece of her died with Cronos to say it.

But Cronos is who helped me decide what was the most important and what had to be let go or redone.

I start with…us.

I close my eyes and envision a protective dome of light over all of us. Like a bubble. And inside that bubble, I keep time where it is now.

"It's working," Hades says.

I open my eyes, and sure enough, power is flowing out of my chest— the same incandescent light that splintered to create the red cracks in time, then came back together inside me. It flows directly from my heart outward, creating a glassy, protective layer between me and Hades. It spreads and grows from there, moving to surround all of us.

With Hades on the outside.

With my other hand, I reach out and flatten my fingers against the thin, soft film made of power. Hades flattens his hand, palm to palm with mine. I can't feel him, though. Only the effervescence of Cronos' power.

"I love you," he says.

I'm so damn tempted to say, "I know." But I have no idea if he's seen that movie, and in this moment, I won't deny him the words. "I love you."

Then I watch him smile one more time.

I don't want to look away. "The water will hit you until I can push it back. Be ready."

Because the moment the bubble I'm making seals the four pillar Titans inside, they won't be able to hold back the deluge anymore.

Hades nods.

I glance to my right, where the sides of the bubble are about to meet. Three. Two. One.

*Bang.*

The water explodes into the cavern, and I almost expect Hades to be violently slammed out of sight, but fire and smoke flare up around him, protecting him, and he stands before me. He's going to stay with me as long as he can. I can see that much in his eyes.

So I go to work.

I picture two things happening, and this is where it gets hard. First, I freeze current time inside our protected bubble.

Immediately, Hades frowns and drops his hand, looking around. "Lyra?" I see him call.

He can't see us now. It's working.

Next, outside of us, where he is and in the rest of the world, including Tartarus, I start reversing time.

"Would you fucking look at that?" Iapetus demands.

No one tells him to shut up.

# 103

# IF I COULD TURN BACK TIME

### LYRA

Cronos warned me, even prepared me for what I'm seeing, but it's still a shock as I watch Hades move backward, watch past versions of all of us appear and interact with him, also moving backward. Watch the past version of myself from only minutes ago argue with him.

I can't watch him go or I'll lose my focus, so I look away, concentrating on Tartarus for that part. When I glance over again, he's gone.

It needs to go faster. The longer I do this, the worse for me.

I speed the outside world up, like watching an old VHS tape rewind. Then our past selves disappear, me up to the Underworld and then Olympus with Hades, the others to wherever they hid earlier.

After a short time, Hades' fire-and-smoke tentacles reform and return to Tartarus, digging in deep, searching for me even though I was no longer there.

"There they are," Mnemosyne whispers.

The gods of death return, reappearing in the cavern, followed by the Titans and Boone and Persephone from where they went to hide.

They all watch the fight in reverse, but it's happening behind me. I'm solely focused on Tartarus in front of me. Waiting for the first of two specific moments in time that I'm looking for. Any second now.

A strangled gurgle sounds to my right, followed by Theia urging, "Don't let go, sister."

Tethys.

We were able to save Tethys.

Relief spikes through me, sharp and uneven, and the world outside glitches—the fiery smoke monster in front of me does the same thing three times before I finally get a handle on it.

"Focus," Rhea whispers.

I nod.

Eventually, our fight with the gods winds down, until our past selves are inside Tartarus with the doors wide open and the gods of the Underworld are before them, their lights wound together overhead already having done damage with Hades' smoke-and-fire tentacles battling them off.

Deliberately, I slow the pace of the outside world's reversal, looking for the moment. The single, perfect moment. Then the debris clears, and the bridge over the abyss is whole. The light of the gods of death pulls out from inside Tartarus, but the gates are still open.

"Now," I whisper. I push pause on the time outside, and the smoke freezes. "Hurry," I say.

Still holding one another within my bubble, we run at full immortal speed. But with every jarring step, I can feel time slipping away from me in here. I can feel the pull of the power from my chest, and each step gets harder, my legs turning heavy.

But we get there, to the massive, open double gates of Tartarus.

A whimper escapes me the second I stop, and I have to take several breaths.

"Lyra?" Concern laces Rhea's voice.

"I'm okay." Except it's taking too much of my energy to make my lips form the words now. I need to work faster.

I press my free hand to the open gates and extend the bubble surrounding us. I picture it flowing through those doors, over the bridge, down the abyss to the seven Locks below, out to the pillars that feed the cosmos, then back into the tunnels, covering every inch of the prison that held the Titans for so long and all the souls still captured within.

By the time I finish, I'm shaking so hard, I can hardly hold up my arm. I slide my hand down the door until it's waist level, then lean into it, pinning it in place against the gate with my body weight.

"Iapetus," I say.

He's standing closest. He also volunteered for this part. He lets go of our chain, linking Mnemosyne and Phoebe's hands together behind him. The fact that he doesn't disappear or freeze is a good sign. Then he closes the gates while we're all still on the outside. Testing them. No Locks snap back into place, and he's able to open them again.

He nods at me.

That's when the nausea hits.

The next sign that I'm being drained too fast. Cronos warned me what to look for.

*Work faster, Lyra.*

Iapetus rejoins us, placing a kiss on Mnemosyne's hand and getting a smile from her. Hoping like hells I've got everything covered inside Tartarus, I hold all of it—us and the prison—in this moment of time after the door was opened and I was given Cronos' power.

Cronos warned me not to go to the past before that. Not even to save him. World-ending, time-breaking paradoxes and all that. I'd lose my power. We would still be trapped in there. He made me promise.

So I made him a second promise to get him out of there. Somehow. In another time.

I try not to think about the underlying sadness and the smile that he gave me when he told me I should do that. He should know by now that my version of stubbornness tends to get shit done.

Maybe I didn't learn my lesson with Isabel after all.

But right this moment, I have no godsdamned choice about it.

I continue reversing time outside my bubble.

Turning the world backward. It takes a while now, even though I'm making it go as fast as I can. Light and smoke and fire duel throughout the chamber. No wonder we were having earthquakes. Then Hades' tentacles leave, and eventually the gods of death behind us take their light and leave, too.

After that, we're not sure what's happening because it's happening outside of this chamber. I'm not even sure how long I've been down here at this point. Thanks to all my time traveling, it feels like lifetimes. But out here? I haven't asked how much time passed, making it tricky to reset it. The only way I know time is still rewinding is the effect on my body.

My head falls forward because I can't keep it up.

"What's happening to her?" I vaguely hear Boone demand.

I'm too busy trying to stay on my feet to care. My legs are shaking so hard, I'm not sure if my knees are going to give out on me.

*I have to keep going. I can do this.*

And I have to see it to know when to stop.

I force one eye open, and the view outside our bubble stutters again. Not like before, though, repeating the same second over and over. It blinks from the solid gates to the rubble and back.

"What the fuck was that?" Koios asks.

"Lyra—" I think maybe Rhea looks at me then. I'm not sure because I'm keeping my one open eye on the gates, waiting for the exact right moment, and if I move even a little, I'm going to lose it. I can feel both sets of time slipping out of my control. It'll be utter chaos.

Cronos warned me about that, too. That once I got started, got too far down this road, I couldn't stop until I was done.

"Lyra?" Rhea sounds worried.

Like a mother.

Tears spill out of my eyes and down my cheeks, but even those are doing strange things, rolling down and then rolling back up.

"Lyra," I hear her say like she's far away.

Then she's telling somebody to hold on to her shoulder.

The next thing I know, two arms come around me from behind, holding me up.

"What's happening?" Mnemosyne sounds scared.

She's never scared. I don't want her to be scared. After everything they've been through to get out of that place, everything they've lost, they've earned the right to never fear again.

"The power to do this is draining her," I hear Rhea say. The sound is up against my ear. "One of the only limitations Cronos had. He couldn't see the future, and the power to see the past literally drained him."

Is she the one holding me?

She lost Cronos today. Partly because of me. I can't fix that. I can't save him. And still she fights to help me.

"Don't worry, darling," she murmurs. "I'll give you all the power you need."

Energy surges into me.

Like grabbing onto one of Zeus' lightning bolts, reminding me of the day I became a goddess.

I don't know how Rhea is doing it, but I gasp long and hard, sucking oxygen into lungs that had stopped functioning.

The world around us stops glitching. The tears on my cheeks roll in one direction.

"If you don't think you can do it," Rhea whispers, "stop it here. It's enough. We'll figure out another way. But it's enough."

"It's not. I don't want him to regret—"

I don't want Hades to regret this one thing. I can save him that much pain.

"Then hurry, love. Hurry."

I keep going. I keep time outside the bubble backing up, reversing. I don't stop until suddenly Charon and Cerberus and Demeter appear in the room.

That's when I slow it down. Then Hades is here. I see the way they had to pull him off the door as he's screaming for me. I manage to stop it then, when they're all standing in front of the closed gates, looking shocked, right after Boone and I were pulled inside.

I stop everything outside.

I would have stopped it sooner, but I needed to see them show up here to know I wasn't guessing at the moment.

"Did it work?" Phoebe asks shakily.

If it did, then Tartarus is still open. Cronos is still dead. Only the world outside of the bubble, outside of us and Tartarus, reversed.

I hope.

I'm still holding our time in the bubble, but I release the outside world. We watch in regular speed as Hades loses his shit, pounding on the doors and yelling my name. Past Lyra would have been on the other side with her hand to it, worried about him. Only she's not in there anymore. Tartarus' timeline is being held on my current timeline—the me now, not the me from my past.

I hope. I really don't want there to be two of me.

I'm almost done.

We have to wait until the others try to drag Hades off, but then he abruptly teleports away. I know where. To go beg his siblings to unseal each of their Locks so I can get out.

And finally…finally…I let go of my grip on time in both places.

The protective shield around us pops like a soap bubble.

I didn't realize how much I'd cut us off from the world until sound subtly resumes and the air moves against my skin.

I stare at the closed gates of Tartarus.

*Please, gods, let this have worked.*

Hopefully there aren't duplicates of all of us who were in my time bubble now, too. Cronos wasn't sure of that.

"Iapetus?" Rhea asks.

He tests the gates again, and they still swing open and closed easily.

Tartarus is still unlocked. And Cronos isn't with them. He would have been if I messed up and duplicated all of us.

Thank the Titans for that much.

Rhea is still holding on to me or I'm pretty sure I would collapse. "Thank the mother goddess," she whispers, echoing my own thoughts.

"Good enough for me," Iapetus says.

Propping myself up on the wall, I draw Rhea around to find that she looks like death warmed over with sallow skin, eyes sunken into her face and dark circles around them. I think I nearly killed her. Thank the cosmos I didn't. "Thank you."

She cradles my head in her hand. "You are as much a daughter to me as you were to him."

To Cronos, she means.

She's lost him, and she doesn't blame me, and I can't deal with it. Maybe later. We still have more to do here.

I give her a watery smile. "Go," I say.

The Titans hurry inside Tartarus, closing the gates behind them and leaving only me, Boone, and Persephone on the outside. They will find a way from the inside to make the prison appear as if it's still locked up tight. No doubt the gods of death are going to come down here to check after what they'll remember happening.

My legs go out from under me, pure jelly. "Whoa, whoa, whoa." Boone half catches me but ends up squatting in front of me. "Are you okay, Keres?"

"Well, ain't that a bitch," I say with a smile. "I don't think I can walk until I recover." I can't feel my legs, or really anything below armpit level.

Boone glances at Persephone. "If they see her like this, they might suspect that she did this instead of Cronos."

Cronos was adamant that we hide my power over time from everyone. The Queen of the Underworld and goddess of glamours is power enough, but time, too? I would be viewed as a threat. Especially after what Hades did. They'll all remember it.

So Cronos is part of our cover story. We need the world to believe that, while dying in the rubble, he reversed time, coming up with a new plan to try to get out, and spitting the three of us—me, Boone, and Persephone— out when Hades bypassed the wards with Pandora's Box. Everyone will assume he did that so that his son wouldn't bury him alive again.

Persephone purses her lips. "I have an idea."

## 104

# NO ONE SAW THIS COMING

### LYRA

Boone holds Persephone in his arms. The goddess of spring is all about renewal. Her idea was to basically give me all her own energy the way Rhea did. She teleported us almost to the surface first. Boone will take us the rest of the way.

That was her big idea.

So I can walk. Mostly. But she can't, now. The plan is to explain her weakness away as something that happened during the fight with the gods of death.

I think we're all mentally preparing to put on a show.

I know I am.

Once we tell our story, once we're reunited with loved ones…then we can all go home and finally rest. Lick our wounds. Process. Grieve. Then figure out what the fuck to do next.

"Ready?" Boone asks.

Persephone and I both nod.

Sound cuts off, but when it cuts back in, it's not to Hades yelling at his siblings to release me. It's not to chaos as they all try to reconcile the memories of what happened before and being yanked back to this moment in time. It's not even to a fight.

It's to Hades on his knees before the gods of death, Anubis' crook around his neck.

"Stop!" I cry out, and I try to run, but I can't move.

Someone or something is holding me still, trapped.

Every god around us, Olympic and otherwise, crouches into a fighting position.

"How did you get out?" Anubis demands of me.

I'm shaking again, this time in fear, my gaze going between him and Hades. This isn't how this was supposed to happen.

"Cronos..." I stutter and stumble over our story.

Anubis' canine eyes are narrow slits by the time I'm done talking.

He remembers...me removing his glamour, even if it's back in place now. We have a story for that, too. But Anubis doesn't ask. Maybe he's not sure what to believe.

Has the Egyptian god already come to the same realization we have? That we need to keep the glamours a secret for now. We need to lull whoever fooled the entire world into complacency so we can hunt them down.

"Go check the gates of Tartarus," he orders Eshu and Hel.

The Norse goddess twitches a shoulder. "I am not your bitch—"

"Fine," Anubis says. "Someone else."

"I'll go," Yeomra says.

It doesn't take them nearly as long as it did us. I keep my gaze on Hades, who stares back blankly, not seeing me.

Not seeing the gods return. Not seeing anything.

"It's locked," they assure Anubis.

"So..." I glance between him and Hades again. "Everything is all right—"

The jackal-faced god draws his lips back, baring his teeth. "I'm sorry, young goddess, but it is not. Cronos'...selfishness...may have fixed the damage, but we all remember what Hades did."

"He was holding back. The prophecy was worse—"

"He showed us what he's capable of and how easy it is to set him off. Power like that cannot remain in the hands of someone who would do those things simply for the sake of a lover."

Horror only adds to my numbness. My ears are ringing. "What do you mean?" I ask through stiff lips.

Anubis doesn't answer.

Instead, he gestures to the other gods of death, and they gather around Hades, a hand on each shoulder.

A set of scales materializes in front of Hades, and then a blue light in the form of an orb also appears, pulling out of his chest. It lands on one side of the scales, and then a feather—white and fluffy but slight—appears on the other. The feather of Maat, the Egyptian goddess of truth and justice.

And I hold my breath as the scales decide.

Only…Hades' power is heavy, and so is his guilt.

His side of the scale goes down.

"No!" I cry out. "Don't kill him."

"Hades," Anubis pronounces in a voice gone almost mechanical. "You have been judged."

No. I will my body to move. I will my legs to run to him. To put myself between him and them. To teleport him away.

I look around for Charon. For Cerberus. They would stop this if they were here. Wouldn't they? But they aren't here.

This can't be happening. The gods can't kill Hades. Not now that we're finally through this. We fixed it. We fixed it, gods damn it. "Don't kill him—"

Anubis holds up a hand. "You are hereby stripped of your powers and your immortality. No longer a god but mortal."

Hades snaps out of his haze, and his head is thrown back on a scream of agony that shakes the very foundations of Olympus, the ground rocking under all our feet.

In a blink, the blue orb on the scales turns as black as death, and the shaking stops. Anubis releases him from the hold of the crook, and Hades collapses on the ground.

Then that black light that was once his power just…fades away.

Leaving silence as still as the grave over everyone gathered to witness. Not a single god or goddess stopped them. None protested.

The gods of death release one another, then, one by one, they disappear back to their own domains until only Anubis is left.

"We can't be without a god of death." Zeus, alive once more, finally speaks. He sounds like he's in as much shock as the rest of them.

He's right. As Queen of the Underworld, I'm limited without Hades' power over death.

"Hold a contest," Anubis declares. "For a new god of death of the Olympic realms. And we will return to grant the winner that power."

The jackal glances at Persephone and me, then holds out a hand. Hades' bident manifests in the air before Anubis. He whispers words to it. The bident glows an incredible bright orange, and then there's a flash of light, and it splits into two.

Two identical bidents.

With another whisper, both weapons fly over to hover before me and Persephone.

"For now," Anubis says, "your two Queens of the Underworld can manage, with help."

Persephone and I look at each other as we each take one. Even through the shock and fear, a small spark of hope ignites. Friends, she's always said, and now I know she was right. Maybe together, we can hold things down long enough.

With that, Anubis is gone, too.

I run to Hades, or the best I can do with jelly for legs. Hades is still unmoving on the ground, and I am so lost.

He's not dead, his pulse steady under my touch. Thank the gods, the stars, the universe, and all of the Fates that he's not dead. But he's mortal now.

He's mortal, and I am not.

I battle back the despairing panic that threatens to take me under. My mind is flashing from thought to thought. Hades once told me that what he sees in Elysium—the paradise that place would create for him—is him and me together with me as his queen. But does he end up there after a mortal death?

Is that how we end up in Elysium together? Do I follow him there?

No. I can't let myself think that way. That's not going to happen.

We can't take Hades to the Underworld. Not yet. His mortal soul will be trapped down there until I can protect him, either with however he allowed the other champions in the Crucible to visit or with the same kiss he gave me.

"We'll take him to his rooms in Olympus," I say.

"No—" The protest comes from Demeter.

I know this because of the way Persephone looks beyond me and pales. Boone must see it, too. He carries her to her mother and sets her in Demeter's arms. "Stay here with your mother," he whispers. "Stay here. I won't be long."

No one else speaks or protests as Boone takes Hades and me both to our home here, laying Hades on our bed. I crawl up there with him, lying so we're facing each other.

"I'll get Asclepius," Boone says next.

"No." I stop him. "No one can know that I'm weakened. Leave us here. I'll recover."

"And him?" He nods at Hades.

Boone is grim and quiet. Not like his usual self. But I don't have it in me to deal with that. Not yet.

Hades' face is only inches from mine. I scoot closer, cupping his cheek with my hand. Do I dare to reverse this, too? I don't think so. The gods would remember.

"I'll be here when he wakes up," I say.

No more tears. No more panic. I have to be strong now. For Hades.

Boone hesitates only a moment before he nods and leaves the room, and I lie here and wait, my gaze on Hades' face. I peel the glamour away while I do, then trace the lines and angles of his face with my fingertips.

He's not dead. Neither am I. We will heal. We will figure this out together.

His eyes flutter and open slowly, and I have to bite back a whimper. Because they are no longer silver.

They are…blue.

Not the otherworldly blue of Cronos or Zeus, but a dull gray-blue.

He focuses on my face, and I see the instant the fog of sleep clears and he remembers what just happened. Then his expression hardens for a beat, and I think I see a hint of silver in the anger that flashes in his eyes before he softens as he takes in my worry. He reaches out to cup the back of my head, leaning closer to kiss me softly.

"Don't worry, my star," he murmurs against my lips. "I have a plan."

# EPILOGUE
# DECEIVER

I glamoured the immortal world thousands of years ago, and those effects are still intact on every face I see around me.

Except Hades, but I think becoming mortal negated the need for that magic.

I *had* to glamour them all, using weak-minded gods to help me do it at the same time, and keep them under my thrall all these ages.

Those monsters, the Titans, deserved the punishment I ensured they received.

But the other gods never would have done it. Not without me forcing their hands. And I was right to. Look at what Hades did, what he became. Even I had no idea what I was unleashing when I sent Persephone to Tartarus. The events I would set in motion. The young goddess of spring may appear ditsy, with all her smiles and sweetness, but she's sharper than she lets on. She was getting too close, figuring out too much. She would have found me out eventually.

In the end, Hades nearly fulfilled the prophecy. He would have, if Lyra hadn't stopped him. He is dangerous. He should have been killed as a child.

Now he is no longer a threat — the world is safe from Hades.

Maybe there is nothing else to do.

Except remain vigilant…and to do that, I will stay close to the one who matters most to Hades.

Lyra.

I will become the sibling she never had, her closest confidant. Perhaps even use her in the way I've used Zeus, if her mind is malleable enough.

Too bad. I've always liked her.

# GLOSSARY OF GODS, TITANS, & MORE

**APHRODITE:** Greek goddess of love, desire, beauty, pleasure, and procreation

**APOLLO:** Greek god of music, poetry, light, prophecy, and healing; often associated with the sun (Artemis' twin brother)

**ANUBIS:** Egyptian god of mummification, the afterlife, and the dead

**ARES:** Greek god of war, physical combat, bloodlust, and protection

**ARTEMIS:** Greek goddess of the hunt, wilderness, wild animals, and childbirth; often associated with the moon (Apollo's twin sister)

**ATHENA:** Greek goddess of wisdom, strategic warfare, and crafts

**BOONE:** Greek newly made god of thieves…and more to come

**CERBERUS:** Greek creature—Hades' three-headed hellhound; guardian of the Underworld

**CHARON:** Greek ferryman of the dead across the rivers Styx and Acheron in the Underworld

**CRIUS:** Greek Titan of constellations; orderer of the year

**CRONOS:** Greek King of the Titans; Titan of time, agriculture, heavens, strength, animal communication

**DEMETER:** Greek goddess of agriculture, harvest, and fertility; mother of Persephone

**DIONYSUS:** Greek god of wine, festivity, religious ecstasy, and theatre

**ERESHKIGAL:** Sumerian goddess of death and Queen of the Underworld

**ESHU:** Yoruba messenger spirit and trickster god

**EURYBIA:** Greek Titaness of all things that affect the seas, including weather and winds

**GAIA:** Greek Primordial mother of the Titans

**HADES:** Greek god of death and the dead; previous King of the Underworld; current King of the Greek/Olympic Gods

**HECATE:** Greek goddess of magic, witchcraft, crossroads, ghosts, and necromancy

**HEL:** Norse goddess of the Underworld and the dead

**HEPHAESTUS:** Greek god of fire, metalworking, crafts, and volcanoes

**HERA:** Greek goddess of marriage, women, and childbirth; previous Queen of the Greek/Olympic gods as Zeus' wife

**HERMES:** Greek messenger of the gods, god of travelers, merchants, athletes, and orators; previous god of thieves

**HESTIA** *(deceased)*: Greek goddess of hearth, home, and family

**HYPERION:** Greek Titan of cosmic order, father of light and the heavens

**IAPETUS:** Greek Titan of life and pain; father of mortals; western pillar of the sky

**KOIOS:** Greek Titan of intellect

**LYRA:** Greek newly made goddess, newly crowned Queen of the Underworld… and more to come

**MEDUSA** *(deceased—or is she?)*: Greek gorgon with snakes for hair who could turn anything living to stone with a look until Perseus cut off her head to defeat the kraken

**MICTLĀNTĒCUTLI:** Aztec god of death and the ruler of the Underworld Mictlan

**MNEMOSYNE:** Greek Titaness of memory

**PERSEPHONE:** Greek goddess of spring, vegetation, and agriculture; previously named Queen of the Underworld

**PHOEBE:** Greek Titaness of prophecy and the moon

**POSEIDON:** Greek god of the sea, storms, earthquakes, and horses

**OCEANUS:** Greek Titan source of all waters: oceans, seas, rivers, and springs

**ODIN:** Norse "Allfather" and ruler of the Aesir gods; god of wisdom, poetry, death, magic, and war

**RHEA:** Greek Queen of the Titans; Titaness of the Earth, fruitfulness, fertility, motherhood, generation

**TA'XET:** Haida god of violent death (Tia's twin brother)

**TETHYS:** Greek Titaness of fresh water, nursing

**THEIA:** Greek Titaness of healing, sight, and prophecy

**THEMIS** *(deceased)*: Greek Titaness of divine law, order, justice, and custom

**TIA:** Haida goddess of peaceful death (Ta'xet's twin sister)

**URANUS:** Greek Primordial father of the Titans

**YEOMRA:** Korean god of the dead and the fifth of the ten Kings of the Underworld (Shi-wang); supreme ruler of the Underworld and judge of the dead

**ZEUS:** Greek god of the sky, thunder, lightning, and overall kingship; original and previous King of the Gods

# ACKNOWLEDGMENTS

Dear Reader,

*The Games Gods Play* is the book that pulled me out of a severe burnout. I thought that I was done, that it was time to give up the dream. And then I got the idea for this book, and Liz loved it, and then the story just exploded out of me, reinvigorating my love of writing, every single word a joy. To have it received by readers in the way it has been has made it that much more special in my heart.

So to my fellow writers out there…there is no right way to do this. Find the way that works for you, that feeds your soul and makes you happy.

Now, about *The Things Gods Break*… The second I finished typing the final words of the first draft of *The Games Gods Play*, I had an epiphany of exactly what I wanted to do for book two. I love stories and characters that are never quite what they seem, the full picture just out of view, because when all the details finally come together, they are even more beautiful. To me, that's Hades' and Lyra's love story, and I hope very much that you loved every second of the journey (one that's not quite over)! (Also sorry/not sorry for another cliffhanger.)

I have so many thanks to give for all the support that got me here.

Thank you to God. What an incredible gift to get to explore and design so many worlds and meet so many characters just through the power of imagination. To then get to see the wider world I actually live in and meet real people who love this genre as much as I do leaves me amazed and grateful every day.

To the incredible readers all over the world…how can I even begin to express how much your support and kindness and enjoyment have meant to me beyond a sincere and heartfelt thank you! I love to connect, so I hope you'll drop a line and say "Howdy" on any of my social media!

To my agent, Evan Marshall…for all your guidance and support and kindness, thank you so much!

To my editor and publisher, Liz Pelletier…for your friendship, your guidance, and for fulfilling all the author dreams my heart could ever have, a thousand thank yous! I'm on for the ride and, damn, what a ride!

To my editing team, Mary, Hannah, Stacy, and Rae, as well as all the internal readers, copy editors, proofreaders, formatter, and everyone who works so hard behind the scenes…thank you for helping make this book the best it could be.

To my publishing family at Red Tower / Entangled…you are all amazing to work with and make what I do an even greater pleasure.

To my international publishers all over the world who are bringing this book to even more readers…thank you. To see my words in so many languages and get to talk to readers from all over is just the most incredible experience. Seriously, all my author dreams realized!

To my artists…Bree Archer, LJ Anderson, Elizabeth Turner Stokes, and Kateryna Vitkovska…I didn't think it was possible, but book two might be even more incredible than book one. I get so excited every single time I see an email from y'all.

To my talented and phenomenal assistants, Pam & Chrissy…thank you for keeping me together, on top of all the details, socialing all the socials so beautifully, and even more for keeping me company and your love.

To all my incredible author friends and writing community…you are my found family and always will be.

To my team of sprinting partners, beta readers, critique partners, TXRW, Cathy's writers group, MAKEs, and awesome writing retreaters… your discussions, feedback, support, and friendships make me a better writer and a better person.

To all my family and friends, both near and far…you are and will always be lights in my life.

Finally, to my husband and kids…you are my stars, the anchor of my life, and the source of meaning and joy in this world for me. I love you!

Xoxo, Abigail Owen
abigailowen.com

# THE WAR IS COMING.

### AND THOSE WHO DON'T DROWN...

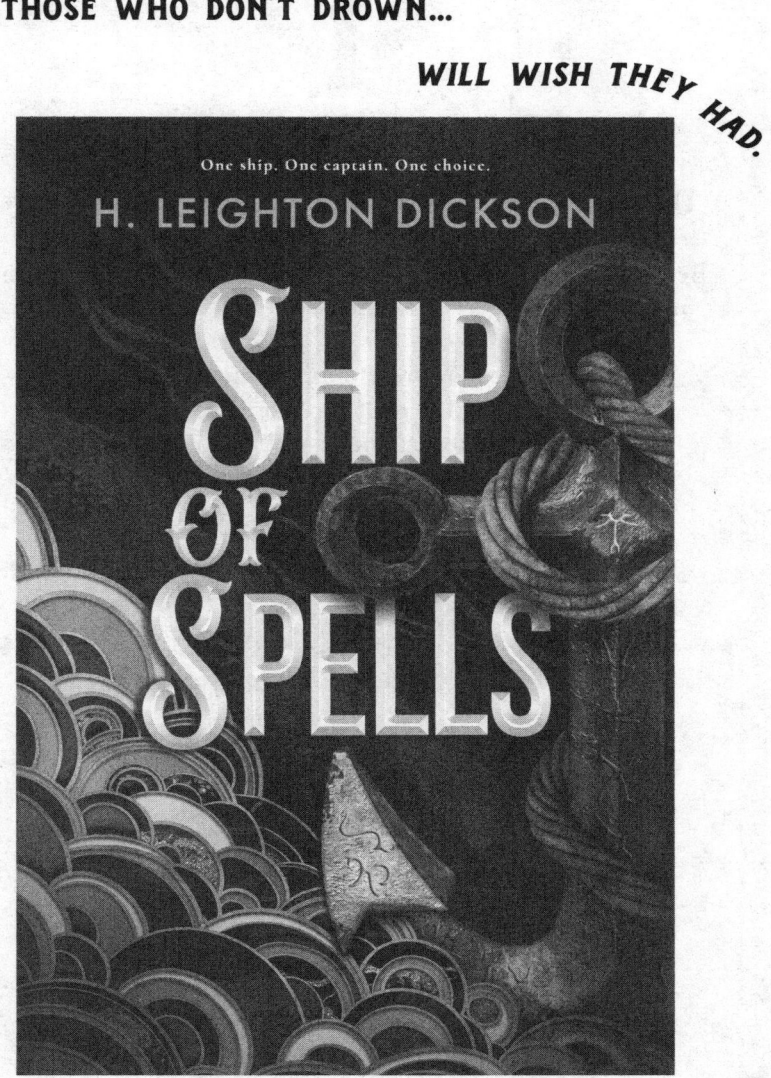

### WILL WISH THEY HAD.

One ship. One captain. One choice.

## H. LEIGHTON DICKSON

# SHIP OF SPELLS

### NOVEMBER 4, 2025

## Doubling the Trees Behind Every Book You Buy.

Because books should leave the world better than they found it—not just in hearts and minds, but in forests and futures.

Through our Read More, Breathe Easier initiative, we're helping reforest the planet, restore ecosystems, and rethink what sustainable publishing can be.

Track the impact of your read at:

### CONNECT WITH US ONLINE

@redtowerbooks
@RedTowerBooks
@redtowerbooks

Join the Entangled Insiders for early access to ARCs, exclusive content, and insider news! Scan the QR code to become part of the ultimate reader community.